Pollute
the Poor

Simon Cann

Coombe
Hill
Publishing

Published by Coombe Hill Publishing
33 Melrose Gardens
New Malden
Surrey KT3 3HQ
United Kingdom
coombehillpublishing.com

This book is a work of fiction. Any resemblance to any person living person or dead, or events is entirely coincidental and unintentional.

ISBN: 978-1-910398-02-9 (paperback)
ISBN: 978-1-910398-03-6 (ePub)

A big thank you to:

■ Cathleen Small for her editorial input.

■ Lawrence Rippingale (lozeng3r.com) for the cover art.

31 July 2014

one

"German efficiency," Boniface spat under his breath, yanking the outer door and launching it like a trebuchet, the hinged piece of wood arcing into the side wall as he started to jog toward his office. His teeth stayed together as his lips continued moving: "Next time I'm getting a client who understands that people are asleep until the sun has risen and should have time to shower, shave, and read the morning paper."

Through the second door on the left—his corner office—the phone was ringing. Behind, with another dent added to the wall, the door stay squealed as it progressively released its load before dropping the weight through the last few inches to slam shut.

As Boniface picked up speed, with each step the smell he had noticed when he opened the door but had tried to ignore was tugging at his nostrils with newfound vigor. A bitter, acrid smell—ammonia fused with filth, fused with never-washed human. It wasn't rotting food or decaying household waste or forgetfulness to apply deodorant or a broken-down heater meaning a missed shower. It wasn't that Montbretia had left something in her trash or that the cleaner hadn't been through last night or the night before, and it definitely wasn't the smell of the new carpet. It was more like a municipal waste dump in the heat of summer to a factor of ten.

Boniface turned into his room flicking the door behind him as he ran to grab the phone. Two steps across the room and he snatched the handset as the door clicked shut. "Guten morgen, Chlodwig. Wie gehts?" He straightened and walked slowly around his desk, careful not to catch the phone cord as he moved to the window. "No, that's pretty much the limit of my German, I'm afraid. So if we can stick with English, I'd be grateful. Anyway, how are you this morning, and how is business in Hamburg today?"

He leaned to rest his head against the cool glass of the window and looked down on Wimbledon Hill Road, his breath misting the pane. From his vantage point two floors up, the perspective of the street was squashed. Everything looked its regular size but somehow flatter, and through the tinted glass, under the dull light with the sun still under the horizon, everything took on a monochrome hue.

The smell wasn't improving.

A bad smell can be acceptable—as much as any smell can ever be acceptable—if you can get away from it and breathe clean air, but for Boniface, the smell wasn't shifting. If anything, it was holding tighter and working its way farther up his nostrils and scraping down into his lungs. He stepped back from the window and looked around as if he would be able to see the source of the smell or at least see the smell floating across the room, then reached for the trashcan under his desk. Seeing a fresh liner in it, he shrugged, replaced the bin, and sat on his desk, pulling out his bottom drawer to rest his feet.

"Greta wanted me to bring you up to speed on an issue we've got and to walk you through our strategy to handle it." He nodded, made some vague noises of affirmation, and continued. "Greta wants me to brief you. Fully. She wants you to hear the problem and the solution together. She wanted to tell you herself and she would have done, but she's in Malta today to sign the deal for the bulk carriers."

Boniface listened. Nodded. Made more noises of affirmation as if to imply he was paying attention to Chlodwig rather than wondering about the smell and being frustrated about the early hour.

"The problem is with the Montenegro Shipping Line." He paused, listening, and then sighed with a knowing acknowledgement, his tone resigned. "Yes, it's always a problem with the Montenegro Shipping Line."

As the German responded, Boniface stood, gently kicked his drawer closed, breathed in slowly as if that might reduce the pungency of the smell, and pulled back his shoulders, still not paying much attention. He had already heard the arguments, and given what he was about to disclose, he wished that Chlodwig's voice had been heard more forcefully before the purchase of the Montenegro Shipping Line was completed.

Feeling the I-told-her-so homily dissipating as it worked its way down the line, Boniface continued. "It's a bit more serious than we might have expected, and the issue is likely to become public any day now. We don't know how or where it will become public, or even when, but we're fairly sure it will."

Boniface stared out of his window again. In the distance he could hear a siren. The monochromatic light of the street below, now with a steady flow of traffic, was illuminated by a gentle flickering light at the lower end of the hill. One, then a second police car came into sight from the bottom end of the hill, their flashing lights bouncing off the storefronts. As they reached Boniface's building, the two cars turned into the road bounding the second side of his office. He watched as they turned, their sirens attenuating as they disappeared from view, and stayed gazing at where he had last seen the vehicles.

"There's a problem. It's a big problem. We reckon there are photos. There's definitely a trail back to the Montenegro Shipping Line. There are dead bodies, but we haven't got a definitive number." Boniface paused, shaking his head as he waited for the question he knew Chlodwig was about to ask. "We don't know. Tens, at least. Probably over fifty. Maybe over one hundred."

He caught sight of his reflection in the window—his face, gray like the street outside, with all signs of joy drained—and registered the tremble in his voice as he tried to say out loud that his client might have been responsible for the deaths of more than one hundred people. One hundred innocent people. Men. Women. Children. He hadn't mentioned the other people who might be hurt: not only those who were visibly injured, but those who would be ill for years to come. Those who might contract cancer. The birth defects. The people whose lives would be blighted through polluted drinking water and living next to a toxic-waste dump.

"Somalia." He tilted his head away from the phone. "Yes, Somalia, and no, we don't know..."

His door opened. Two police officers—uniformed and wearing stab-proof vests—entered the room: a man in his mid-thirties with a younger officer, almost certainly fresh from the Peel Center, the Met's training college, standing nervously behind. They both stood at the far end of the room, apparently unwilling to step forward.

"Alexander Boniface?"

"Hold on a moment, Chlodwig." Boniface put his hand over the mouthpiece. "Could you give me a couple of minutes, say ten minutes, to finish this call? I'm sure Montbretia can fix you a cup of tea or something while you wait."

"Would you end the phone call, please, sir?" It sounded like a request, but Boniface understood that the officer was giving an order.

"Chlodwig, something's going on. I'll call you straight back in a couple of minutes."

Boniface placed the handset back in its cradle without making a noise. "You're looking pale, sir."

"Death is never easy." Boniface exhaled.

"So you admit..."

The younger officer looked admiringly at the older officer as Boniface's voice took on a new urgency. "Admit what? I was... Never mind, different conversation. Why are you here?"

"We've had a report of a murder."

"A murder?"

"Yes, sir. A murder."

"Where?

"Here."

"Who has been murdered?"

"I was rather hoping you could tell me, as you are apparently the murderer."

Boniface let his body fall into his chair back and waited for the room to stop spinning. "Here? Murder? Me the murderer?"

"Yes, sir. You. Alexander Boniface." The older officer took a step farther into the room; the younger man jumped, apparently to keep his human shield in place. "We had a phone call," he glanced at his watch, "thirteen minutes ago, informing us that you had committed a murder in your office."

two

"There's no dead body here," mumbled the man who appeared to be Alexander Boniface.

The sergeant pulled out a notepad from under his stab-proof vest and checked his watch before starting to make some notes. He surveyed the man who was sitting as if he had been dropped into his chair, his tie cocked, his eyes looking tired. "A few preliminaries, please, sir. You are Alexander Boniface; that is correct?"

The sergeant watched as the man slumped in the chair nodded, his mouth still slightly open.

"This is your office?"

The seated man nodded again, as if the effort to move his head required all his energy.

"You say there is no dead body here?" The sergeant made no attempt to moderate his volume. The young constable beside him stood up straighter, nodding as if to affirm his agreement with the sergeant's approach.

Boniface's head jolted and he stared up, pulling his tie straight. "There is no dead body." He sounded as if he was explaining a simple fact to a child. "I'm sure Montbretia told you the same thing."

"Who is that, sir?"

"Montbretia. The lady who let you in."

The sergeant relaxed his posture. "I'm sorry, sir, it wasn't a lady who let us in. It was a gentleman."

"A man? No man works here."

"It was definitely a man, sir. Unless this Mon-whatever-her-name-is has a thick, bushy beard." The sergeant scowled at the constable, whose mouth wriggled like an overexcited child telling a silly joke.

"What do you mean? There's no man here and definitely no one with a beard. Did you stop him? He's an intruder. If there's any murdering..." Boniface's voice became strained and the pitch rose. He leaned as if to stand up.

"Sir. Please. Let's start with the basics." The officer kept his tone calm but commanding. "We've had a report of a murder, and so we're under a duty to make some inquiries."

"But Montbretia." Boniface sounded nearly panic-stricken.

The sergeant stepped forward, positioning himself squarely in front of Boniface, and waited.

"Yes. Of course." Boniface leaned back in his chair. "Where do we start?"

The sergeant sniffed, flaring his nostrils.

Boniface was oblivious or ignored the implicit criticism. "The smell? I haven't got a clue. I noticed it when I opened the door, but my phone was ringing so I ran for that, and then you arrived. I thought it was the new carpet or perhaps some leftover food, but I've been here for..." Boniface made an exaggerated movement to see the time on his phone, "eighteen minutes, and it's not getting any better. I haven't had a chance to sniff out the source yet. Shall we go and have a look?"

Boniface leaned forward but rocked back when the sergeant remained motionless. "Questions first." He waited for Boniface's affirmation: a slight nod of the head. "Are these offices all yours?"

"This suite, on this floor. Yes."

"What have we got here? In terms of rooms in the suite, sir?" The sergeant emphasized the word *suite*.

"There's this office." Boniface held his hands up and looked around the corner office, bare apart from his desk, the table with three chairs on each side, and the coat rack. "Montbretia's office is next door, and then there's the reception area at the end, next to the door you came through."

The officer stepped back, twisting in the direction of Montbretia's office.

"Next door, in the other direction, we've got the conference room, and across the passage there are two smaller rooms for clients to use, and the kitchen area."

The officer's eyes followed the direction of Boniface's hands as he pointed toward the other rooms. "Nothing else, sir?"

"No. The washrooms are communal: Go out through the door, and they're next to the elevator."

"Well, let's take a look around, shall we? See what we can see. If you would care to follow us, sir." The younger officer moved swiftly out of the office, followed by the sergeant, turning to walk backward and fixing his gaze on Boniface as he followed into the corridor where three other officers—their white shirts covered by dark stab-proof vests, each with a radio attached at shoulder height—spread across the hallway at the far end.

"Some might suggest that's a rather poor use of taxpayer resources for a bad smell," said Boniface, his voice calm, his posture straight. He had the look that the sergeant would expect from a business professional—tall, slim, wrapped in a blue suit with a subtle stripe, topped by dark brown hair, well enough cut to know that it had been cared for, but not so much effort that he would own a manicure set if they searched his home, and finished by a highly polished pair of black shoes. While Boniface had the full business armor, the sergeant knew that the best criminals went to the same tailors these days.

"Shall we look in Montbretia's office first?" Boniface reached for the handle and pushed the door open. "Aaaahhhh." He took a handkerchief and covered his nose. "I think we've found the source of the smell. You boys can go home."

The sergeant held up his arm, pinning Boniface in place without needing to touch him or utter a word, and stepped into the room. Where Boniface's office was bare, this was crowded. On the walls were framed newspaper articles. There were stacks of paper on the desk and table, and a large potted plant sat in the corner, leaning toward the window that ran the length of the far wall.

On the left, a body lay on the floor. A man, with a long, unkempt gray beard streaked with food, wearing a knee-length dirty green hooded coat held closed by several pieces of string knotted around his waist. Trousers that might once have been brown or perhaps blue, but now were dirt colored, poked out from the coat but didn't quite reach the two old shoes with holes in the soles. Under the shoes, the man was wearing one sock. Over his left eye, the weathered face tanned with dirt was broken by a gash, the top of his head now looking crumpled.

The sergeant turned to find Boniface had followed him in. He pointed toward the corridor and followed Boniface out. "I think we had better call this a crime scene, Mister Boniface." He looked to the tallest of the three officers lined across the entrance. "Call it in."

three

The lawyer removed his steel-rimmed glasses and laid them on the table, an imitation Swedish furniture store piece, its cheap blonde veneer darkened through wear and chipped to match the gouges in the gray steel legs.

He glanced up at his new client, Alexander Boniface, who was slipping his blue suit jacket over the back of the thinly padded chair. The meticulous tailoring of the jacket with its subtle stripe was in stark contrast to the factory-made, one-size-fits-all chair on which it was being hung. He understood why Boniface presented himself in this manner and appreciated the understated sophistication, which allowed his client to become invisible when he needed. He also knew that the police would not recognize the utility of Boniface's appearance, but would instead see someone they thought they could bully.

"How long will this take, Stephen?"

The lawyer kept his reply gentle. "A while."

"Quantify."

"Hours, definitely. At least eight hours. Overnight, perhaps, but unlikely. Almost certainly you'll be out within twenty-four hours, thirty-six if an inspector agrees to an additional twelve hours, and longer still if they apply to a magistrate."

Boniface flinched, slowly starting to pace across the anonymous room. "Can't you make it go faster? You're a criminal lawyer, you're used to dealing with this sort of thing—there's got to be a way to speed things up."

The lawyer kept any emotion out of his tone. "Plead guilty. Plead guilty, and we can all go home." He waited a beat. "Well, I say *all*. Of course, I mean all of us apart from you. You'll go to jail for fifteen or twenty years. Maybe more."

The lawyer felt his face twist as he suppressed a smirk while Boniface turned, pacing like a frustrated caged wild cat.

His client turned back to face him, his tone warmer, more conciliatory, perhaps. "I wasn't specific enough. Forgive me. Is there any way…"

Stephen cut off his client. "Let me make this simple. The cops' perspective will be that either you are responsible for the body, in which case they've got their man, or you know something about how it got there." He watched his new client, calibrating his responses, before continuing. "The idea that the body was dumped and it was bad luck that it was dumped in your office won't sound like a plausible explanation."

The lawyer replaced his glasses and looked over the lenses to fix Boniface with his stare before he continued. "If the body was dumped, then that's one thing and it's harder to link you, but if he was murdered in your office, then you've got a whole heap more explaining to do."

Boniface spun to face his lawyer. "What do I do, Stephen? What do I say when the truth is that I am ignorant about how the body got there, who he was, or how he died?" The anger ripped through.

The lawyer's tone remained calm. "Despite what you see on the TV, homicide detection is usually simple. Most people are killed by someone who knew them or was close to them. It usually is the husband, the wife, the boyfriend, the spurned lover, or whoever. You were in the room next to the body—in their eyes, with no other explanation, that makes it virtually unquestionable that you did it."

Boniface stared back at him, incredulous. "You're saying I'm guilty by proximity?"

"No. I'm telling you how the police will see things. I don't like how they will think about your situation, but I prefer that you understand the battle we're fighting."

"This is crazy." Boniface's voice was rising to a crescendo. "You're seriously telling me I'm guilty because I was close and in most cases that would mean I'm guilty?"

Boniface loosened his tie and dropped into his chair. The last time the lawyer had seen the man who was now his client was after a mutual client had been arrested. Boniface had been a man on a mission. He had listened intently, asked some questions—smart, insightful questions, questions that showed he was thinking not one step ahead, but at least three or four, as if he was playing games of chess simultaneously with a range of people, each with a different playing style—and then when he had a grasp of the facts, he had taken control.

A few relaxed conversations, full of humor and kind words, and the press soon concluded that there was no story. Or rather, there was a story—it had taken three phone calls by Boniface to find a far more interesting, and true, story for the journalists who gleefully turned in this new tale to their somewhat surprised, but nonetheless delighted, editors.

But now as he viewed the man in front of him, he could see that the initial disorientation of being taken to a police station was wearing off, and all that was left of the adrenalin surge that came with the shock was the gnawing little voice in his head saying, "What if I never get out? What if I go to prison?"

He observed more closely, trying to divine the other man's feelings: fear, confusion, panic as he tried to get enough information to understand the parameters of his situation, but not having the experience of his predicament to know what question to ask. Boniface rested his elbow on the table with his hand over his eyes, his thumb and middle finger massaging his temples. "Why can't they question me and get this over with? I'm here. I've got my lawyer. What's stopping them?"

The lawyer began slowly. "It doesn't work like that. All murder, manslaughter, and infanticide offenses are dealt with by Murder Investigation Teams from the Homicide and Serious Crime Command."

Boniface sat back in his seat. "So where are they?"

"Could be anywhere, but I'm guessing that the forensics guys will be taking your office apart piece by piece, and the detectives will go there first."

"These detectives are the murder whatever people?"

"The Murder Investigation Team, yes. They'll go to the scene—your office—first, and see what they can find. But there's a good chance the crime-scene guys won't let them in unless they've managed to create a safe path." Boniface frowned, questioning his lawyer. "They must ensure that the detectives don't contaminate the scene, so they'll get them into bunny suits, like all the SOCOs..."

"SOCOs?"

"Scenes of Crime Officers. The CSIs. The forensics guys. Whatever you call them, they'll always be SOCOs to me."

"These are the sensible shoes and practical haircut types?"

"Scientists is the term you're reaching for, I think, Boniface. And the SOCOs won't let the detectives onto the scene unless they're sure there will be no contamination, so normally they won't let them in until they've taken their samples."

"So why do the detectives bother going there?"

"The SOCOs will have done some field tests and have got those special 360-degree cameras that let them record the whole scene so the detectives can look at the output, and they'll want to have a look around outside."

Boniface sighed.

The lawyer continued in his matter-of-fact tone. "To be honest, you're also being left sitting around to soften you up. The cops know it's disorientating and unpleasant to be held in a police station."

He paused, making sure he still had Boniface's attention before he continued. "They'll make sure you're looked after—you can have refreshments and food. You've got access to a lawyer. When they start the questioning, they'll let you take breaks when you need, and everything you do will be recorded on their computer so they can prove they have discharged their duty of care. But it's still their house. They have a psychological advantage if you have to ask permission to take a piss."

Boniface sat fixed in his position, his eyes locked on his legal adviser. As the lawyer paused, Boniface leaned back in his chair with his hands behind his head, the sides of his mouth pushing upward. "I was a complete numpty. I followed them meekly like a lamb. When I got here they took my fingerprints, which is when I panicked and decided I needed a lawyer—I didn't know what else to do."

"You did the right thing." The lawyer followed down his scrawled notes before looking up. "Getting back to the body: You're sure that you have never seen the dead guy before?"

"I barely saw him this morning. They were so busy bundling me out of there. I smelled him more than saw him, and as for what I saw, I only remember the gash over his eye."

"A gash. How big? Was there blood?"

Boniface moved his hands as if positioning the scene. "Look. I saw the body for a moment. Yeah, there was a gash over his..." He looked up, his eyes flicking from left to right. "Yeah. A gash over his right eye. The whole area looked a bit...flattened? Like someone might have hit it."

"Was there blood?"

"In the wound. I think."

"Anywhere on his face or on the floor. Was there any blood there?"

Boniface slowly turned his head from side to side. "Not that I can remember seeing." He shook his head once. "No. I don't think there was any blood. At least none that I saw."

The lawyer nodded, scratching a few notes on a yellow lined pad. "Montbretia?"

"I called her. She called you."

"That I know," said the lawyer. "So she wasn't in the office when this all happened."

"Correct."

"The body was found in her room?"

"Also correct."

"And you don't see a link there?

"Don't be stupid." The lawyer could hear the anger behind Boniface's assertion, and if this was insufficient to convey his client's disgust, the sneer was unambiguous.

He put down his pen and stared at Boniface, waiting for his client's annoyance to ebb. "Listen. You are my client. You, not Montbretia, and I'm making sure your best interests are served." A blink affirmed Boniface's acknowledgment.

The lawyer paused before continuing. "Can you trust Montbretia? The body was in her room—she doesn't have some axe-murdering secret that she's keeping from you?"

A mildly amused look spread over his client's face. "No. I'm fairly sure she doesn't keep an axe in the office, and she doesn't murder people as a hobby."

"Now be serious, Boniface. Can you trust her?"

Boniface stared straight, dropping the pitch of his voice as he quietly intoned, "I can trust her."

"Can you be certain that she's not involved?"

Boniface's voice kept its somber tone. "I trust her."

The lawyer sat motionless.

"I trust her. I work with her. I've seen her under stress. I've seen her in pain. I saw her when I told her that her sister had been killed. I've seen how she reacts. We lived under the same roof for five months, so I know something of how she thinks and feels, although I know enough to know that there's much more going on inside. But her thought process, her decision making, her values, her beliefs, her priorities all tell me that I can trust this person."

The room fell still, both men staring at each other. There were raised voices outside the room, what sounded like banter between two colleagues at opposite ends of the corridor. A rumble of traffic outside and trains passing nearby.

Boniface broke the stillness, his voice scarcely above a strained whisper. "I trust her. If there was anything else, anything, I needed to know, she would have told me."

"Okay," the lawyer mouthed. "Who else should we point the cops at? For instance, which clients are you presently working with?"

"They're off limits." Boniface didn't seem to offer any option for discussion.

"Still, it would be good to be assured that no client of yours is involved in all of this."

Boniface exhaled. "You don't get it, Steve, do you?" Stephen continued to take notes as the room again fell quiet again. He glanced up to see Boniface staring straight at him, apparently waiting until he had his full attention before continuing. "If this story gets out, my business is dead."

The lawyer frowned.

"Think about it. If you were a potential client, would you hire the guy who may or may not have killed a bloke and then left the dead body in his own office?"

"But you're innocent, Boniface."

"I know that, you know that. But think about it from the client's perspective—they ask me to represent them, and the first thing the press will say is 'Company A, represented by Mister Alexander Boniface, who was accused of killing a man and dumping the body in his office.'" Boniface relaxed, almost as if all his physical strength had drained from his body. "Would you hire me if you knew that's what the story would be? It's hardly a declaration of innocence or an illustration of good judgment."

He started to speak, but Boniface continued. "If I blab about a client—even once—then whatever tattered reputation I still have will be incinerated." His breathing seemed heavier. "Whatever happens, if news seeps out that I'm involved it will kill my business. Stone dead.

Immediately. That means I lose everything—my business, my home—and I end up in a deeper financial hole of debt. Plus, it's not just me: Montbretia loses her source of income, and the people who have relied on me, the people who have helped me financially, they lose too."

"I hear you." The lawyer picked up his pen. "But you do realize that the cops will ask about your clients?"

Boniface returned to the standing position, stretched, and then leaned against the wall, the fine blue stripes in his white shirt highlighting its crispness against the dulling white of the wall.

"You're sure your current client has nothing to do with this whole situation?"

"My client wouldn't do this kind of thing. It's not as if they've got a chief killing officer on the staff. No one has 'disposing of dead bodies' on their job description."

The lawyer scribbled.

"I know that the next thing you're going to advise me is to keep quiet." Boniface pushed away from the wall with his shoulder and started to pace. "I know the general idea here: Police and press, say nothing and it will go away. Can't be misquoted, can't unwittingly give them a lead. I know. I've told enough clients not to say anything. I was a journalist long enough to realize that opening your mouth is often enough to hang you. But I don't want ructions. I'm innocent and I need to be free—I've got a client with a problem—so I want to be as helpful as possible and get this over with."

Boniface rested both hands on the table. "I can see the disappointment in your eyes when I tell you that, but I need to get back to work."

The lawyer sat up straight, facing Boniface directly, and began, "You've never done this before."

Boniface winced.

"I was forgetting. Sorry."

"It's not you that should be sorry, Steve; I was the one driving the car. I was the one who had been drinking. But the difference then is that I was drunk, so I didn't notice what was going on around me, and second, I was to blame, and I knew it. So you are right, this is my first time: the first time I've been interviewed by the police when I'm sober, and the first time when I was innocent of whatever it is they might think I've done."

"But are you happy to submit to questioning about a possible murder charge without preparation?" He fixed his gaze on Boniface. "What would you say if a client told you they wanted to talk to the press without preparation?"

Boniface's visage softened. "I don't need practice. I've got you by my side. What can go wrong? They come in. I tell the truth. We all go home."

"You don't get it, do you? What they want to do is to get a chronology of what happened. Their aim is to lock you into your story. They don't care what the story is; they want you to commit to it. Once you've committed to your story, that's it; then they'll pick at it and keep picking."

"I get it."

"No you don't." There was exasperation in the lawyer's tone. "In the last half hour you've changed your story—you've added, you've clarified—call it what you will, you've changed your story."

"I'm trying to tell you everything."

"Sure. But once they've locked you in your story, every change will be used as a weakness to lever you open. Any minor error or discrepancy will be a lie as far as they're concerned. Any lie proves your guilt. Any assertion without proof infers guilt. It's a one-way street. You can't clarify without saying you lied. If they have any evidence that contradicts your story, then they'll think they can prove their whole story, however fanciful or inaccurate it may be. Remember, you have no evidence to prove your innocence, do you?"

"What?"

"You can't prove that you didn't kill the guy. You can't prove that you didn't dump the body. Think about it and stay quiet, please."

four

"Hello boys!" Montbretia let the glass door swing behind her as she stepped into the street-level office two floors under Boniface's. Mentally she reminded herself: The Brits call them estate agents, not realtors.

"The delightful and fragrant Miss Armstrong. Your radiant beauty casts us poor wretches in the shadow of the misery of our meager subsistence without your dazzling looks and charming personality to shine light on our impoverished living." The man behind the first desk stood as he spoke, moving out and rolling his left hand as he made an exaggerated bow.

"Oh, Charles, you are full of shit, but do carry on. It makes a girl feel good." A broad grin broke across her face as Charles stood from his reverential Elizabethan bow.

"See. You're full of shit, Charlie boy." The second man turned to face Montbretia. "So when you coming out with me, Monty-girl?"

There was a hardening in the older man's voice. "Zahir, I..."

Montbretia cut them short. "Now boys, let's not get in a fight. Two scrapping estate agents isn't pretty." The joy on her face now felt forced. "You know I love you both equally." Her tone was of a mildly exasperated parent.

The warmest part of the not warm day had passed, and the plate-glass windows on two sides of the room let the gray light seep in. The property details hanging in clear folders suspended in straight rows acted like blinds blotting out any chance of brightness, and the strip lights in square blocks between the ceiling tiles seemed to cast shadows inside the office, not bring light.

Montbretia stood in her fitted, faded jeans and white shirt with a tailored brown jacket. Her eyes flicked between the two men. Charles, with his blond, subtly wavy hair, in his blue chalk-striped suit with a red silk handkerchief in his top pocket, and Zahir, in his less well-fitting suit. But you wouldn't notice the poor fit; all you would see is the dull green open-weave fabric with an electric blue lining, the chunky gold watch, one of many similar gaudy pieces, and the chunky rings, all topped by the rough-cut spiky black hair.

Zahir broke the silence. Keeping his arm by his side, he twisted his hand to point upward. "So?" His eyes followed his finger to indicate Boniface's office. "What's Mister Grumpy been up to?"

"He's not grumpy, he's preoccupied."

"He doesn't like us."

"Doesn't like you," said Charles under his breath.

Montbretia laughed, bringing her hand over her mouth, then paused as she tried to regain her composure. "No. He's got a business to run and clients with problems that need fixing. He's serious about what he does." She hoped she had sounded sincere. "He's one of the good guys, Zahir."

Zahir's left eye twitched, pulling the rest of his head around: an involuntary spasm that Montbretia had noticed always followed a disagreement. "Think about it. When my sister was killed, he was the one that gave me a place to stay—he gave me the keys to his front door, emptied everything out of his spare room, and told me to stay as long as I wanted and refused any rent. Even though I've got a place."

"You mean the place where you haven't invited me?"

"I mean the place where no one is invited—it's my home. It's the first home I've ever had, and I never planned to own a home, but the way it came about..." Montbretia's voice trailed off.

"Of course. Of course. What with your sister and that awful business," offered Charles in the voice Montbretia recognized as intending to be reassuring.

Montbretia bowed her head for a few moments in contemplation. "He was a real help—the only one to give me the help I wanted—when Ellen died." She looked to Charles for support. "You know that Boniface was the one who told me that Ellen had died?"

The only sound was the noise of cars passing outside the window and the buzz of a light in the ceiling. "In the weeks after Ellen—not just the immediate few days—as well as giving me a room rent free, he gave me money. Gave, didn't lend, and won't let me pay him back, and he's given me work when I want it."

Zahir had the look of someone desperate to say something. "Yeah, but I bet he's got spy cameras filming you, Monty-girl."

"He doesn't have spy cameras."

"You looked!" Montbretia felt her cheeks light up like two beacons. "See! You looked. You knew he let you have the room so that he could spy on you. Mister Grumpy is also Mister Pervy-cam."

"I looked, and there was nothing." She lowered her voice from the defiant tone she had used to respond to Zahir. "Within a few weeks I had figured that he didn't have the knowledge to install cameras and wasn't that sort of guy anyway."

Zahir gave an uncommitted sneer, half lifting his shoulders in apathetic acceptance. "Okay, so he's a saint, and he's not into women." He took a moment to take in Montbretia. "At least he's not into *hot* women, so what has he been up to?"

"Yes, we thought we had all the news for you," said Charles, stumbling over his words like a five-year-old with a new secret to divulge. "What with the burned-out van up on the Common, but it seems that you have the biggest story. What's happened? They say the police arrested Boniface."

Montbretia sighed and stepped backward to rest on the edge of the desk opposite Charles. "I don't know. What Boniface said didn't make much sense: He was on the phone, and the police came in and said there had been a report of a murder. When they looked, they found a dead body in my room."

"Wicked." The younger man in the unpleasant suit had a self-satisfied smirk. "I'm gonna ask those crime-scene dudes if I can have a look when I next meet them for a ciggie."

Charles flashed a look of anger at his younger colleague. "Gracious, that's quite shocking."

"So did Boniface do it? Is that why they've arrested him? Don't worry, I'll look after you when he's gone." Zahir seemed barely able to contain his enthusiasm. "So when you gonna come for a ride in my car?"

"I'm sure Mister Boniface will be touched with your concern, Zahir." Charles turned to Montbretia. "That sounds dreadful. Is Boniface alright?" Montbretia looked down. "What can we do to help?"

"You've got cameras here," began Montbretia.

"Sure. We've got CCTV."

"Can I have a look?"

Zahir looked up. "You look after the shop, Charlie-boy. I'll take her out the back."

Montbretia stiffened, and Charles continued. "It's alright. Thank you, Zahir. I think we'd all be better served if you keep your killer sales presence here, just in case a customer comes in."

"He's jealous because I sold three houses last week." Zahir held up three fingers, saluting like a boy scout. "Three. Two of those were big sales, 2.5 mill and 3.8 mill." He dropped his fingers and clenched a fist, holding it over his heart. He beat his chest twice with his fist. "Boy from Bangladesh sold well. One week, over seven million pounds in sales." He turned to Charles, raising his eyebrows. "What did you sell?" He waited expectantly. "Yeah. You're right, better keep the salesman in the shop, and when you're ready, Monty, you can come out with me. I'm the one that can afford to treat you right."

Montbretia gave a weak smile and continued her conversation with Charles. "Where are the cameras?"

"That's a secret," said Zahir. "If I tell you that..."

"You'd have to kill me," said Montbretia, trying to keep the tedium out of her voice.

"No. I could never hurt the woman I love." A self-satisfied look spread across his face. "No. You'd have to marry me, so I knew I could trust you."

"We've got two that record outside," said Charles, stepping between his guest and his overly pushy colleague. "The first one is there." He faced the door on the front elevation of the property and pointed to the top-right corner. "That looks across the door, pointing up Wimbledon Hill Road."

He pointed in the diagonally opposite corner. "That's the second one; it points along the Mansel Road window toward the junction."

"You mean it points away from our door?" Montbretia's voice was deflated.

Charles paused and flushed slightly. "Mmm."

"You don't have one on that outside corner? Pointing in our direction? Or anything else that might help?"

Charles sounded apologetic. "We're worried about people breaking the window. He twisted through 180 degrees and pointed up at a black bubble in the ceiling. "We've got a third camera there, but that records everyone who comes through the door, so I don't think it will help much."

Montbretia chewed her bottom lip, lost in contemplation. "Okay, well, let's see what you've got. Take me to the recorder."

"This way." Charles held out his arm, directing Montbretia to the door in the rear wall.

"See you later, babe." Zahir flashed a lascivious grin as Montbretia passed. "I better make some calls. Someone needs to bring in the cash to keep those cameras running, and it ain't gonna be you, is it, Charlie-boy?"

Charles led Montbretia down a short corridor and into a small, windowless room. "I'm sorry about him. I try...but you know." He gave a what-are-you-going-to-do shrug.

"It's alright. I can handle him, and despite the bluster, he's quite respectful. I spent an hour and a half across the road this morning. That was..." she searched for the word, "wearing."

Charles grimaced, pulling his chin back. "You mean you spent time with Jason, Declan, and Trevor."

"I think you mean J-man, D-man, and T-man." A mock admonishment. "Anyway, it was only Jason and Declan, although I can never remember which is which. One's taller and the other's heavier. Both have got bad haircuts that they think are trendy. Each wears a cheap, rather shiny suit they think is catnip for the ladies. One suit was more silver, the other more pewter in hue. Each wears chunky gold-like and platinum-like jewelry and probably sourced it from the same..."

"...online retailers that Zahir patronizes," Charles finished.

Montbretia's face reddened subtly.

"But you didn't break any fingers today." Charles looked slightly shocked, as if he had surprised himself by making the comment, and was even more surprised that he hadn't been punished.

"I only needed to do that once, and the lesson was learned; they've all been very wary about physical contact since then. It's the puppy-dog helpfulness that got to me." Charles frowned, waiting for Montbretia to continue. "I was going through their CCTV, and every three minutes one of them would be in. Did I want a cup of tea? How about coffee? A Danish? Lunch? Did I want company or cheering up? Did I want to take my mind off...? Well, I'm not sure exactly what I was meant to take my mind off, but there you go. And when that didn't work, they started with their stories and the brags about the houses they've sold, and..." She sighed. "As I said, it was wearing."

Charles's face took on a look of concern. "Did you find anything on their CCTV?"

"A man with a beard leaving the building. The significance of this man is that he left after Boniface arrived."

"So Boniface saw him?" Charles beamed as if he had solved an ancient mystery.

"That's rather the point; he didn't." Montbretia watched his face fall and continued. "But the police did."

Charles's face registered horror. "The police." A flicker of hope passed across his face, and the horror turned to enthusiasm. "So they arrested this fellow?" Montbretia shook her head once. "But they at least know what he looks like?"

"They were concentrating on looking for a dead body and were scared about the dangerous murderer who was still on the premises. Apparently the guy held the door open for them, and that was the last they saw of him."

"Gracious." Charles appeared to be back to his normal bumbling self. "So did the cameras across the road give you a good look at this man?"

"No—that's what I'm hoping to do with your cameras. To be honest, I only know the man's a man and bearded because Boniface said so; their cameras were too blurry to see much more than a figure leaving around the relevant time."

"Well, then, welcome to the beating heart of our empire." He gestured around the room, highlighting the table, several four-drawer filing cabinets, the stacks of papers and brochures, the computer and printer, and the single chair, triumphantly finishing like a game-show hostess revealing the monitor screen split into four with the first three quadrants showing the live feed from the three cameras.

"Show me how it works, and then you can go back. Zahir needs some adult supervision, and it's going to be a long, tedious process to watch not much happening."

five

"Are you alright to get started again, Mister Boniface?" Standing just inside the door, Detective Inspector Raymond Talbot looked for affirmation from Boniface and then looked to his lawyer, Stephen Holding, sitting next to him.

The lawyer nodded once. "Let's go," said Boniface. "But I'm afraid the story won't change." He stared at the detective, overweight, over forty, and over confident of the effect of his own force of personality, while being underpaid and underwhelming in the sartorial elegance department.

The supermarket suit was an unfortunately chosen shade of gray: If he splashed when he washed his hands, it would look like he wet himself. The polycotton easy-iron but never ironed shirt was thin, starting to wear and, despite being labeled white by the same supermarket that supplied the ill-fitting suit, was showing the ghost of too many stains, mostly from food eaten by hand or dropped from a fork as he gesticulated while eating. A polyester tie, ineptly tied, served to draw attention to the messy ensemble. Only his well-polished but cheap shoes suggested any sign of discipline.

Boniface passed a glance at his lawyer: cheap suit, cheap shirt, and cheap shoes. If he didn't know this was a show, put on so that people would underestimate this unprepossessing and otherwise utterly modest man, then Boniface would have reflexively sneered at his appearance in the same way that he now sneered at the detective inspector.

The detective inspector appeared to be enjoying himself much more than he had been when they broke. "While you've been enjoying a cup of our very finest tea, I've been having a chat with our scene-of-crime guys."

Boniface stared down at the half-finished and now abandoned plastic cup holding the swill the station's vending machine labeled as tea. In his disgust, he almost missed his lawyer speaking: "You will be making a full disclosure of everything you have found at the scene." Clearly the lawyer had also picked up on whatever was lifting the inspector's mood.

The policeman nodded his head, a look of smugness spreading across his face. "It will be my pleasure," he said as he sat down. The second officer, younger but with less hair, slimmer, and dressed equally—if not more—cheaply but with better-fitting clothes that had been cleaned more regularly, assumed his seat beside the boss.

He hit the record button. "Interview recommencing at seven-fifteen PM. Present are DI Raymond Talbot and DS Kevin Hitchcock."

"Stephen Holding."

Boniface sighed audibly. "Alexander Boniface."

"So, Mister Boniface. Shall we start again, from the beginning?"

Boniface sighed, again. "I arrived at my office a minute or two before seven. No, I didn't have a watch; I didn't check a clock. It was gray; it was after dawn. I reached the door to my office on the second floor at seven AM precisely. I know it was seven AM precisely because as I started to punch the security code, the phone in my office started ringing. My client is a stickler for punctuality: If they make an appointment to talk at seven AM, then they expect to talk at seven on the dot. Not at six-fifty-nine. Not at seven-oh-one. But at seven."

"Okay. We've got it. It was seven AM. Who did you speak to?"

"That's not material. As I've said, I will not disclose the name of my client, nor the name of the individual with whom I was speaking, without first discussing the matter with them and getting their agreement in writing. However, I can assure you that my client is a well-respected company that operates on a global basis, and I was talking with one of the board members who has an unquestionable reputation."

The inspector rolled his eyes. "You arrived, and there was no one in the office?"

"That is correct."

"You're sure, Mister Boniface?"

"I didn't do a full search of the office; I was running for the phone. But it was dark in the office. The central passage has no natural light. The lights are on motion sensors, and none were on when I arrived. There was no light coming from the rooms with open doors, and no light coming from under the doors that were closed. From that I made the assumption that I was alone, but as I said, I didn't check because I was running to answer the phone."

"So was the light on when you went into the office where you found the body?"

Boniface paused, thrown by a question he hadn't been expecting. "I can't remember." His eyes fixed on a point in the distance, even though the room was a small box with not quite enough space for the four occupants. "No, I can't be certain. Instinctively, I would say it came on when the door opened and the sergeant stepped in, but that room has a window, so the contrast between the light being on and off is less noticeable. To be honest, I was more worried about what we might find in there."

The policeman sat back in his chair. "You know what, Mister Boniface?" Boniface met his interrogator's gaze. "I don't find your story plausible."

Boniface remained subdued as the detective inspector continued. "Sure, you come across as a nice enough kind of guy. A bit of a problem with your drinking in the past, but you say that you don't touch the stuff anymore, and you haven't blipped on our radar since that, shall we say, unfortunate incident. In fact, that incident is the only record of you that we could find—you don't even seem to have a parking ticket."

"Not that I could get one of those at the moment," interjected Boniface.

The inspector looked momentarily confused before continuing. "True. But I still don't believe what you're telling me." He leaned forward. "I'll give you, you don't look like a murderer. But I've been wrong about murderers before, and just because you don't look like a murderer, that doesn't prove your innocence."

Boniface remained still.

"I accept your logic that it would be crazy to dump a body in your own office. But again, that's hardly proof-positive of your innocence. And you're right that there is no obvious link between the body and you, and again, that lack of a link does not give us any suggestion as to your innocence, especially as we have yet to confirm the identity of the deceased."

The inspector leaned in, his voice becoming quieter. "But here's the thing: You do have someone who you suggest could vouch for you, and yet you won't tell us who he is. You say it's a client, but you won't tell us the name of the company or the name of the individual you were speaking to. If you can give us a name, we can speak to them and get confirmation that you were talking the whole time. Sure, it's not irrefutable proof—you could have been murdering and talking—but it's the only evidence you've offered up."

The detective inspector waited.

He sighed and slumped back in his chair. "I get the notion of client confidentiality, but you understand we can get a warrant and check your phone records." The detective inspector looked to the lawyer as if seeking his agreement. "You recognize we'll be able to trace this person, and so that leaves me wondering why you're not being more forthcoming. Why don't you give us a name, and we'll all go home?"

The detective inspector drew his hand back through his hair, roughly combing it. "You assert that someone unknown to you must have dumped the body of someone else unknown to you in your office—in the room next to yours, which you say is usually occupied by your associate, Miss Armstrong."

Boniface felt his head involuntarily moving to nod.

"Are you offering nothing to back this suggestion?"

"The man with the beard," said the lawyer.

"The accomplice with the beard?" The inspector softened his voice so it was more of a whisper you would use when trying to comfort a child and regarded Boniface with soft eyes. "Look. Maybe it wasn't murder. Maybe it was the other guy: You were there, but it was an accident."

He stopped talking, apparently hoping for a response. "But if it was an accident, this is your opportunity to tell me now."

Boniface relaxed in his chair. "As I've said before, I can't explain how a dead body got into my office. All I can tell you is that I have no idea who he is, and I had nothing to do with whatever happened."

"Alright, then. We tried. Now let me tell you what we've found." The edges of the detective's mouth twitched vaguely upward. "We've had the crime-scene people in all day going inch by inch through your office. I don't have the full details at the moment, but once I do we will make a full disclosure." He stared pointedly at the lawyer. "But for the moment, let's stay with the big picture."

The lawyer nodded.

"The crime-scene programs on TV where the forensics guys find the villains? It's different here; our forensics guys stay at the crime scene, and we do the detective work. But where the TV does get it right is with the spray. You must have seen it when they spray a surface and hold ultraviolet light over it. If there are blood traces or traces of any other human fluids, it lights up."

Boniface softened his stare.

"Luminol. That's what it's called, and as you might expect, they sprayed luminol around looking for blood." Boniface looked to his lawyer, who was scratching notes on his yellow pad. "The body was found in Miss Armstrong's room. Next door, the corner office, is yours?"

The inspector paused, looking at Boniface as if expecting a response. "That is correct." Boniface's voice was quiet but firm.

"Well, when the crime-scene guys sprayed the carpet in your room, it lit up like the Blackpool illuminations. No, this wasn't Blackpool; this was more like Las Vegas. A whole great strip, about eight feet long."

Boniface remained impassive.

"You know what I think?"

With a small movement of his head, Boniface confirmed that he did not.

"I think that's where you killed him, and once we've analyzed that piece of carpet we'll be able to tie you to the murder scene."

six

She watched as her knuckles made contact with the door.

The door of her ex-husband's apartment.

A delicate, controlled impact—enough to make a noise, but not enough to wake a sleeping person or to hurt her hand. Again, skin on dark wood. Again, silence with no light under the door to suggest human occupation.

She turned her ear toward, but not touching, the door and pressed the doorbell, startling herself with the vulgarity of its ring, which decayed, leaving the sound of movement within.

Veronica stepped back, smoothed her fitted dark-green dress, and checked her reflection in the window over the stairwell. She flicked her head, watching her dark auburn mane pulse over her shoulders, then stood squarely facing the door as it cracked open.

"Hi."

The face of a younger woman looked through the slit. Her body, wrapped in shades of pink, was positioned with her weight behind the door.

The older woman made eye contact and smiled. "Montbretia?"

The tension in the younger woman's face released, breaking into a broad grin. "Veronica?"

"That's right."

"Call me Monty." The younger woman stood back and opened the door. "He's still not back, but do you want to come in?" Veronica took in the faded fuchsia sweatshirt and dark-pink sweatpants as she stepped forward—the click of her heels silenced as she passed over the threshold and onto the carpet in the hall—turning in the direction suggested by Montbretia's look.

The hall was dark and became darker as the door shut. Stepping into the living room, the sole source of illumination was the light pollution forcing itself from outside. Reflexively, Veronica turned on the lights as she passed the switch inside the door, dimming them as she started to scan the room.

It was as it had been last time she was here. Two perpendicular sofas: The one on the left had a crumpled triangle of cushions—probably a sign that Montbretia had been sitting there, and given the lack of light, probably in deep in contemplation. A cup of coffee—cold, Veronica guessed—sat on the low table shared by the two sofas.

"Can I get you something?"

"A tumbler, please," said Veronica, slipping her bag off her shoulder and reaching inside. "He doesn't stock what I like." She slid out a bottle of whisky and placed it next to Montbretia's cold coffee, then sat on the sofa, keeping her ankles and knees together as she delicately lowered herself.

"Won't you join me?" she said as Montbretia placed a crystal tumbler on the table.

"I'm fine, thank you. Water? Ice?"

Veronica looked up at Montbretia, pulled a mock frown, and shook her head imperceptibly. "This is the good stuff. You don't dilute it." She released the frown. "Are you sure you won't have a sip? You look like you could do with a drink."

The younger woman dropped onto the pile of cushions on the opposite sofa, pulling her knees under her chin and wrapping her arms around her legs. "I can't drink anything at the moment."

"Come on, dear." Veronica's expression was one of concern. Her head tilted, her mouth half open. She leaned in. "This is Boniface. He will be fine. He's at the police station, and he's probably only still there because he's boring them with his stories." She smiled softly and slid around the table to sit next to Montbretia, putting an arm around her shoulders. "He'll be fine." She felt her lips twisting. "But he might break a few things on the way to being fine. You know Boniface."

Montbretia sat up straighter and dropped her feet to the floor. "I'm only here because I don't know where else to go or what else to do. I can't go to the office, I don't want to go home, and I figured he'll come here as soon as he's out. I've called him, and there's no reply,"

Veronica took a sip and placed her tumbler back. "I'm the same," she whispered. "I didn't know what else to..." She let her words fade to silence without finishing her sentence.

The older woman took another sip and disturbed the quiet. "I know it's been a few months, but I was so sorry about your sister. It was dreadfully shocking."

Montbretia bowed her head, biting her lower lip, and whispered, "Thank you."

The room fell still, noiseless apart from the sounds from the road outside. Veronica walked to the window, felt behind the curtain for the drawstring, and closed out the night. She tapped the dark fabric to knock out a few wrinkles, then walked back to the table, poured herself another whisky, and returned to her seat across from Montbretia, who looked up, forcing a look of confidence across her face.

"You're living back at..."

"Ham Common. Ellen's old place. I didn't want to go there—at first I cried every time I went there, and when I stopped crying I got scared—but now I find it comforting having Ellen all around me." Montbretia's voice trailed off, the only sound the noise of Veronica lifting and replacing her tumbler. Montbretia looked straight at the older woman. "Did you find anything?"

"No." Veronica kept her voice soft and tried to let her slight Scottish burr resonate. "It's hard to ask questions when you realize that by asking you're tipping off journalists. But I found nothing—no one seems to have picked up the story." She took another sip. "What did you find out?"

"I spent all of my time in the realtors'—sorry, if I don't use the English, someone who's not here will correct me—I mean estate agents' offices."

"Oh. Are you thinking about selling when you get probate?"

"No, it's just that Wimbledon... What is it with Wimbledon?" Her voice became more inquisitive. "Before I came here, I'd heard of Wimbledon because of the tennis. But now I've lived and worked in Wimbledon for a few months, I realize I was wrong: It's the land of tennis *and* realtors."

"Not forgetting the Papal embassy," offered Veronica.

"Tennis, realtors, and the Pope's London home-away-from-home on the Common," said Montbretia, her body relaxed as she continued. "There are three realtors in the storefronts under the office, two right across the street, another two further down the block, and they all seem to have CCTV."

"That sounds like fun." Veronica made no attempt to keep the sarcasm out of her voice as she raised her eyebrows. "Which was worse, watching the CCTV or dealing with the estate agents? I presume they all fit the stereotype?"

"So much testosterone. So much need for a public sterilization program," said Montbretia, exasperated. "But at least they don't grab. One tried it once during the first week I was with Boniface. He put his hand on my ass."

The older woman grimaced.

"So I told him, 'Touch my ass, and I'll break a finger.' He thought he would be funny and said, 'What, like this?' and placed his hand." Montbretia twisted to indicate where she had been touched.

Veronica sighed, still nodding.

"I didn't mean to break his finger. I only meant to twist it back and make him look a bit foolish." She held her hands out, palms turned up. "But I misjudged it." She became more serious. "In the end it was quite useful: I made my point, and no one has touched my ass since then."

"What happened to the guy with the broken finger?"

"Same as the other guys, he moved on to another job, but he moved on a bit more quickly than normal. He had lost face by getting beaten by a girl, and as it had happened in public, there was no way for him to deny it. But the rest of the guys love me for it, and so it was easy when I wanted to see their CCTV."

"And?"

"And it's very boring. But I did see a few things."

"Do tell." Veronica sat forward on her seat.

"I can do better than tell." Montbretia put her hand through her sweatshirt collar and pulled at her shoulder, dragging out a blue lanyard with a small oblong piece of silver plastic at the end. "I can show."

seven

Boniface looked across the road and up at his office. Under the street lighting, the yellow/beige 1970s brickwork layered between the brown-framed tinted windows had lost any sense of color, instead becoming lighter and darker stripes.

The estate agent offices on the ground level were empty: Apparently Charles and Zahir had sold enough houses for one day. Or more likely, Zahir had sold, and Charles had fussed and soothed the upset customers who were never intending to buy a property in the first place.

There was one light, somewhere in the heart of the building, on the floor between his and the street level—and that was likely a faulty sensor—but apart from that, as far as Boniface could see, the building was in darkness.

He crossed Wimbledon Hill Road, turned into Mansel Road and followed the side of the building to the parking lot behind the office, where he stared at the rear elevation. "How would you get a body in?" he muttered under his breath, looking up at the fire escape. "Or did they go through the front door?"

Boniface pulled out his key and entered the lobby from the parking lot side, locking the door behind him. A small, faceless lobby with magnolia emulsion walls, concealed lighting, and enough space for a tiny security desk that was never used, probably explaining one factor in keeping the rent down.

He looked back at the back door—a single aluminum-framed glass panel—then at the front door, two brown aluminum-framed glass panels; then he gave rear door a firm shake. He wasn't sure what he expected. A final scan of the lobby, and he started on the stairs, ignoring the elevator.

Two flights, turning at an intermediate landing next to a floor-to-ceiling picture window, and he arrived on the next-floor landing, which was a facsimile of his landing. Two further flights, and Boniface was outside his office. "Good evening."

"Good evening, sir." The officer looked to be around the same age as the young constable who had been in Boniface's office that morning, and if she was charged with standing outside his office overnight, there was every chance she was equally lacking in experience.

"What happened here?" asked Boniface.

"There was an incident, sir."

"An incident?"

"An incident." The officer was definitive, offering no apparent hope of elaboration. Perhaps she wasn't as guileless as the constable this morning.

"Can I go in?" Boniface tried to peer through the reinforced safety-glass panels in the door.

"Mister Boniface, I presume." She had evidently paid attention when she was briefed.

"That's right."

"I'm afraid you can't."

"And if I wasn't Boniface?"

"Unless you're a scenes of crime officer, then you're not going past." Her delivery remained emotionless and her message absolute.

"What about the fire exit, or should I say the non-fire entrance? Can I go through there?"

The officer's voice had an edge of exasperation. "I'm sure that any fire exit will have been sealed, sir. But please remember that this is a crime scene—do you want to leave your fingerprints and DNA in all the places that you know the SOCOs will be looking tomorrow?" She reached under her stab-proof vest, pulled out a notebook, checked her watch, and started to make notes, looking up at Boniface as she continued. "Procedure, sir."

Boniface raised his eyes. "What have they found? These scene-of-whatever people."

"I don't know, sir. You would need to talk to the senior investigating officer or one of the officers involved with the investigation, such as Detective Inspector Talbot."

"We're acquainted," said Boniface. "What about the carpet?"

The officer frowned. "Was there anything else I can help you with, sir?"

eight

Boniface fumbled as he pushed the key into the deadlock in his front door and twisted. The lock didn't move. He twisted the key counterclockwise. It moved. As he twisted back again, he could hear feet running inside. He tugged the key out of the lock as the door swung open and two women embraced him.

"So this is my welcoming committee to celebrate being sprung from jail? What have you got lined up for me? There are things an incarcerated man misses. He has needs, he has wants."

Veronica let go and stood back, looking up at him. "You're trying to tell us that the tea in the cop shop was awful?"

"That's about it," said Boniface kissing the top of Montbretia's head as she clung to him and leaning to kiss Veronica. "Shall we go inside?"

Boniface moved slowly, with a lump of varying shades of dark pink clinging to his side. "Why didn't you call when you got out?" asked the pink bundle.

"Because the nice, kind policemen escorted me out of the office this morning before I could plug in my charger," replied Boniface, reaching into his pocket and tossing his inert phone onto the sofa. "If you've ever seen the sort of person who doesn't carry a phone, you'll understand why I didn't go looking for a phone box." He grimaced. "Added to which, I didn't want anything to slow me from getting to see my two favorite gals."

"Even though you didn't know we'd be here," said Veronica.

"But in my heart, I did know where you were," responded Boniface lightly. They sat, Montbretia still hanging on to Boniface and Veronica, on the perpendicular sofa, reaching for her bottle of whisky. "You were expecting a long wait, I see."

"Preparation," said Veronica. "Anyway. Tell us. How did you manage to escape?"

"I dug a tunnel."

"Alexander." There was a sharpening of Veronica's tone as she held her tumbler away from her mouth.

"Horseradish."

"Will you stop with the horseradish-gate! Don't bring up that story—just tell us how you got out." Montbretia let go of Boniface and leaned back to stare at him.

"I'm being serious," said Boniface. "I'm free because of horseradish."

Montbretia continued to stare.

Veronica took a sip. "Let's get past this horseradish thing, then you can tell us about the police."

Boniface leaned back and relaxed. "It's good to be in a relaxing seat. The chairs at the police station are bloody uncomfortable."

"Horseradish."

"Right. Background. When I was sorting out my head," Boniface made quote marks with his fingers, "last year, I was friendly with a guy called Quentin. I got out and set up my own PR agency; Quent got out and decided to start making organic horseradish. Two months ago he called me. The first batch of organic horseradish was ready, and he wondered if I could give him a few pointers or a few suggestions for how to market it."

Montbretia leaned, like a sprinter getting ready on the stocks.

"I made a few phone calls and suggested a few other people Quent could call. Literally, I spent fifteen minutes. Anyway, long story short, Quentin's organic horseradish got mentioned in an article in the *Daily Mail*, and as a result, everything went wild for him. His internet server got swamped, crashing his website, but that didn't matter because he sold out the whole year's supply in under ninety minutes. So Quentin is hugely grateful and thinks I'm a marketing god, and to express his gratitude, he sent me a box of horseradish."

"But he sold out his supply. Also, horseradish doesn't come in boxes."

"That's why you're a journalist," said Boniface to his former wife. "Quentin sent me a box with 12 jars of horseradish. The horseradish was fine, but the jars were the test packaging."

"Which had some issues," interjected Montbretia.

"I had this box of jars sitting in the office for a few weeks, and I figured we should try this stuff, so about ten days ago Montbretia and I decided to have roast beef sandwiches. That way we could try the horseradish in its intended context." Montbretia seemed ready to butt in as Boniface continued. "So Montbretia offered to go to the sandwich shop while I finished something off."

"When I got back," said Montbretia, picking up the story, "he was in his office, ready for my return—he had two plates, a teaspoon, and the roll of paper towels. I walked into the room with the sandwiches, freshly made, and he's there like a simpering little kid, whining that he can't get the lid off."

"It was the test packaging. There was a fault with the lids. They were tight, and she distracted me."

"Distracted you!" Montbretia's voice rose in pitch and volume. "You were being a whiny little kid. 'It's too tight. Help me. Help me. Help me.' He was holding the jar up near his face and getting all red and angry."

"Which is when you distracted me."

"Which is when the seal gave way."

"You distracted."

"The seal."

"Move on." Veronica was firm.

"She distracted me, the lid flicked off, and I lost my grip on the jar."

"There was no distraction. I happened to be there when he let go of the jar of horseradish, which flipped up and then headed toward the floor."

"So there's a jar of horseradish heading toward our new carpet, and I reacted instinctively."

"He tried to catch it on his foot."

"I tried to break its fall so it wouldn't smash."

"Note how he says 'tried'. Because what he actually did was catch the corner of the jar with the edge of his shoe. Now, I'm no physicist, but I believe what he did was convert linear vertical motion into rotary motion. So instead of going down, this jar was now spinning like a wheel and going horizontally." Montbretia laughed loudly.

"End result," said Boniface, "we got an eight-foot streak of horseradish across the carpet."

"So how did this get you out of jail?" asked Veronica.

"Well," said Boniface. "On TV cop shows you get the science people coming along, and they spray stuff that shows blood trails."

"Luminol," said Veronica.

"That's the stuff," said Boniface. "Apparently it gives a false positive when sprayed on horseradish. So we're going to find a new cleaner, because when the crime-scene guys sprayed the carpet, they found the murder scene. Or at least what they thought was the murder scene. When I told the detective inspector about the horseradish, he was pretty deflated. Five minutes later, I was out the door with some gruff words to behave myself." He clapped his hands together once. "So that's my story. What have you two been up to?"

"I've been at work, Boniface," said Veronica. "However, Montbretia has been very busy on your behalf."

Boniface turned to Montbretia. "Did you get into the office and see the damage? I got the impression that the carpet in my room has a big horseradish-shaped hole in it now."

Montbretia twisted her head like a lighthouse, arcing left-to-right-to-left-to-right. "You can't get in. There was yellow crime-scene tape everywhere with a policeman at our door."

"There was no tape at the front when I went past, but there was a rather stern policewoman outside our suite."

"So in your heart you didn't know we were here, and instead you went to the office before coming here," said Veronica, looking disapprovingly at Boniface.

Boniface ignored the comment as he continued. "What next?"

"Next?" Montbretia rolled her eyes in an exaggerated manner. "Next,

I went and talked to your favorite people."

Boniface shut his eyes. "I'm sorry for the suffering I put you through. I understand the sacrifice you're making."

"They're not that bad, Boniface."

"They're an indistinguishable morass of under-educated, ill-disciplined liars with no concept of their own ignorance or limitations. They all wear the same awful suits, nasty jewelry, and drive those appalling cars as if the laws of physics and death don't apply to them."

"They're not all like that."

"True. Charles is different, but he's even more ineffectual than the rest. I still don't get why you talk to them."

"Charles is sweet and the rest of the guys are fine. I talk to them because they're friendly and they show me around properties that I could never afford. I'm not taking risks or making compromises. None of them knows where I live—my house is still registered in Ellen's name—and they all move on to new jobs every couple of months."

"You didn't make any compromises today?" With a single turn of her head, Montbretia confirmed the negative. "And have you bathed in disinfectant since you saw them?"

Montbretia raised her eyebrows. "Relax, there were no compromises, and the only thing I flashed was a smile. I have had a shower; I did feel the necessity to wash myself down after swimming through all that testosterone. You don't think I went out dressed like this." She indicated the mismatched shocking-pink ensemble.

"What did you find?"

"CCTV and a burned-out van, which probably carried the body to the office—it's in the Caesar's Camp parking lot on Wimbledon Common."

Boniface turned to Veronica. "Have you got a driver?" She nodded, taking another sip. "Then let's go and have a look. You can tell us about the CCTV on the way up."

"There's not much to see up there," said Montbretia.

"There may not be, but I'd like to have a look, and then we can grab something to eat."

"You go," said Montbretia. "I'm in for the evening—I'm not dressed for dinner."

"It doesn't matter how you're dressed," said Boniface. "We're not going anywhere fancy. Wear what you wore today."

Veronica made an exaggerated sigh. "Bring me out here only to say we're not going anywhere nice." She sighed again, the extremity of her lip lifting as she winked at Boniface.

"You've got catching up to do," said Montbretia, "and I'm tired."

"But you're the one with the knowledge," said Veronica. "And you can't leave Boniface on his own. He needs adult supervision."

nine

"It's the obvious place."

"Why?"

"It's the closest isolated location and has the clearest access. Given the direction the van left the office, pretty much every permutation of any possible route avoids CCTV cameras." Montbretia stepped back from the burned-out Mercedes Sprinter van and held out an arm, rotating in a circle. "Standing here you're in the middle of a one-mile radius of the major road into and out of London, not to mention you've got five train stations, four subways, three hospitals, a cemetery, several supermarkets, a windmill," she smiled at Veronica, "and the Papal embassy, all within easy walking."

"Some of those are quite a distance," said Boniface.

Montbretia sighed. "If you've gone to the effort of lugging a dead body into an office, driving up here, removing the plates, and torching the van, then walking a mile or two, even in the dark, isn't going to cause you the sort of stress you need to talk through in therapy."

"Can't argue there," said Boniface. "So which way did they go?"

"A guess," said Montbretia, "would be that anyone would have walked toward the bypass—it's the major road into and out of London. If you go the route we came, then you're into a residential area pretty rapidly. But if you go that way," she pointed into the wooded area, a mass of shadowy black shapes in the nighttime, "then you've got the cemetery, a supermarket, and student accommodation blocks."

Boniface exhaled, nodding to suggest he knew where Montbretia was taking her logic.

"In other words, you've got an area where you will be unnoticed, and if you sit by a bus stop you're invisible, even to people standing next to you."

"And once you're on a bus, you're gone," said Boniface. He pointed back along the road they had been driven along. "Is that the only access?"

"For a van this size, yeah. There are other tracks, but they're gated, and you would want a four-wheel drive or a bike."

"Is this your route?" asked Boniface.

"You come through here?" Montbretia could hear the disquiet in Veronica's voice.

"Often—once or twice a week. It's the shortest route from home."

"But you live on Ham Common."

"Yup. And if you draw a straight line between my house and the office, you go straight through Richmond Park. There's a slight kink because there isn't a convenient gate, and apparently I'm not allowed to knock down the wall and go through people's backyards."

"The English are like that," offered Veronica, her Scottish brogue thickening.

"But when I get out the gate, I go over the bypass, and it's straight through." Montbretia kept her back to the road that led to the parking lot, holding out her arms in a V-shape. "There's the shortest track, but that's pretty bumpy." She indicated with her right arm. "Or," she indicated with her left arm, "I take the longer route, but it's a much better track and there are usually people around—dog walkers and horse riders."

"So which route did you take today?"

"I took the long route and was about 500 yards over there." Montbretia felt the disappointment tinged with hope in Boniface's and Veronica's looks. "I saw nothing." She watched as the hope left them.

"Question," said Veronica, startling Montbretia. "You reckon the van driver went away from the approach road. Away from the office."

Montbretia moved her lower jaw from left to right, contemplating. "It's a guess and a pretty weak guess."

"The guy you showed me in the CCTV with the fake beard went up the hill."

"That's the direction he appeared to be heading," said Montbretia. "But we're extrapolating from there. He could have jumped out of the camera arcs, ripped off the beard, put on a jacket, then turned back, and we wouldn't be able to recognize him. He could have kept the disguise and walked around the block, doubling back on himself—there's too much CCTV footage and only one of me."

"But he was last seen coming in this direction?" Montbretia nodded, allowing Veronica to continue. "If he did come in this direction, then why would the driver walk in the opposite direction?"

Montbretia lifted her shoulders, keeping them raised as she started to respond. "As I said, I'm guessing. Also don't forget, there was nearly two hours between the van leaving the office and the guy with the beard walking out. And to guess even more, I guess that the driver got here, set the van on fire, and left. I doubt he saw any necessity to hang around, especially as he won't have known when his fake-bearded buddy would be free, if that guy was waiting for Boniface to arrive."

Veronica hugged herself, apparently feeling the chill as she contemplated.

"There's one other thing," said Montbretia. "In fact, there are three things."

"Three things, and then let's get something to eat," said Boniface.

"Point one," said Montbretia. "We don't know what the driver did. We can speculate, but that doesn't take us forward. All we can hope is that someone saw him, so I'm coming back here tomorrow morning to find anyone who's here at the same time every day."

"That's crazy," said Boniface. "This isn't a good place to be alone in the dark, and that sort of sniffing should be left to the police."

"The police who haven't put a 'police aware' sign on that burned-out wreck? The police who think you had something to do with the body dump?" said Montbretia, not managing to keep the annoyance out of her voice. "Someone, somewhere must have seen something."

"There's..."

Montbretia cut off Boniface. "Point two. The driver and the bearded guy seem to have a different approach. The driver doesn't get seen. By contrast, the bearded guy waited until the police turned up and then left, crossing the arc of a CCTV camera."

"She makes a good point, Boniface," said Veronica. "These are professionals, and if a professional is happy to be seen on CCTV, then there's a reason for that." She turned to face Montbretia. "Point three?"

"We've discounted any notion that they might have left a car here." She looked up at Boniface and Veronica; both seemed confused. "It's not a smoking gun—I'm just pointing out that there are even more permutations, and the only way we're likely to find anything is by finding someone who actually saw something, which is why I need to get back here in the morning."

ten

"Nothing, until six-fifty-eight when you scamper past. Then at about ten-past-seven, two police cars scream round the corner, and two minutes later a guy with a big bushy beard crosses from our side of the road and turns up the hill."

"Can you see his face?" Boniface raised his voice over the sound of talking and cutlery clinking on plates as people ate.

"This is the best view." Boniface reached over the starched white tablecloth, now spattered with yellow grease stains, as Montbretia passed her phone. He squinted as she continued. "If you flick through to the next picture, you can see the top of the beard coming off under his right ear. He's trying to push it back as he walks."

"I see," said Boniface.

"But that's not the interesting thing," said Montbretia. "As he lifts his right hand, the sleeve drops and you can see a tattoo poking out. Not enough to see what the tattoo is, but there definitely is a tattoo and not a bit of wrist decoration."

Boniface squinted, then looked up. "I'll take your word. On this size screen it could be a smudge."

"Zoom in," said Montbretia.

"What, to see a smudge of a tattoo?"

"The previous shot—where he's pushing back the beard." Boniface fiddled with the screen. "Zoom in on the hand that's pushing the beard."

Boniface felt the muscle in his jaw lose tension. "Is he missing a finger?"

Montbretia nodded. "Still doesn't tell us where he went, but if we ever see him, he should be pretty recognizable." She held out her hand for her phone and continued. "That's pretty much it for the CCTV."

"Where does all this leave us? You've worked hard and risked your physical and mental safety spending time with those horrible children who are desperate to sell any property in Wimbledon, all to give us zero leads that we can follow." He read the disappointment on Montbretia's face. "Don't misunderstand: What you've done is helpful—you've chased every bit of evidence you've found to its logical conclusion—all I'm saying is where do we go next?" He surveyed the near-empty plates, the debris of saffron rice, near orange-colored chicken, and thin unleavened bread, all interspersed with serving dishes containing potato, cauliflower, chili, green peppers, onions, and other vegetables Boniface had difficulty recognizing. "More food for anyone?"

"It leaves us with a simple question." Veronica spoke as if she hadn't heard Boniface's offer. Her voice was measured, her focus fixed on her former husband. "Who is trying to get at you, Boniface? You don't leave a corpse unless you're trying to make a point. It's not a lighthearted April Fool."

Boniface remained quiet, letting his gaze fall on the dark-red flocked wallpaper.

Veronica continued. "Let's start with the people you've upset."

"That's a long list." Veronica narrowed her eyes as she always did when she didn't get a straight answer. "Where do you want me to start?"

"At the beginning." Boniface knew this look. He had been evasive, and so Veronica had flipped into interview mode. She had stopped asking questions and was now expecting answers.

"You probably know better than me," said Boniface. "You remember who I turned over when I was a journalist—you were married to me. People might have hated me, but the stakes were never big enough to get at me like this."

"Start with the simple guesses," said Veronica. "Your story forced Stan Gadson to resign as an MP, and his researcher went to jail for six months. Do you think it could be him?"

"Nah. That was far too long ago. Also, he had a heart attack the year after, and when I last heard, his health wasn't great—not that it was good when he was in Parliament."

"What about the researcher who went to jail?" asked Montbretia.

"Again, too long ago, and he never had the brain power to think things through, which is why he ended up in jail rather than Stan."

"He still mentions you on Facebook," said Montbretia.

"Really?" Boniface snorted. "You're kidding."

Montbretia gave a firm shake of her head in response to Boniface's grin.

"If it's not something you did when you were a journalist, then is it something to do with your time working with Gideon?" asked Veronica, still in interview mode. "You did some unpleasant stuff then—did you upset someone enough that they would send you a cadaver?"

"I upset people, but I didn't have any power." Boniface felt like he was whining. "I was handling the press, Gideon was the minister making the decisions. Someone might have wanted to get back at me for being a smart-assed pain, but a dead body seems rather extreme."

"You might think you were an angel, albeit an angel with a loose tongue, but does everyone else see it that way? The Honorable Gideon Latymer, Member of Parliament for some metal-bashing corner of the West Midlands, was involved with fairly dubious decisions. Contracts were canceled, new contracts put in place, and there was lots of cash getting passed in brown envelopes." Veronica sat back in her chair, plainly with a mild distaste in what she had said.

"Gideon was clean, but he was naive and made some bad decisions. There's a reason his political ascent stalled."

"Sure, but is there anyone who thinks that you were captaining the ship, even if you were taking orders?"

Boniface exhaled as if trying to blow out a candle across the room. "Politics is a contact sport and I was an enthusiastic team player, but why me and not Gid? Why now? It doesn't make any sense, but I'll call Gideon in the morning and see if he's heard anything."

Veronica reached down to her bag, pulled up her bottle of whisky, refilled her tumbler, and returned the bottle. "It's alright," she said to Montbretia. "We have an understanding in this restaurant. As long as I don't let other patrons see, then I'm not creating a precedent." She turned to Boniface. "While we're talking about alcohol, what about your fellow rehab inmates, Boniface?"

He chuckled softly. "Yeah, there are some pretty obsessive-compulsive, angry guys there. None that could get their life together sufficiently to organize this. But more to the point, they all loved me there."

"If it's not your past, then it's your present and it must be an angry client." Veronica took another sip of whisky. "Who is your current client?" She dipped her head, looking up at Boniface, and spoke in clipped tones. "By the way, I was a good girl. I didn't put matchsticks under Montbretia's fingers to make her reveal."

"It wouldn't have done any good," said Montbretia, her voice very matter-of-fact. "He doesn't tell me what he's up to unless he wants me to get involved." She flicked her head to face Boniface, her eyes sharp, her tone surprisingly bright. "What about the rapist?"

"What sort of clients are you taking on, Boniface?" asked Veronica, staring at Boniface. "Is money really that tight?"

"I didn't take on a rapist." He broke eye contact with Veronica. "I spoke to a rapist's father."

"And he was big and incredibly scary." Montbretia indicated height, width, and depth and started pushing and pulling her face into grotesque shapes.

"Yeah. He scared me, too, and nearly broke my hand when he shook it. Anyway, he threw down his business card, and I was too busy looking at his description of services—metal recovery and recycling, ferrous and non-ferrous including brass, lead and copper, domestic and industrial, nuclear decommissioning..."

"Stop."

"Seriously, nuclear decommissioning." He paused. "Then I read the name and twigged."

"So who was he?"

"Tommy Newby."

Veronica's voice took on an urgency. "Tommy Newby? Tommy Newby, father of Angelo Newby, who beat that poor girl to a pulp?"

"Yes, that Tommy Newby. That Angelo Newby who was found not guilty." Boniface fell back in his seat, his voice timid as he continued. "There was a delay in the trial, so Tommy got his driver to bring him down to see me. He thought it was time for a bit of PR input."

"What did you say?"

"There wasn't much I could say. Angelo had already been crucified in the press; anything I would have put forward would have made things worse. Added to which, I was busy and I don't take clients who pay in used fifty-quid notes."

"So you turned him away."

"I told him that my services wouldn't help. I suggested he hire a lawyer to start suing anyone in the press who might defame his mild-as-a-lamb son and to make a conspicuous donation to a women's refuge to show how seriously the family regarded the issue. You know the line, violence toward women is terrible, but our Angelo is a little angel who loves his mother—just look at his tattoos. In between the picture of the devil and the stripper who gyrates when he flexes, there's her name."

"So you turned him down."

Boniface grimaced. "I thought I gave him a more positive course of action, and I didn't charge him."

"This isn't about you, Boniface. This is about Tommy, the hand-crushing father of a violent rapist." Veronica fixed him with a stare as she continued. "Did Tommy Newby think that you refused to help his son at the very moment when he thought you were the one person who could help? I'm not asking whether you did the right thing, or even whether you made the right decision for yourself. I'm asking whether Tommy thinks you refused to help him."

Boniface deflated. "I don't think so, but I couldn't read the guy. He's used to getting his own way. He doesn't often hear the word no, or at least when he does, it is conventionally followed by the sound of breaking glass and breaking bones."

"You don't think it's Tommy?"

"I doubt it's Tommy. Look what happened next."

"You mean the witness didn't turn up and hasn't been seen since? Or you mean the case had to be dropped because of the lack of said key witness, and then Angelo went to Saint-Tropez, where he is currently in jail, having been accused of raping and murdering a hotel chamber-maid?" She sighed and continued, her volume soft but the tone sarcastic. "Remind me again, how did that all work out for Tommy and Angelo?"

"What I mean is that Tommy took my advice to make a charitable donation." He watched Veronica's reaction: Without a doubt, she was disgusted by the notion of the man. "Tommy's a leg-breaker. Leaving a body would be far too much of an ambiguous communication."

Boniface scrutinized Montbretia and his former wife, who was refreshing her tumbler again. Montbretia broke the silence. "Is that it?"

Boniface squirmed. "No. I'll speak to Tommy."

eleven

Montbretia led into the entrance hall and waited for the reassuring click as Boniface closed the front door behind them. "Isn't it a bit weird?" She turned, trying to keep him in position without taking an aggressive stance.

"What? Having a new person in the office who's been sleeping on the job? Sleeping in your office." Montbretia's feet remained stationary, her head swiveling as Boniface walked past her into the lounge. He checked his phone that he had put on to charge before they left for Wimbledon Common, then reached for a CD. "Music I think."

He hit the play button, unleashing guitar power chords over the speakers.

"That joke wasn't even funny the first time. And don't you know that people don't use CDs anymore, grandpa?"

"People may not, but CDs still sound better than MP3s." He twisted his face. "I would have preferred vinyl, but a good dose of Dutch prog rock on CD keeps me happy."

"Really?" Montbretia could feel incredulity mixed with frustration in her voice. "You really want to go through the pain of listening to a whole album of this stuff?"

Boniface sighed. "No. Not really. This lot only did two tracks that are worth listening to."

"You mean this and that piece of yodeling shit?" Boniface had a wide and sometimes eclectic selection of music. Most dated from the 1970s. Most was tolerable if you were in the mood, but trying to use music as a joke was annoying Montbretia.

"Yes, this track, and the name of the other piece is 'Hocus Pocus,' I think you'll find."

"So, the yodeler's delight and 'Sylvia,' and that is it?" She glanced as Boniface gave a single curt nod, like a defiant child. "Well, 'Sylvia' isn't funny."

"No, but it is a great track. Listen to the melody: so much joy, hope, expectation, elation, but underneath it's tinged with melancholy. There's heartbreak and sadness. It's a whole story in one melodic phrase. Without using words, you understand exactly what the guy's telling you." He let the track continue, listening. "The world is always different after listening to this track."

"And its title is my middle name." She regarded the crumpled mound of cushions on the sofa where she had sat, deep in contemplation, in the fetal position—her knees under her chin and her arms tightly wrapped around her legs, with a cup of coffee that she let go cold as she waited for Boniface to return.

But he hadn't returned when she expected him to, and it had been dark when Veronica had arrived and rang the doorbell, rousing Montbretia from her numbed inaction.

She dropped into the spot where she had sat earlier. "Great. I've got the joke. Can we go back to no music and you promise never to play 'Sylvia' again? Or at least can we turn down the volume so we can talk like civilized human beings? If you don't want to answer the question, you can say so."

"What question?" said Boniface.

Montbretia tilted her head—the social-worker look, as Boniface called it. "I'm not trying to pry or be judgmental, but you and the ex—don't get me wrong, I like her—but isn't it a bit, well, weird?"

Boniface flopped onto the sofa where Veronica had sat earlier in the evening. "What? You mean it's weird that my former wife and I are not scratching each other's eyes out?"

"Sort of." Montbretia wished she had planned this conversation before asking the question. "But isn't it a bit weird that she arrived without prompting. You could have had a chick here—that would've been embarrassing."

"She rang the bell, though, didn't she?"

"How do you know that?"

"Because although she's got a key and could have let herself in, by ringing she makes sure that there are no embarrassing incidents."

"She's got a key?"

"So have you."

"But we weren't married."

Boniface's tone was dismissive. "Is that important? Am I required to cease to trust everyone from whom I'm divorced?"

"Don't be like that—that's not what I'm trying to say," said Montbretia. She continued, hesitant. "Shouldn't you be...over? Finished? No longer involved? It's not as if you've got kids."

Boniface paused, looking as if he was weighing what he wanted to say and how he intended to present his perspective.

"Our divorce was different." He sat forward. "We didn't split because we hated each other, and we never fell out." He stopped talking, his hands still moving as if giving directions in a conversation he was having with himself.

"There was a time when it was bad. Very bad. We shouted. A lot. Before that there was a time when we drifted, like two separate ships on a desperately foggy night, each seeing the other on the radar, but not getting close enough to see or touch. Something like that or some other cliché. But ultimately, we can't be married to each other."

Montbretia frowned. "Explain."

"The split was the final step before I went over the edge, not the cause. When I sorted myself out and had stopped drinking, things changed. Veronica can handle her drink, but I can't, and I can't remain in control when alcohol is around. That's why there's no alcohol here and she brings her own bottle and takes it away."

"But you wouldn't drink it if she left her bottle here."

"Probably not. But she understands the risk—it's rather like leaving a knife on the floor. Sure, the baby probably won't stab itself, but if it did, how would you feel?" Boniface fixed Montbretia with a stare, breaking as he continued. "So yes, it's kinda strange, but we're both big enough to work it out, and we both still care for each other, which is why she came around here."

Montbretia nodded tentatively.

"Does that make some sort of sense?"

Montbretia nodded more firmly. "I didn't want to intrude, it's just... well, you know..."

"Weird."

Montbretia snorted. "Weird. But okay weird, I guess." She put her hand through her collar and pulled at the blue lanyard with a silver memory stick.

"Before you show the CCTV footage, there's something I want you to do tomorrow." She let herself sink back into the sofa, flicking her eyes from left to right.

"Sounds like I'm on a mission tomorrow. Do I get a disguise? Do I get a codename?"

Boniface narrowed his eyes. "No. All you have to do is do what you do well: talk to people and put them at ease."

"Sure. Who?"

"Whoever is taking our office apart."

"But you saw, Boniface: There's a police guard. How am I meant to find anything?"

"Clearly you were never a smoker."

"Neither were you."

"True. But I know many smokers—or at least, I did before they died or got nagged to stop smoking by their worried spouses—and one thing all smokers do is go outside for a cigarette during their break. All you have to do is stand outside our office and wait for someone in a bunny suit to come down and find out what they know."

"I'm not a detective, Boniface. What am I meant to ask them?" She felt an emotion that was somewhere between annoyance, confusion, and incredulity.

"Every employee feels overworked, underpaid, and that their boss doesn't appreciate them." He let out a small sigh. "It's a law...it's written down somewhere, and if you're a science geek scrabbling through crime scenes, you must feel very aggrieved. You're likely to be about a thousand times more intelligent and better qualified than the administrative people who run your lab, and your pay is decided by politicians you will never meet."

That seemed logical. Boniface didn't need to continue, but he did. "Find someone and say something that makes them know that you feel their pain, and you'll be in. Then follow up with some direct questions about the body—who is he, where did he come from? If we can't find who dumped the body, let's see if we can find out who the dead person is and work back from there."

twelve

Montbretia checked her phone. Seven AM. Two hours gone, one hour left.

It was lighter than when she arrived—it was now between dawn and sunrise—but she still couldn't feel any change in temperature. It wasn't so much that it was cold—in fact, it was a near-perfect temperature if she had been cycling—but it wasn't warm, and that mattered because she had been in the same place since she arrived. The farthest she had moved had been from one side of the lot to the other—that wasn't going to be more than fifty feet.

She stared at the burned-out van. It looked very much like a burned-out version of the van she had seen on the CCTV. The van that had entered their office parking lot at about 5:30 yesterday morning—it was the first thing to enter the parking lot after her and Boniface had left at around 10:30 the previous evening. Montbretia knew—she had checked all the CCTV that was available from the businesses up and down Wimbledon Hill Road.

Ten minutes after arriving, the van was gone.

It seemed a pretty standard panel van. A Mercedes Sprinter, white. A brief internet search yesterday had suggested the van was used by any number of delivery firms, construction firms, and wannabe rock bands on the road. The number of vans on the road and the uses the van was put to seemed endless. It seemed to be the van that was used by everyone for everything and anything. In short, it was ubiquitous and anonymous.

There was nothing else on the CCTV apart from a few pigeons, until 6:58 when Boniface hurried past on his way to the office. At about 7:15, two police cars had rounded the corner, and two minutes after that, the man with the beard had passed.

Except he didn't have a beard. But he did have a tattoo that was exposed as his sleeve dropped when he slapped the fake beard back into place, and the top half of his ring finger on his right hand was missing.

After they had watched the CCTV, Boniface's mood had hardened. He had never been happy about Montbretia coming up to the Common, but after seeing the CCTV footage last night he had become quite insistent: no risks, no danger, nothing stupid.

She had agreed: no risks, no danger, nothing stupid. However, Boniface hadn't clarified what constituted a risk or danger, and stupidity was only relevant if you were caught, so she was happy to agree to his terms. Or rather, she couldn't see the point in arguing with him when she would do what she wanted in any event.

Boniface would be busy today. He had two leads to follow and a client—a client whose identity Montbretia still didn't know—to resign from. While he was running around in the center of London, she agreed to see if she could find someone in a bunny suit, and since he was focused elsewhere, he wouldn't notice that she was first doing what he thought she had agreed not to.

During the first two hours of doing what Boniface thought she wasn't doing, Montbretia had spoken to six people and gleaned no useful information. She slipped out her phone to flick through the stills from the CCTV again. She stared, hoping for a new insight.

She zoomed in: a white van; it looked the same as the one in front of her, except that the one here was burned out. She had seen it in the dark, seen it at the time it was dumped and set alight, and she could see it now. Whatever might have been in the van was burned, and she was no closer to knowing who the driver was.

A few more flicks and she got to the pictures of the man with the false beard, the tattoo, and a partially missing finger. However hard she stared, there was no more detail—what was she meant to do? Show it to people and ask, "Have you seen this smudge?"

She walked back to her bike and rested on the crossbar, waiting. It was still chilly, misty, and being surrounded by woods on two-and-a-half sides made her feel halfway to being in the middle of nowhere. Another time check. Still not time to go.

Along the approach road, two headlights were bumping on the rough track cutting through the golf course. Eventually the car pulled up, a German station wagon, but Montbretia was dubious about the make.

A small man wearing a worn blue waxed jacket and a crumpled flat-cap got out. Montbretia was talking before he noticed her. "Hello there. I'm so sorry to bother you. Were you here yesterday morning?"

The driver appeared startled, then froze. The only visible sign of life was his still-moving eyes, looking Montbretia up and down, scanning nervously around as if he was expecting an elaborate practical joke. Finally he spoke. "Yes."

"At this time?" Montbretia tried to keep her galloping enthusiasm out of her voice.

"No." His face had a look of awe, as if he was about to relay a tale of biblical proportions and unimaginable, incomprehensible tragedy. "I had a flat tire. It took an hour for the guy to arrive to fix it." Montbretia felt the appropriate response was a series of facial expressions to convey the acknowledgement he apparently craved. "By the time the tire was changed, the dog was too upset and she had crapped on the carpet, so I had to clean that up."

"Gracious." In her few months staying with Boniface, Montbretia had learned that the word "gracious" seemed to be used by the Brits to imply some shared understanding of suffering without needing to calibrate how much understanding. She waited a beat before continuing. "Was the van here when you arrived?"

"The van and the firemen who were blocking up the place. I turned round and parked over by the pub." He threw his hand loosely in the direction of the road he had driven along.

"So you didn't see what happened here?"

"No." His head twisted and his eyes narrowed. "Is that an American accent I can detect?" Montbretia felt a resigned smile cross her face. "Where are you from?"

"Virginia. Richmond, Virginia."

"Ha! You've come all this way to be near to another Richmond. Have you been to our Richmond?"

"I have," nodded Montbretia, raising her eyebrows to point at the old Labrador standing patiently in the back of the car. "It looks like your dog wants to get walking, so I'd better not delay you any further. Thanks for your help." She spun away—she was bored, but not sufficiently bored to waste the next five minutes of her life comparing two places that just happened to have the same name.

thirteen

His phone rang.

He ignored it.

After the sixth ring, it stopped.

He stretched and felt his right leg kick out the sheets and fall over the frontier of the bed. Strange. Sheets tucked in. He stretched his left leg: There were no sheets to hold it as it fell over the opposite extremity of his berth.

Still tucked-in sheets, and he could reach both sides of the bed without going full starfish. Something was wrong.

Then he remembered: It had been a good night last night. A very good night. But however much fun you might be having, if your companion's husband's company owns an executive jet and he's the CEO, you can never be sure what time he'll get back. So while you can rationalize to yourself that it was acceptable to entertain his wife—and she was a game girl who liked her entertainment in so many and such varied ways, all so pleasing to him—and that it was quite acceptable to choose one or two of the best bottles from the CEO's hand-picked wine-cellar (read, wall full of climate-controlled cabinets in the basement), it simply wasn't appropriate to still be there if said CEO arrived home before he was expected. So when the mutually beneficial activities came to a close, he was packed off in a cab and had spent the night in his club.

Hence the bed that had been made before he got into it.

Hence the single bed.

He yanked the sheets over his head and tried to get back to sleep again.

His phone rang again. His phone, not the phone in the room. He ignored it again, pulling the sheets tighter over his head, trying to stop the noise and keep out the traces of daylight that had made their way around the curtains.

The noise stopped, then started again.

"What?" Clearly the only way to get rid of telemarketers trying their luck this early was to shout. His face relaxed into a smile. "Boniface, my dear fellow. Where are you?" He glanced around but couldn't see a clock. "Here? Now? Where? Reception? Never heard of me? Definitely not staying? Pass me over to Brenda. It's bound to be Brenda; she always looks after me." He heard some mumbling and the sound of the phone being bumped as it was handed over. "Brenda, darling, I most humbly apologize. I should have told you to wear your best silk knickers. *That* is the famous Mister Boniface standing before you. He's quite harmless—you can send him straight up." He rolled onto his side. "By the way, and exclusively as a matter for the record, Boniface is rather Church of England in his tastes, so I'm pretty sure he'd be grateful even if you're wearing your comfortable old cotton knickers."

He dropped his phone, turned over, and tried to get back to sleep.

There was a knock on the door. Firm contact between wood and knuckles. Gideon pulled the sheets tighter. Another knock—this one more vigorous. Gideon threw the sheets back, leaving his trailing foot still on the bed as he took the half step to the door, which he opened without checking the peephole first, and stood, naked, to greet his guest.

"Boniface!" He watched as Boniface took in his state, then flicked his hips, his nakedness allowing skin to slap against skin at the top of his thigh. "You're lucky I don't have a boner; otherwise I would be pointing you in the wrong direction. Come in. Sit down." He pointed to the lone seat in the room, next to the bathroom door, then closed the door to his small room and walked past Boniface into the bathroom without closing the door behind him.

"First stream in the morning. Isn't that best to check whether I'm pregnant?" Gideon stood, leaning forward, arms outstretched, hands at roughly head height resting against the wall, aiming straight for the center of the bowl in front of him. "Sounds like a mountain stream in full flow, doesn't it, Boniface?"

Gideon shook, tore off a few sheets of paper, wiped, dropped the paper, and flushed before he moved to the sink. As he dried his hands, he caught sight of himself in the mirror and looked down at his wrists. "She was considerably more enthusiastic than I expected."

Boniface grunted from his seat outside the bathroom.

Gideon continued to examine his wrists. They may have been silk scarves, but he wouldn't be rolling up his sleeves today. At least not in public. "Have you got a comb there, Boniface?"

"Sure."

"It's this chocolate, stuck in my...well, look..." Gideon walked out of the bathroom, head down, both hands pulling apart pubic hair like he was the first explorer in a newly discovered jungle.

"Gideon, please." Gideon could hear Boniface's distaste as he replaced his comb in his pocket, looking away. The host remained standing at the extreme of Boniface's line of sight and continued to explore, his hands at the height of his former pressman's head.

"She was a game girl."

Boniface sighed expressively. "Is there some new law that I'm not aware of which obliges me to listen as you tell me about last night's exploits?"

"I'm sure there is, Boniface." Gideon slapped him daintily around the cheek, his feet unmoving as he placed his hands on his hips. "You know how much you enjoy hearing about my fun and games."

Gideon paused and watched Boniface as his head turned cautiously. "It's too early in the morning to have your cock pointing at me."

Gideon hoped there was a glint in his eye. "You're in a dilemma, aren't you, Mister B? You are desperate to ask me to put some clothes on—and you probably want to make some disparaging comment about my awful behavior—but you recognize that means you first have to acknowledge your discomfort at my nakedness..."

"You're in your own room," muttered Boniface without conviction.

Gideon continued, "You also know that asking me is likely to provoke me to take a step closer to you. And you're weighing up whether I'm staying naked to provoke you or if I'm lacking clothes because that's the state you found me in."

Boniface remained still with his head turned away.

"Really, Boniface, for such an old lush, you always were far too buttoned-down...or was it buttoned-up? I never got to figure what your kink was, and I always thought it would be bad form to ask the delightful Veronica to illuminate. How is dear V, by the way? Still the ex? Still haven't found a way to be sober and married?"

"Still haven't." Boniface looked Gideon in the eye, his voice slightly strained. "Try some clothes, please."

"There's no pleasing you, is there, Boniface? Anyway, I haven't told you my tale of last night." Gideon stepped into the bathroom, grabbed a toweling robe hanging behind the door, and returned to the bedroom where Boniface was sitting. "You're not playing this game very well."

"I didn't realize..."

"Shhh." Gideon finished tying the belt around the white robe as he walked along the narrow passage around the bed. "My story." He sat on the bed and faced Boniface. "You remember that Swiss guy with the aluminum company?"

"Moritz Leisy." Gideon nodded as Boniface continued. "You introduced us. I pitched for business. He decided he didn't like me...which wasn't so bad because I found him to be a truly tedious individual."

Gideon tightened his mouth and furrowed his brow as if contemplating Boniface's assessment of the man whose wife he had spent most of the night with.

"You boffed his wife." Boniface dropped his head into his hand and massaged his temples.

"Boffed. Really, Boniface. You're so animalistic. For you intimacy is about ejaculation. One spurt and it's the end of the story as far as you're concerned. But yes, Allegra and I enjoyed each other's company, and to be honest, I don't even remember whether there was coitus. There may have been, there may not have been. But what I can tell you is there was much nakedness, a huge amount of fun over a long period of time, and the dear lady was very satisfied by the time I was packed off."

Boniface glanced up, then dropped his head back into his hand.

"She was very enthusiastic—much more enthusiastic than I had expected. Marks for enthusiasm. Bonus credits for willingness to participate. Gold stars for being open about what she wanted to try. But she lacked finesse. Look at my wrists."

Boniface raised his head as Gideon pulled back his sleeves to show the friction burns around his wrists. "There's something sticky in my hair, and of course the chocolate stuck..."

"I get it. There was food, including melted chocolate."

"That's my point. You're not meant to put melted chocolate on your partner's cock...or near anywhere else where hair grows. Jam, cream, whatever, but nothing that is liable to set. Nothing that won't come out in a quick shower." He pulled down the shoulder of his robe. "I was already nursing a war wound: I don't require any more problems."

"Ouch. What happened there?"

"Hot wax that went a bit too far on the night before."

"Allegra again?"

"No, that was a far more adventurous young lady who really enjoys pain."

"Jesus, Gideon. You're going to break the internet if you create any more new perversions. You do know that at the banquet of human sexuality and experimentation, you don't have to try every dish."

"Relax, Boniface. I haven't tried all the dishes." He paused, hoping for dramatic effect. "But I do have a to-do list."

"Is Allegra on that to-do list again tonight?"

"Oh no, no, no, no, no. You would never go to the same restaurant for two nights running. You would never go to the ballet two nights running. Especially not when you live in London and can go to the theater or the opera the next night. So why would I limit my activities on consecutive nights to one person? Besides, my allure is the new, the daring, the outrageous." He sighed mournfully. "The forbidden fruit ceases to be forbidden if you can get it on demand."

Gideon leaned forward before continuing. "I also get the impression that the husband is a bit like you. She's got to be lying at a right angle before he can begin. There are rules to be followed. Minimum standards to be met. If that's the case, then a bit of tedium will make her even more keen."

"You know how they warn teenagers about risky sexual activity?" Gideon could hear the disappointment in Boniface's voice. "Every time we talk, I feel like I'm becoming your disapproving mother telling you that your been-there-seen-that-done-her list will present, shall we say, issues for you at some point."

Gideon pushed out his bottom lip and waited for Boniface to notice. "You didn't wake me up with the sole purpose of telling me off." He brightened. "Come on. Why are you here, Boniface?"

"I'm here because I need to talk, but I can't talk when you keep flopping out. Get the chocolate off your gonads, and I'll be back in an hour."

fourteen

A few more people came through in the last hour Montbretia spent in the parking lot watching the burned-out Mercedes van. By the time she left, she had spoken to fifteen people.

No one had seen anything apart from a burned-out van and what the Brits liked to call the fire brigade. One person had seen the fire burning—or at least the end of the fire; that person had made the call to the emergency services—but they hadn't seen anyone around.

Before she went looking for people in bunny suits she needed to go home. The route out and the route back gave her two opportunities to check the paths that the van driver may have followed.

It was a long shot, and the track she followed from the parking lot gave her no clues—she would try the alternate on her way back. When she got to the main road, she crossed at the horse crossing before heading into Richmond Park. As she liked to point out to her friends who visited from New York, this was a proper park: three times the size of Central Park. For that matter, even Wimbledon Common was bigger than Central Park. She felt herself bristle at her friends' assumptions; then she realized how much she was going native, siding with the Colonists. She put the thoughts out of her head and made for the main path bisecting the park.

In just over three miles, she exited at Ham Gate, followed the road around the perimeter of Ham Common, past the church, and was home.

While it was home, it still didn't feel like home. Her house had become hers when her sister was accidentally killed five months earlier, and technically it still wasn't Montbretia's house and wouldn't legally be hers until the formalities of probate had been completed, which, according to the lawyers, would take another nine months or so. Until then, it was still owned by her sister's estate, of which Montbretia was the sole executor.

The house was still decorated to Ellen's taste, furnished with Ellen's furniture, the kitchen filled with Ellen's kitchenware and cookbooks, and the closets filled with Ellen's clothes. It was a comfort having Ellen still around, but it also made it harder to accept that she had gone, and would make it harder to ever move on from here.

It was also the site where Ellen's friend, and Boniface's client, Nigel Trudgett, had been murdered. Apparently there had blood spattered across the front of the house after he had been shot. Montbretia hadn't seen it, but according to Boniface, Hilda Longthorne, her next-door neighbor, had cleaned the whole area the minute the police had told her she could.

Montbretia walked up the path between the two homes with entrance doors on the side of each house facing the other, and leaned her bicycle against the wall. She opened the door and picked up the mail on the mat, flicking through the pile before she threw it on the side next to the answering machine with its red flashing light.

She hit the play button. "Hi Monty, it's Nathan..."

"He sent you flowers last month."

Montbretia hadn't heard Hilda behind her. She turned to see her next-door neighbor standing outside the open door. "Hello, darling." Montbretia jumped down and embraced the older woman. "How are you?" She stood back, beaming at her neighbor, who was straightening her faded green cardigan, pulling it tight over her brown floral dress.

Hilda's voice was stern, rising above the burbling message from Nathan, which was still playing. "You need to ensure that you are clear with these young men. They must understand that while I'm very grateful to receive their flowers, and I do love the flowers—but you should take them because they were sent for you—my acceptance doesn't mean that I have agreed to have sex with them."

Montbretia let out a short, surprised burst of laughter at her septuagenarian neighbor's comment, as she looked at the wrinkled skin and colorless gray hair, which disguised a youthful vigor and biting sense of humor. Nathan's voice droned on in the background. Montbretia wasn't quite sure what he was talking about, but she understood enough to realize that if he hadn't understood the word goodbye, then she had insufficient time to call him back. Ever.

Hilda returned Montbretia's smile. "I've had some more flowers."

"From Nathan?"

"No." She held the edge of a card with the local florist's logo. "One bunch was from Russell." She handed the card to Montbretia. "The second bunch was from Oliver."

"No card?" said Montbretia lightly.

"No card," affirmed Hilda. "No card because Oliver hand-picked the flowers and then delivered them in person. I promised I would pass them to you the moment you got in."

"Such a wuss," said Montbretia under her breath.

"It's sweet," said Hilda.

"No. It's annoying. I told him if he ever picked me flowers, wrote poetry, cooked me anything more than a boiled egg, or did anything else designed to show me his emotional side that I would puke. On him."

"Doesn't the car suggest some manliness?" asked Hilda. "When I was young enough to care about those things, I would have said yes to any man who drove a TR6"

"It's a lovely car," said Montbretia. "But it's forty years old, and he's such a simpering girl about it. The primary purpose of a car is to get from A to B, in the warm and in the dry. You can do that in a TR6 if it's a warm and dry day. If it's not, then you get cold and wet in that car. The car belongs in a museum, not on the streets of London."

"The flowers are lovely. Won't you take them?" Hilda's face almost begged. "Please?"

Montbretia sighed, trying not to be annoyed. "I like flowers, but I kill flowers and I'm never here, so I would rather they went to a good home. Your home. It's a favor to me and a small thanks for being such a super neighbor."

"I think these are meant to be special," said Hilda in an almost apologetic voice, a slight reddening coming to her creased cheeks.

"He didn't, did he?" Montbretia could hear the annoyance in her own voice.

Hilda's face softened as she gracefully conceded.

"You're telling me that Oliver hand-picked a spray of montbretias," said Montbretia. "I told you he was sickening. Now do you see my point?"

"I do," said Hilda.

"What did Russell send?" asked Montbretia.

"Stargazer lilies."

"Now that would have been a good choice," said Montbretia, "if I actually cared about Russell." The answering machine beeped behind her. "But like Nathan and now Oliver, he too is history. I've got other more important things to do."

Hilda had an inquisitive look on her face, but Montbretia knew she would never let her curiosity intrude, and at the moment she didn't have time to explain.

"I need to pick up one of Ellen's suits and get back to the office." She stepped inside, turning to face Hilda. "If any more flowers arrive, please give them a good home."

fifteen

Boniface walked down the creaky and uneven stairs, wary not to catch his foot on the thinning carpet, before he passed through the reception area. Dark wood and old marble—wipe-clean surfaces seemed somehow appropriate for Gideon.

Gideon who, while remaining a Member of Parliament, was now taking full advantage of the end of his Cabinet responsibilities by leading a campaign fired by his passion. On first blush it might seem strange for Gideon to be the leading campaigner for victims of sex crime, but when anyone heard him talk on the issue, there was no doubt of his commitment. For Gideon, a sexual omnivore with a biological need for frequent and varied stimulation and many experiences with many partners, sex crimes were an abomination.

Gideon's campaign embraced all such forms of sex-related crime. He wasn't only a supporter of the more obvious victims that the press could relate to—primarily women who suffered abuses on a spectrum from verbal intimidation, through groping, all the way up to rape and murder—he was concerned with male rape, with a focus on the victimization of rent boys, the exploitation of children in all the forms it took, people trafficking for sexual exploitation, and the least trendy area of all: the sexual exploitation and sexual rights of the vulnerable and mentally challenged, in particular, their rights around pregnancy.

To Gideon, in all its forms, however Clinton-equse one wanted to be in the definition, sex had to be a consensual shared act, and having shared a consensual act last night, he had then slept at his club, which Boniface was now leaving, and from where Boniface usually would have been quite happy to take the first cab.

But not this morning.

The first cab had what he didn't want: one of the younger cabbies with a bluetooth headset stuck in his ear who spent all day on the phone and never remembered to switch off the intercom, forcing his passenger to endure half a conversation around the details of the boy his fourteen-year-old stepdaughter had slept with and how if gun laws in the UK were like gun laws in the States, he would have put her honor beyond doubt.

In the third cab he stopped, he found what he wanted: short, fat, old, gray cardigan, flat-cap. Old school. Someone who would not only know all of the back doubles but would have the temperament and the patience to go up every back street, happy in the knowledge that he was racking up his fare.

The downside was that rather than listening to tales about potential bastard children, Boniface had to hear about the cabbie's wife's "women's problems, you know" in graphic detail. He was grateful when Tommy's vintage Bentley came into sight.

"Is that a Blower?" the cabbie asked as Boniface stepped out of the cab.

"Definitely a Bentley. Definitely authentic, but beyond that, I'm never sure what differentiates a Blower from a conventional Bentley." Boniface pulled out his wallet and pulled out two notes, which he handed to the driver.

"Thanks, gov." The cabbie continued to stare longingly at the Bentley. "Didn't know there was a difference; thought all vintage Bentleys were called Blowers."

"I know even less," said Boniface, "but if I find the owner, I'll ask him and let you know when I next get in your cab."

Recognizing the unlikelihood, the cabbie winked and started to pull away. "Cheers, gov. You have a good day." The diesel engine throbbed up the street as Boniface started walking past the Bentley, taking his time to admire the immaculately restored vintage machinery. He tilted his head in acknowledgement to the driver, who had been polishing the front headlight with a handkerchief—nursemaid and guardian of the antique while it was on the public highway.

As Boniface passed the front wing, the driver dropped his visual lock on Boniface, apparently now searching out the next potential threat to his responsibility. As the driver dropped his stare, Boniface became aware of his own apprehension: pounding heart, tightening in the stomach, and a loosening in the bowels. He stepped through the café door and stopped, scanning the rows of Formica-topped tables bolted to the floor, interleaved with bench seats covered in dark red leatherette as immobile as the tables, filled with people engrossed in eating.

He was grateful for the cabbie's wife's problems. If she had been a normal, healthy woman, Boniface's mind might have wandered, and it would have wandered to think about Tommy. But thanks to a middle-aged woman with a middle-aged problem married to a middle-aged man who liked to moan at great length, there hadn't been any space left in Boniface's mind.

Then Boniface saw him. He knew he had seen him because he could hear his breathing: fast and deep. He held his breath for a moment, then breathed out slowly and in slowly.

Boniface watched as Tommy lifted his paw up to his mouth. It was probably quite a large sandwich that he was eating, but in his hand it looked like a delicate cucumber sandwich with its crusts removed that a well-to-do Edwardian lady might consume at tea. As the food went into his mouth, Tommy saw Boniface. The big man's brow furrowed.

He replaced the sandwich and stood, wiping his hands. As he reached his full height, the only term that came to Boniface's mind was "bear." This was truly a bear of a man—a rather overweight bear wearing a sober charcoal suit, but a bear nonetheless.

He unknitted his brow, and the light of recognition sparked in his eyes. "Mister Boniface, what a coincidence." The bear smiled and offered his hand to Boniface, who felt his right hand get swallowed by the bear's paw. "Please." He pointed to the bench on the opposite side of his table. "Join me."

Boniface slid in, nervously watching Tommy sit down, very aware that he was in a place he hadn't been before, sitting with his back to the door, with a man who may have dumped a carcass in his office just over 24 hours ago. "And it's Boniface, not Mister anything."

Tommy nodded. "Have you had breakfast?" His voice was soft, concerned, reassuring, like a grandfather with his grandson. "Have a bacon sandwich. The best bacon sandwich you'll get in London."

The big man twisted in his seat to face the stainless steel and glass counters at the end of the café. Three men, all southern European in appearance—Turkish, Boniface guessed—with swarthy skin, hairy arms, and very dark hair, apart from the older boss man who had gone gray on his head and arms. All three looked like they could handle themselves in a fight, but at the moment, the younger men were busy cooking over a griddle. "Another bacon sandwich for my friend," said Tommy to the older man. "And could you make him a fresh pot of tea with boiled water, not that warm stuff that comes out of the tank?"

"Coming right up," said the older man, ripping a page off a small notepad and passing it to one of the cooks.

"I remember that girl of yours. Monty, is it? She gave me a pot of tea... said you liked proper tea, properly made."

Boniface acknowledged as the older man came across the red-and-white-checkered floor carrying a bacon sandwich. "That was quick. Thank you."

"For my favorite customer." He winked at Tommy, who managed to communicate his thanks without using words. "He can wait." He cast a lazy glance across the room at a man wearing a misshapen sweater, engrossed in the sports pages of a tabloid.

Boniface took a bite. "Good?" Tommy seemed in need of reassurance.

"Good," said Boniface, replacing the sandwich on its plate and dabbing his lips with the paper napkin that came with his breakfast. He stared straight at Tommy, who met his gaze. "I'm one of those people who prefers to meet face to face. If there's a phone call or any other interaction that doesn't involve two people in a room, I'll avoid it if I can."

"You're sounding like me. I always want to look someone straight in the eyes." Boniface could hear the softening of Tommy's accent, the gentle

Derbyshire tones smoothing the edge of his big voice, making him sound almost like a modern BBC television announcer: correct pronunciation but with a regional accent.

"It leaves less of a trail. Electronic communications leave a nasty mess that can be sold to the press." The big man nodded but remained quiet. "Tommy, I've got to know. Did I upset you?" He scrutinized Tommy—small creases fluttering across his weather-worn brow. "If I did, I need to make things right."

"Upset me how, Mister...I mean Boniface?" Tommy's eyebrows lifted, emphasizing that he was asking a question. "You were the only one who treated me with any sort of dignity when Angelo was arrested. You didn't take my money, you understood my son was suspected of the crime—not me—and you weren't intimidated by my reputation. You gave me advice—and it was good advice that you gave me in about three minutes. I respect that, and I respect you."

The two men sat facing each other, the only sounds around them the noises of quiet conversations and people banging their cutlery against their plates as they ate.

"Why the question?" The big man waited, continuing when Boniface was not forthcoming. "I presume today's meeting isn't a coincidence?"

Boniface took another bite of his sandwich before continuing. "It's not a coincidence, Tommy, although it is a pleasure to see you again. I wish it was under better circumstances...for both of us."

The big man leaned in, his voice lower, his tone richer. "I know what my problem is: my boy. But what's your problem and what is it that brings you to me?"

Boniface paused as a teapot, milk jug, and mug were delivered to the table. He thanked the older man and proceeded to pour his tea, waiting until he was out of earshot. "It's a problem, but you should focus on Angelo today."

"Come on, Boniface. You're here, you might as well tell me. A problem shared and all that."

Tommy's voice was hypnotic. Boniface felt himself being drawn while still trying to hold back. "I've got a problem." Tommy nodded as Boniface forced himself to continue. "I can't be certain, but I think someone's trying to send me a message."

"How?" Tommy tilted his head. The concerned grandpa, not the angry bear.

Boniface hesitated. "Let's just say they led the police to my door for a crime I didn't commit."

Tommy nodded, after a while raising his eyebrows. Boniface sat mute, pursing his lips and giving a single, staccato nod in reply to the question raised by Tommy's eyebrows.

"You're not going to tell me what the problem is, but it's the sort of thing you think I might have been capable of if I had been angry?"

Boniface felt his cheeks redden slightly. "It's not that I'm refusing to tell you. It's that it's questionable as to what the problem is, and if there isn't a problem between us that needs to be sorted, then I don't see the necessity of boring you with my issues."

Tommy sat back, but his voice remained low. "Let me lay it on the line for you, Boniface. My boy did a bad thing: I've never said otherwise. When I was in trouble, everyone was happy to help. Everyone. But they didn't look at the help I needed—we needed as a family—all they saw was a guy who didn't have the greatest education, who didn't work in the most glamorous of industries, but who had done reasonably well for himself. And when they saw me, they had only one thought: money."

Tommy took a last bite and finished his sandwich, then washed it down with a slurp from his mug of tea.

"But you didn't take my money, even when I wanted to pay you there and then. Instead, you sat down with me, talked to me like a real human being, and gave me some advice. Good advice, which we followed. It's a shame that Angelo..." His voice became wistful. "Well, here we are fighting so that he doesn't get extradited back here." He voice trailed off as he stared into the distance. "That girl of yours. I shouldn't call her a girl, but you know...Monty?"

"Monty is what she calls herself. Short for Montbretia."

"Montbretia? That's..."

"Yup. A flower." Boniface clocked a look on Tommy's face that he took as bafflement. "Hippie mother," he offered by way of an explanation. "One daughter called Hibiscus, the younger Montbretia."

"I suppose I got away lightly with my wife insisting we call the boy Angelo." His tone was rueful. "Anyway, Montbretia was a true delight, even if she didn't realize."

Boniface tried to keep the astonishment out of his face, but failed as Tommy continued. "I know that with my size and my reputation I can come across as a bit scary, but she looked after me while you were busy."

"I think I was on a call," offered Boniface.

"You might have been; all I remember is talking to her and being impressed. She didn't judge me based on my reputation or based on what Angelo was accused of. She didn't judge Angelo based on the stories that had been in the papers. But she didn't ignore the seriousness of the case. She wanted to hear the facts, and she understood that there were two truths in the room on the night of the incident."

Tommy paused. "For that I am grateful to her. She also made a great cup of tea," he pointed to Boniface's pot, "which is where I learned about how you like your tea." He lifted his head and stared straight at Boniface. "So it's cards-on-the-table time. You know I've got a number of skills and that I was a bit of a boy when I was younger. I behave myself now, but I've got friends I can call on, and I reckon it would always be good to be owed a favor by you. So how do you need me to help?"

sixteen

Montbretia laid the headband and the plastic hairclip on the counter, and pulled her towel tighter, re-tucking the corner under her right arm.

She wasn't sure why, but somehow a hair accessory felt necessary. More proper. Isn't that how people who work in offices dress? A not really practical suit and something ugly and plastic to hold your hair in place. She felt like a twelve-year-old on bring-your-daughter-to-work day, trying to dress like someone else's image of a grownup.

And in her image, you needed something in your hair.

And a suit.

In her case, one of Ellen's pantsuits.

She had been there when Ellen bought the suit. Ellen had clearly felt put-upon by her younger sister and had been unsure in the shop, but when they got home she had been thrilled.

Montbretia went to her bedroom—the spare bedroom in his apartment, as Boniface would likely see it—and blow-dried her hair before putting on the white cotton blouse, hers; and the blue pant suit, Ellen's. She pulled the pants around her waist, breathed in, pulled each side together, fiddled with the button, and released her breath.

This was a level of discomfort she hadn't expected.

Ellen was shorter, with bigger boobs. Not much—a cup size, perhaps—but enough to notice, not that Ellen was aware when guys noticed. But surely bigger boobs equated to a bigger waist. It was a basic law of nature, wasn't it? Indisputably, it was the law of natural justice.

They had lived apart for years, not that they had been the kind of sisters to swap clothes when they lived together. When they had gone shopping together during Montbretia's visits to London, she never understood the English way of sizing—and to be honest, she didn't fully understand it now—but she had always assumed that Ellen had the larger waist.

But apparently not.

And now Montbretia was left with a pair of pants that were too tight, not quite long enough, and which rubbed at the top of her inside left thigh.

The choice was no choice: the ill-fitting pants, her jeans, her sweaty cycling gear, or her mishmash of pink gym clothes that she had yet to move from Boniface's apartment. The pantsuit would let her look like she might work in an office, so she slipped on the jacket and a pair of Ellen's sensible wear-all-day-in-the-office low-heeled pumps—the wrong size, but who cared; she was only going to be wearing them for a short while—before returning to the kitchen and picking up the headband.

She looked in the mirror as she combed back her hair and systematically fitted the headband, the burgundy arranging her chestnut hair in a way that made her look about eight years old. She would have preferred a headband with Minnie Mouse ears, but that probably didn't fit the office-worker look.

It was 10 AM, and she was clean, no longer sweating, refreshed, and dressed in a way that suggested, to her at least, that she might plausibly work in an office. She walked from Boniface's apartment down Wimbledon Hill Road to acquire her last few props.

It felt weird for Montbretia, buying her first pack of cigarettes in her mid-twenties. Somehow she still felt like a kid doing something forbidden, not that much had ever been forbidden when she was growing up. Their mother was what others liked to call a free spirit, which was something of a euphemism for a hands-off parent who felt she had two younger sisters and not two children. But some conditioning kicked in: It would have been less stressful to buy porn.

She paid for the cigarettes and left.

Two minutes later, she returned when she realized she would need a lighter.

Two minutes after that, she wondered whether it would be easier to start a conversation if she didn't have a lighter.

Then she figured she wouldn't be smoking anyway, so it wouldn't matter.

As she waited in the coffee-shop line, wriggling with the poor fit of her blue suit, she toyed with the cigarette packet and pulled off the cellophane. Flipping back the lid, she picked out the paper to expose her props. Would it look better with a less full packet, she wondered.

"You no smoke here." The barista's accent was thick Eastern European. "It's the law. You smoke outside." He pointed to the tables outside the door.

"I..." I what? I don't smoke? I'm holding these for a friend? "I...I'll have an Americano."

seventeen

"I almost don't recognize you with clothes on." His guest faked a look of shock. "Look at you: suit and tie, polished shoes—I expect no less—and you've even coordinated the handkerchief in your top pocket with your tie. A bit 1980s, but I appreciate the effort."

"Boniface." Gideon stood to greet his guest. "I thought the library would be best. The old duffers either aren't awake or are still getting breakfast so we won't be disturbed, and I've got a pot of tea for you. Sit down." Gideon indicated a wing-backed chair, positioned to mirror his own, forming a triangle with the unlit fireplace. He watched his former colleague across the room—uncharacteristically looking somewhat hesitant—then turned to a small side table and poured from a silver teapot.

Gideon placed a cup of tea on a side table next to Boniface. "Whatever your question, dear Boniface, I'm sure we can find the answer in this room." He pointed to the expanse of bookshelves covering an entire wall of the narrow room. The shelves were old and showing signs of wear, especially at ground level, where the frequent scuffing had chewed holes in the uprights. But the shelves were packed with books. Old books, new books, hardbacks, paperbacks, English, foreign language, literature, reference.

No two books were the same size. "Anything you want, but exercise some vigilance if you want any books from that end column."

Boniface frowned.

"Woodworm met wet rot. Some of the books still smell a bit, and it's all rather precariously balanced. If you lift one end, the other is likely to fall apart. They were ready to fix it, but some of the longer-serving chaps were unhappy with the minor addition that would be levied through the annual fee, so it's a rather make-do-and-mend solution at the moment. Very wartime spirit, which puts the old boys in a good frame of mind." Gideon vigilantly lifted over his own cup of tea and sat across from his guest. "What occurrence demands that we talk so urgently?"

"I've got a problem."

"Ointment."

"A serious problem, Gideon." Gideon watched Boniface squirm in his chair, seeming to find it impossible to achieve a comfortable position.

"Lots of ointment." Boniface's mouth tightened. Gideon felt a small pang of guilt, unsure whether he might have misjudged his reaction. "Sorry." His voice was straining to be more than a whisper. "What's the problem?"

"Someone is sending me a message." Boniface paused. "Maybe I'm being dramatic, but it feels like someone's trying to destroy me."

The only movement in the room was the breathing of the two men. Gideon broke the impasse, raising his eyebrows and tilting his head in an inquisitive manner, hoping to encourage Boniface to elaborate.

"I don't know." Boniface's speech was rapid. "It may be nothing. But it might be something, and if it is something, then I wonder why it's not your problem too—and if it's nothing, I don't want to waste your time."

Gideon smiled sympathetically. "For an articulate man, you can lose your powers of communication at quite a pace." Boniface mouthed the word "sorry" as Gideon continued. "You don't wish to elaborate—that's fine, but a few questions."

Boniface's mouth twitched—not quite a fully formed emotion, but enough to imply the affirmative to Gideon.

"Are the police involved?"

A nod.

"You're the suspect?"

Another nod.

"So this is something going after your reputation. Could this put your name into the public domain?"

"That's what seems to be happening." Boniface shifted in his seat. "Whoever has done this is smart: If this leaks, people will always remember me for the story. They won't remember that I was innocent; they'll simply attach my name and the event."

"With a click of their fingers, your reputation is trashed."

"Precisely. I can't be the behind-the-scenes adviser if my attachment to every client will lead to a news story linking that client to me, and me to this case."

"You're here because you think it might be related to some of the stuff you pulled when you ran my press and media at the Department?"

Boniface's voice was rising. "I'm here, Gideon, because I'm in freefall. Messages are usually signed or have cards. This one had neither: The first I knew was when the cops showed up at my office yesterday morning."

Boniface stood and took a few steps away from his chair.

Gideon kept his tone soft. "I get that something bad is happening. I get that you think I can help or might be a target too. But what task do you want me to perform?"

Boniface sighed, keeping his back to Gideon. "If it's not you and me, then it's me. Me alone." He started to pace beside the tables arranged along the central spine of the room. "If that's the case, can you call in some favors? Keep your ear to the ground? See if anyone's heard anything?"

"You recognize that I'm..."

Boniface regarded Gideon from the far end of the room. "I know you're not a minister, because if you were I might have a job with you." There was a ringing echo as Boniface stopped talking. When he continued his voice was calmer. "I know it's hard to call in favors, but is it that much of an embarrassment for a guy who's happy to dance naked around his bedroom while I sit there?"

"Boniface, you know..."

"I know everything you're going to say. It's hard. It relies on personal relations—which in your case is doubly hard because, as a rule, you've shagged the wife of virtually everyone who might be useful. You're not a minister anymore, so you don't have the same influence." He continued his path around the central tables. "But do you think it's easy for me? I've been to see you twice, and it's not even 10 AM."

Gideon kept his tone soft. "Alexander, you're going red in the face." Boniface's head twitched reflexively at the use of his first name. "Come and sit down and quietly tell me how far you've got so I don't waste any effort."

Boniface walked slowly up the room. Apparently lost in thought, his feet dragging along the thin carpet, hand to his face, holding his chin. As he sat, Gideon said, "If we're looking for people who don't like you, then I suppose we've got to begin with Stan Gadson."

Boniface released his locked position slightly, the trace of a pleasure showing. "Dear Stan. My first big scoop." His tone conveyed a tinge of melancholy. "Already ruled out him, and the researcher."

"So who else?"

"No one. There is no one from my time as a journalist that I can think of who would have a hunger for destroying me like this. There are a few of the old-time politicos and their hangers-on who still pull faces at me, but nothing more. Have you got any ideas?"

"You had a certain reputation while you handled the Department's press. To understate how you were described, some might have thought of you as pugnacious."

"Committed?" Boniface's tone was light.

"Committed." Gideon lowered his voice. "But you were a mess and you made mistakes. Not that I'm criticizing as I sit here is this glass house making sure there are no stones lying around."

"I think the end result is sufficient proof of how much of a mess I was. But can we get to the point here?" There was agitation is Boniface's voice. "Sure, I pissed people off, but I didn't have any power. I was handling the press; you were the minister making the decisions. Someone might have wanted to get back at me for being a smart-assed pain, but ultimately any decisions were yours, not mine. So why would they get at me and not you if this is a political problem?"

"That would be my assumption, but that only leaves one option, doesn't it?" Gideon paused for dramatic effect. "It must be beyond question that one of your clients is trying to mess with you, and since you haven't been in business for that long, I must congratulate you on upsetting someone so completely and so rapidly. I know upsetting people was once sport for you, Boniface, but you have exceeded all of your previous records."

"I'm ahead of you on that one. My first thought was Tommy. Tommy Newby."

"Tommy Newby? Tommy Newby, father of Angelo Newby, who beat that poor girl to a pulp after..." Gideon recalled Tommy Newby's name.

"That Tommy Newby. That Angelo Newby, who was found not guilty."

Gideon's voice had an angry edge. "Was found not guilty after a delay in the trial because they couldn't find that afternoon's witness." Gideon felt his eyes drawn to Boniface, trying to suppress the feelings of disappointment. "Was money such an issue, Boniface, that you needed to make these compromises? Is that what's making you so highly strung?"

"Hold on. Let me explain." Gideon took a deep breath before nodding for Boniface to continue. "The afternoon that the witness didn't turn up, Tommy got his driver to bring him down to see me. He thought it was time for a bit of PR input."

"A bit late, but what did you say?" Gideon could hear the incredulity in his own voice.

"There wasn't much I could say. He was already crucified in the press; any active PR campaign would have made things worse. Added to which, I was busy."

"So you turned him away." Gideon grimaced and held his arms in a gorilla position while talking in a deep voice. "I'm Tommy, and I let some southern softie in a suit turn me down."

"I told him that my services wouldn't help. I suggested he hire a lawyer to sue anyone who might defame Angelo, and that he make a conspicuous donation to a rape-crisis charity to show how seriously the family regarded the issue."

"So you turned him down."

"I turned him down, but I thought I was at least pleasant about it, and I thought my advice had been taken when a sizable donation was made to a charity."

"So it's you we have to thank for thirty pieces of silver going in the right direction."

"I didn't think about your work; I suggested a solution for Tommy." He continued, his voice softer. "You know what came next: Angelo went to Saint-Tropez, where he is in jail, having been accused of raping and murdering a chambermaid, and there's an application to extradite him back here to face numerous other charges, most relating to violence toward women." Boniface threw his hands in the air as if surrendering. "I offered some advice, for free, but given the way events turned, I wondered whether Tommy was upset with me, and whether he took it badly because his son is going to spend the rest of his days in prison."

"So when will you be meeting Tommy?"

"I've been. He's in court every day with the extradition hearing. I had breakfast with him while you were scraping chocolate off your cock."

"And?"

"And I'm his new best mate. I was the only one who didn't take his money. If I've got a problem, he can help, and if he can't help, he knows people. As in *people.*"

"Do you believe him?"

"That he knows people, yup." Boniface tilted his head from side to side. "That he didn't do it, probably. But I'm not sure I could trust him, and I absolutely don't want to be under any obligation to him."

"So if it wasn't Tommy, then who? Which lowlife client has been causing you problems?"

Gideon could make out the slightest shake of Boniface's head. "Not a clue. Most of my other work has been corporate strategy and general communications. You know, media training, how we want others to see us. Nothing in the least contentious."

"And your present client?"

"It's not them." Boniface shook his head vigorously, relaxing as the subject moved from Tommy. "They're in it, deep. As in deep, deep, deep, deep. The last thing they need is me and the police causing them any grief."

"Who is the client?"

"Big problem, big secret, I'm afraid."

"How long have you been working with them?"

Boniface defocused, as if the answer were written where the far wall met the ceiling. "About nine months."

"That's quite a while; that's long enough to upset someone. Who knows about the work you're doing for this mystery client?"

"Me. The CEO. I was literally telling the first person outside of us two when the cops walked in yesterday."

"Has Montbretia done any work for the client?"

"She's done lots. But she doesn't know who she's been working for."

Gideon frowned. "How is the delightful Miss Armstrong, by the way?"

"She's fine. She sends her regards."

"Regards and nothing more?"

"Nothing more."

"Do you think...?"

Boniface cut him off. "I don't think. I'm not her boyfriend; I'm not her pimp. I have no influence over her choices."

"Oh." Gideon felt the disappointment. "The delightful Miss

Armstrong must have seen a bill or some sort of financial transaction for this client."

"Nope. No bills. No paper trail."

"Montbretia must know who she's working for."

"Nope. Not a clue."

"Come on, Boniface, she's not stupid."

"She's anything but stupid. She turned you down—that must say something about her level of common sense and understanding of risk. But that still doesn't mean she knows who she's working for. She thinks we're being paid—and hence her work is funded—by an overseas charitable trust, and indeed, that's true. What she doesn't know is the arrangement our paymaster has."

"I'm intrigued. Explain."

"My client has a charitable trust, which is ostensibly their Hail Mary pass to wave when they are called to account for their sins. Added to which, it looks good in the corporate social responsibility report."

"What? You think no one will make the link from the charitable trust to the associated company?" Gideon scowled, incredulous. "You do know that the charity will lose its tax status when that comes out."

"I do, or at least, I would. That's why we're not being paid by the charitable trust." Gideon sat back as Boniface continued. "Our CEO has a friend who is CEO of a packaging company in Spain. That packaging company also has its own trust and was about to make a donation to an infrastructure project in Chad, to help with the refugees from Sudan's Darfur region."

"So they swapped projects?" Gideon felt the realization showing on his face. "Two strangers on a train."

A slight smirk of self-satisfaction formed at the edge of Boniface's mouth. "Absolute disconnect. Timing and amounts are totally unrelated. Two people—two friends—had lunch in Madrid nine months ago, end of story. No investigative reporter could spin any inference, but we get paid."

"What happens when you turn up at their offices, or are the meetings all secret squirrel?"

"They think I'm the CEO's life coach. And on that happy thought, I will leave you."

"I'll be in touch," said Gideon, rising and shaking hands.

eighteen

Montbretia scanned, hoping not to see Zahir.

When she passed, he didn't seem to be in the office, which would mean he was in one of three places: in the back rooms of the office, out having a smoke, or haranguing a client into considering a property he was forcing them to view.

Feeling guilty about the poor soul who would have to endure Zahir's sales pitch, she hoped it was the third option as she continued to wonder whether to have a full pack or to remove one or two cigarettes as she stood outside the office.

She put her coffee on the sidewalk and took out the cigarette packet. She didn't even know how to hold a cigarette. Holding a short tube isn't that difficult, but how did smokers hold these things? Was it between the thumb and first finger? No, that seemed like pantomime villains who always sucked too hard. She pinched out a cigarette and tried it in the V between her first and second fingers, the tip of the filter a small way above her palm.

She had only met Gideon twice, but with him meeting Boniface today he had taken up residence in her head, and why was this? Both times they met, he had propositioned her. Each time she had declined, politely, and he had accepted her rejection without question, carrying on the conversation as if he had asked whether she would prefer red or white, only to be told that she would prefer a glass of water. As for the stories Boniface had told, they sounded like urban myths, until she met the politician. After that, she suspected Boniface underplayed Gideon's past and his tastes.

"Light?"

Montbretia glanced up, surprised. "I'm sorry?"

"Do you want a light?"

A tall, thin, somewhat unhealthy-looking man was talking to her. It was another moment before she realized he was wearing a white plastic one-piece suit, like a baby's romper suit, zipped up the front and with elastic cuffs and an elastic hood that he slipped back. Boniface's comment made sense now: She had found someone in a bunny suit. She had found her target, a scientist.

She gave her best slightly-shy-so-as-not-to-scare-the-geek smile. "Thank you. But I'm trying to quit."

He frowned, the new information not computing in his scientific brain.

"I come out here, and I follow the ritual for the bit of smoking that I enjoy—the break from the office, the fresh air—but I try not to smoke." She smiled softly. "Day two and I haven't cracked." She gazed up at the scientist. "I might have done it if you hadn't stopped me. Thank you." She bobbed down, bringing back her coffee. "But coffee. Some addictions can't be cured."

"Oh...well...umm...er... You're welcome." He put his lighter away and zipped up his bunny suit. "You're right. We should all smoke less."

"I haven't seen you before, so I'm guessing you're one of the crime-scene guys."

"The bunny suit didn't give it away?"

"You mean this isn't your best suit for work?" She sipped her coffee, watching as the scientist mirrored, sipping from his thin plastic cup of indistinct brown liquid.

"This is business casual," said the scientist. "If it was best, I'd be wearing a tie."

"Of course." Montbretia was mindful to ensure her voice was solemn before she continued. "Dreadful business in there."

"Mmm."

"They say he was murdered. Is that true?" Her voice still solemn, her heart pounding.

"Don't know." Montbretia looked up, hoping he sensed her question. "It takes a few days, longer if there are chemicals—drugs and the like—that require analysis."

Montbretia wondered how good the scientist was with uncomfortable silences and waited, staring expectantly.

The scientist cracked first. "But we do know he was alive two days ago."

Montbretia stepped closer, cocking her head. "How do you know that? Is there some clever scientific technique?"

A vaguely nervous look spread from his lips. "I would like to say there is, and when they took the body away there was no noticeable decomposition that would come with someone being dead for longer, but the truth is far more mundane: He was arrested in Tilbury two days ago. That's why his prints were on file and they were able to identify him."

The pitch of his voice dropped, and he spoke with less haste. "That's why they think it was murder. But as I said, the autopsy won't take place for a few days, and the real difficulty is that we almost certainly don't have the murder scene, so it's hard to tell whether he died and was bludgeoned, or whether he was bludgeoned and that killed him. I mean, common sense says you don't beat a dead body, but they dug up Oliver Cromwell's corpse so they could hang him."

Montbretia calculated: Was there more he could tell her? Probably not. "Where is Tilbury? This place where you said he was arrested?"

"You're not from around here, are you?"

"You found me out, science boy," she said, cracking a broad smile, hoping he had some sort of a sense of humor. For the first time, the nervous look lifted from his face, and she saw a hint of a goofy grin. "As you've guessed, I'm from across the pond. Virginia. Richmond, Virginia."

"Richmond? Like..."

What was it with the Brits? Two places, one name. "Like Richmond up the road, but I haven't been to Richmond in the U.S. for quite a while. I was travelling, and I've been here since..." Her voice trailed off. She caught herself with another memory of Ellen. "So, yeah, I'm a foreigner. Where is this Tilbury place?"

"You've got London." The scientist held his fist in front of him at chest height, turning toward her as if showing her a map. "With the River Thames going through the middle." He drew a horizontal line across his fist with his other hand. "Then you've got the M25, the big motorway that goes round London." Montbretia watched as he drew a circle in the air around his fist. "Where the M25 and the Thames cross in the east..." he started making hand gestures, one crossing the other, "if you go about two or three miles further out down the river, you get to Tilbury. It's part of the Port of London."

"So it's close?" Montbretia tried to keep the excitement out of her voice.

"Physically, yes. But speaking as a scientist in terms of evolution, no, it's not close." Montbretia reached into her pocket and pulled out her phone. "That was a science-boy joke, by the way," he said apologetically. "I've never actually been to Tilbury."

Montbretia gave a quick flash of her teeth to acknowledge the attempt at humor. "You're right, it's close. But it seems to be in the middle of nowhere. It's totally separate from London; all that connects it is a train line."

The scientist leaned, trying to peer at the screen, then snapped upright as Montbretia slipped the phone back into her pocket. "Not smoking makes me want more coffee. I've wasted enough of your time, and I can see you want to get back to work. There's a mystery that needs solving." She held out her hand. "It's been a pleasure."

He shook her hand weakly and started stammering. "Perhaps... coffee...later..."

Montbretia hesitated, then reached for her phone, unlocked it, and handed it to him. "No promises," she said firmly. "Put your number in, and I might call."

He tapped and tutted, then handed the phone back. "I put it under 'science boy' so you'll remember who I am."

"Well, science boy, thank you," said Montbretia, turning to leave, knowing that she would almost certainly never see him again unless she needed something more from him.

nineteen

Leaving Gideon's club for the second time that morning, Boniface followed the side streets through St. James's, heading north, and had soon crossed Piccadilly, diving into the warren of streets that was Mayfair.

He never enjoyed visiting Mayfair.

Each property in Mayfair was, without exception, gorgeous: lots of old townhouses, many examples of perfect architecture crafted in Portland stone several hundreds of years ago. What wasn't to like? In a word, Mayfair itself, and what it had become.

But for Boniface, the problem was more practical: Mayfair was sandwiched between Oxford Street and Piccadilly, with Park Lane and Regent Street stopping the filling from spilling out from each end. Even before you started getting snooty about the Bond Street divide—and Boniface didn't care whether it was east Mayfair or west of Regent Street—the space comprising Mayfair was finite. On the Monopoly board, Mayfair had always been the most expensive location, but when you started cramming prime London real estate, a fixed resource, with hedge-fund managers and corporate headquarters in between some of the choicest residential locations in Western Europe, you made money the condition of admission.

Large piles of money were not enough. This wasn't the place for professional soccer players or rock stars, although Jimi Hendrix did live there almost fifty years ago, when the location was still considered faintly bohemian, but now it was the place where the super-rich—those for whom a billion was a mere rounding error—kept their London houses. This was now the land of the oligarchs. The place to find the people who controlled the world's energy supplies.

With the heritage of the architecture, planning laws had evolved to severely limit any external alterations to any properties, which gave the super-rich only one option: renovate internally, and if they wanted more space—if they needed a gym, sauna, Jacuzzi, or swimming pool—then dig.

Never mind the nightingale singing in Berkeley Square, all Boniface could hear and see as he threaded through the narrow streets of Mayfair were the signs and sounds of construction workers. White vans delivering, trucks being filled by hand with dug-out soil because there wasn't enough space to get proper machinery in, scaffolding and safety hoardings all covered with notices proclaiming how considerate their construction workers were—those acclaimed staff all wearing dirty high-vis jackets and hard hats but seemingly incapable of finding a pair of jeans to cover their ass cracks.

Boniface passed a group of workers chatting on the street, none speaking English, as he began the gentle slope up to the Weissenfeld Shipping global headquarters. It sounded grand. In reality, it was a converted house in Mayfair that was rumored to have once been the home of a famous sailor, but no one was quite sure who he was or which battles he might have won. As far as Boniface was concerned, it was a good-sized house but a comparatively small office.

He walked beside the red-brick wall, stopping to hit the intercom button before looking up at the camera. A buzz confirmed the unlocking of the wrought-iron gate, which clunked shut behind him as he passed over the stone path crossing the small garden—the raised beds, manicured shrubs, and trimmed mature trees a green oasis in the heart of the West End. For some reason, he couldn't stop himself from wondering how Greta Weissenfeld would get on with Gideon Latymer: There was something in the domination of her personality that would make her such a challenge, and such a thrill, for Gideon.

Stepping through the front door, Boniface crossed the black-and-white marble floor and jogged up the stairs, two at a time.

"Mister Boniface. I thought you'd abandoned us when you didn't turn up yesterday."

"I wasn't scheduled, Lennie. The lady wasn't here."

"That's true, but you could have come to see me. My life could do with some coaching." The security guard's manner matched his appearance: sixty-something, 5-foot-9, heavyset, graying and thinning on top, but still military smart. "She's got Mister Regenspurger with her at the moment."

"Oh." Boniface felt the tension is his jaw as he grimaced. "Whose kneecaps is he going to break today?"

The security guard remained impassive, then conspiratorially whispered, "She's got *another* new secretary."

"It's something we're working on," lied Boniface as he started on the next flight of stairs.

"Mister Weissenfeld wants to see you," he said. "Immediately, he told me to tell you."

Boniface stepped back down the stairs. "Mister Weissenfeld? As in Chlodwig."

"Him." Lennie nodded definitively. "When I mentioned you were expected, he said he wanted to see you when you arrived."

"He's here?" Boniface could feel the tension in his voice.

"In the conference room."

Boniface heard himself swearing under his breath. He hesitated, collecting his thoughts. "What does he want?"

"I guess you'll find out when you see him."

"I guess I will. Catch you later, Lennie."

As far as Boniface had seen, every room in Weissenfeld's London office was awkwardly and inconveniently shaped. This was not all that surprising, given that the building had been designed as a family home more than 200 years ago.

Two hundred years ago, all houses in London had fireplaces: it was that or get cold. Fireplaces required chimneys, and chimneys took up lots of space as the pipes from the lower floors traveled through the upper floors, eventually finding freedom through the roof. Every room had a fireplace standing proud on the wall, and every room had chimneys passing through, so no room had four flat walls.

Couple that with the changes since the house was built—walls moved, bathrooms added, back staircases repurposed, plumbing for central heating, gas lighting added, gas lighting removed, electricity—and you ended with a situation where, depending on your attitude, each room was either unique or inconvenient. The conference room was even more inconveniently shaped, with the addition of an overweight German who looked close to tears.

As Boniface came through the door, the German stood, apparently trying to speak but making stammering sounds, which were muted when he moved a shaking hand to cover his mouth.

"We killed those people, Boniface. Us...we... It didn't just happen. We did it."

Now standing, the German remained immobile: an overweight statue covered in a crumpled beige suit with hints of yellow and green, but somehow avoiding brown tones.

"I keep thinking that I should have done something. I could have done something." Boniface felt ashamed to witness the soft, puffy face exaggerated by the swollen red eyes, the neatly trimmed near-white goatee quivering as the German tried to articulate his thoughts. "If I had acted, those people would still be alive. I could have stopped Greta."

Boniface tried not to show any shock on his face. The notion that someone could stop the unstoppable, that a force of nature could be controlled or managed, didn't sound plausible. "It is my fault. I should have stopped Greta, but I behaved like our father."

Boniface remained still, like a birdwatcher observing a rare species, watching as Greta's older brother tried to recover some dignity. He tugged the lapels of his suit jacket, the fabric tightening around his shoulders before he straightened his tie. Boniface made a small turn of his head to encourage the German to continue.

"Whenever Greta would come home, father would always sigh. He disapproved of how she behaved, but he would never tell her because he couldn't stand the argument. If you tell her she's wrong, she will keep arguing until you apologize and tell her that actually it is you that is in the wrong and not her. When she has bullied you into submission, she will then tell you about all your faults and how much you have hurt her by criticizing her, and you must be wrong in criticizing her because you have just admitted you are in the wrong."

He sighed. "Father spent four hours one night after he challenged Greta on one little matter. Somewhere in those four hours, she told him that he clearly loved the rest of us more than he loved her." There were tears again in the big man's eyes. "She was the baby—she was his favorite, and this broke his heart. He never argued with her again."

He inhaled, almost a sob, his physique again crumpling like his jacket as he sat down. "When Greta told father she should become chief executive, he didn't argue, and he accepted it when she removed him from the board two years later. It was his own fault, he said. He let her get like this. He had indulged her, so he must pay the price."

Chlodwig rested his elbows on the table that dominated the room while he held his head. Boniface couldn't figure whether the table was too big or the room too small—either way, the light-colored wood with an open grain pushed the surrounding chairs against the walls.

He squinted against the autumnal sun, sliced into julienne strips as it pushed its way through the single sash window. "What are you doing here, Chlodwig?"

The other man looked up, surprised. "You told me about all those people dying, the police turned up, and I couldn't get hold of you..." His voice trailed off. "What was I supposed...?"

Boniface turned away from the damp eyes; he knew what was waiting for him when he saw Chlodwig's sister.

"So I came, and I bought Sophie to help Greta."

In other words, Greta would be annoyed that Chlodwig was here, and that annoyance would be compounded by the imposition of a new secretary.

"Chlodwig, I think you should know that I will be tendering my resignation. I will tell Greta face to face: That's the reason I'm here today."

The puffy face nodded, a look of confusion forming. "Why, Boniface?"

twenty

Boniface ascended to the top floor and followed the maze to the secretary's desk outside Greta Weissenfeld's office. A head bobbed up—it took Boniface a few moments to realize that she was standing.

She came out from behind the desk, holding out her right hand to greet him. "I am Sophie Driesdorfer. Pleased to meet you, Mister Boniface."

As Boniface shook her hand he checked: She was short. Shorter than Greta, and if he was being brutal, dumpier. As she walked back behind her desk, he tried to guess her age but failed, settling for somewhere in the range of twenty to fifty.

"It's Boniface. Not Herr Boniface, not Mister Boniface. Just Boniface." He tried to convey reassurance, tilting his head and softening his smile. "You must be Greta's new..."

"Yes." Boniface hoped she was as efficient as her response. "You started today?"

"Yes. Herr Weissenfeld... Do you know Herr Weissenfeld?"

"We've just been chatting."

"Herr Weissenfeld thought I would be suitable to work with his sister. She doesn't trust English secretaries." Realizing what she had said, she started gabbling; her English was good, but with a rip of a German accent cutting through. "Herr Weissenfeld feels that it would be beneficial for Fraulein Weissenfeld to have a secretary who understands her language and the work ethic that she is accustomed to." Satisfied that she had given a good account of why she was hired, she jerked her head forward to emphasize each word. "So I am here."

There were voices in Greta's room, and the door opened.

A figure exited. Slim, dressed darkly, marginally shorter than Boniface. He moved without making a noise, and Boniface suspected if he walked through water, there would be no ripples and no wake.

Boniface had heard the rumor, ex-Stasi, but had never felt able to ask a direct question from anyone who might know—after all, why would a life coach care?—and so had to be content with throwaway lines and odd adjectives: "sorts problems," "practical," "on the ground," "local knowledge, local contacts," "no nonsense," and Boniface's favorite, "pragmatic." The figure continued to pass; dull skin hung loosely over the skull, contrasting with the two dark eyes that fixed Boniface, igniting a primeval urge to confess every secret he knew.

Sophie had stepped into the room and was holding the door open.

"Fraulein Weissenfeld, Herr Boniface is here."

"Boniface, I need you to start talking to people. Today. Now." Boniface had yet to enter the room, and orders were being given. He knew Greta would be sitting behind her desk—her Louis XIV reproduction desk, an abomination in Boniface's mind, showing a Mayfair victory of money over taste over practical function—reading from a list in her notebook that she carried with her everywhere, gold pen checking off each task as she gave her command without looking up to ensure the instruction had been received. That she had uttered the words was sufficient to absolve her of responsibility. Failure on your part to hear did not constitute an excuse or even reasonable grounds for a delay in implementation.

Boniface advanced into the room, the door shutting as the secretary left.

He had one option to slow the oncoming torrent: distraction. "That's new." She looked up. "Stand up, let me see."

As Boniface warily positioned himself in the uncomfortable Louis XIV–styled guest chair, Greta stepped out from behind her desk.

The dress was a simple design. The skill was in fitting it to her figure, and Greta's dressmaker showed formidable skill in cutting and stitching the lemon-gold fabric, which stopped half an inch above the CEO's knees. Boniface assumed that, as was usual for Greta, the dress would be sleeveless, but that detail was hidden under the embroidered, almost metallic gold jacket edged with three-color twisted piping: one line matching the gold of the jacket, one a deeper coppery gold, and the last a more ivory tone. If he were feeling less charitable, Boniface would have described the shoes as slut-wear, but given that she was still the client, he felt he could be more generous and acknowledge to himself that these heels were probably most suitable for the bedroom and could only be worn outside the bedroom if your chauffeur dropped you at your office door.

Boniface never knew what to say in these situations: He didn't care for her dress sense, but he appreciated that she had very distinctive taste. Over the last few months, he had learned that he needed to openly notice what Greta was wearing if he wanted her to feel good about herself and so be in a reasonable mood. He had also learned that an earnest look on his face accompanied with a measured nod of the head would communicate the appropriate response, even if he didn't understand the full extent of what he was communicating.

Irrespective of her talents, Chlodwig had made a wise selection of secretary for his sister. The uncharitable would describe Greta as being squat. She addressed the issue through her attire. By contrast, Sophie was shorter, stockier, and far less well groomed. She wore sensible shoes and a dress that you would forget while you stared at it. Chlodwig instinctively knew—with his sister's compulsion to compare and to calibrate her emotions through comparison—that Greta would always feel good about herself when she saw Sophie.

"Before you..."

Greta silenced Boniface, her approach strident. "First tell me what Chlodwig is doing here. He says he spoke to you yesterday, and because of that conversation, he got on a plane and came straight here. And he bought me a present: a fat present that dresses badly." She paused, continuing with more measured tones. "But she's only been here for three hours, and already she's done as much work as that other useless girl did in three weeks, so maybe she can stay."

"I need to exp..."

"No, Boniface." Her voice was hardening again. "What you *need* to do is to make Chlodwig go home." She continued, striking the desk with each word for added emphasis. "You created the problem. You, Boniface. You! You need to fix the problem."

She seemed tired from the exertion and exasperated from needing to explain, but still she continued. "You spoke to him, and as a direct result of that conversation, he is here."

She fixed a glare on Boniface, as if encouraging him to acknowledge that she was correct. "I'm not missing something, am I Boniface? It's not my fault that he's here, is it? It's not that I did anything?"

"No, but..."

"You're right, Boniface. No buts. Fix it. Make him go home." Her tone became more conciliatory. "Take him to dinner tonight. It's not a problem; he's on German time, so he'll be in bed by 10 PM. Let him stay a night so that he knows his ugly little girl has got settled, then he can go home tomorrow morning."

"I'll do it," said Boniface. "But there's something I have to say first." His voice was timid, almost apologetic. "I am tendering my resignation."

There was a twitch as Greta's head turned to face him. He noted that her straight blond, shoulder-length hair moved as one helmet-like structure. It was expensive to have such a simple look—and Boniface was sure that one afternoon in the salon would cost more than he spent on his hair in a decade—but all he could see was a Wagnerian Brünnhilde character. He could readily imagine her standing in her helmet with horns, gold body armor shaped to her figure, carrying a big stick and singing very loudly.

He tried not to let any emotion register on his face.

"You're not resigning, Boniface. There's work that needs to be done. First, you've got to make sure Chlodwig goes home."

"I'll deal with Chlodwig. But the last thing you need is to be represented by someone who has been arrested for murder. It won't support the right image for the context in which we're trying to present the events in Somalia."

Boniface explained the events of the previous day, starting with his phone call with Chlodwig. Greta listened impatiently, becoming increasingly frustrated.

"But this is all a problem for you, Boniface. Not for me. Why are you resigning at the time when I need you?" Boniface ignored the rhetorical question as Greta continued. "I've been paying you for nine months with nothing going on, and now that this issue is about to break…now…now that we are putting your plan—*your* plan, not my plan, *yours*—into action, now you decide you want to resign."

Boniface thought she was pausing, but he was wrong. "You told me you could handle the press. You told me you were an expert in public perception." Boniface squirmed in his uncomfortable chair. "Now you're saying that there's a dead body in your office and that it's going to affect me. How stupid do you think I am? You're like a little girl"—she affected a squeaky voice—"I don't know how he got there, I don't even know if he was murdered." She dropped the affectation and reverted to her normal voice with added thunder. "Of course it's murder, Boniface. You don't find a dead body in a street and decide to dump it in some stranger's office."

"I…"

"No, no, no. You are not resigning, Boniface." She started pointing, a disapproving finger was being waved. "Get out your notebook and write this down—you need to brief all the executives today. The story is about to go public, so you need to make sure they all understand the strategy and are following it without deviation."

Boniface reached into his pocket and pulled out a small notepad. He clicked the button on the top of his pencil to extend the lead and readied himself to take notes, aware of the contrast with his principal: Where she recorded detailed notes, written with archival ink containing carbon particles—ink designed to be read in 1,000 years—in a notebook that contained all her records and was always with her, he wrote with a pencil, as many left-handers did, and once actioned, he tore and shredded his used pages for additional security.

"Task one, Boniface." Greta's voice was clipped and fast. "Meet with each executive individually: Jeremy Farrant, Joanna Baines, and also for these purposes, Brad Phipps. Explain the background to the Somalia issue—broad strokes, avoid details. Tell them your strategy. Tell them what the line is we're taking and what they're doing next. When the story breaks, it must be minimized, and there's no scope for confusion through conflicting accounts."

"I saw that Mister Regenspurger is here. Should I brief him?"

"No. Why would you? But get a hotel. I want you close, and I don't want you to waste time traveling. And before you send Chlodwig home, make sure he understands the situation. This time, I want no confusion and no blubbing big brother."

Boniface scribbled and lifted his head.

"You've wasted enough time today, Boniface. Stop discussing, stop asking. Go. Do. Don't talk, just do." Boniface put his notebook into his pocket as he stood. "You had the police visit you yesterday. Is there anything else I need to know, Boniface? Is there anything you haven't told me? Are there any more surprises that you should tell me?"

Boniface reflexively tightened his lower lip.

"What is it, Boniface?"

"It's..." He sighed. "The question is not so much as to whether there's anything else." He spread his hands. "I mean..." He clasped his hands together. "We've all got a history. It's more a case of how far they'll look, how deep they'll dig, and how much they'll attach my name to what they dig up."

Greta nodded, holding the silence. "That sounds like a yes to me, Boniface."

Boniface mirrored her slow nod. "I suppose it is."

twenty-one

The full extent of Montbretia's knowledge of Tilbury had been based on the maps of the place she had consulted on her phone during the train journey and science boy's comments—and he had never been there.

After talking with science boy in his bunny suit, Montbretia had walked to Wimbledon station without delay: She had covered the less than half mile walk in eight minutes. In less than five minutes the train had arrived, which dropped her at Waterloo Station seventeen minutes later. It took a similar amount of time to get across London on something Boniface called the Drain, but which seemed like "the Tube," as she was learning to call the subway. Whatever they wanted to call it, she changed at Fenchurch Street station, where she got on a very slow train that resentfully dragged itself out to Tilbury.

Total journey time: about 90 minutes. Final destination: the 1970s, apparently. Change in Montbretia since leaving Wimbledon: one headband left behind, blue pantsuit still intact and rubbing, annoyingly. Reason for visit: That was where Montbretia wasn't sure. If she was honest, she had acted on impulse; it was probably because she didn't know what else to do, and it was the only lead she had.

She stepped off the train and saw one other passenger disembark at the same time. She followed the path he took through the station, coming out onto what she presumed, having squinted at the map, was a main road. Her fellow traveler had already disappeared.

On sight, Tilbury was the most depressing place Montbretia had ever visited. It was desolate. It was a wasteland. It was as if the aliens had come, killed all the humans and all the vegetation, and then departed, leaving behind concrete, tarmac, and steel but no forms of life.

She looked left. She looked right. Blacktop. Closed stores. No people. No trees.

She looked again. This was wrong—she needed to find the details, she needed to perform a mental inventory.

Three cars, parked. No signs of drivers.

John's Leather and Casual Wear. Shutters down. Notices posted on the shutters. A Chinese takeout. Shutters down. A faded sign. Shutters down with posters stuck to the shutters. Another Chinese. Another shutter. A mission, probably Christian. Shuttered. Even God had given up on Tilbury. Shipping agents. Shuttered. A car-parts store with a dropped curb at the front. Shuttered. Another Chinese. Yet another shutter. Dental surgery. Shuttered. A social club. No shutters to shut, but a closed notice pasted to the door. A combined post office/travel agent. Shuttered. A tattoo and body-piercing parlor. Shuttered. Beauty salon. Shuttered. Liquor store. Shuttered. Chicken, pizza, burgers. Shuttered.

There were more shuttered stores on the right than on the left, so she followed in that direction, passing seven more cars, all stationary, all without drivers. The variety of stores expanded: fish bar, community center, taxi office, drugstore, all shuttered. The shuttered commercial properties turned into blocks of apartments as she continued. Comparatively new blocks of apartments, but still all without any sign of life.

The new blocks gave way to older properties, mostly houses, the transition marked by a flophouse. This had been out of commission for a long time. Unlike the storefronts, there were no rolled-down metal shutters; instead, this had been boarded and was thick with posters offering cash for gold and check cashing.

Apparently someone had once thought human beings might pass this way, but that must have been a long time ago.

Montbretia kept walking, remaining on the road with the familiar sights of humanity—houses, cars—but without any signs of human inhabitation, even though this was meant to be a comparatively busy time for human beings: lunch time.

She had walked little farther than half a mile when she decided to head back to the station—there had to be some humanity there. Added to which, she wasn't comfortable with what she was wearing: Ellen's pantsuit wasn't her style, and their different body sizes meant that there was chafing. And while the shoes were sensible wear-all-day-in-the-office low-heeled pumps, they were the wrong size and were really beginning to pinch.

The walk back felt longer than the walk out, but as she approached her destination, she saw a small café tucked in the side of the station. If you knew it was there, it was obvious. If you were walking out into Tilbury and looking around, it wasn't.

Montbretia stepped in. It was small: four Formica tables crammed into a tiny room, and behind the counter the kitchen area, with what looked like a side window opening onto the main route out of the station, which would explain why she didn't see the place as she passed through. An old gated wooden sign leaned against the wall: "Trev's fried chicken—7 PM 'til late." It at least implied that some form of humanity might pass this way at some point.

The man behind the counter—the second human Montbretia had seen in Tilbury—leaned with his back against the counter, reading a newspaper.

"You must be Trevor." Montbretia was pleased to find someone to quiz about Tilbury.

He turned and nodded, a graying goatee hiding any emotion.

"I'll have an Americano."

"Coffee comes out of tin." He dropped one side of his paper and clumsily lifted a catering tin of instant coffee. "The only question is, do you want milk?"

"Coffee with milk, please," said Montbretia meekly, feeling chastised.

He grabbed a white mug, tossed in a teaspoon of coffee, opened the tap on the boiler, then splashed in a slug of milk and banged the mug on the counter as he put it down. "One pound twenty."

Evidently service was extra. Montbretia reached for her cash, feeling Trevor's eyes appraising her. She placed a few coins on the counter and turned, picking up her mug. "Thank you."

"I'd go home now." He nodded as if that affirmed the wisdom of his opinion. "Drink your coffee, then go."

twenty-two

Boniface had already been in one gentlemen's club that morning, and stepping into Jeremy Farrant's office was like stepping into a second. Crossing the threshold at his office door was like crossing the threshold into a time when Great Britain was the sole global super-power and Britannia really did rule the waves.

He hadn't been into all the individual offices in the building, but those that Boniface had visited—including the CEO's—possessed a single door. Farrant's opened through a double door, giving the feeling of a room that required a servant for each door.

Office carpets had never interested Boniface—or at least they hadn't until the SOCOs apparently cut a big hole in his. They were things you had because you couldn't *not* have something to cover the floor. What was the alternative? Bare wood? Polished metal? Floating on air? In his experience most floors—except in the executive suite—were either covered with mismatched tiles with a high nylon content, delivering a static shock whenever you earthed yourself, or by a single piece of carpet, which was then ripped up and shoddily refitted when someone decided that the ethernet cabling needed to be upgraded.

Boniface had never paid attention to the carpets in the Weissenfeld office, which was another way of saying that nothing in the carpeting had ever drawn itself to his attention. The carpet was a flat piece of fabric, well laid and with no bumps or wrinkles, clean, and without any marks where furniture had been. Thinking about it now, its color was a lemon/yellow/gold that was not dissimilar to the color of the dress Greta was wearing today.

He wondered whether that was intentional and whether he should have mentioned it. Probably not.

But walking across the carpet in Farrant's room, Boniface noticed the difference. It was as if he had rolled off a bed of nails and onto a mattress of feathers. With each step the carpet enveloped and supported his foot, making sure it wasn't too much effort or too much of an inconvenience to walk across it.

The feel of the carpet distracted Boniface from noticing that a different-color carpet had been fitted. Instead of a lemon gold covering, this was the color of crushed green olives with a broad border, about eighteen inches deep and expertly fitted, having a dark red and burnished gold pattern.

Boniface's eyes followed the border, watching how it followed the irregular features: the old fireplace, the alcove, the next room jutting into this. He noticed the border going around the bookcases. "He can't have done…" Boniface walked over to the bookcases and looked down the side.

The wall bowed—the building was several hundred years old, and every wall bowed—but the bookcase had been fitted perfectly to the wall with the far flank of the upright carved to reflect the imperfections of the wall. At the foot, the baseboard had been fitted around the front of the bookcase, and only then had the carpet been added.

Boniface moved in closer to appreciate at the handcrafted piece of furniture. It was impressive: one single structure, constructed in situ. He examined the end panel—there were no joins, and the only ornamentation was some exquisite rosewood fretted inlays. Either this was a single plank or a good piece of veneer. Boniface laughed at his own stupidity: He was starting to get a feel for Jeremy Farrant—there was no way this would be veneer.

He was right; the end panel was a single solid piece of mahogany: The corners gave him the proof he needed. There was neither the join of two pieces of veneer, nor the unnatural grain when veneer is rolled around a corner. Instead, you could see the grain crossing the corners where the wood had been cut. He twisted his head to peer under a shelf, then under the next, and under a third. If you bought a bookcase in a store, the shelves were adjustable. These weren't. These shelves had been positioned in full knowledge of the library they were to hold.

Boniface surveyed the library, which covered the whole wall on either side of and above the double doors, acting like insulation against the rest of the company. From floor to ceiling the shelves were lined with leather-bound law books, labeled by year, an unequivocal statement that the resident in the office was a lawyer.

Boniface sneered.

In the twenty-first century, legislation was so extensive, complex, and changeable that all lawyers referred to online sources when reviewing legislation. This allowed members of the legal profession to know they had the most up-to-date reference, with all changes tracked so they could see what legislation was in force on any day in the past. Not only that, but computers allowed a lawyer to follow links—legislation made frequent cross-references. For a computer-based lawyer, a cross-reference was as much of a challenge as clicking with a mouse. For Farrant, a cross-reference would require that he stand up, go to his library, and pick out the next book, which would then likely be out of date.

This wasn't convenience. This was risk. Using paper—even leather-bound paper—meant this man's knowledge would go out of date. "Dangerous," muttered Boniface under his breath.

The light from the two sash windows on the outside wall drew his attention to a small collection of framed pictures on the side wall behind the desk. He walked past a wall safe—which appeared to be of the same nineteenth-century vintage as everything else in the room—to have a closer look at the paintings. Two were portraits of family groups; the third picture showed a large gray-stoned house, the sort of building that was now used for period dramas on TV and hired out for corporate bonding sessions. Boniface had heard that Farrant owned a castle in the Scottish borders—he wondered if this pile was it.

He turned from the wall, glancing at the desk as he passed. Unlike the bookcases, this looked genuinely old—if it had been commissioned, Farrant would almost have got something more in proportion with himself and the room, thought Boniface. It looked sufficiently battered to be at least 200 years old, with drawers out of alignment and not fully closed. This explained the safe.

Crossing the room, he reached the seating area: a club chair and a sofa, both scroll-armed with buttoned dark-green leather, angled toward each other. Boniface dropped into the club chair, which faced toward the far corner past the desk. It was good to sit in a comfortable chair—the one at Gideon's club had been thin and old, the one in Greta's room had been designed for looks rather than comfort, but this was comfortable.

Boniface felt a vibration inside his pocket and reached for his phone. "Gideon." He listened. "I know it... Late lunch... Sure." He took the phone away from his ear and checked the time. "I can't be there until at least three, maybe later." He closed his eyes, listening. "Where would we be without your juvenile sense of humor? I'll see you later."

He stood and slipped the phone into his pocket as the door opened. A man, perhaps six inches shorter than Boniface, entered. He was older—he had the appearance of a spritely 80-year-old—but Boniface pegged his age as late sixties. Slim and well-dressed in a dark gray pin-striped three-piece suit. "Mister Boniface, I believe. So good to meet you." The voice sounded like a caricature of a BBC radio announcer from the 1950s. Exaggerated Received Pronunciation tones, but in this case slightly high pitched.

He pulled a small silver box from his pocket, flipped the lid, took a pinch from the contents, held his fingers to his left nostril and inhaled. "I'm sorry you've had to wait, Mister Boniface, but I'm afraid any conversation will have to wait until tomorrow. Say first thing tomorrow morning?"

Boniface kept his tone calm. "The matter that I need to talk about is both urgent and highly important."

"Oh, I'm sure it is—that is why I will see you so expeditiously."

twenty-three

She wasn't quite sure what she had expected when she left Wimbledon, but she hadn't expected unconcealed hostility. She hadn't expected to be told to go home when she only wanted a cup of coffee, which was now on the first Formica table where she was intending to sit.

"You're not the first social worker, researcher, do-gooder, or whatever you want to call yourself to come around here telling everyone how sorry you feel while you try to boost your own career." Montbretia found she had lost the ability to talk as he continued. "You look around and say, 'Oh, the depravation, the docks have gone, what will the poor people do?' Well, the docks are still here, and they're busier than ever."

"I know," said Montbretia.

"But it's the work that has gone..." He paused, apparently catching on that Montbretia had replied.

"You're talking about the impact of containerization." She kept her approach calm. "People say it's globalization and they're wrong, it's containerization. Where it would have taken days to unload a ship and would have required an army of stevedores, TEUs can carry more cargo, and that cargo can be loaded and unloaded faster and requires less skill."

"You know what a TEU is?" The man behind the counter had a slight crack in his goatee where Montbretia guessed his mouth might be.

"I do," said Montbretia.

"Seriously, you know what a TEU is?" A bemused look had turned to outright cynicism.

"I'll call them intermodal containers if you prefer," said Montbretia, straining to keep the satisfaction out of her voice. "Intermodal containers, TEUs or twenty-foot equivalent units, or shipping containers; shipping containers that you see everywhere on ships, on trains, dragged behind tractor-trailers, by the side of the road, for storage, and in any number of uses. How do you want me to describe them?"

She sat, twisting into the hard plastic behind the table and turning to better see her inquisitor before continuing. "If you want me to talk about the economics of containers and shipping, I'm happy to. I'm happy to talk about bigger ships, which can carry more cargo more efficiently, meaning that the fuel footprint per ton of cargo is reduced. Or maybe you'd like to discuss the paradox of the huge benefit of global trade while local businesses—particularly businesses around ports—are destroyed?"

He came out from behind the counter, wiping his hands on his stained red-and-white striped apron and grooming his goatee. "I think

I had you wrong, didn't I? I'm sorry." He offered his hand. "I'm Trevor."

Montbretia stood and accepted the handshake. "Monty."

She sunk back into her seat. Trevor mirrored at the next table. "Why the interest in shipping?"

"My job."

"Come on, girl. No one takes a job in shipping unless they've got no other options."

Montbretia gave a soft laugh. "Well, I'm not in shipping as such, and the shipping link was a fluke." Trevor frowned as Montbretia continued. "I was traveling and came to London. Long story short, I've been staying for longer than I thought I would."

"I sense a man," said Trevor jovially, his face falling as Montbretia felt her breath leave her body and her heart slow.

He started stammering: "It didn't work out. I didn't mean to put my foot in it." He held his hands up as if holding back her sadness.

Montbretia felt her eyes misting. "Sorry. I wasn't expecting this conversation." She dabbed her eyes with a tissue from her pocket. "It wasn't a man. It was a death." She wiped her eyes again. "My sister."

"My dear God, I'm sorry."

The two sat in silence, Montbretia taking the occasional sip of coffee. "I had to stay to deal with—I'm still dealing with—probate, and to be honest, after Ellen...I couldn't keep moving. I wanted to spend a few months reflecting...remembering..."

"Mourning." Trevor's tone was smooth, comforting.

Montbretia continued, her voice still strained. "There was this guy who was with my sister at the end, and he's been great. Boniface, that's his name. He had set up his own business a few months before, and he needed someone to help, but he didn't want the hassle of an employee. I needed money but didn't want to be tied down with a job and didn't want to work in a bar, so the arrangement works for both of us."

"So he's in shipping?"

"No," shrieked Montbretia, moderating her volume as she continued, shocked by her own reaction. "Definitely not. Boniface isn't the physical labor sort. No, he's...if I call it PR it would give the wrong impression. He's not the issue-a-press-release, get-a-pretty-girl-to-stand-next-to-your-product kind of guy. He's much more into strategy, big messages, crisis management—that's a big thing for him. He's an ex-journalist, ex-government press guy, so he's got a lot of contacts, a lot of experience."

"I don't see the shipping link."

"That's because it's not that obvious," said Montbretia, her face softening. "When I started working with Boniface, I did the easy stuff. Week one I sorted his filing. Tedious, but he gets scared by paper." She hung her head, shaking it in disappointment. "Such a wimp. Then week two, I sorted out his technology—made him use a phone that was built in this century, taught him how email can benefit his clients. Week three I sorted his website, which was when he figured I could help his clients, and so I did a bunch of websites for his clients, which is how we come to shipping."

Trevor sat stroking his goatee as Montbretia continued. "One of Boniface's clients...well, it's not so much a client as a group of concerned companies all somehow associated with shipping, are worried about the reputation of businesses involved in global logistics."

She took a sip of coffee before continuing. "He figured that each organization had similar public perception issues, but he also saw the irony that a public which disapproves about shipping companies moving toxic waste is the same public that wants cheap consumer goods. Boniface's argument was that if you want your iPad or whatever, then there will be consequent chemical waste that needs to be disposed of safely, and a public discussion was needed about the two sides of the coin—his point was if you don't want the nasty chemicals, don't buy the electronics, but since consumers want gadgets they should take some responsibility for the consequence."

"He sounds like a bright guy."

"He is," said Montbretia. "But he's also practical—he helped set up what's called the Global Logistics Forum, which is meant to be a place to discuss these issues."

"I'm with you so far, but how did you get involved?"

"The website—I set it up. Boniface wanted a place where respected and identifiable individuals could put forward their perspective and other people could discuss the matter in a dignified manner. The way we started this discussion was by setting up a website and encouraging academics and experts to submit papers on their subject."

Montbretia felt the enthusiasm for her work as she explained. "I'm a go-with-your-gut, go-with-your-heart kinda gal, but pretty soon I was reading a wide range of papers from an even broader array of very clever, very informed, and very experienced people, and I got to know the subject. So I started asking people to contribute. For instance, I found a chemist in India—she's a PhD—to talk about the challenges of managing production but also the ethical considerations around the chemicals that are involved in production. She got a grip on the difficulties with noxious substances in countries where the infrastructure isn't in place to deal with the amount of waste that is created."

Trevor's head nodded.

"In a roundabout way, that is how I came to know about TEUs."

"What brings you to my humble establishment? Are you reviewing the economics of running a greasy spoon where the only passing trade goes through the station or is white van drivers delivering crap that people have ordered from the shopping channels?"

"I'm afraid not. I'm after a bum." Trevor's eyes opened wide. "A vagrant, a tramp, one of the homeless…"

Trevor sat back. "Got a few round here, and when they come I tell 'em to…" He stopped himself. "I tell them to go away. I mean seriously, do I look like a charity?" He lowered his voice, his tone questioning. "Why do you want a vagrant? What's it got to do with shipping? It's not some clever new strategy of your boss?"

Montbretia felt a sharp intake of breath through her teeth. "It's quite bizarre. We had a dead body dumped…near where I live." She didn't like blurring the truth, but she couldn't think of a better excuse. "Nobody knows much about the bum. In truth, there is only one fact of which we're certain: He was arrested in Tilbury two days ago, and I figured he might have…" Montbretia realized she wasn't quite sure why she had come to Tilbury or what she was hoping to find. "I dunno. The police are doing nothing, and I wondered if he had friends or someone who knew something about him. Someone, somewhere must care. Someone must want to know that he's gone."

Trevor let out a slow breath. "Asking about one guy is a bit like asking about a raindrop. We get a lot of outsiders through here, and no one has a home. Sailors don't have a home; they're always on the move. People you might think of as vagrants are often sailors who've been stuck in port for too long. Usually they'll find another ship and the next tide will take them away."

"What happens to the ones that don't get back on their ship?"

"Most of them move on—that's what they've done all their life; that's what they keep doing. Most head for wherever they think of as home, and the rest go to London—we're close enough, and that's a much better place to be homeless. There's a better passing trade if you're out begging."

"What about the ones that don't move on?"

"They die." Montbretia couldn't hide her shock. Trevor's voice softened. "They don't stop-die." He clapped his hands loudly as if to emphasize the speed and finality of death. "But soon they're gone. It's Darwinian: The strong ones get back on a boat, and the weak stay here. You see them around—sometimes there are small groups of them around a fire. Nobody knows them, and without the structure of being part of a crew—without a captain giving out orders—they drink too much, don't wash, don't eat enough, get ill, and die. For men who are used to hard, physical labor, it's sad. Most don't make it through their first winter."

"You said they sit round a fire. Where?"

Trevor raised his shoulders, shaking his head. "It changes. They move on. Wherever they are, they'll be out of sight. It'll be somewhere that can't be seen from the road and somewhere that they won't be noticed. But honestly, Monty. Leave them alone. You're a lovely girl, so go home. They won't talk to you, ever. They hate strangers…"

He grinned. "And they'll know you're not a sailor."

twenty-four

"Mister Pitcher for Mister Catcher."

Gideon's puerile humor hadn't improved over the years, especially when he was seemingly trying to add a veneer of discretion, although it wasn't evident to Boniface why Gideon would want a meeting with Boniface kept off the radar.

At least for the acne-ridden juvenile—forced to wear a clean white shirt and waist coat, or vest as Montbretia would insist on calling it, then made to stand behind the reception desk and be helpful—the innuendo, weak as it was, made no sense. He grunted in a manner that the French seemed trained for from birth and waved his hand with Gallic disdain, leaving Boniface to find his way from the faceless dark wood and marble reception to room four.

Room four was up the stairs and along a corridor. It was easily recognizable: It was the room with an open door with Gideon sitting in view. "Boniface, old chap. Come in, come in, but do shut the door."

The door clicked as he shut it, the sound bouncing off the hard surfaces in the room, and his feet echoed on the floorboards as he walked to greet Gideon. "Still or sparkling?" Gideon pointed to the two bottles on the circular table covered in a crisp white linen cloth.

"Sparkling." Boniface pulled back the free dining chair and sat as Gideon poured.

"You old hell-raiser. Sparkling mineral water, and during school lunch time. Are you going to amp yourself up a bit more and have a small herbal tea later?"

"What's with all the codenames, Gideon?" Boniface surveyed the small, featureless room—his attention drawn to the view of St James's Park, the park the Queen looked over when she pressed her nose to the front windows of Buckingham Palace.

"In clubland there are certain standards. Discretion is understood. But we're in the jungle here, Boniface: We're in Westminster. We may be overlooking the Palace, but we're looking from the jungle. Normal rules of etiquette don't apply; I mean, they let journalists become members of this establishment." Gideon beamed at his self-conscious attempt at levity. "When you have staff who don't understand discretion, then I'm afraid precautions are called for."

All humor evaporated from Gideon's voice as he continued. "I've made some enquiries: You've been associating with very bad types, and you've got yourself in a dreadful pickle, Boniface." Any remaining mirth fell from his face. "This is hard, Boniface, but I'll come to the point: I can't be seen with you until this whole thing blows over."

Boniface felt like he had been punched. In the space of six hours, Gideon's attitude had changed.

"This isn't goodbye, Boniface, but it is definitely *au revoir*." Gideon took a sip from his glass. "It took me two phone calls, Boniface. Two phone calls to find that the earthly remains of a recently departed derelict have been left in your office and that you're the prime suspect." He paused, continuing when Boniface made eye contact. "You, Boniface. You are the prime suspect. Do they think you did it? Probably not. But are you involved? Do you know more than you have told them? Definitely. Do you know why the body was dumped in your office—which is not an easy feat, by the way? They don't know, but they suspect you probably have a good idea."

Boniface fought to quell the anger, feeling every sinew tighten as he tried to maintain his outward composure.

"You told me you had a problem. You told me that you thought someone might be trying to destroy you. I get it. I guessed it was something financial or grubby—photoshopped pictures of you in rubber, something like that. But no...murder."

"You know..." Boniface began, but was cut off by Gideon.

"I know you didn't do it. I know you're innocent. I know you're being set up." He slowed, looking around as if he might find instructions for what he was trying to say written on the walls. "But you've been a royal pain in the you-know-where. You've come up with some cock-and-bull story about a mystery client whose details you won't disclose on a project you can't talk about. That's the sort of stuff that annoys cops."

Gideon had a pained expression. "You understand my big problem. I'm leading a campaign against all forms of sexual violence. You've even suggested ways we can make sure the campaign has more resonance—how it can matter more—to the average person. And I'm grateful." Gideon sat back in his chair, his voice becoming more animated. "I'll give you a practical example. I'm talking at a conference," he checked his watch, "in forty-five minutes, about child prostitution."

Boniface listened.

"You know my view. There is no such thing as child prostitution. No such thing." Boniface knew and agreed with the argument. "What there is, is horrific exploitation of children by adults. Whatever you think about prostitution and the social, gender, and political issues around it, there can be no doubt that a child does not have the capacity to make an informed decision to work as a prostitute. Your high-end call girl is quite an entrepreneurial young lady, and this is more so since the days of the internet. Your so-called child prostitute does not get self-motivated; they are always, *always* forced into the life by an adult who then takes their earnings. Call it what it is: It's child sex slavery and nothing less."

Gideon paused. He had been emphasizing each point by banging on the table with a single finger. When he continued his tone was modulated. "So look at it from my point of view. How can I be anti–sex crime but pro-murderer? How can I take a public position of support—or even association—with you without the discussion in the press moving from extreme child exploitation to whether Gideon Latymer supports murder if it's committed by his friends? You were a journalist, you remember how it works."

Boniface, his head lowered, became aware of his breathing.

"I'm all for fair trials, most particularly in the court of public opinion, and innocent until proven guilty. But here's the thing: I don't want my day in court. It's little comfort to be proved innocent when you are wrongly accused." Gideon continued, his tone almost apologetic. "All this and you're working for a client where you're covering up your money trails, which makes it sound like you're into international money-laundering. Are you staying on the right side of the street with this one? It's one thing to take a risk when your business is spotless, but it's a whole other thing when you're accused of murder...." His voice trailed off.

Boniface stared out of the window, through the lush trees and across St James's Park. He didn't notice when Gideon continued. "If there's a chink of light, as a former minister, I am due a certain amount of respect, a limited number of privileges, some courtesy, and I can beg a few favors. But there are scores to settle against me. Also, with some of my tastes, I have a few acquaintances with shared interests on whom I bring pressure, although the irony is that they might enjoy it if I play rough. Having pulled those strings, I'm satisfied that it's not us."

Boniface frowned, questioning.

"It's not MI5. And for the record, it's not MI6 or any other of our lesser-known and somewhat more furtive and off-the-books chaps that you can think of. This is your foul-up, not some establishment conspiracy."

Boniface sat quietly. When he spoke, his voice was hardly audible. "Thank you."

"I know this sounds cruel, but I know you understand: I can't be associated with a murderer. I know that if you were doing my PR you would tell me to do what I'm doing." He stood and stepped to the door. "Come out to the country when this dreadful business has blown over." His face lit up. "Bring Montbretia."

He had half stepped out of the door when he turned around. "You will remember to leave by the back door."

twenty-five

"Have you come to give me a blow job?" Montbretia felt herself tremble and her face burn. "Then fuck off. If you're gonna call yourself a social worker, then be social," he started as if to unbutton his trousers, "and get to work. If you're not going to be social and you're not going to work, then fuck off."

The man with a thick Glaswegian accent sneered to the second man standing behind a burned oil drum, as if giving him a cue for the correct emotional response.

"Fuck off, lassie. We're not a project for you. And for future reference, I prefer my girls with bigger..." He held his hands as if holding a basketball to his chest with each.

"He's very picky about his ladies." The other man's London accent cut through. "I ain't..."

Montbretia had relented and accepted a second cup of coffee from Trevor. It was no better than the first, but it was tolerable—and this time free.

Most of the cup of coffee had been spent with the café owner urging Montbretia to turn around and go home. In the end, he had agreed that he couldn't stop her walking along a public road. For her part, Montbretia had agreed to check in with him before she left Tilbury.

Before beginning her walk, she had used his restroom. It wasn't a public restroom, but it was what he used. It was filthy and the door didn't shut, which was less of a problem because the light didn't work. However, the greasy floor—it felt easier to assume the floor was greasy when she considered the alternatives—or rather, the mechanics of using a restroom with a greasy floor when she was wearing pants and using one hand to hold the door half closed while still letting enough light in, was a problem.

After she finished scrubbing her hands in the café's sink, she looked at Trevor's first-aid kit and found only a two-pence coin, which apparently was what used to work with public phone booths. There being no Band-Aids, she padded her shoes with some paper napkins she found. It didn't stop the shoes rubbing, but they dug into her feet in a different place so she had a different discomfort to distract herself from the minor pain she already felt.

As she walked, the discomfort had itself become a pain.

But then again, that was expected. Trevor had suggested she continue down the road she had walked earlier. It led to a footbridge over the railway line. Montbretia demurred; she wanted to cover the ground she hadn't seen, and so she had turned left and walked up to the roundabout where the Tilbury town road and the main road to the docks joined. Trevor had said the roads were disinteresting and not designed for pedestrians.

He hadn't lied.

He hadn't exaggerated.

Having walked for a mile or so, all Montbretia had achieved was to draw parallel with the station, but on the other side of the railway line from the café. During her walk she had seen lots of blacktop roads, ugly shuttered cement walls around Tilbury docks, and lots of tractor-trailers pulling TEU containers—lorries, as Boniface always called them. Lorries speeding to and from the port, every lorry that passed kicking out black clouds of sooty diesel fumes.

Despite having covered some distance, she hadn't seen any signs of humanity. Sure, there had been people in the many lorries and the few cars that passed, but apart from that there had been no signs of any human habitation. Before coming to London, she had been traveling for two-and-a-half years. She loved cities, the buzz of people, and the mix of cultures. She also loved getting away from everything—following a trail for days and being totally isolated.

But the road to the Tilbury docks gave her neither of these experiences. She was on her own but she wasn't alone. It wasn't like being in the city with lots of people around, providing safety in numbers. It wasn't like being the only person following an old trail when there's security because there's no one else around to be a danger. Here she felt the worst of both worlds—no crowd for security, but lots of individuals passing, any of whom could be a predator and would be out of the country in hours.

She thought about the pantsuit again. This was dangerous. As well as bad shoes, which would stop her from running away. She looked so anomalous that she might as well be wearing a target. If she was to get in trouble, these clothes offered no defense: They could be quickly and easily ripped by an attacker.

At least if she had jeans on, they couldn't be ripped. And if someone tried to attack her, especially when she wore a belt, it would take too long for an attacker to get her jeans off—and even longer than that when she was fighting. And she was prepared to defend herself—boots were good for kicking people.

But a pantsuit—a pantsuit that rubbed the top of her thigh—gave no protection.

She made up her mind to walk for another ten minutes before she turned around and went back to Trevor, the train, and home. After seven minutes, she saw two men, both roughly dressed and dirty, flanking a burned-out oil drum.

As the Scotsman greeted her and encouraged her to get on her knees, she realized the danger she was in. It was the Londoner talking now. "So if you're not up for a blow job, how about a hand job? Two of us, one of you, and a nice time skiing." He let the implicit threat hang in the air.

Montbretia stepped back.

"How about a cup of tea?"

It was the Scotsman who spoke. "I'd prefer a blow job."

"And a bacon sandwich," offered Montbretia. Neither responded. "Perhaps while you have your tea and bacon sandwich, we could talk about the guy who was arrested two days ago. I know what happened to him."

The Scotsman stood up quickly. "You know, you really are starting to piss me off."

twenty-six

"I'm sorry to say, Boniface, but I'm very disappointed." The gentle German voice was as a kindly uncle delivering a rebuke; it was caring, helpful even, but firm. In reality, it was a body blow to Boniface. The tone was light—the gruffness and the lower frequencies were naturally filtered out of Chlodwig's voice—but the sadness was unmistakable. "Honestly, Boniface, I thought more of you."

Boniface remained still, sitting across the overly large conference table in the too-small conference room watching the German as he continued. "What is so upsetting is that I like you and respect you. You are bright and engaging, and you are an honorable man with the highest moral concerns." He paused before continuing. "This morning you told me that you were resigning, but now you tell me that you didn't follow through, and indeed, it is your intention not to resign."

Boniface had recounted the events of the previous twenty-four hours—from their telephone conversation to the arrival of the police, the discovery of the body, and his becoming a suspect for murder—when he talked with the CEO's brother that morning. It hadn't been an easy conversation, but it was clear to both men that it wouldn't be tenable for Boniface to represent Weissenfeld Shipping.

He looked up into the puffy eyes of the German, no longer red as they had been this morning, but the disappointment was wounding. "I understand your reaction. Really I do, Chlodwig. I understand what I'm saying is a turnaround, but that's why we should talk, and talk somewhere away from the office."

So far, so Greta. He was doing what he had been instructed to do, he just wasn't sure in his mind that he was here because he had been bullied by Greta or because he was looking three steps ahead and was concerned about the damage an angry client could create.

It is one thing to deal with bad publicity surrounding a corpse: Boniface could at least try to explain the situation to any potential new client. A slim hope, but some hope. However, trying to find new work when your last client publicly criticizes you for walking away from the project that you were hired for and had been paid for, at precisely the moment when your talents are required, is a whole other issue.

It was time for the textbook negotiation opening. Unfortunately, this textbook was being rewritten by a man who was negotiating his way into doing what he didn't want to do, what he had specifically set out *not* to do this morning, and which would upset Montbretia when he told her that he wasn't yet able to devote all his time to trying to find who had left a cadaver in his office. "I, too, believe you are an honorable man, Chlodwig, so I hope you will hear me out and will consider my suggestion, which I think might have advantages for both of us."

It was low calling to his sense of honor, but Boniface was running out of options, especially now that Gideon had severed diplomatic ties. "As I said, it would be good to chat somewhere away from the office. Could we have dinner tonight?"

twenty-seven

"When the ship took the cargo to Rotterdam, the payment was to have been made electronically, company to company."

"Standard payment practice," said the CFO.

Boniface continued, "But when the ship left Brindisi for the second time, they were carrying dollars—sports bags stuffed with greenbacks."

"Who signed off on the cash payment? Who signed off on them even carrying cash?" Joanna Baines, Weissenfeld Shipping's chief financial officer's speech was deliberate, considered, some might say aggressive, but punctuated by odd pauses: She eschewed the usual errs and umms that often filled spoken communication, choosing instead silence, as if she would be charged for each wasted sound. When she continued, her manner was quiet, small, cautious, as if using the minimum energy necessary to convey her point. "It's not practice for crews to carry this much cash." Her tone became insistent without any increase in volume. "There are policies in place to ensure no unauthorized cash payments are made, and how did they get that much cash?"

Boniface was content to let her continue: She was repeating what he already knew, but in accountant-speak. He rocked his head forward as if he might care, but in all honesty, he never got excited by anything the bean counters said, particularly the bossy, controlling types like Joanna Baines.

"Is this so hard for these people to understand? I mean, it's not like this was a mistake—someone consciously decided to take the dollar bills. Even Regenspurger understands the process."

"Regenspurger?" Boniface's post-lunch stupor and post-Gideon contemplation was immediately forgotten. "How is Regenspurger involved with money?"

The CFO paused, apparently not expecting a question. Boniface looked on as the rather hefty, somewhat inelegant woman repositioned herself. She made a few hand gestures, like a nervous actor mentally rehearsing her cue, then began. "You've probably heard about his reputation."

Boniface tried not to appear too sheepish. He had heard rumors, nothing more, and nothing that could be substantiated.

"Some of it is almost certainly true, and that reputation can be useful."

"So he does...?" Boniface held up his fists as if going into a fight.

"No. But as I say, his reputation is useful." The woman's voice was calm and definitive as she got into the rhythm of her explanation. "We're a big company in the world of shipping, and we go to many places where the rule of law is not implemented in a way that we might hope."

Boniface let his head nod, degree by degree, and he tried to bring some levity. "What we might loosely categorize as lawless hellholes."

She mirrored Boniface's nod. "You might say that. I couldn't possibly comment." Her face took on a more serious air. "These places present a challenge—again, being euphemistic, the challenge might be termed local culture and custom." She rubbed her fingers against her thumbs, seemingly becoming more circumspect.

"If I understand what you're telling me, Joanna, you are seen as the big, rich shipping firm, making you an easy target for someone looking to raise an additional bit of local taxation."

"Precisely."

"And Mister Regenspurger?"

The CFO leaned forward. "We have legitimate interests to protect, and it's important—staying within the confines of local law and ensuring compliance with international non-bribery laws—that we send a message that we are not a firm to be messed with. Time is money and all that, and if we offer a bribe once, then we'll be on the hook every time we pass through that port. And even if we don't pay, we'll waste time; that delays shipping, and we get fined." Boniface could see the pain at the thought of spending money with no equivalence in return. "Mister Regenspurger's skill set is in negotiating between the locals and our crew in order to find a mutually acceptable solution, which doesn't cause us any problems down the line."

"A fixer," offered Boniface.

"On a logistical front, he fixes problems." The ungainly woman dropped her voice. "I'm not trying to say that there has never been a situation where a couple of bottles of scotch were accidently left behind five minutes before one of our ships was cleared to leave port, but most of the time all you need is a big lad or two to stand there. If the locals know they can't push the crew around, they'll go and pick on someone else."

"So what happens? You get a problem and Regenspurger jumps on a plane?"

"Rarely—we only unleash the big beast if there's a big problem. More often there's a niggle that needs to be sorted then and there, and we don't have time to waste, so it's a case of getting local ad-hoc help. Reliable help that won't cause problems for us down the line. It's a specialized market: You need people who have an incentive to drop whatever they're doing and go and help our guys."

Boniface winced. "What's the issue with cash and Regenspurger?"

"Bluntly," she looked like she was trying to stop her eyes from involuntarily rolling, "think of the services that Regenspurger acquires for us as being a twenty-four-hour call-out service. These people must be paid in cash, and we are obliged to pay a retainer in expectation of future services."

Boniface felt the tension drain out of his body. He had been sitting with the CFO for he guessed about twenty minutes, and he was becoming increasingly fixated on the furniture, starting with a 1960s linoleum-topped desk. Linoleum topped so the surface could be replaced. The 1970s office chair Boniface was sitting on, fashioned from a single tube of steel with a thinly padded seat and backrest, each covered with loose nylon covers, which could be removed for washing. The only good thing he could find about his chair was that it rocked—it was sort of like an adult rock-a-tot for the office. But what had been taking almost all of Boniface's attention since he arrived were the filing cabinets. Two walls were covered with cabinets of different vintages and different shades of brown, gray, and green. The bottom layer, four-drawer cabinets; the top layer placed atop the bottom layer, two-drawer cabinets. Every single cabinet had a flaw—a patch of rust, a drawer not fitting, out-of-kilter corners.

Boniface drew his gaze away from the filing cabinets to find Joanna Baines staring at him, a look of stifled excitement in her eyes. "How much?"

"I beg your pardon?"

"How much do you think I paid for all the office furniture in this room: the filing cabinets, my chair, your chair, this desk?"

Boniface pushed out his bottom lip, slowly shaking his head. He didn't care, but he felt he should make a show of considering the question. "Go on. Tell me, Joanna."

"Fifteen pounds."

"Fifteen quid?" Boniface could hear the barely disguised shock in his voice as he nearly shouted.

"I had to pay a man sixty-five pounds to collect the furniture, which was quite a bargain, what with him having to bring it up two floors and the load not fitting in the van, meaning he had to do a second run."

Boniface wasn't sure whether to be impressed or horrified. "This looks ex-Civil Service, ex-government."

"That's where I got it, Boniface—government surplus."

Boniface looked up and down the cabinets, then back to the woman, her brown suit jacket not reaching her wrists. "You've heard of computers, right?"

"Computers don't give you the advantages of paper. I have everything, *everything* available to me. There's no waiting for it to boot up, and nothing's as compatible as paper. We run a global business, Boniface, with hundreds of different offices all using different standards, formats, and languages. Everyone understands paper. Nothing is quite as compatible as paper: You never have to worry about converting data into one format from another. My paper is never incompatible with your desk."

Boniface didn't know what to say.

"Paper can't be hacked and altered. If someone changes one of my files, I can see the change—I don't have to pay some IT geek to tell me about digital signatures or electronic fingerprints." A look of smugness spread over her face. "Plus, I can start checking the records—or rather Brian and I can start checking the records—as soon as you leave here, and we'll be able to see what cash the Montenegro Shipping Company has paid out."

Boniface tried to restrain himself, knowing he would regret asking the next question, but he couldn't hold back. "Why spend fifteen pounds on furniture when you could get something..." He tailed off, thinking of the lawyer's office. "New. Different. Better. Custom built."

The CFO pondered before answering. "Me? I don't care about my office. One desk is the same as the next. One filing cabinet the same as the next. I honestly see no difference between a brand-new filing cabinet and one that might be forty years old and rusty. If you look at the function that they've got to perform, they are the same."

Boniface faced the woman square on, listening as she continued. "I bring people here when they are trying to spend company money. The conversations are always the same: They talk about 'investment,' which is their code for vanity spending. But when you're sitting here looking around my room, it's hard to argue that you absolutely have to spend 10,000 pounds on a mirror to go in a bathroom. I don't have to argue; this room makes the case."

"So why didn't you bring Jeremy Farrant in here to talk about his shelves?"

Baines half-laughed. "I did. Surprisingly, those shelves weren't that expensive. If you know a good cabinetmaker and he has a good source of wood, then the job is done to a much higher standard and much swifter than if you get a bodger in who breaks things. I'm not suggesting the guy was cheap—simply that in the context of the finished product and the extent of the work he undertook, we got incredibly good value. The carpet, however..." She shut her eyes, shaking her head. "I wince whenever I walk on it, knowing how much it cost and how much we wasted pulling out the old carpet, which was three months old."

She opened her eyes. "The desk has been in his family for generations, ditto the seats, which he had reupholstered at his expense about six months before he was hired. But he's not here for the law; he was hired for his contacts, and his office is like his suit. He has to present a certain image. You see, Boniface, it's all about form and function, and form can have function in context, so that was money I was happy to spend." She relaxed, her tone changing from that of a crusading missionary. "We didn't accidentally spend the money on Jeremy, and we won't have accidentally passed cash to someone in Somalia."

"So are you saying this is fraud?" asked Boniface.

Baines pointed to the filing cabinets. "I doubt it, but that's why I've got the paper, and you can be assured I will check before I do anything else."

twenty-eight

Boniface stared through the plate-glass window onto the poorly lit emptiness of the street outside. The occasional passersby passed by; most looked in their early twenties and on their way to seek out cheap alcohol and the company of others who couldn't stand their own company either. They would reach the end of the night drunk and unhappy, but tell themselves they were having a great time with lots of friends.

"Your bratwurst, gentlemen." The owner of the deli meticulously positioned a plate before each diner. Her German accent was thicker and her tone far more assertive than Chlodwig's. "Can I get you anything else?" As Chlodwig thanked her, Boniface scrutinized his dinner: bratwurst, coleslaw, and a crusty white roll.

The deli was empty apart from the two men and the owner. Any sound—a moved chair, a glass replaced on the hard table—reverberated on the hard surfaces without any human or other soft object to damp the resonance. Anything above a low voice ricocheted around the room, and a whisper became a sibilant snake sneaking into sunlight-starved recesses. Without the usual background noise providing anonymity, Boniface felt exposed.

The German looked up and gave a nervous smile. "I very much appreciate the opportunity to talk, and I'm sorry if this food is not what you're used to. If I change my diet too quickly, my stomach..." He pulled a face. "Let's just say my stomach can be a bit delicate."

Something changed in the German's tone; he seemed to be beginning a story or maybe a moral fable. Boniface continued to eat. "When Greta removed Father from the board, it broke him. He was a proud man, a resourceful man. After the disaster for our country of the Nazis, who Father always hated, and the war, he built up his own small business, which became a very successful shipping company in the Baltic. It was small, well managed, and efficient. It generated good income, which supported the family and paid for all of our education. Losing his business—even to his daughter, but particularly in the way that she snatched it—broke him."

Boniface scanned the room: three tables lined against the window with a counter separating the cooking area. Chlodwig and he were still the only customers, and he suspected that as soon as they left, the deli would close for the evening. Five minutes to finish the meal, five minutes to tell Chlodwig what he had to say, and he could be gone.

A wistful look came across the German's face. "I know everyone remembers their childhood as being perfect, but we really did have a perfect childhood, and much of that happiness was because we had a successful father who was well-respected in the community, and we all loved him dearly."

Chlodwig fell quiet, gazing into the distance, apparently looking back over fifty years. Boniface continued with his dinner, not wanting to interrupt.

"This wasn't enough for Greta. She didn't want small, however successful. She wanted a global business. She had a vision of a fleet. Different ships for carrying different cargoes: grain, coal, even wine or beer. You name it, she wanted to carry it. Once she had all these cargo ships, she bought Regal International Cruise Line, which, quite naturally, had to have the biggest passenger liner. Have you seen the pictures of the ship? It has seventeen decks; it's bigger than an aircraft carrier."

Chlodwig paused. "As a businessman, I understand her strategy. She had a vision for the business and grew Weissenfeld Shipping by buying other shipping lines and then running the combined fleet more efficiently. And you know what? She realized her vision, and she has built a global shipping empire that is hugely successful. But it is nothing like our father's old business. Without her, we would still be running boats across the Baltic."

He hesitated, then continued weakly. "Without her, our business probably would have crumbled because we wouldn't have taken advantage of the efficiencies that are necessary to succeed in business today." He nodded as if agreeing with a conversation going on inside his head. "But this is not the business that Father set up, and it is not that business because Greta's will must prevail. She will always be that spoiled child who was indulged because she was the baby. Because of that force of will, we bought the Montenegro Shipping Line, and those people are all dead."

He stopped, a slightly self-conscious look across his face, his eyes reddening. "I'm sorry, Boniface. I'm going on rather, but my point is simple: Greta gets what Greta wants, irrespective of the costs to others." He fixed his stare on Boniface. "I hope your change of heart isn't because of pressure Greta has put on you."

Boniface sized up the man across the table. There was ten years in age difference between him and his sister. In attitude, it felt like ten generations.

"Of course Greta wasn't happy with me resigning. But, in the very short term, there is a job to be done, and I felt I couldn't walk away from that." Boniface paused, making sure the German had processed the information before he continued. "I will resign. I will resign as soon as I can, but until everyone understands their roles, until the strategy is in place, I can't leave the job incomplete."

He looked to the German, waiting for his confirmation that he could deliver the final line of this argument. "Say this whole thing explodes tomorrow. Half the people implement the strategy, half don't. What have you got? Chaos." He softened his voice. "I'm only there to coordinate—I'm not the one in front of the camera—and I'll be gone in days, not weeks, not months."

"I'm not sure, Boniface."

Boniface tried to keep his voice calm, knowing he was about to take a risk. "Maybe we should bring in Greta? I would suggest we go and see her to discuss this, but I saw her heading out five minutes before we left. From the way she was dressed, I guess she's on a date."

"That was over an hour ago," Chlodwig lifted his wrist and deliberately looked at his watch, "so it will be over by now, and the gentleman will be history."

Boniface was shocked to hear this patrician man become so dismissive. Chlodwig appeared to notice. "It will not end well. She does not respect any man that shows her kindness—all she sees is the weakness that can be exploited, and she detests that." He softened his voice before continuing. "On a Darwinian level, she knows that a kind man would never protect her, so he's no good for her. But if he's the sort of man who does not show that level of kindness—if he is the sort of man who will not bend to her will—then in her mind he cannot love her."

Boniface listened, processing the double negatives. "That's an unwinnable dilemma. What man could ever be good enough for her?"

Chlodwig's voice became very soft, almost a whisper. "When our father died, it was a terrible time. We were all very upset, but Greta—the baby—was in pieces."

He stopped, composed himself, then continued. "Greta was in a terrible state when she heard the news and tried to get hold of her husband, Wolfgang, who was locked in negotiations. He was doing a huge deal with his company. Literally, the doors were locked—the negotiators cut themselves off from the outside; there were no phones, no messages until the deal was sealed."

Boniface finished his last mouthful and listened as Chlodwig continued. "Greta hated that Wolfgang was not available to her. She shouted and screamed at all of us, at the people where the negotiation was going on. We were already hugely upset, and this made everything worse."

"No messages were passed?"

"None. But a message was left at reception, and as soon as Wolfgang heard the news he came home to be with Greta. He was a good man—a kind and loving husband. But when he arrived home—it was a three-hour car journey in winter—all Greta could do was berate him for not staying behind to keep looking at the details of the deal." He took a sip of water. "So you see, it will not end well. She will end the relationship tonight, it will be his fault, and she will line up another man, any man, for tomorrow evening. Poor fellow, as you English would say."

"This is all men?"

Chlodwig paused, looking as if he were making a shameful admission. "There is one person who Greta has yet to dominate and exploit by her force of will, and I'm not convinced that he will win."

Boniface raised his eyebrows.

"Her pet, Regenspurger." Chlodwig spoke with a tightened mouth. "I cannot abide having Stasi thugs on the payroll. Father never would have hired such a person; he's nothing more than a Gestapo man with a different uniform. I understand the necessity for practical people on the ground to sort out problems, but I disapprove of having thugs."

The two men sat in silence as their plates were cleared. Boniface waited until the owner was out of earshot. "Chlodwig, there's a noticeable tension with your sister. Perhaps if you were to go home tomorrow, it would de-escalate the situation?" The flash of tension across Chlodwig's brow passed. "I could be your man on the inside for the next few days."

The German didn't respond.

"Will you at least consider the situation please, Chlodwig? I know you're not happy with me remaining, and I hope you can see that I'm not happy with the situation either. But perhaps, as a short-term fix..."

Chlodwig spoke in measured tones: "Boniface, you are unmistakably trying to persuade me of something—that is your job. But while you are doing that, I think you are missing the simple message that I'm trying to communicate in my slow and ponderous manner: You need to protect your own best interests, and I'm not convinced you're doing that."

twenty-nine

"What do you mean you didn't resign? You need to resign, Boniface." Montbretia looked up at him. He was getting bored with other people's disappointment, but at least Montbretia had the courtesy to show some annoyance in her eyes, scolding him like he was a child. "Phone them now and tell them."

"I can't," Boniface felt himself mumbling. "Not now."

"Can't? Can't!" Montbretia seemed to be moving from exasperation to anger. "Boniface, slavery has been abolished. Nobody can force you to do something." She relaxed, seemingly trying to be more understanding, or perhaps conciliatory. "I thought we agreed. You would see Tommy and Gideon, and then you would resign, leaving you free tomorrow. Or did I not understand this correctly?"

He knew he was in for a pounding. It was almost as if she was tag-teaming with Chlodwig, even though she had never heard of him. It was best to sit back and take a few punches, then when she was tired he could try to explain.

Montbretia's annoyance finally appeared to ebb.

Boniface started gradually, trying to keep his demeanor calm, reassuring, engaging. De-escalate, move past the provocation, get to a better place. "To be honest, I thought they would want me out. Immediately. For them, there is huge potential reputational damage in having me there."

Montbretia flicked out a hand as if saying, "Of course!" Her eyebrows raised—the look of a teenager, but a paragraph of argument communicated without the necessity of speech.

"I was wrong." Montbretia's fixed face fell as Boniface continued. "I can't walk away."

"Do you want me to show you how, Boniface? It's not difficult."

When he had spoken to Montbretia before he left for dinner with Chlodwig, she had said she was in Tilbury, which in itself was surprising. They agreed to meet and talk—the story she told sounded quite alarming. Knowing what he would tell her, he suggested somewhere that wouldn't annoy her—somewhere she would feel comfortable—and undoubtedly, she felt comfortable expressing her disapproval here.

He had chosen well.

A traditional pub in the heart of London's West End, one block north of Shaftesbury Avenue, the London street best known for its preponderance of theatres. The pub was small, with an L-shaped bar giving two ends where customers could find relative seclusion, but it was still big enough for there to be background hum wrapping you like a warm blanket, unlike the Teutonic austerity of Chlodwig's favored bratwurst deli.

The brass fixtures, dark wood, patterned burgundy and blue carpet, and brown leather furniture with alcoves and screening all said "relax, kick your shoes off, and make yourself at home—you're not on display here." He shuddered to think of the reaction if they had met in a hotel bar. Montbretia was allergic to bar nuts, light jazz, and interior design executed on an industrial scale. He knew what she would have said: "It's like the Apple Stores—they bring me out in hives: all that uniformity, all the conformity. I can't stand rooms designed for a cult and filled with smiling dead-behind-the-eyes automatons."

Boniface leaned closer to start his explanation.

"Don't say that it's more complicated than I understand."

Boniface wasn't sure whether Montbretia had issued a threat or an instruction, but he tried to keep his voice light. "Am I allowed to say there are things you don't know, because I haven't told you?"

Her eyes brightened for the first time since he told her that he hadn't resigned. "Yeah. You can say that, Boniface."

Boniface relaxed into his seat. "I've been working with this client, as in getting paid by this client, for about nine months now. Before we met, I was working with the client. While you were still in Turkey and wherever you were before that, and while Ellen was still"—he faltered—"they were paying me."

"This is the same client that you won't tell me who it is?"

Boniface grimaced.

"And for whom there is no documentation in the office?"

"You looked?" Boniface's calm was broken.

"Mmmm." Montbretia stared down, a slight warmth appearing to radiate from her cheeks. "Is this the same client you said you would go and see this morning and resign?"

"I did offer my resignation." Boniface could hear his desperate indignity. "It was the first thing I did, and it was rejected, but believe me, the first thing I'm going to do tomorrow is offer my resignation again."

Montbretia sat with her mouth half open. "Now you're sounding pathetic. How hard can it be to resign?"

"You don't take the money and then resign because it's inconvenient to you." He sat back and exhaled through his nose. "We're ninety percent done. We've rehearsed, and show time is any day now. If they want me to stay, I can't walk away without making them very upset, and an upset client potentially kills the whole business."

"But when we talked you were going to resign. Now you tell me you've been to dinner and that you're staying in a hotel so you can start early. All with a client whose identity I don't know, and apparently can't know."

Boniface opened his mouth—Montbretia held up a finger, commanding him to stop.

"What use are you to your client if you're in jail? Won't it be far more damaging to your client if this whole dead-body-in-the-office issue blows up and spatters onto them? If you've sorted it, then you've immunized them against damage."

She dropped her finger, keeping Boniface fixed in her gaze.

"Let me tell you about Tilbury." Boniface remained still as she continued. "I met science boy in his bunny suit outside the office."

"Science boy?"

"To my shame, I didn't get his name." She brightened. "I got his number."

"Science boy?" Boniface felt able to take a sip of water for the first time since he had begun his conversation with Montbretia.

"He put it in my phone and he put his name as science boy so I wouldn't forget." She looked down. "I don't think anyone has ever cared enough about him before to give him a nickname. I felt like such a cow taking his number. It gives him hope—I could see it in his eyes—hope that will never be fulfilled. If I call him, it will only be because I need something."

She met Boniface's gaze for assurance before she continued. "I started at the Common—I went early."

"I said..."

She shushed him. "I know what you said, and you also said you would resign. Anyway, I took care and didn't get murdered. After that I went to the office, where I met science boy. It sounds like it's going to take a long time to analyze the place, but what he did tell me was that the guy whose body was dumped was alive two days ago. They know that because he was arrested in Tilbury. So I went to Tilbury."

Voices, indistinct but clearly conversations punctuated with the sound of glasses, creaking and squealing doors, and the occasional laugh all faded as Boniface listened to Montbretia telling him about her trip to Tilbury.

"I don't like you taking these risks, Monty. It scares the hell out of me."

"I'm a big girl, Boniface. I spent over two years traveling around the world on my own. I think I know how to look after myself."

"You're missing my point." There was a sharpness in Boniface's retort. "You can do what you want to do—that's fine with me. On the whole, London is one of the safest places you can go. It's not dangerous to walk down a street. It's not dangerous to walk on the Common. But when you go and poke people with a stick, when you seek out dangerous people who may have committed murder in order to poke them with a stick, when you seek them out in isolated places and come back and tell me that some aggressive vagrant asked you for a blow job while you were wearing clothes that could be ripped off and shoes that you couldn't run in, when the only reason you went was to help me—then I get scared, and I think I'm allowed to ask you not to take any risks on my behalf." He fixed her with a stare. "Take risks for yourself, not for me."

"You need to get off your ass. You don't get to change the rules, Boniface. Not when you're ignoring the rules and when you're not defending yourself." He sat straighter. "I do have a stake here. Whose room was the body left in? Are you sure that it's you they're after?" She pointed a finger apparently for emphasis, continuing in a calmer manner. "I would have gone with you. It would have been fun to take you along to the god-forgotten hole that is Tilbury, but, oh yeah, you were working with your special client."

"You make it sound as if I've done nothing all day."

"No. *You* make it sound as if you've done nothing all day. You don't get credit for doing the complete opposite of what you said you would do, no matter how much you try to spin it."

"But I did go and see Gideon and Tommy—Gideon three times, once without clothes on."

"Yuck!" Montbretia sat open-mouthed.

"For the whole conversation, while he was telling me about his exploits with last night's paramour, and picking chocolate... Anyway, I left and came back when he was dressed."

"Yuck, yuck, yuck." Montbretia shuddered. "Please tell me you got something useful from these two."

"I did." Boniface leaned toward Montbretia, looking left to right, and whispered. "Tommy loves you."

"What?"

"Tommy loves you. Seriously. Thinks you're a charming lady who treated him well and didn't judge him on the basis of how he looked or because his son is a murdering rapist."

"Gideon? What did you get from him apart from an image burned into your brain, which they'll find if you donate your brain to medical science?"

"Good news, bad news. Which do you want first?" asked Boniface.

Montbretia thought for a moment. "Shall we start with the good?"

"Gideon has offered his body for your pleasure."

"I thought we were starting with the good news." Montbretia had the look of someone who had just eaten something unpleasant and was looking for somewhere to discreetly spit it out.

"The good news, as much is it's good, is that he's pretty sure it's not political."

"How's that...?" Montbretia stopped herself. "So what's the bad news?"

"The bad news is he's backing off. The cops think I know more than I'm telling, and with his sex-crimes campaign he wants some distance." Montbretia frowned as Boniface continued. "In short, he can't be portrayed as being anti-rape but pro-murderer."

"But..."

Boniface stopped talking and waited for Montbretia to play the scenarios in her head. When she relaxed back into her seat without offering any argument, he continued. "I think we both need some sleep. Do you want me to get you a room at the hotel?"

"Nah. I prefer my own bed." She waited for a beat. "And I really want to wear my own clothes tomorrow. There's a reason why you don't see me in pantsuits."

"You can stay at my place if you want."

"Thanks, but the only clothes I've got there are my pink gym clothes, and I won't be seen in public wearing those."

"What? You've got photographers following you?"

"No. But I have standards, Boniface, and there's stuff I've got to get for tomorrow."

Boniface let his eyelids affirm his agreement. "Will you at least let me pay for a taxi to take you home?"

"Deal," said Montbretia.

"Let's have dinner tomorrow night. Hopefully the situation will have moved forward by then."

thirty

The dark blue Mercedes, approximately the size of a Dutch barge, wallowed up the road, drawing to a halt outside the Weissenfeld offices. The driver got out and held the door open for the passenger with very high heels, who exited without acknowledgement as she continued her phone conversation while passing through gates and doors that automatically opened, subsuming her within the building.

Within thirty seconds Boniface was at the gate. The gate was closed, the car gone, and there were no people to usher him inside. He waited for the gate to unlock, passed through the garden, entered the former house, and took the stairs two at a time. "Morning, Len. I need to catch the lady; I'll be back for a chat in two minutes." Reaching the top floor, he followed the winding passage to Sophie's desk.

He stretched for the handle to Greta's office. "She is on the telephone."

Boniface straightened and turned to see Sophie's unsmiling face. Beside her desk a tall, skinny man in his early twenties stood, his eyes unnaturally open like he had a permanent surprise. His brown suit camouflaged him against the office furniture, and the large stack of files he clutched, like a mother holding a baby who had been pulled out of the rubble after a natural disaster, offered some sort of protection.

"I'll wait." Boniface moved away from the door, becoming aware that he could hear the otherwise noiseless man breathing in but not out. With each inhalation, his head twitched.

"She is busy today," said Sophie in a flat voice.

"All day?"

"Yes, Mister Boniface, all day." Sophie looked down at a day planner, running her finger over each appointment listed. "All day." She raised her head from the planner, her eyes looking away from Boniface and toward the stranger who turned, noiseless apart from his inhalation, and started to walk away from them, his steps uneven beats as if he were about to break into a canter.

"No gaps? No slivers of time?"

"No." Sophie was using vocal sounds but without attaching any emotion. Boniface wasn't sure whether that was a "no, I'm sorry" or maybe a "no, let me see what I can do" or even "there's loads of free time, but Greta doesn't want to see you."

"Can we change her schedule? Slip in five minutes here or there?" As the words fell out of his mouth, he realized he was suggesting something Sophie knew to be impossible. Boniface was the person telling the Nobel

Laureate that, in truth, gravity doesn't exist.

"Why would we do that? What do we do with the meetings that have already been scheduled?" Sophie slipped along a path between baffled and bemused.

It was too early. Boniface had done what was expected—he stayed in a hotel and was at the office at 7:30. That was enough drama for the day. "Can you tell her I want to talk to her as soon as possible? If she's looking for me, I'll be with Brad Phipps."

He dropped down the steps to the security desk. "Lennie."

"Boniface."

"I'm looking for Brad. Where would I find his office?"

The guard pointed downward. "But he's not there yet."

"Could we?" Joanna Baines, the joyless CFO with the £15 filing cabinets, ascended from the floor below, a finger pointing Boniface in the direction of her office.

thirty-one

"Boniface." Joanna Baines had her back to the door and hadn't turned around when Boniface entered. "MV Paranoid."

"I beg your pardon." Boniface wasn't sure whether he was more surprised by the CFO's utterance or by the gangly youth Boniface had last seen with Sophie Driesdorfer, but who was now sitting at Baines's table, his pile of files looking ready to fall and crush him.

"Motor Vessel Paranoid," said Baines.

"You've lost me," said Boniface, looking between her and the acned face of the young man who was still twitching as he inhaled.

"The previous owner—indeed, the founder—of the Montenegro Shipping Line was a big fan of Black Sabbath."

Boniface wasn't sure whether she had finished speaking or if she had paused for dramatic effect. He watched as she rounded her desk, then met his gaze.

"He christened each ship in his fleet after Sabbath albums, so we've got MV Master of Reality, MV Sabbath Bloody Sabbath, and MV Sabotage, which is a really stupid name for a ship that you are intending to insure through Lloyd's of London." She gave a look that he took to be embarrassment, the first time Boniface had seen her express any emotion. "MV Paranoid is the ship that went to Somalia."

"That's good, isn't it?" asked Boniface.

The muscles in Joanna Baines's face faltered. "We've only been able to go so far through the records since we spoke yesterday." Her head swiveled to look at the thin man sitting at her desk before turning back to Boniface. "By the way, have you met Brian? Brian Singleton."

"I saw you up..." Boniface stopped himself—better to remain diplomatic and not mention where he saw the younger man. "I've seen you around. Good to meet you."

The younger man mumbled something and continued to twitch as he breathed in noisily.

"You can blame Boniface for not going home last night," Baines addressed Singleton before she turned back to Boniface. "To confirm, the dates you told me yesterday were?"

"Leaving Brindisi on 10 October, dumping in Somalia on 15 November."

Baines glanced at Brian Singleton and nodded. "We've been through the papers we've got here, and the Paranoid was definitely in Somalia—there are expenses recorded." She extended her arm, waiting until Singleton put a piece of paper in her hand. "The full itinerary that we can reconstruct from our records is: 21 September leaves Brindisi, 30 September stops in Rotterdam, 10 October back in Brindisi, 25 October Ivory Coast."

Boniface glanced up from his notepad, where he was busily scribbling the details as Baines recounted them. "Ivory Coast?"

"Correct, Ivory Coast, the last stop before they arrived in Somalia on 15 November."

"So that's it?" asked Boniface. "That's the proof that the Montenegro Shipping Line sanctioned the dumping?"

"Quite the opposite," said Baines, her voice strident. "That's the evidence that MV Paranoid visited those ports. We have transactions that can be traced to each location. What we have no evidence to suggest was that there were any substantial cash transactions."

Boniface inhaled sharply through his teeth. "In that case I had better get out your way and let you do some more digging."

"I think you misunderstand, Boniface." The CFO's voice was firm. "I'm telling you that we are not the source of the dumping. Our ship may have carried the waste, but we didn't pay for the waste to be taken."

Boniface put his notebook back in his pocket before he continued. "You carried the waste. You dumped the waste. It's enough to crucify the company, and this is why I need us to get to the position where everyone understands what happens next and how we run this thing in a way that minimizes the damage for the business."

"This, I'm afraid, is where I have a problem," said Baines.

"Go on," said Boniface, trying to keep his tone measured.

"There are several aspects here. First, the strategy you outlined yesterday is to essentially throw our hands in the air and say, 'Yup, we did it.'" Boniface raised his eyebrows slightly as the CFO continued. "In other words, you want us to legally admit guilt and assume an open-ended liability. When I hear the words unquantifiable loss, I come out in a rash. I also know that as an officer of this company—a publicly listed company—I am required by virtue of my directorship to ensure that we make an immediate report to the Stock Exchange because I have information that may have a material impact on our share price."

"I don't think you've got the strategy quite right," said Boniface. "Can I explain?"

"Hold on a moment," said Joanna. "Before you explain, could I bring up my second point?"

"Please." Boniface sat back and listened; out of the side of his eye he caught Brian Singleton pushing himself back into his chair, his unnaturally wide eyes making him look shocked at the objections coming from his boss.

"We've got a marketing and PR guy. You've probably heard; his name's

Brad."

"I was on my way to see him when you diverted me," said Boniface.

"The point of Brad, if you will, is to be a central resource to remove duplication and to bring efficiency. As you can guess, it was my idea to create the role."

"Makes a lot of sense," said Boniface.

"I'm not sure how much work you've done to date, Boniface, but going forward it should be Brad that handles these issues. It seems like you've glossed over some of the fundamentals, like the necessity to talk to the Stock Exchange, so why don't you go and have a chat with Brad and leave us to it? Send your invoice directly to Brian, and he'll deal with it without delay."

thirty-two

After five minutes Boniface gave up listening.

The call had come in; Brad had answered.

That annoyed Boniface, but he could tolerate a brief interruption—he wasn't sure whether the tall, slim All-American kid who was in reality Canadian had an assistant who would take messages, and voicemail can be very impersonal. He was more annoyed when Brad didn't ask to call back, instead launching into the conversation as if there wasn't someone else he was already talking with.

Boniface might have been more accepting—perhaps it was a genuinely important call. However, apparently Brad took all his calls on speakerphone and, while talking, walked around the room playing basketball with the small ball that seemed to live on his desk and the matching small hoop—which Boniface was sure was meant to go over a wastepaper basket as a weak joke—that was attached to his door, which the Canadian closed with a hefty kick.

After the first minute, Boniface was convinced Brad was talking to a friend. By minute three, Boniface was sure it was a supplier to Weissenfeld—someone who had to suck up to the company to keep getting paid. By minute four the stomach-turning realization hit him that this was someone who Brad was trying to positively influence. This was someone on whom Brad was unleashing his full marketing and PR arsenal.

Boniface was used to conversations with nouns and verbs. Sometimes adverbs and adjectives could be thrown in with more sophisticated audiences, but when he got away from nouns and verbs, he became twitchy. By contrast, Brad's conversations used words he didn't understand, punctuated with a number of vocal noises and with a regular supply of words that didn't mean anything. "Yo" was employed both as a greeting and as a replacement for the word "your"; "awesome," "dude," and "bro," which appeared interchangeable; along with the equally flexible "yer feel," "cool," and "alright." Except Brad didn't say alright. Instead, he tended to say alllllll-riiiiiiiide. He pronounced Ts as Ds, but then again, so did most country singers.

He knew it would be a painful experience when the conversation began. "Yo, man! You're that Boniface guy, right? Good to meet you, man." But when Boniface started to explain the problem and Brad called it "awesomely gruesome," Boniface felt himself begin to die inside.

Boniface felt no more enthusiastic about the discussion that would follow. As he tried to ignore the phone conversation assaulting his ears, he looked around the room, paying attention to the details, but couldn't find a space larger than three inches square. The rest of the room was covered with sports memorabilia—Brad was manifestly both a keen participant and an enthusiastic follower, particularly of hockey.

Boniface made a mental note to call it ice hockey. He knew it would upset Brad.

Between the autographed hockey sticks and many pucks, there were several basketballs, all autographed and in glass cabinets, awards, and photos, most of which were autographed, and those that weren't had a man who looked remarkably like Brad growing up over the years—tall, blonde, slim but fit, with clear skin that always had a slight tan from being outside.

The phone call ended, and Brad continued without a pause. "Look Boniface, I'll be honest. In this company they're a bit...I don't wanna say slow, but y'know...they're kinda old school." He inclined his head as if concluding after deep cogitation—his sign, a hint to Boniface: professional-to-professional, chewing the fat. "They don't get how you do business these days. I told them we need to get the company name on soccer jerseys. The premier league—the English league, right—is the biggest league in the world, right? We should be there, right?"

"When you say we, you mean Weissenfeld Shipping?"

"Who else could I mean, Boniface?"

"The people who charter ships go to the subsidiary companies, like the Montenegro Shipping Line, so they have no knowledge of the Weissenfeld brand."

"Precisely, Boniface. They don't know the brand, which is why we need to be on soccer jerseys."

Boniface was figuring out how to respond to the basic *who's your customer—which brand do they recognize* misunderstanding, but Brad was continuing. "You try telling them about search engine advertising—you know, keywords when people search Google—and it's like you're speaking a foreign language."

"But aren't there a limited number of shipping companies, and a limited number of people who charter ships, so everyone pretty much knows everyone already?"

"Precisely, Boniface. So when someone searches for shipping, they should find us, and if we don't advertise, they won't find us. I mean, it's obvious, isn't it? But apparently not to them upstairs."

It wasn't obvious to Boniface what the benefit to Weissenfeld would be, so he let it slide and tried to get back on track. "So, Somalia."

"Yeah. Like bad. Just *the* worst." Boniface marveled at how the English language could be mangled by a man who seemed to have a total lack of any real empathy beyond a slogan.

"We're still clarifying details—"

"Whatever, dude. There's a boat in Africa, I get it." Brad was back in his chair, spinning and rocking. Boniface suspected he was medicated for ADHD symptoms as a youngster, whether he needed the treatment or not.

"No one knew what the cargo was—and still no one knows what the cargo was. No one cared what the cargo was, so the locals—as far as we can tell—unloaded it and moved it from the port and left it where they drop all their other waste, right next to a squatter town."

"So why don't we say 'Yo! Yo deal with it!' and come home?" He thrust his chest forward and shoulders back, swaggering.

"Well..." Boniface counted to ten, then continued. "It's a tricky legal situation. There is culpability, there is a money trail—although there is some dispute—and there are photographs. Also, let's not forget the dudette-in-chief." He noticed Brad's eyes flick as he tried to mimic the other man's language. "There is the desire on Greta's part to do something, but it's not as easy as reaching into her pocket. There are implications. You can't say 'We're responsible for ten percent of the problem' or 'We only killed eighty-six people.' It doesn't work like that. As soon as you admit any liability, you open yourself up to all liabilities. Those liabilities could bankrupt the company or tie it up in incredibly complicated and tedious litigation for years, and no one knows what reputational damage that would do."

Brad looked blankly.

"So that's the background. But we didn't want to force the problem prematurely into the open, and we can't be flat-footed if the story breaks, so we've been working to provide context around..."

"What context is there?" Brad seemed agitated. "People died, right?"

Boniface stopped himself from sighing. "People died. But dangerous chemicals don't happen in a vacuum. People don't say, 'Hey, let's go and find some nasty chemicals to move around the world.' Noxious chemicals are a byproduct of the manufacturing process, so what we are trying to do is reinforce the causal link between consumer consumption and waste products."

Brad frowned. He had the look of a confused man who didn't know what question to ask.

Boniface continued. "In short, we want to say, 'If you don't want the nasty chemicals that require disposal, then stop buying electronic gadgets.'"

Brad nodded, as if he was pleased to see that Boniface had reached an understanding that was self-evident to him.

Boniface tried to hide his annoyance as he continued. "We've also done a lot of work to manage the information people will find when they search."

"What? Like when they Google?"

Boniface wondered whether he could have his head fitted with an exasperation valve. "We wanted more than that. What we wanted was a central forum where all the issues associated with globalization could be discussed. All the issues: the manufacturing process, economics for the producer countries, economies of the countries exporting jobs, the logistics, the product benefits, and so on. The first manifestation of this forum was a website, but naturally, the intention is to build into the real world starting with conferences and some high-level summits."

He saw nothing in Brad's eyes. Nothing. No spark. No recognition. No understanding. No thought about how this tool could be exploited for his own advantage. Nothing. Whatever was there before had slipped away.

"The first step has been a website where we have encouraged some interesting discussions, and I think we've also been able to demonstrate a level of independence by coordinating criticism of the industries and calling on academics to submit papers, but we've also made sure there are enough realists that the necessities and the pragmatism are seen."

The word "website" elicited a response in Brad in the same way that a loved one's voice might elicit a response in a coma victim. But as with a coma victim, you never knew whether they were responding to the stimulus or having a dream.

"Now, because the website is so authoritative since it has leading experts contributing and linking to it as they discuss the issues, the site has been gradually rising up the search engine rankings. As it has risen, more people have linked to it—so now, for instance, we have links from the BBC, the FT, CNN, and The Wall Street Journal. With those links we're now showing in the top two or three listings in the search results for all the major search engines, in all territories."

"Big whoop. You set up a website. That's like, what? An afternoon's work?"

Boniface contemplated the hockey sticks: It wouldn't be the first time that one had been used in a murder, and he was already suspected of murder, so why not be accused for one he *did* commit?

"It's not like selling widgets. We're trying to do something with a lot of moving parts. First, we've created a forum with a network of experts discussing the issues. Some are more disposed to us, others more against, but if the press contact them, they will give a rounded view of the issue. And that's the other half of the story: If you search for any related issues—so if you drop Somalia, toxic waste, and Weissenfeld into a search engine—what pops up at the top of the list? So we don't just get found: The right message with all the complexity around the issues and a bunch of sympathetic experts gets found. It ranks way above any conspiracy nut-job site."

Brad sighed. "Man. You are making it way, way, *way* too complicated.

"SEO—y'know, search engine optimization—ain't rocket science, Boniface. You get an agency to buy links."

"Which get blocked by Google for trying to pervert their system." Boniface heard his snappiness. "This isn't search engine optimization—this is about creating a sympathetic community of experts to push our case."

"Man, I hear what you're saying. But, y'know, you're starting to sound old school—there's a much faster way to solve this problem." He picked up his mini basketball. "I should be leading this, right? I do PR around here, yeah? I'm the new broom brought in to shake stuff."

He turned, dropping the ball. "I mean, like, when something goes wrong, I know who to call." His eyes moved to his unnaturally tidy desk, from where he picked up a plastic folder. "See. I've got a list of all the people I can call at newspapers." He brightened. "Joanna paid some dude on the internet like twenty bucks to research this list, so we're covered."

thirty-three

Boniface stepped into the corridor, closing the door on the Canadian.

He tried to keep his feet firmly placed on the black-and-white-checked marble tiles running across the floor as he felt the tension at the back of his head—the anger boring into his brain stem—and waited, willing the pain to subside. When he felt he could turn the pain into an ache, he swore under his breath, and kept swearing as he walked up the stairs to the security guard's desk.

He stood in front of Lennie, motionless, his eyes wide.

Lennie nodded.

Boniface's look became more aggressive—his head lowered, and he continued to fixate on the guard, his eyes looking up.

"I'm an old soldier. I was hired to take orders. Orders come down from the lady general; I pick up my weapon, attach the bayonet, and go over the top into battle. I don't ask questions."

"But he's a..." Boniface let out an infuriated sigh, his eyes drifting up to the next floor, where Sophie and the rather odd man he now knew to be Brian Singleton were standing at the top of the stairs facing each other—as far as Boniface could tell, neither social misfit was speaking.

"I follow my orders." Lennie winked. "But in the fog of war there are accidental casualties." He let out a long and heartfelt sigh. "You can be assured that I would carry out my duty and bury the dead." A look of satisfaction had appeared across his face, which fell away as Boniface's phone rang.

"Boniface." He answered. "Tommy." He felt surprise in his voice, becoming aware he was talking too loudly. He moved away from the security guard, holding his phone closely, talking in a soft voice. "I can. I'll see you there."

A cantering step and the sound of inhalation caught Boniface's attention, and he nodded to acknowledge Brian Singleton as he walked past, his head twitching as he inhaled. Boniface replaced his phone in his pocket, turning back to Lennie as he continued. "What's your take on him?" He tilted his head in the direction that Joanna Baines's galley slave had cantered.

"An odd one, but he's meant to be very good at his job and incredibly detail focused, which I guess is what you want in a numbers man."

"Odd how?" asked Boniface.

"Lives with his mother, who makes him sandwiches. Fixed routines—has to go for a walk at twelve-forty-seven each day, always leaves the gate and turns left, returns after precisely twenty-six minutes." The security guard stepped back and looked from side to side before leaning toward Boniface to continue. "I've never had a conversation with him, but as I say, odd with routines and probably harmless."

Boniface took in Lennie's comments. "Catch you later," he said, moving toward the staircase.

For the second time that morning, Boniface wound around to Greta's office, managing to touch the door handle before he heard Sophie's sharp tones. "Was I not clear? She is busy all day." Boniface had not seen her behind her desk.

"I need to see her. You will let her know." The dumpy German made eye contact with Boniface and continued with her work. "I'll be with Jeremy Farrant, but I want to get a breath of fresh air first."

"In London?" Her head oscillated slightly as she laughed to herself, and seemingly having answered her own question, she looked up at Boniface. "Why are you telling your movements? Fraulein Weissenfeld doesn't want to see you. Do you think I am responsible for you?"

thirty-four

"I'm like you; I like to speak face to face."

Boniface scanned the café. It hadn't changed since yesterday. In truth, it probably hadn't changed much in the last 50 years. Some of the clientele might be different, but the red-and-white-checked tiles, the Formica tables with bench seating, and the stainless-steel counter, they were definitely unchanged.

Tommy's suit had changed—Boniface noticed the different belt, which led him to see a fractionally different fabric color.

Tommy whispered. "I had a word. You know, *a word*, with some of my former associates who may—not saying are, but may—be on the wrong side of certain lines from time to time, and who know people who definitely are. That's why I thought we should, you know, face to face."

Boniface mentally calculated the time he had wasted getting a cab halfway across town to listen to Tommy's tales from beaten-down criminals who didn't have the sense to get out of the game. "Thanks, Tommy. I appreciate it," he lied.

"Anyway," Tommy was still whispering, although Boniface couldn't figure why. "I've had a word, and they all say that this is an outsider job. No one has been asked to do any work in Wimbledon." He continued, louder but with an almost apologetic tone. "If I knew what had happened, I could ask more direct questions."

Boniface sat back and took a sip of tea—Tommy had ensured a freshly drawn pot was delivered between the time Boniface entered the café and when he sat down. He exhaled, then spoke quickly and lightly. "A dead body was dumped in my office."

Tommy looked visibly shocked. "A dead body—your office?"

"Montbretia's office, actually. But definitely a body. Very definitely deceased."

Individual muscles in Tommy's face twitched as he seemed to process what he had just heard. "That's serious. You don't leave a body unless you have real need to say something." He had another thought. "The cops think you're involved?"

Boniface exhaled again. "Yup. I am their prime suspect, and if I didn't do it, then I know more than I'm telling them."

"Do you know who he was? The dead bloke."

"All I know, Tommy, is that he was dead in my office, but he was alive and well, and arrested in Tilbury, two days before we found him. He was a vagrant."

"Tilbury? Town or docks?"

"Docks, I think. Does it matter?"

"No, but you've got big trouble, Boniface." Tommy sat back, visibly shaken, as if someone had given him a diagnosis that he had three months to live. "I said this was an outside job. It is, and it's professional." He stared straight at Boniface, his voice low and measured. "Who do you know with connections to shipping?"

Boniface let a silence fall between him and Tommy. The rest of the café still resonated to the sound of cooking, chinaware, and conversations about sport, but an icy chill surrounded Tommy and Boniface.

"You're being crazy, Tommy." He caught what he had said. "I mean that in the nicest possible way. But surely you're exaggerating."

"I know Tilbury docks, Boniface. One of the reasons why I moved down from Derbyshire was because there was good scrap-metal business going through the London docks, and you know I've done well out of my business. I've done well because I've got to know the people at the docks. Some of them are lovely lads…some of them…"

"Really, Tommy? Is it that bad?"

"It's like anywhere. Most of it is fine. But around the edges, that's where the problems come, and Tilbury has more edges than most places." He took a mouthful of his bacon sandwich and continued. "You see, Tilbury has vast numbers of people coming through—they're either coming or going. Nobody ever stays in Tilbury—they're always passing and passing quickly."

"That's what Montbretia said," offered Boniface.

"Why does she know Tilbury?" There was concern in Tommy's voice.

"She went there yesterday."

"You idiot, Boniface. I thought you cared for that girl." Tommy's face reddened. "It's not the sort of place for someone like her."

"She's tough," offered Boniface.

"I don't care how tough, she ain't a criminal, she won't think like a criminal to avoid getting in trouble." Tommy looked up. "I'm serious, Boniface—you look after that girl."

Boniface mumbled some sort of affirmation. "So people come, people go. That doesn't make it bad."

"No. But it makes it easy. Say you decide to send someone a message. Say you drop a stiff in someone's office." Tommy lowered his voice. "If you know someone who can get people in and out on a ship without paperwork, you import a couple of guys from East Europe or somewhere. Give them an old van. They pick up the first vagrant they see near the docks and beat the guy over the head." Tommy looked up at Boniface. "The body was beaten over the head, wasn't it?"

Boniface felt his lower jaw hanging loose.

"Beat them over the head. Take them to wherever. Drop the body.

Take the van somewhere. Burn it. Get back to Tilbury and get on a boat. They'll be out before the cops have found the body. Whoever dumped the body will be gone by now."

Boniface still couldn't speak.

"And if they want someone to disappear, having access to a boat is a great way to dump a body. They don't last long on the North Sea, and any sailor who might witness what went on ain't British and will be out of the country for months, if not years or forever."

thirty-five

He flipped the small silver box out of his pocket, opened the lid, took a pinch, put his fingers up his left nostril, and sniffed. Then repeated with his right nostril. As he had been yesterday, the small man was immaculately presented, wearing another tailored three-piece suit, this one charcoal with a narrow herringbone stripe, and a silk handkerchief in his top pocket. However, this piece of silk was worn with more of a peacock flourish than Gideon would have welcomed, having a lighter shade than the politician would have settled on.

"For you?" Jeremy Farrant held his silver snuffbox between his thumb and his index finger and looked over his half-moon glasses at his guest. Boniface declined. He was sitting on the same green leather scroll-armed club chair that he had sat on yesterday, but today he contemplated the room in a different light. Remembering what Joanna Baines had told him, he somehow felt less uncomfortable knowing he was sitting on Farrant's family furniture. But he also recalled the often-used definition of new money: Someone who bought their own furniture.

"You're an interesting old chap, aren't you, Boniface? Far more interesting than I expected after our brief exchange yesterday." He took out two green files, dropping one on the far side of his desk and opening the closer one as he sat down behind the huge lump of old wood.

"Soooooo. A journalist. Made your name with the Stan Gadson affair. Your research led to the MP resigning and ultimately his researcher receiving a jail sentence, and as their stars fell, yours rose and there followed ten years of what can only be called great success. You were a very well-regarded journalist, and through that time you were married to another journalist: Veronica Rutherford, now the editor of the *European Daily Herald*, owned by the charming Ivan Kuznetsov."

Boniface could hear the attempt at sarcasm as his host said the word "charming."

Farrant looked up, keeping his finger on the page. "But this isn't news for you."

"It's only news that you care about what I did fifteen years ago."

"It behooves me to check. It's important that we know who we're dealing with, wouldn't you agree, Mister Boniface? Telling you what you already know is hardly useful information, but it does give us an opportunity to have a discussion." He lifted the side of the file that was closer to Boniface. "Here. This copy is for you."

"Thanks, but I don't feel the compulsion to read the file—I was there. I saw the movie; indeed, you may say that I was the author and the screenwriter."

"Quite so." The small man gave a patronizing smile, wrinkling his nose and narrowing his eyes. "So you are expecting that the file will cover the end of your marriage, the meltdown, the alcoholism, the time with Her Majesty's Government, that unfortunate incident and the brief relapse, and the establishment of your own business?"

Boniface sat up straighter, twisting to face Farrant. "If when you say 'unfortunate incident' you mean the one with the car, the solid object with which the car came into contact while I was in charge, having more alcohol than a distillery in my veins—indeed, I think it would be more accurate for you to say I had blood in my alcohol—with the resulting and continuing driving ban, and the additional treatment, then yes. That seems a fair summary."

The older man wrote a few notes on his file as Boniface continued. "But that was the day when everything changed, and since then I've been a good boy with no relapses."

"I must say, for an alcoholic—sorry, for a *former* alcoholic—you are incredibly well presented, Mister Boniface. Good skin, no weight problem—as you know, there is a tendency to balloon or wither, depending on the chosen poison—and you can unequivocally dress yourself and have found yourself a good tailor."

Boniface's eyebrows flicked.

"Your belt, Mister Boniface. Or rather, the lack of a belt and the absence of belt loops. Always a definitive giveaway. But also, the suit fits you. You can see it when you move—there are no odd wrinkles or pulls as you flex."

Boniface relaxed as the small man continued. "If I may make a suggestion, however. Your shoes. Beyond doubt you bought those in a shop...and they look like a suitably stout pair of brogues, but you would appreciate the difference if you found yourself a decent cobbler. A small luxury, but worth it. I'll get my assistant to give you details of mine."

Boniface found himself almost ready to thank the man who had refused to talk to him yesterday and in the intervening period appeared to have carried out a detailed background check worthy of the security services. But as Farrant continued, Boniface lost the urge.

"Now you have your own firm." He stopped scratching notes and returned the lid to his pen. "I thought public relations, whatever that means, was the domain of well-mannered young ladies who went to a good school before being finished, but who would never amount to much in the employment field, and yet had a yen to prove—however fallaciously—that they weren't wholly dependent on daddy's money before they married into the role of breeding the next generation of the aristocracy and the moneyed classes."

The lawyer stood, leisurely starting to walk around his desk toward the windows. Boniface gazed at the hand-stitched leather on his feet gliding over the olive green expense that upset the CFO so desperately.

"I looked at your website, and I saw that PR is so much more than well-turned-out girls and press releases: There's crisis management." He held his hands up, his mouth open, aping a cliché of a shocked person. "Communications." He pulled a serious face. "Strategic advice." He held his chin in his hand as if thinking. "Apparently we're living in the electronic age where stories can't be squashed, so we should all embrace engagement and openness." He shook his head in a theatrical flourish. "It's all quite beyond me, which is why our glorious leader called you, I presume."

"If you've finished patronizing," muttered Boniface without bothering to move his eyes toward the small man. "That's how it started."

"I spoke to Joanna last night. She briefed me after you had your little chat. Then I told her I wanted to spend fifty pence." The lawyer moved the muscles in his face as if trying to express happiness. "She's like a boring grandparent. A boring grandparent who doesn't want to spend any money but feels we are obligated to immediately report this matter to the Stock Exchange."

He turned and looked out the window. "Let me be sure I've got this right. Dollars were paid, and there are photographs."

"Dollars paid, but Joanna disputes their source," said Boniface. "The photographs and documentary evidence of a Montenegro Shipping Line vessel having been in Somalia are beyond disputable."

He seemed peeved at Boniface's interruption but continued. "We have Weissenfeld—one of the biggest global shipping concerns—and we believe there are people who assume we have very deep pockets from which they can extract money due to the apparent facts."

"That's about it," said Boniface. "But there is an ironic twist." The lawyer turned to face him, apparently intrigued. "The irony is that most dumpers drop their waste into the sea off Somalia. For all their faults and foul-ups, our crew at least tried to do the right thing and pay for their waste to be taken. If they had dumped it, we wouldn't have this issue."

"So, quite literally," the lawyer spoke evenly, "we have people with enough brains to be dangerous." He paced forward and sat on the sofa opposite Boniface with the same caution he would employ if he were wearing a short skirt. "Now, Boniface. Your approach?"

"My strategy is the long game. In short, avoid any flash points so the issue can be managed."

Farrant nodded.

"The difficulty for Weissenfeld is if the story suddenly blows. If there are headlines saying Weissenfeld has killed hundreds, the reputation damage would be immense and lasting." Boniface relaxed, feeling able to explain with greater detail. "But if a story breaks about a company standing up and taking responsibility in an industry with a high death rate, working in a country with an incredibly high death rate, well...it's not news. Also—and this is the bit you'll like—it changes the definition of loss, so it immunizes you against court action."

The lawyer continued to nod.

"There are other benefits to this approach," said Boniface. "By having a process which you are proactively managing, you are keeping your hand on the cost lever. It's the ongoing nature of that cost which has upset Joanna. She's far more in favor of determining—and paying out—the cost now and amortizing it, ironically, over the future life expectancy of the victims."

The lawyer pursed his lips. "That's a very detailed and well-thought-through strategy, Boniface. Take a problem, morph it into something else—something else that greatly reduces the risk of court action and makes you look like the good guy over a sustained period. Very smart." He sat back in his chair, his voice becoming snappy. "But we can't do it. It's not practical."

Boniface jolted.

"Look, Boniface. We appreciate your hard work thinking about possible solutions, but this is incontrovertibly a legal matter. The determination of whose liability it is and of the amount of liability...those are all legal matters which fall within my purview, so I'll take it from here. I think the first thing is to get an injunction to prevent any publicity. I'll instruct counsel on the matter this afternoon; there is no reason to delay."

"But in the age of the internet..."

The lawyer cut him off. "In the age of the internet, the law of the land still applies." His tone became soothing, reassuring. "Look Boniface, I like your strategy—it's very clever in theory. But we don't have the time to wait. We can't keep implementing that program over years—over years where there are no guarantees about the amount of our liabilities. No, the only solution is to get an injunction and to cut this off in the courts."

thirty-six

Boniface's back was toward the corner of Weissenfeld Shipping's London office as he contemplated the buildings across the road intersection.

He slipped out his phone. 12:43. He cast a glance up the hill to the entrance gate to the office before returning his gaze to the central London streets.

Mayfair, where business and residential overlap, is a strange place at lunchtime. Residents either are inside eating or have gone out to eat. In either case, they're not on the street. Construction crews tend to sit in a line on the curb to have a smoke and share a two-liter bottle of warm soda.

The executives in offices need to support the conceit that they're too busy to be away from their desks, even for the time it takes to pee. They can scientifically prove this assertion by bragging about the cost of rent for their office. The only group of people who go out to find something to eat are the administrative staff from the offices, in particular, those sent by their too-busy bosses to get them some food.

Since the administrative staff will walk to the nearest sandwich bar, there is little requirement for motorized transport, which means that apart from a few delivery drivers, the only vehicles on the road are those passing across Mayfair or taking advantage of a shortcut to avoid the jams on the four main roads bounding the rich man's ghetto.

Boniface checked his phone again. 12:46. He watched the second count, clicking over to 12:47. Thirty-eight seconds later, the lolloping figure in the brown suit came out of the gate and started walking down the gentle hill. Boniface tried to pace his steps: one long, one short, one long, one short. He lightly tapped his hip with each step and found himself tapping a classic shuffle rhythm, as Brian Singleton drew toward him.

"Good afternoon, Brian." Boniface relaxed his face, trying not to intimidate the accountant. A sound dropped out of Singleton's mouth, but nothing Boniface could understand as English.

The interaction did nothing to slow the younger man's pace as he passed Boniface, crossing the street and heading down the hill. He continued without breaking pace, without looking back. Boniface observed, sensing the rhythm—long stride, short stride—as Singleton moved, not limping, not showing any disability.

He had covered about 20 yards before Boniface started to jog, slowing as he drew level, and matching his pace. "I heard you like to walk. Mind if I join you?"

A noise came from the other man. Nothing specific, only a noise, but enough to suggest to Boniface that his swift-cantering companion had not dissented.

They reached the next intersection and crossed diagonally, turning right into a small mews-style road with street-level garages under townhouses on one side, and bijou terraces on the opposite. "I've got a bit of a delicate matter to discuss," said Boniface. "I think you've got an admirer in the office."

The younger man continued, his rhythm steady.

"It's Sophie."

Boniface listened as the accounting galley slave's rhythm missed a beat, quickly recovering and continuing at its brisk pace.

"I need your help. Could we slow down or pause for a moment?"

The accountant slowed, then stopped. Boniface felt his heart thumping as he pulled in extra oxygen, pleased that the physical exertion was over. He turned to stand face to face, not quite sure where to focus as he looked into the over-open eyes.

He paused for a few moments, gathering his thoughts, making sure he put forward the most compelling argument he could. The truth could wait for another day. "She likes you, but she's too shy to say, and she can't compromise or jeopardize her position in the office by being seen wasting time with you."

The wide eyes blinked. Boniface took that as a positive sign.

"So what we require is a reason for you to spend time with her. She's far too nervous to go on a date and she's only been in the country for a few days. But I can find a way for you to spend time together, where she will feel safe."

The eyes narrowed, inquisitive.

"It's her feelings we need to think about," said Boniface.

Singleton dipped his head once as Boniface contemplated how to lay out his proposition. He stepped back and turned, gesturing to the accountant. "Walk. But walk slowly, as I explain."

The skinny man followed Boniface's lead as they paced along the street. Boniface caught the younger man's eye, then pointedly flicked his eyes at three construction workers standing outside their site's hoarding having a cigarette. Singleton nodded and the two continued in silence, rounding a left turn before Boniface spoke. "They tell me you're very good at what you do."

The accountant looked blankly at Boniface, his eyes over-wide again as he gave a single nod and mumbled something. Boniface didn't understand what he said, but this was definitely an attempt at direct communication.

The left turn turned again, doubling them back and funneling the two men onto a road wide enough for a single car to pass and no more. "You've been looking through the files," said Boniface. "The files about the Montenegro Shipping Line."

Boniface fixed eye contact with the junior accountant. A blink was sufficient acknowledgement.

"You must have noticed something odd."

Eye contact was broken.

"Look. I'm a PR guy. My strength is not in detecting problems with the accounts. But I know there's a problem." Boniface made sure he still had his companion's attention. "Do you know how I know there's a problem?"

The other man's head vibrated. Boniface was hesitant about whether he was encouraging Boniface to continue or inhaling.

"I know because Greta told me."

The accountant stopped, confusion across his face, vague syllables falling out of his mouth.

"This is quite simple," said Boniface. "At some point, someone will figure where the problem lies. When that happens, you're either with the angels or with the devils." He waited a beat before continuing. "I think you're on the side of the angels, but I would hate to see someone keeping something from you and then blaming you for a problem."

Singleton muttered.

Boniface leaned closer so the other man could hear. "We can't identify where the problem lies and I'm not blaming anyone. However, until we can identify the problem, we can't trust anyone. That's why Greta has involved me, an outsider."

Boniface waited while the accountant balanced the ledgers of risk and reward, and weighed the numbers.

"Joanna's paper is a great haystack to hide a needle, and as she said herself, it's hard to audit a handshake." Boniface continued. "My interpretation of what she said is that she agrees that her records may not be complete."

The accountant mumbled. Boniface wasn't sure, but he thought he said, "That's one explanation."

"I need you to go back and review this Montenegro issue with a critical eye. Get forensic. Find out whether there is a paper trail from Montenegro Shipping to Somalia. I don't care how obscure, how well hidden the trail is, you need to find it. When you've found it, come to me first."

Boniface calibrated the accountant's look as suggesting reluctance.

"You come to me first because I'm the outsider. You come to me because I make sure it gets taken directly to the person who hired me— Greta." Boniface stepped back, trying to keep his body loose. "You come to me, and I'll make you a star in Greta's eyes. I can't take credit for your work—I won't understand what you're telling me, and it will have more credibility coming from someone who understands all the detail—but I will get you in front of Greta to help clear up the mess."

The accountant didn't seem to have twigged what Boniface was suggesting.

"Once you're a star in Greta's eyes, you will spend all of your time going in and out of her office. That means lots of waiting outside with Fraulein Driesdorfer, and it means the chief executive will be telling Fraulein Driesdorfer how smart you are."

Boniface watched as Singleton's skepticism gave way and the look of an over-excited schoolboy spread across his face.

"If someone wanted to pull this off," said Boniface. "How would they hide the paper trail? When you're doing double-entry bookkeeping, do you put a nod in one column with a corresponding wink in the other?"

thirty-seven

"Is it nature trek day at school?" The Glaswegian barb was as inviting as it had been yesterday, although she wondered if she could detect a tiny reduction in the aggression of the delivery.

Montbretia felt much more confident this morning: She had dressed in a way that was comfortable and practical. A shirt with a jacket for warmth, jeans for comfort and added protection, and her boots—if anyone wanted to fight, she could kick, and if that didn't work, she could run. She was still going somewhere secluded with people who hadn't shown much respect or didn't have any idea of boundaries, but at least today she was prepared.

And there was no chafing to annoy her.

"You look different today." The Londoner spoke. "See. It's much easier for her to get on her knees."

Montbretia ignored the comment and took off her backpack.

"Look, Angus. She's changed her hair. Yesterday it looked as if it had been held in place by a band. Today, look. She's washed it and it's free-flowing." He nodded knowingly. "Women communicate through their hair."

"What?" Montbretia exploded.

"Well-known fact, love, even if you won't admit it."

"You are communicating shit." Montbretia squatted by her backpack and pulled out a small stove.

"I think she's communicating to you, Angus, that she's up for it. Her hair is saying if you want a blow job, it will erotically caress and stroke you as she longingly accepts your shaft down her throat."

Montbretia had lit the stove under a dented cooking pot into which she had poured a dark-brown liquid with solid lumps. "It can't simply be that this is how I usually have my hair?" she asked.

The Londoner, taller and more gaunt than Angus, stood and stretched, then pulled his dirty gray coat tighter. "See how her hair swooshes, Angus. It's thick and rich, a gorgeous shade of chestnut, cut to about shoulder length, looks naturally straight, but with a slight inward curl at the end—it's like she came out of a shampoo advert." The Scotsman nodded as his companion continued, now addressing Montbretia. "Each time you move your head, your hair flicks. But you move your head in a very definite way. As you turn your neck, you slow until your hair catches up."

Montbretia stirred the soup with a wooden spoon, lifting and inspecting a carrot before returning her focus to the broth. "As I said, this is how I have my hair."

"So you usually have it ready for giving blow jobs, and yesterday you flattened it to tease us." The Londoner had a victorious smirk. "You're a little minx, aren't you? But I respect that—much as I enjoy a woman that will drop 'em on command, I always feel a bit...I dunno, dirty, afterwards. Chase is better than the catch and all that."

Montbretia threw the spoon into the pot and raised herself from her squatting position, taking a step toward her tormentor. "Can we be clear? The only sexual contact that will ever occur between you and me is my boot and your bollocks. Anything beyond that is in your dreams."

The Scotsman laughed loudly as the thinner man blanched.

Montbretia reached into her backpack and took out three mugs and a brown paper bag. "What's this?" asked Angus.

"Breakfast? Lunch perhaps," said Montbretia.

"You think that heating up some tins of soup will make us your friend?"

"It's not tinned. I made it myself, and I'm not asking for anything in return. But if I may pick you up on a point of etiquette, I haven't actually offered you anything yet."

"Well, hurry up and offer," said the scolded Londoner, stretching his neck to look in the pot.

Montbretia stirred her pot and took a step back, wooden spoon still in hand. The Londoner moved closer, reaching his hand toward the pot. Montbretia tapped him on the back of the hand with the spoon—he jumped and stepped back, as if realizing that Montbretia was looking for their attention.

"Gentlemen. I think we got off on the wrong foot yesterday, and I feel that sad state of affairs is my fault for not introducing myself properly to you." She glanced left and right, making sure she made eye contact. "My name is Montbretia, and it would be my honor if you would join me for some soup." She half paused before continuing in a less formal tone. "As I said, it's homemade soup—beef with some vegetables. And I've also got some bread, some nice rolls...but unfortunately they're not home baked."

"I hope the vegetables are organic," said the Scotsman, noticeably trying to keep his face straight. "I've tried to keep all pesticides out of my diet since I made my lifestyle choice to pursue outdoor living."

Montbretia appeared slightly embarrassed. "They are."

"Well in that case, I'd be pleased to break bread with you. I'm Angus, pleased to meet you, Montbretia."

"Gerbil," said the Londoner. "They call me Gerbil."

"It's my pleasure to meet you gentlemen; please call me Monty." She stirred the soup and tasted it. "Now, if someone would be kind enough to arrange something for me to sit on, I'll sort the soup."

Gerbil returned dragging three palettes, which he stacked and offered to Montbretia as she handed him a mug of soup.

"This is good," said Angus. "You can come back tomorrow and bring us some more." He put his mug down and pulled his coat tighter around him. "Think of it as your entry fee to this very exclusive club."

"A very exclusive but kinda chilly club," said Montbretia, feeling the rawness of the day as she cooled from her brisk walk from the station.

"Chilly?" The Scotsman continued in his nearly indecipherable twang. "We're at the docks. That's the North Sea out there. What do you expect?" He softened, giving Montbretia a reassuring glance. "But there is a bit of a bite to that wind."

A lorry thundered past, dragging a container behind it, shaking the three soup drinkers. "An exclusive club in such a pleasant location." Montbretia mirrored the Scotsman's joviality.

"Aye." He said, his eyes looking over the scrubland where they sat, past the road, and over the concrete wall enclosing the docks. "I've been in the middle of the ocean and found it less desolate than sitting here. It's like an urban desert with the mechanical camel trains passing." He gestured as another lorry went past, moving at about forty miles per hour, but with the size and bulk of metal traveling at that speed, bumping and rocking over the worn-out road, looking as if it were traveling at the speed of a spaceship.

"I'm sure our next location will be even more salubrious," said Angus, winking. "We like to move the club every two or three days...so the riffraff don't get in."

"And so we don't get hassled," said Gerbil, coming back to life.

"Is that what happened the other day?"

"What?" Gerbil's reaction was reflexive.

"The guy who was arrested...was he hassled?"

There was a rasp of annoyance in Angus's tone. "Why are you so interested in this guy?"

"Because he's dead and his body was dumped in my office."

"You're serious?" Gerbil spoke and Angus stayed motionless.

"Albie was telling the truth, then." Angus looked across to Gerbil— an unspoken conversation passed between the two. He looked back to Montbretia. "Sailors tell stories. You travel the world, you see a lot of things, most often in cheap places where people with few choices do anything for a few dollars, so you see some wild stuff. Wild." He paused, lost in silent contemplation. "But then you spend weeks on a ship with nothing to do but talk, and that's where you learn to embellish your stories. That's assuming you can talk. Most of the crews are Filipino these days. I know a few words—enough to say 'where's the brothel' and 'where's the beer'—but not enough to have a proper conversation."

Gerbil picked up the tale. "Albie came here. He was agitated..."

"It wasn't agitated." The Scotsman cut in. "He was fucking upset." He turned to face Montbretia. "Albie and this other guy were sitting there when this van pulled up. Two guys got out and bundled Albie's mate into the back of the van."

"What sort of van?" asked Montbretia.

"A white one," said Gerbil. "Albie ain't so good with the lingo. That's why he was with this other bloke: They both spoke the same language."

"Which is?"

"Albanian, I presume," said Gerbil. "I get by with English, French, German, Polish, and like Angus, some of the Southeast Asian languages, but I never understood when those two were speaking. Anyway, these guys gave Albie a good kicking."

"Who..." Montbretia paused, unsure what to ask.

"You need to speak to Albie," said Angus. "He saw what happened, and if you give him enough alcohol, he might remember something. If you get him enough alcohol, he'll tell you that the two guys were acting on orders."

"Albie? Short for Albert," asked Montbretia.

"Just Albie." His speech slowed as he lost himself in thought. "I haven't seen him since that night."

thirty-eight

"Where have you been, Boniface?" It wasn't a question as much as a full frontal attack. Boniface pulled out his phone, glanced at the screen, and Greta exploded: "Sophie looked and you weren't here."

"I..." Boniface tried to find the right way to start his sentence.

"I run this company. I paid for your hotel, so you are here when I need to speak to you. I'm not here to fill a space in your schedule." Her voice was forceful; her German accent became stronger when she was angry. He moved to the Louis XIV chair. "Don't sit—you're not staying. Brief me and then get back to putting your makeup on or whatever it is that you do while I'm paying you to work."

Boniface stiffened as Greta continued. "Why is Chlodwig still here, and why is Chlodwig still very unhappy? I gave you a simple task, Boniface, and you have failed." She looked up. "Have I failed to pay you?"

"No," said Boniface, his voice a movement of his jaw and a weak aspiration of air.

"Good." She was firm. "Now tell me the execs all understand the strategy. Tell me they all understand what they must do."

Boniface took a calculated risk and sat. "There are a few jitters."

"Jitters?"

"Nothing long-term...it's people getting used to a new idea."

"Did they understand the strategy, Boniface? Yes or no. Either, or. Black, white. Answer without gray, without maybe, or perhaps. Answer in a way that I understand, and which gives me confidence that you are money well spent."

Boniface checked his notebook and was returning it to his pocket as he started. "There are jitters—they're focusing on their own responsibilities instead of looking at the broader issue, so Joanna wants to know who authorized the payments and to ensure any future payment over five-hundred bucks is countersigned by her, and she wants to tell the Stock Exchange; Brad is upset that he's not running the PR operation; and Jeremy thinks you should be focusing on strategy and leaving him to handle what he sees as a legal matter." He paused. "What was the question? Yeah, I've told them, and none of them like the strategy, but I'll give them twenty-four hours to mull it over and take another run at them tomorrow morning."

"Another run at them tomorrow?" Boniface could hear the anger dripping, like molten lead burning holes in the carpet. "We don't have time. Sort the problem. Earn the money I've already paid you."

Boniface hesitated. "Who do you want me to deal with first?"

"Don't test my patience, Boniface. You get like a whiny little girl." Her voice took on the tone of a young child. "You can't have two priorities; you can only do one thing at a time and you have to do them in order." Her regular voice returned to pierce Boniface. "This isn't a joke, Boniface. Sometimes I think I'm the only one taking this seriously."

"I'll get straight on it," said Boniface. He brightened his voice. "By the way, how was your night last night?"

"You're changing the subject, Boniface. You only ask that question because you can't compliment me on my dress because it's the afternoon. But since you ask, he wasn't the man I expected. And since we're talking about last night, tell me why Chlodwig is still here."

"He's cautious. If I'm honest, I think he wants to be supportive but doesn't know how to show it."

Greta threw her head back and cackled. "You are funny, Boniface." She grabbed a breath and continued, her voice deepening. "Chlodwig wants to appoint a COO. That's madness. A chief operating officer. Who do you think looks after operations at the moment? If he paid attention, he'd see that's what I do. I know more than any COO ever would about this company, and I care more than some outsider would. He's looking for me to make a mistake, then he can act."

Boniface frowned. "I got the impression that..."

"Stop there, Boniface. You're making excuses. Go." She pointed to the door. "Get rid of him. Get the execs sorted. I've been paying you for nine months, and the progress is going backwards, and everything I ask you to do ends in failure." She sighed. "Have you even sorted out the mess in your office yet?"

"It's not been my focus."

"Why not? How difficult can it be?"

Boniface sighed. "The police haven't released my office yet. But we do have a lead on the body. Apparently the dead guy was seen alive in Tilbury."

"I can't see what's holding it up. Now go and sort the execs."

Boniface opened the door. A slight rustling at Greta's desk made him glance back to see her looking directly at him. "You're coming with me to the opera tonight. Covent Garden." She scanned up and down, assessing him, judging. "You'll need your tuxedo. Sophie will give you the details." Her head dropped and she was focused on the papers in front of her.

thirty-nine

"What do you mean where am I? I'm with Angus and Gerbil, of course." She felt an imp-like grin working its way across her face. "Gerbil." She beamed. "You heard me correctly. They're my new best buddies. It was a simple equation: Food plus the human touch equals men who are happy to spend time chatting. You're in PR—you should try it sometime."

She looked back at Angus and Gerbil, about twenty yards away, sitting and chatting. Having returned after going for a walk and to find somewhere to relieve herself, she saw that the two had broken up some palettes, ready to light a fire after the evening drew in, when the smoke would be hidden.

"I've spent most of the day trying to decode broad Glaswegian—I'm pretty sure it's Glaswegian mixed with a hefty dose of alcohol. Do you know what neeps and tatties are?" Her face was incredulous. "How do you know that? I had to do a search for it when I went for a pee, which, by the way, is not a pleasant experience if you're a girl wearing jeans and in this place that time and humanity forgot." She felt sheepish. "I did go and use the restroom in the café by the station that I went into yesterday. I felt I had to order a cup of his awful coffee—but I learned after yesterday and got it to go, then poured it down the first drain I passed."

Another lorry rattled down the road. Each truck had its own signature defect that manifested itself as a subtly different noise. This one had a low squeak, but the squeak didn't seem to be synchronized with the movement of the truck or have a regular rhythm. Montbretia struggled to hear Boniface as the squeak squawked into the distance.

"What do you mean, 'Are these guys that relevant'?" She unclamped the phone from her ear and held it in front of her as she pulled a face. "Boniface, it's not that the guy who was murdered was a vagrant and these guys are vagrants too…" She tried to keep her voice calm, but she could feel the annoyance rising. "Boniface, Angus and Gerbil actually met the guy who was murdered."

Another two trucks went past as Montbretia strained to hear Boniface. "Angus and Gerbil met the guy, but there's another vagrant around here who was on good terms with the guy who was murdered and who tried to help him. He got a good kicking for his efforts by the sounds of things." She listened. "Albie. Albie the Albanian."

She removed the phone from her ear for a second time and pulled an even more grotesque face. "I'm with a homeless man called Gerbil. Do you think I asked for identity papers to confirm Albie the Albanian is his real name? They call him that because he is Albanian and they can't remember what his birth name is. He said it once and they didn't understand what he said, so now they call him Albie and he answers to it."

The temperature in Tilbury felt ten degrees colder than it had felt when Montbretia left home that morning. Montbretia figured the temperatures were similar, but with the constant sea breeze and the damp from the river, what had been a nip in the air was starting to become uncomfortable. It had been worse when she was sitting, but now that the sun was dipping, she could feel the temperature falling further.

She hunched her shoulders against the chill. "Look, I don't care what his name is. All I care about is that I find the Albie guy and see what he can show us. I don't know if he'll tell us anything useful—and for that matter, I don't know whether Angus and Gerbil have uttered a word of truth today, but I'll hang around for a while longer and see if I can find Albie. So I might not have found anything, but I thought I should tell you what I've been up to and that I'll head out of here in about an hour. Where are we meeting for dinner?"

She strained to hear. "I can't hear you, the wind is getting up. Where are you, anyway? It sounds like you're standing in the middle of the road." She listened. "In a car. Near your apartment. But what about dinner?"

Montbretia had found that anger had warming properties. "So you're going somewhere tonight—dropping me without actually bothering to tell me—and you're going somewhere secret with your secret client who you said would be your ex-client by now."

She found her breathing becoming fast and heavy as she listened to Boniface.

"No, Boniface. No. You don't get to make recommendations. Get here and help; then you can recommend to your heart's content. But you're not here, and while I'm doing all the work, I make the decisions. I'm a big girl—I've got myself out of plenty of scrapes." She held the phone by her side, shaking her head in disbelief, then continued. "I know there are risks, and of course I'm concerned. But what makes me scared is that you don't seem to get that what you're doing is much more dangerous."

forty

Detective Inspector Raymond Talbot put out his hand to slow his bag man, as he liked to call him. "Wait. Watch." Detective Sergeant Kevin Hitchcock nodded to acknowledge that he had seen the object of their observation as Boniface got out of the large chauffeur-driven Mercedes that had swept into the drive around the front of the block.

The two officers paused under the canopy at the front of Boniface's apartment block, standing back on the dirty white stone porch, disappearing into the camouflage offered by the unlit hall on the other side of the dark wood-framed glass doors behind them.

Boniface held his phone in his hand and leaned into the window of the dark blue Mercedes to talk to the chauffeur. "Notice that?" asked Talbot.

"What? That they seem to be arguing?"

"No. Big car, clearly a chauffeur from the way he's dressed. But he's a chauffeur giving Boniface some lip, and he didn't get out to open the door."

"You mean Boniface has pissed him off, too?" asked Hitchcock, pulling out his notepad and recording the car's plate. "Someone else's car and chauffeur. Do you want to bet it's got something to do with that mystery client?"

"Precisely. Gives you the warm fuzzies about the national computer, doesn't it?"

Boniface waved his hand in the direction of the rear of the block as the car drove in the direction indicated, leaving Boniface walking toward the entrance, head down, phone clamped to his ear. "Hi Monty." His tone seemed subdued. "Look, I'm sorry, I was...I was out of... Look, I was wrong. Could you call me when you stop being angry at me?"

Boniface glanced up to see his way blocked. "Detective Inspector. Detective Sergeant. What a pleasant surprise." His eyes were dull, bags starting to form underneath. The vigor he had shown during his interview two days ago seemed to have deserted him.

"The pleasure is all ours, Mister Boniface, isn't it, Sergeant?" He looked to the younger man, not sure whose fake bonhomie would crack first; he suspected Boniface's, looking at his condition. "We were just having a look around your office, and I said to the Sergeant, 'You know, Sergeant, that nice Mister Boniface lives up the hill—why don't we go and have a look and see if there's anything to see,' and so we walked up, not thinking that we might have the good fortune to bump into you."

"I'm pleased you did, and I look forward to the next time the stars align and our orbits collide." Boniface moved, seemingly intending to walk past the two.

"Ah, Mister Boniface, are you not going to stay and have a chat with us?" Talbot liked to adopt unusual speech patterns; he felt it unsettled suspects, giving them two issues to consider simultaneously: the question and why the officer was talking in a strange manner.

"I'm..." Boniface indicated along the driveway around his brick-built block in the direction the Mercedes had driven. "I'm in a hurry, I'm afraid. Apparently if I'm one second late, I turn into a pumpkin and my carriage will depart without me, so if you don't mind."

"Mister Boniface, that's not a chat." Talbot exaggerated a frown, turning his head. As his head twisted, he could feel the connected muscles in his back rubbing the jacket of his overly tight suit. "That's you not telling us what you know."

"Again," offered the Sergeant.

"Come on, Boniface. We're all reasonable men. Can't we have a reasonable chat? Out here. In the open air. No nasty tape recorders or anything like that." Talbot sniffed, damp air mixed with the fumes of the traffic up and down Wimbledon Hill Road, getting increasingly heavy as the afternoon moved into the rush hour.

"Alright Detective Inspector. I'll begin with a question," said Boniface. "When can I have my office back?"

Talbot held his hand open, as if suggesting everything was beyond his control. "You know those scientists."

"You mean the ones who have difficulty differentiating between blood and horseradish?"

The Detective Inspector tutted. "Mister Boniface, I thought you were better than that. But if you want the scientists to finish all of their tests before they release your office, it might take a little while longer. But it's funny that you bring up your office." Talbot struggled to contain his joy that Boniface had set up his next line. "We've had a lovely chat with some friends of yours."

"At your office," added Hitchcock.

"Well, they said they were friends of yours, Boniface, but you know me, plodding old policeman, I get suspicious." Talbot puffed up his chest and rested his thumbs in his belt. "They didn't dress like you, and to be honest, we thought they were sizing up your office, which is why we had a chat, and as we talked, they told us they were your friends." His face cracked and he exhaled while sneering—a technique he had spent long perfecting. "Actually, the big guy said he was looking for Mister Bonnington, but his comrade-in-arms corrected him. So I'm guessing they weren't friends, but what? Business acquaintances? Clients?"

Hitchcock turned to his detective inspector. "You know what, gov,

I've been thinking. You remember we were suspicious about Mister Boniface's clients because he wouldn't tell us anything about them, and this made it sound like they were a bit, you know...maybe not on the right side of, you know...legal."

"Mm hmm."

"Well, I was wondering. Did he refuse to tell us about his clients because they're all, you know...complete knobheads, and he's ashamed to be seen in public with them?" He turned to Boniface. "Knobheads is a technical police term, Mister Boniface. It means..."

"I think I understand the gist of what it could mean," said Boniface, his tired, featureless face cracking.

"Interesting gentlemen," continued Talbot. "And d'you know what, Mister Boniface? It was very lucky we turned up, because they were criminals." He made two small emphatic nods.

Hitchcock jumped in again. "I love the police computer, Detective Inspector. She makes me feel happy inside."

"I haven't got a clue who those two could be," said Boniface. "Can I go now, please?"

"Relax, Mister Boniface. This is far more interesting than having a conversation with that chauffeur..."

"And whoever owns the car," added the younger officer, scratching at his notebook.

"We've got so much to talk about, and I know it will interest you: There have been lots of calls to the station about you. You're a popular guy, Mister Boniface," said the detective inspector, scratching his stomach as he remembered it was at least two hours since he had eaten.

"I know I'm meant to do the whole poker-face thing, but this is news to me," said Boniface.

"Funny thing. Very next morning after we had our last little chat, within three minutes of getting in, I had a call. Assistant Commissioner. For me. Directly. Wanted to know about you and the case. Didn't make any suggestions, just wanted details. Funny that. Don't often get the brass calling, and definitely don't get the third most important man in the Metropolitan Police Service calling with no reason. But here's the odd thing—I couldn't make out whether he was a friend or an enemy of yours."

Boniface's lips twitched at one end. "Never met the man. No clue why he would call."

"Then this afternoon, we started getting these calls from newspapers. Calls plural. Asking lots of strange background questions—nothing specific, and no one knew what the right question was to ask." He waited, letting the revelation sink in before continuing. "But here's the odd thing—it was like we got called by the work-experience kid each time. By the third call we realized that they were all asking the same questions in exactly the same order."

"Exactly the same?" Boniface was frowning quizzically.

"Exactly," said Talbot. "No derivation from the script. No intention to get further details or even listen to the answer. Just a list of questions."

"Now, Detective Sergeant Hitchcock and I are exceedingly vigilant." Hitchcock nodded in an exaggerated manner as Talbot continued. "We're very keen to make sure the good name of an innocent man isn't besmirched by an unintended conversation with the press. Having read a bit more about your background, I think you know something about the press saying bad things.... But it does seem to me, Mister Boniface, that you have a very interesting group of people—diverse in their concerns— who have an interest in your well-being."

forty-one

He watched as Boniface was raised up. A solitary figure ascending from below—bleary-eyed with his head slowing turning to scan his environment. Tired, but he still had some innate sense to present himself in a way that was simultaneously professional, believable, but at the same time sufficiently uncontroversial to allow him to fade into the background like a chameleon.

Boniface stepped off the moving staircase and walked over to his table, pulled out a flimsy metal seat that twisted too much to give any support and yet didn't bend in the right places; he sat without waiting to be asked and talked without paying attention to his host. "I've had a gutful of Gideon's cloak-and-dagger shit. Can't we have a normal meeting like normal people? Do we have to meet in a train-station café?"

"Did you enjoy the opera last night?" He indicated across the round metal table—its surface fashioned like a piece of engineered steel, which only served to catch the dirt—to the second cup of tea.

"What was that?" He heard a rasp of annoyance in Boniface's voice.

"You went to the opera last night. I asked if you enjoyed it. This is what people call conversation."

"No. This is what people call..."

"Shhhh." He sat calmly, waiting for the fire in Boniface's eyes to show some sign that his head wasn't about to combust. "Gideon went to the opera last night. He didn't know that you would be there, and indeed, he was as surprised to see you as you are that you were seen."

Boniface had fixed his host with a blank stare.

"Gideon saw who you were accompanying and felt it best for all three of you that he stayed in the shadows. But you will understand—with the company you have been keeping recently—that Gideon was very concerned when he saw who you were consorting with, and wondered about whether one could find a connection with your current...challenges."

"Really? This is your excuse?"

"Shhhh, shhhh, shhhh." He held a finger over his lips. "Inside voices. I'm speaking. You'll get your turn when I've finished." He pointed at the tea he had bought for Boniface. "You can drink you tea and listen."

Boniface returned to his sullen teenager look, steadfastly ignoring the tea.

"Will you let me finish?" He waited for Boniface to make eye contact before continuing. "You've had a rough couple of days, Boniface: dead bodies, police think you're a murderer, association with a known criminal who has the ability to dispose of bodies and his dangerous son, and a client with big problems. Gideon understands, but he's worried. Worried that people may take advantage of your good nature, worried that people may exploit your short-term needs in a way that damages your long-term interests. I could go on, but can we accept that Gideon is worried?"

"You know this because you're your own little one-man Gideon Latymer tribute band." Boniface's voice was calm, but his words spat fire. "You wear his clothes, but you lack his natural charm, flair, wit, and intelligence. In other words, you lack everything that makes Gideon, Gideon. If you want a career in politics—which I presume you must if you've got yourself up a few rungs to being Gideon's personal flunky—then if you want to take that next leap, you need to become you. Reach inside and find your inner you, however unappetizing he might be."

"And find my own personal Boniface to do the Machiavellian string-pulling behind the scenes?"

"Wouldn't hurt, would it, Benedict?" Boniface paused. "It is Benedict, isn't it?"

Benedict nodded.

"Surname?"

"O'Reilly."

Boniface continued, his momentum moderated. "Don't get me wrong, you're clearly a smart boy. But if my experience over the last few minutes is anything to go by, then the first step for you is to learn some serious presentation skills. And I don't mean *can use PowerPoint* presentation skills, or TV interview skills, I mean being able to connect with people. The ability to find the message and focus on it. Get to the point before I die of boredom."

Boniface kept his focus as he continued. "Drop the pitch of your voice—get some power and take elocution lessons for the timbre. All I can hear is this nag, nag, nag, nag sound in my head. Power. Authority. Gravitas. Humor. That's what you need. You have to be the kind of person the public want to identify with. Even if you're not one of them, they need to like you and think you understand them—they need to know your name is Benedict and not say 'that bloke who hangs around with the sexual deviant.'"

O'Reilly paused, giving Boniface a chance to finish his monologue.

"A voice like a squeaky flywheel will never make you likable." He sighed. "See what happens when you deprive me of sleep by calling me at 4 AM? I get annoyed and give you some free advice." Boniface's gaze focused, his face looking quizzical. "Why did you call me at 4 AM if you knew I'd been out late?"

"Be grateful. You at least got to bed." O'Reilly took a sip of his tea, again indicating to the cup across from him. "Me? I got a call from Gideon when he saw you at the opera. I've been doing the background research for you since then."

He held up a manila folder and tapped it.

"We must assume that this trip to the opera wasn't pleasure—no one actually goes to the opera for pleasure. Even Gideon. This suggests an obligation on your part, and the logical extrapolation is that you were required to play the role of the gracious consort to someone who has a hold over you. One person who might have such a hold, at this time, is a client. When Gideon saw you with Greta Weissenfeld last night, he put two and two together and assumed that Weissenfeld Shipping is your client with 'a bad thing' waiting to break."

Boniface growled. "You're doing that pain-in-the-ass condescending talking again. Cut it out or I'm off."

"I'm sorry, Boniface, but Gideon is worried: These are not nice people." Boniface went to say something, but his host continued. "You're a big boy, we know. We reckon you've got a pretty good idea about what you're dealing with. Gideon is concerned that Weissenfeld's resources are greater than yours, and they could literally spend you into the ground with their pocket change."

Boniface held his hands over the table between the two men, turning them. "See that." He carried on slowly turning his hands, like a small-scale oscillating fan. "I know I'm playing with fire, but I haven't burned myself. Yet."

"Yet... And while it's not a good reason for you to listen, I have spent the whole night pulling this material together, so, as well as being polite, it might be useful to make sure I haven't found anything that you don't already have a detailed knowledge of."

"Go on. Let me hear it." Boniface sat back in his chair, sweeping a hand through his hair.

"I'm sure it goes without saying that Greta Weissenfeld is highly talented and highly driven." He looked for Boniface's confirmation before he continued. "Many who have dealt with her are less complimentary; the word 'sociopath' seems to be a common choice." Boniface seemed ashamed as he wrinkled his nose in acknowledgement. "But what about the lawyer, Jeremy Farrant? What do you know about him?"

"Pompous ass," said Boniface. "Likes to spend money, mostly on carpets it would seem. Thinks he's it. Owns a castle in Scotland. Is there more?"

"He's dangerous. It not that he's a shark, it's that he brings an unfortunate combination of competence and incompetence, mixed with greed and ruthlessness, all polished off with that pompous arrogance you have noticed."

"Thinking about it, he also did a background check on me. It was pretty thorough."

"No, he didn't." O'Reilly paused, trying to inject some dramatic effect in a dreary station café. "Tamsin Smales-Mainer, his so-called secretary, did."

"So-called?"

"Yup. She's not a secretary."

"We're talking about the same woman—triangular with narrow shoulders and a 1980s big-hair perm that looks so odd that it must be natural."

O'Reilly reached into his manila folder and pulled out a photo, which he showed to his guest.

"That's her," said Boniface. "So if she's not a secretary, what is she?"

"She's a lawyer. Young, but very well-regarded lawyer. Will be going places if she passes the Jeremy test."

"Why would a lawyer work for him and pretend to be his secretary or assistant or whatever she is called?"

"Most young lawyers get all the grunt work, Jeremy's grunt work is at a much higher level. The grunt work is the top-level stuff that Jeremy should be doing—it's great experience for any lawyer." He considered the situation for a moment. "How many junior lawyers get to do a background check on Alexander Boniface? Working for Farrant, you get all the introductions and the contacts you could ever need, and everyone knows that if you survive Jeremy, then you really are good. So after two years, Jeremy gets a new slave, and the one who has survived the ordeal by fire and kept Jeremy out of jail gets rewarded with gold."

"Does he," Boniface twisted his hips forward awkwardly in his chair, "give them practical lessons in how to interface with senior lawyers?"

O'Reilly turned his head. "As far as we can tell, Jeremy is asexual. He keeps these people around so he can look good and puff his chest out."

"But Jeremy must do more than hire good staff," said Boniface.

"Jeremy's main role is his contacts. That's where the castle helps: He takes those who need to be influenced hunting, shooting, fishing, or for a few rounds of golf, all within his very private and very exclusive estate with ample and sumptuous accommodation, lots of good food, and lots of very pleasant alcohol. In the long run, it's much more persuasive that kneecapping."

"Good people skills," said Boniface, his tone flat.

"Indeed, but Jeremy isn't an idiot. He's smart man: street smart—which is odd given that he hasn't been on a street since the late 1960s—but not intellectually smart. He simply does not know the law. His arrogance is his Achilles heel, and that Achilles heel is where we started digging the dirt on him." O'Reilly tapped the manila folder. "Botched work—covered up by the old boys' network, trips to his castle, work to other law firms, you know the score. In the end he was ousted as partner from his old law firm because he became too much of a risk." He dropped the manila folder, making the table rock. "It's all in here."

Boniface stared at the folder on the swaying table.

"There is one other thing you should know about."

Boniface's gaze lifted from the folder.

"Lots of journalists—from different news outlets—have been calling Gideon for background on you. The basic story is the same, and it all ties back to your time with Gideon."

"Did it seem like they were all asking the same questions?"

"Funnily enough, Boniface, yes. They all posed the same questions in the same order. Why do you ask?"

"That's what the police told me yesterday."

"That's interesting," said O'Reilly.

"What's more interesting is that my client…"

"You can say it, Boniface: We know it's Weissenfeld. By the way, it's only me and Gideon who know about that detail, and you can rely on us to remain mute on that issue."

"Thanks," said Boniface. "Anyway, what is interesting is that Weissenfeld—most notably, their PR guy who takes all the calls from the press—hasn't mentioned the issue."

The two men sat in wordless contemplation.

"This is for you." O'Reilly picked up his manila folder and laid it on the table before Boniface. "Now, you do understand—and it saddens me as much as it saddens Gideon—but this is the end of your relationship with Gideon, at least until after the next election. This research is your going-away gift."

Boniface's tone was incredulous. "What do you mean my going-away gift, you little turd?"

"This is a token of the esteem in which Gideon holds you, or rather used to hold you and hopes to hold you again, but not in this decade. Not until you are far less radioactive. He's disappointed about your choice of friends, and the choices of those friends' friends. Because of those friends, he cannot be friends with you. In short, Gideon cannot be seen with you and cannot communicate with you. He would have liked to tell you himself, but it's the whole being seen talking with you that he has to avoid."

"This is…" Boniface stood, pulling out his phone. O'Reilly reflexively grabbed it.

"Gideon has been courteous." O'Reilly stood, returning the phone to Boniface. "Please extend the same courtesy to Gideon."

Boniface snatched the phone and walked off. O'Reilly made out his first few words above the hum of the station. "Monty. Can we meet?"

forty-two

"Nothing?"

Boniface was standing in an office he hadn't known existed in Weissenfeld House.

From the size of it, he guessed the windowless box hadn't been an office until recently, when it had been converted from a storage space. The walls and ceiling had been painted white, a piece of standard-issue corporate carpet—Boniface wondered if it had been recycled from Jeremy Farrant's room—had been thrown across the floor, and dark wood shelves went from floor to ceiling on two walls.

Brian Singleton sat behind his desk—or what Boniface assumed would be his desk underneath the stacks of files—and shook his head.

"Nothing?"

Singleton grunted and mumbled as Boniface scrutinized the office, looking for any detail to deflect his frustration. The shelves looked familiar. "Did you and Jeremy get a job lot of shelves?"

Another series of grunts and mumbles—Boniface was getting better at translating; he was sure he heard the words "off-cuts" and "same carpenter."

Boniface reflected on the shelves in a new light. "He really has done a good piece of work." He examined the detail of the carpentry before flipping back to the junior accountant, unable to contain his frustration. "Could someone else be funneling cash and so misrepresenting the transactions?"

Singleton remained behind his desk, staring at Boniface with his overly wide eyes silently saying, "I'm an accountant; do you think I haven't considered that option already?"

Boniface met the stare and locked eye contact, breaking when he realized the younger man's slightly shocked, somewhat sarcastic look wasn't an act he was feigning—that was how he looked.

"What...?" He felt the constriction in his throat as he rasped. He lifted the stack of files on the side of the desk, placed them on the floor and sat in their place, resting his right foot on the pile. He leaned toward the younger man and spoke slowly. "You've done me a favor, and I'm grateful."

He waited for some acknowledgement from the accountant. "I'm grateful, but we need a story for public consumption. You have one task: Slay a dragon. They don't make movies about the really nice guy who was good at mathematics and went looking for a dragon but couldn't find one."

Boniface calibrated the response on Singleton's face: a slight twitch at the edge of his mouth masked by the twitch when he inhaled.

"We're all agreed there is a problem. You, me, Greta," continued Boniface. "But if you can't find something, then I can't make you look like a hero in front of Greta, and if I can't do that, I can't get you next to Sophie."

He mumbled—Boniface leaned to hear better, becoming aware of the changes crossing the man's face. He wasn't sure what he was reading between the acne. His best guess was fear and anger—at least, that was what Boniface hoped. If he was right, these emotions would make the accountant work harder and faster.

"I need you to understand, Brian, this isn't about me. It's helping you, too." Boniface leaned back, making sure the younger man was paying attention. "There's a difference between no evidence of fraud and evidence of no fraud."

The other man thought, then looked up at Boniface, a look of hope forming in his eyes. "You understand your basic challenge—either find the money trail or confirm that there is no money trail. Don't confirm that you haven't found a trail—confirm that one does not exist."

The younger man picked up a file and started flicking through.

"Remember," said Boniface. "We know there's a problem, and if you don't find something, then you're the one being set up by Joanna."

forty-three

Boniface closed the door as he left Singleton's office on the middle floor of Weissenfeld House, meeting Brad Phipps as he descended from the top floor.

"Brad, hi. How y'doing?"

"Cool, bro, cool." Brad's lazy, non-specific North American accent, coupled with his inability to construct even the most basic sentences without adding the words "yo," "dude," "bro," or "awesome," challenged Boniface's ability to divine meaning where there probably was none.

Boniface stopped and walked back to Brad, facing him across the open space that was more of a four-way intersection next to Lennie Watkins' desk. "Have you had any calls over the last few days? Odd calls? Perhaps several calls from different people, but all asking similar questions?"

"That would be, y'know, like, weird."

"You mean no?"

"No, dude." Brad's head flopped from side to side. "Why?"

It was the first sensible question Boniface had heard Brad ask—ever—he thought he would have longer to prepare an answer. "Just, like, y'know. Sometimes these things. Y'know."

"Sure, dude. No probs." Brad turned.

"I'll see you around, Brad. I've got to find Jeremy." Boniface stepped, expecting Brad to move.

"He's not there, dude."

"What?" Boniface moved back to face the large Canadian fidgeting awkwardly in his beige chinos and blue button-down shirt, looking even taller than normal as he balanced on the bottom step.

"Not there. He's gone to court, or is it Counsel? I dunno, it's like..." He seemed incapable of standing still or applying any focus.

Boniface felt his fists clenching. "Why has he gone to Counsel, or court, or whatever?" He slipped his hands in his pockets to get some control.

Brad's face tightened up as if the pressure would help him think better. "He's applying for one of those, y'know things. With the..."

"An injunction," said Boniface, straining to keep his voice calm.

Brad snapped his fingers and pointed at Boniface. "One of those."

"Who authorized this?" Boniface tried to sound nonchalant...casual, even conversational.

Brad blew air out of his mouth, his lower lip flicking open.

"Does Greta know?"

"You mean the dudette-in-chief?"

Boniface regretted using the term yesterday.

"Not a clue, man. Why would she care?"

"Because she runs the company? Because her name's on the letter-head?" Boniface felt the back of his skull throbbing.

"I've got stuff to do, man, I need to call people about this..."

"Injunction?"

"Yeah, I've got to call people about the injunction."

Boniface couldn't keep the rage out of his voice. "Why are you calling people about the injunction? Isn't the point of an injunction to stop people talking?"

Brad stood, eyebrows raised, mouth half open, his head almost shaking. "Dude. The point is to stop *other people* talking."

"No, an injunction..." Boniface stopped. He continued in a lighter voice, but aware that his question was barbed. "Why are you calling people, Brad? It wasn't part of the strategy."

"It wasn't part of your strategy, man. But now I'm running PR. I told you yesterday."

forty-four

Montbretia rested on her crossbar, balancing against the additional weight strapped to her bike. The autumnal chill was catching her after her physical exertion to reach the rendezvous. Her eyes scanned in an arc as she zipped up her fleece, hunching her shoulders against the cold.

At the north side of the park, coming down from the Mayfair edge Boniface appeared, dressed in his trademark suit but with his hair looking disheveled. He usually only displayed this look after he had spent the day sitting at his desk, resting his head on his hand, intermittently gripping his hair as he tried to focus. It was barely 10 AM, and already his hair had given up on the day.

He loosely balanced the handles of a small brown paper bag on his fingers. As he stepped closer, she could see his eyes were having difficulty focusing and his facial expression looked forced. "You look like shit."

His face relaxed. "Thank you and good morning to you." He held out the bag. "Peace offering."

"A muffin? You hate muffins, Boniface."

"They say these are the best muffins—the bakery is in all the tourist guides, and at that price, I hope it's good."

"Am I really a muffin kind of girl?" She kept her tone soft, trying gentle mockery to keep the atmosphere light. "If it were a cupcake you'd be in serious trouble." She took a bite, keeping her lips together as she chewed. "Why here?" she said, trying not to spit food, as she pointed around with her eyes.

"Green Park? I like it. Piccadilly over there; you've got the sweep of green leading down to the Palace. Good morning, Your Majesty, if you can hear me." He bowed his head in the direction of Buckingham Palace. "You've got these gorgeous old houses here." He vaguely indicated the properties a few hundred feet away on his left. "You've got Spencer House—the historic home of the Spencer family." Montbretia frowned, waiting for him to elaborate. "Spencer as in Diana Spencer." Montbretia's frown remained. "You young people know her by her married name: Diana, Princess of Wales."

"Oh," said Montbretia.

"It's owned by a hedge fund manager or something now. That Australian newspaper tycoon lives somewhere over there, and then there's Lancaster House—where the agreement was signed giving Rhodesia independence and thereby creating Zimbabwe."

"And?" Her voice was muffled as she chomped.

"And it's not that far from the client's office."

"For crying out loud, Boniface." Half-chewed muffin fired out of her mouth. "Why haven't you got out of there?"

Boniface was like a scolded child. When he started speaking, his voice was quavering. "I came to apologize and to try to..." His hands circled as if he was trying to communicate but couldn't recall any commonly understood body movement. "Let's say clear the air, because I can't think of a better term. I know you're angry. I know you're upset. But please, I hate arguing with you. I want to...to get past whatever this is."

Montbretia put the last lump of the muffin into her mouth, wiping the crumbs around her lips.

"What's all this?" Boniface pointed to the load strapped to Montbretia's bicycle.

"It's some of Ellen's old stuff—blankets and a few old pieces. It's cluttering the house, so I'm giving it to the hobos in Tilbury." She fixed Boniface, sensing that he wanted to caution her but was holding back. "They were helpful yesterday—and I...we, still need their help."

It was Boniface's turn to question with a frown as two people on rollerblades wobbled between them, the his-n-hers matching black helmets, red jackets, and padded elbows proclaiming their coupledom as they passed through the green space following the path toward the Palace.

"The guys know Albie...Albie the Albanian. They're out looking for him."

"Can we rely on this Albie?"

"I've never met him, so I can't answer that." She inhaled, pondering. "I can't say with any certainty that we can rely on any of them: It's like drunk Chinese whispers trying to have a conversation with them. But Albie saw what happened and understood what the guys in the van said."

"So they spoke in Albanian?"

"Maybe." Montbretia made an exaggerated shrug, throwing up her hands. "All the sailors speak a little bit of lots of languages. They know how to get a drink and..." She stopped, feeling her cheeks faintly redden as she remembered the scope of Angus's linguistic requirements. "But it beats me how they understand anything—I don't understand most of what Angus and Gerbil say, and they're speaking English, apparently. So I'm getting this secondhand tale about Albie, and they keep talking about some guy called Reagan."

"Reagan?"

"Reagan. As in the president." She flapped a hand dismissively. "He's like some ghost or big scary ogre or something. According to Gerbil he sent the guys in the van. It doesn't make sense to me, but maybe once I've seen Albie it will."

"It sounds dangerous, Monty. You make sure you take care."

Montbretia kept her voice soft. "If it's so dangerous, why don't you come with? You can hear what Albie has to tell us, directly from the horse's..."

"I would but I've got to..."

No longer feeling any necessity to attempt to be conciliatory, Montbretia blurted. "You would but your super-secret client has clicked their fingers and so you've got to go running."

Boniface remained motionless, looking down at the ground. He started talking without looking up. "Gideon sent his flunky to talk to me. Benedict. The guy called me at 4 AM."

"No wonder you look so rough."

"Thank you again for the compliment."

Montbretia pushed forward. "Where was Gideon?"

Boniface hung his head. "Gideon doesn't like my friends, so he won't play with me anymore." She scrutinized his face—she wasn't sure whether she was reading shock, disappointment, or anger. Maybe it was acceptance? "He thinks my friends are bad people."

"Are we talking Tommy and Angelo?" A multicolored dog with a piece of cloth tied around its neck scampered up to Boniface and dropped a stick at his feet. When Boniface didn't seem to notice or care, the dog picked up his stick and ran off.

"Yes," nodded Boniface, "and he's very twitchy that I've been talking to Tommy when the extradition case is going on, but he's also made a guess as to who the client is, and he doesn't like it."

"The client whose identity I'm not allowed to know?" Montbretia fixed Boniface. "You're saying that Gideon knows who the client is?"

The side of Boniface's mouth twitched involuntarily. "He's made a guess."

She laughed, a single, joyless exclamation. "So who is it?"

"You don't need to know—and once I've resigned it won't matter."

"So this client is important enough that Gideon has broken off diplomatic relations, but I'm not important enough to know who it is." Montbretia couldn't look at Boniface.

Boniface sighed. "That's not the case. If I don't tell you and something goes wrong for the client—which I expect to happen, very soon—then I can put my hand on my heart and say, 'Montbretia definitely didn't know. Montbretia was not the source of the problem.' I'm not suggesting this benefits you, but it makes me feel better."

Montbretia turned her head and tried to make eye contact at Boniface.

"Benedict, Gideon's flunky, was pretty damning about the client. Nothing much that I didn't know—or couldn't extrapolate." His eyes focused into the distance. "But the information he gave me—the direction I'm being pointed—all seemed a bit simple, straightforward. Packaged with a bow on the top."

"Do you trust what you were told?"

"Yes. No. Perhaps. But I don't know why I'm being given this information. Is Benedict trying to break Gideon's relationship with me? Or is this Gideon protecting himself?"

Montbretia watched Boniface, a man who always seemed so confident in his analysis, so sure of his next step, even if he knew that he didn't know where the next step would lead. Now, standing in a public park in central London, he seemed able to figure all the permutations, he seemed able to grasp his options, and yet he seemed unable to figure how to move forward.

"Come on, Boniface. There's more. What aren't you telling me?"

Boniface chewed his bottom lip and started talking, his lip still held between his teeth. "The cops came round last night."

"Why didn't you tell me?" Montbretia asked.

"Because, honestly, it doesn't matter—they were yanking my chain. It was an exercise for their enjoyment. Something they do when they're bored."

"But still."

"And you shouted at me on the phone..." Boniface straightened. "They did say one interesting thing. They've had calls from the press about me."

"I suppose that was to be expected," offered Montbretia.

"It was. But what surprised them was that the questions were the same—it was as if they were being read from a script." He squinted at Montbretia. "And nobody asked about the body."

Montbretia went to talk and was cut off by Boniface. "Then when I saw Benedict this morning, he said Gideon had received similar calls—low-grade journalists reading questions from a script."

Montbretia felt her jaw hang loose. "So that means..."

"Still not finished." Boniface half lifted his hand. "That alone doesn't mean anything, but here's the interesting bit: When I told the CEO that I was quitting, my resignation was refused. We talked about the situation, and the last thing the CEO said was, 'Is there anything else I need to be aware of?'"

"What does that mean?"

"The CEO wanted to know whether there was anything else from my past that could be negatively connected with the company. As we know, my past is not without blemish."

"But it's all in the public domain?"

"The varnished truth, yes. The less varnished truth, no. The less varnished truth is known by people who were there or who know me—you, Gideon, Veronica, and now the CEO."

"Okay, I get why you told the CEO, but where's the link to these journalists?"

"These scripted questions all seem to be pushing toward the less varnished truth that I discussed with the CEO." Boniface looked down, kicking an invisible stone. "It's not proof, but the coincidence is interesting."

Montbretia sighed loudly, trying to make sure Boniface noticed. "Are you paying attention, Boniface?" She glared at him: no response. "You need to get out now. They're the source of your problem. Your client is killing you, Boniface."

Boniface raised his hands to his face as if in silent prayer. "One last attempt to explain. They've been paying for the last nine months, so if they're genuine, I've got some sort of obligation not to walk away."

"No," said Montbretia. "You've got an obligation to sort yourself out. Then you can fix your client. Remember, a dead man can't administer first aid."

"But if they're dirty, then I've got to stay on the inside and figure out what's happening."

"Okay," Montbretia tried to sound reassuring. "If you won't come to Tilbury, then let me come with you and we'll sort out this client."

Boniface's mouth twitched.

"Come to Tilbury or I come with you now," Montbretia was resolute. "We fight this together."

"I..." Boniface was motionless apart from his eyes, flicking.

Montbretia counted to ten in her head, and counted to ten for a second time, then threw her leg over her bike. "It's obvious you don't want me involved. I don't understand why, but it hurts like hell."

forty–five

Boniface wondered whether she was born with an asbestos mouth, throat, and gullet or if some specialized, albeit very cheap, treatment had been applied. Or maybe she drank gallons of water or was oblivious to pain.

He was sure he could feel his hair starting to singe while she pinned him into the corner with fire spilling out of her mouth as she roared. "You didn't trust me. In fact, you positively suspected me of fraud." He was sure the flames were licking him as she bellowed.

Brian Singleton looked embarrassed as his boss continued to shout at Boniface, but it wasn't clear exactly what the source of the young man's embarrassment was. Boniface was grateful for the conundrum to run around his head as he tried to distract himself from Joanna Baines' onslaught. The simple explanation was that Singleton had blurted and was embarrassed that Boniface now knew that he had blurted—that knowledge being gained by Boniface as a consequence of the metaphorical thrashing he was now receiving.

He tried to figure—as much as he was able to concentrate with the fire-breathing woman berating him—if he could tell her that he never suspected her: Boniface had only told the younger man not to trust her to give him an incentive to carry out his task in secret and without delay.

He couldn't, so he continued to distract himself while trying not to draw Baines' attention to the fact that he was looking for clues from the underling sitting behind his desk. Perhaps he was embarrassed because he didn't like displays of emotion. That would be very English and would fit with Singleton's rather inelegant social dysfunctionality.

"You didn't trust Regenspurger." Boniface was confused by her statement; he struggled to find a reason why he, or any sensible person, would ever trust Regenspurger to do anything other than inflict pain. "We've got the records—you gave us the dates, he wasn't spending money in Africa. We've checked the travel expenses—he wasn't there."

As his ears prayed for relief from the barrage they were receiving, Boniface let his eyes sweep the room in the search of any exit from the tiny box, or any pretext he could use to divert his tormentor. There wasn't enough space for one person to exist in comfort, let alone three, especially when one was snorting flames and the preponderance of wood and paper made the room highly combustible, while its origin as a closet meant that no one had thought to invest in extending the sprinkler system.

"But more significantly, Boniface, you didn't trust the system and the processes in place. You didn't trust the company—your client." Boniface was beginning to regret not spending more time with the CFO figuring out her dragon-like tendencies. If he had, he would have revised his investigative strategy, but as it was, she had now given him enough time to make another guess about Singleton's embarrassment. It was clear that he was embarrassed to be watching someone being pounded as much as he would be embarrassed to be caught watching pornography.

Boniface relaxed, pleased that he had found a plausible explanation to the conundrum that only served to distract him during the unpleasantness, while growing increasingly aware that the CFO appeared to be running out of breath. Her speech was becoming measured, almost calm by the standards of the last few minutes. "Your conspiracy theory that Regenspurger was running an operation off the books or that I'm trying to set up Brian is daft. No, it's not daft, it's offensive."

She stopped and picked up a file.

"Bookkeeping is simple—it's addition and subtraction. There's no multiplication or division. There's no projection. We take facts—provable facts—then add up and subtract numbers."

She seemed to be waiting. Boniface felt an involuntary forward movement of his head. Singleton gingerly looked up to witness the interaction between the two visitors in his cell.

"We know what we started with. We did an audit—we counted. That's what bean counters do."

Another involuntary nod. There was a perceptible cause-and-effect link between his nodding and her calmness of delivery.

"We know what's come in." She hesitated, but not long enough for him to appear to give consideration before nodding. "We know what's gone out."

A nod.

"We know what is left—what we started with, plus what came in, minus what went out."

A further nod.

"Brian told me he was trying to prove that the money trail didn't exist, not to prove that he couldn't find it."

At the mention of his name the younger man looked away.

"He didn't rat on you—he didn't have to tell me anything. As soon as I heard those words, I heard your voice." She opened the file she was holding and laid it in front of him. "Here is the summary of our records—they give you the proof. If you think the records are wrong, then call the police and tell them we have been the victim of an elaborate fraud."

Boniface heard the words but couldn't break from his trance: Now he understand Singleton's embarrassment. He had been caught for the schoolboy error of copying; he had copied Boniface's words. Now the embarrassment made sense.

"Stick with doing what you do, Mister Boniface." Joanna Baines was moving toward the door. "And why are you still here? Brad should have taken over by now."

forty-six

Veronica clamped her phone between her ear and shoulder and pulled at the bridge of her spectacles, drawing them farther down her nose as she stared over the half-moons to see the person her assistant had led to her office door.

Montbretia hesitated in her doorway, looking slightly flushed as if she had been exercising. Her jeans and fleece said otherwise; only her running shoes suggested she may have endured any physical exertion, and they were hardly the sole preserve of gym junkies. Then again, maybe she cycled.

"Mmm. Um hmm." She raised her eyebrows, looking at Montbretia, who stood uncomfortably in the doorway, clasping her hands together, her shoulders hunched like a meek child who needed to ask to go to the bathroom.

Montbretia swayed in and out of the doorway, then mouthed "It's okay" and turned. Veronica snapped her fingers and pointed at the leather armchair across from her desk.

Tentatively, the younger woman crossed the room, her eyes darting from corner to corner, looking at the meeting table, the potted Japanese maples, and the television on the wall. Veronica watched as she sat, balancing on the front of the seat, before turning and then looking past her and out of the window, raising herself up to better see the view. Veronica knew that Montbretia was looking over her left shoulder at the sight of Big Ben 500 feet below them.

"I'll call you back," said Veronica, hanging up the phone. "I'm sorry to be so rude and click my fingers at you." She released her frown. "How are you, Montbretia? It's good to see you again."

"Boniface said you had a good view, but wow!" The self-assurance, the poise, the attitude, the confidence of the other night were missing.

"It *is* quite something, isn't it?" said Veronica. "I never get tired of the view."

"I shouldn't be here; you're busy." Montbretia stood: again, the cowering, jumpy girl. There was no power in her voice, and its pitch seemed higher than Veronica remembered.

She softened her face, her eyes asking to the younger woman to sit.

"I feel like the kid who says she's getting bullied," said Montbretia, still standing. "But actually nobody can be bothered with her because she's a whiny little bitch, and so she keeps going to the headmistress to get attention."

Veronica tilted her head and tried to bring some warmth to her eyes—the typical journalist's pose whenever you're interviewing the subject for a human-interest story. "Well, speaking as your headmistress, is there anything you feel you should tell me?" She looked up at Montbretia, peering over her half-moons.

Montbretia moved toward the door. "This was a bad idea—I'm wasting your time."

Veronica flicked her eyes back to the leather chair facing across her desk. "Sit." She kept the instruction ambiguous, allowing Montbretia to interpret it as an instruction or an invitation, but her continued eye contact hinted strongly. Almost imperceptibly, Montbretia rocked back and forth before turning and gradually walking back to the chair.

"You wouldn't be here if something didn't matter," said Veronica, trying to keep her voice gentle, her tone reassuring. "You don't go to someone's office, without an appointment, without calling ahead, and you don't go to see the ex-wife of the guy who you work with and who is happy for you to use the spare room in his apartment, if it doesn't matter."

Veronica watched as Montbretia sunk into the chair, almost as if she was hoping it would hide her. She continued, "This must be something to do with Boniface."

Montbretia's cheeks lit up and she bowed her head, hiding her face.

Pleased to have hit her target—not that it was a hard target—Veronica continued. "Shall I talk a bit and tell you where I stand? Perhaps I can tell you a few things Boniface won't say or doesn't know."

A small face poked up in front of her. A delicate movement of her lips suggested agreement.

"We're never going to be the kind of girls to sit around doing each other's nails. We're never going to go out on the lash and have a dare about who will pull and sleep with the ugliest guy, who she will then dispense with in the most cruel manner the next morning."

"True." Montbretia's voice was little more than a breath.

"I could be wrong, but I get the impression that you're the kind of lady who would get bored hanging around when I'm enjoying my favorite hobby."

Montbretia frowned.

"My favorite hobby is drinking whisky." Montbretia's mouth formed a perfect circle. "By the way, would you like a drink?" asked Veronica, reaching into a drawer and putting a half-filled bottle of whisky on the desk.

"No thanks," said Montbretia hesitantly. "I'm on my bike...hence the clothes. Not my regular office getup." She smiled, apparently trying to hide her embarrassment. "Who am I kidding—it's not that far off."

"We don't really know each other, but I like you and hope we can be friendly, perhaps even friends." Montbretia tilted her head as Veronica continued. "However, there are...boundaries."

Veronica paused, waiting for Montbretia to make eye contact. "Boniface is off limits as a subject matter."

Montbretia's face paled, her shoulders tensing.

Veronica tried to keep her voice reassuring. "I'm sure you didn't come to talk about Boniface, but I think it helps to make sure we're clear."

The visitor visibly relaxed.

"I'm not sure how Boniface and I describe our relationship now, but he didn't stop being smart, witty, intelligent, and funny just because we divorced. He didn't lose his integrity or stop believing what he believed because we divorced." Veronica paused. "That's where I stand."

Montbretia's head seemed to be involuntarily acknowledging what Veronica said.

"Boniface is off limits, but let me tell you this: With the divorce and the meltdown, things changed for him. He's become darker on the outside, more mournful, but he's happier on the inside now that he's not fighting his demons." She sighed. "The thing to understand about Boniface is that when he worked for other people, he was an introvert trying to behave like an extrovert, but now he can behave as an introvert, so he's happy. He's happy inside his own head, which is where it matters."

The room fell quiet.

Montbretia's eyes seemed to brighten. "Is Gideon setting him up?"

"Gideon?"

Montbretia pushed her eyes up, questioning.

"What? As a sex slave to keep Gideon's women warm in between courses?"

Montbretia grinned, swiftly pulling her hand to hide her emotion. "No. More serious. I don't really understand. It's...I don't know... It was something Boniface said."

Veronica pondered the question before answering hesitantly. "I have no reason to believe that Gideon is acting against Boniface, but that doesn't mean much." She drew her mouth tight.

"What about strange calls from journalists?" asked Montbretia.

"All the time," said Veronica. "However, they work for me."

"Of course," said Montbretia. "But has there been anyone asking questions about Boniface? Anyone reading questions from a list?"

"A list? No." said Veronica. She passed a business card to the younger woman. "I'm not being much help, but put my numbers into your phone, and if you find out more, call."

forty-seven

Boniface positioned himself in front of Sophie Driesdorfer's desk as the dumpy secretary, wearing a different but shapeless and forgettable dress, burned through the pile of work beside her.

The male voice inside Greta's room moved to the door, which then opened. Regenspurger ghosted out, his gaunt figure clothed in darkness, moving without creating a breeze as he passed. "Fraulein." He dipped his head to Sophie, a half bow; Boniface noticed as she drew in her elbows, shivering as the figure disappeared.

He tried to give her a reassuring smile as Greta's voice, coming from her office, pierced him like a shard of glass. "Boniface, come here and stop wasting Sophie's time."

Greta was running down the list in her notebook as Boniface entered, concerned that he would now be required to explain that his ascribed task—a simple task, get the executives to understand the strategy—had yet to be completed. The question was how to present the issue to Greta. Ironically, for a man whose career was built on presentation, he couldn't figure out the best way to present the topic to his principal.

He became aware that he was speaking, but didn't know what he was saying. His mouth was on autopilot while his brain was in freefall. In his hand, his notepad and pencil were furiously making notes.

"According to Brad, Jeremy is applying for an injunction."

"He's a lawyer, Boniface. Isn't that what they do?"

"But if we're trying to prevent people from talking, it confirms that there is something worth investigating. Once we've stated in writing for the courts what we don't want people to talk about, we can't later argue we didn't know about the problem."

"You're talking in riddles, Boniface." He could hear the nib of her pen dragging over the page in her notebook.

"Joanna refuses to discuss the funding aspects until there has been a statement to the Stock Exchange."

Boniface was relieved that Greta's head was still down as she wrote notes—his facial expression may have hinted that Baines had other issues.

"Brad wants to do something that I don't understand. He seems to want a campaign when the injunction will prevent any public comment."

"An injunction wouldn't apply to us, would it, Boniface?" Greta looked up, her piercing blue eyes framed by her helmet-like hair. "You're making it sound like everything is our fault and nothing is your fault, Boniface. You remember when I hired you, I told you that was a conversation I never wanted to have. We're committed—you need to do what you said you would do."

Boniface sat mute as Greta glared.

She broke the silence. "The other issue, your office. Is that sorted?"

Boniface relaxed. "It's not sorted but there's progress. Montbretia has found someone who knew the dead man who can also identify the two guys who picked him up at Tilbury. It should all be sorted this afternoon."

"That's good," said Greta, standing and walking to the door. "I must just give something to Sophie."

Boniface pondered: Maybe Montbretia was right. Maybe he should resign and live with the consequences if Greta wanted to go public and let all future clients know he had walked away when the going got tough.

"Is there anything else?" Greta returned, closing the door behind her.

"A few strange calls, but nothing specific."

forty-eight

Boniface closed Greta's office door behind him.

"I need somewhere to sit and do a bit of work. Is there a free desk somewhere?" he asked Sophie. Her fingers were moving at a speed that Boniface was sure was a fire risk.

"The cubbyhole. Is that how you pronounce it, cubby?"

"It is," said Boniface. "Sounds good. Where is it?"

"Back here," said Sophie. She moved backward, alerting Boniface that she was standing. She took two steps and pointed to a space that would be a storage area in a normal office but was a makeshift office here. White painted shelves lined the far wall, and an expertly cut plank had been fitted as a desk across one of the side walls, with a drawer underneath.

"Herr Regenspurger usually sits here, but he left immediately after Fraulein Weissenfeld spoke to him."

"When?"

"Just now. While you were in with her." She turned toward her desk, allowing Boniface to pass. "Don't touch anything. It makes Herr Regenspurger angry." She involuntarily pulled her elbows in. "He gets very angry."

"He's a bit territorial, is he?" offered Boniface, his pencil already in his hand as he took out his notepad and started to flick through the pages.

Sophie shook her head. "It's not like that. He..." Boniface glanced up from his notepad as the highly efficient woman shrank before him, her voice a whisper. "He scares me."

"I'll be careful. Very careful." Boniface ripped three pages out of his notebook. "Could you shred these, please?"

"Yes," said Sophie, taking the pages and turning.

Boniface clicked his pencil to extend the lead as he sat at the narrow desk. He glanced down—the lead had stopped extending. He pulled the end of the lead out of the pencil and clicked to load the next lead. Nothing. He rattled the pencil. Nothing. He cursed under his breath and then pulled the drawer under the desk, looking for something to write with.

It was a matter of lore, and Boniface was prepared to argue it was a matter of law, too: When you find someone's passport, you are required to laugh at his photograph. Boniface's arm moved, even though the voices in his head were shouting not to pick up the passport that was sitting in the drawer before him.

Boniface hesitantly leaned out of the cubbyhole. No Sophie. He opened the passport: The lifeless eyes of the unsmiling Regenspurger stared out at Boniface. Accusing, interrogating, disapproving, preparing revenge...

Boniface flipped the page to hide the photo; he felt like a child hiding under the pillow, as if closing his eyes would make the monsters go away.

He surveyed his find. Stamps: passport control stamps and visas. He flicked a few pages, taking in some of the locations Regenspurger had visited: Panama, Venezuela, Mauritania, Liberia, Equatorial Guinea, Argentina, French Guiana, Yemen, Georgia, Lithuania, Philippines, Iran, Vietnam, Indonesia, Somalia, Iraq, Djibouti, Ivory Coast, United Arab Emirates, the stamps and visas continued.

"Shit. Shit, shit, shit. Shit, shit, shit, shit, shit, shit, shit, shit." Boniface could hear himself cursing under his breath. "It was Regenspurger."

He flicked back through the passport, checking the stamps, looking at the dates. His route was clear: The first stop was the Ivory Coast, arriving on 17 October. 19 October his passport was stamped in Mauritania. The next day, Liberia. The following day he was in Equatorial Guinea, and then on to Somalia, arriving on 22 October and departing on 24 October, when he returned to the Ivory Coast.

Twenty days later, on 13 November, he was back in Somalia. The date wasn't lost on Boniface. MV Paranoid with its toxic cargo had arrived on 15 November. According to his passport, Regenspurger then left the country on 17 November but had returned since, his last visit being ten days prior.

There was the sound of footsteps. As he hurriedly stuffed the passport back into the drawer, Boniface leaned out of the cubbyhole to see Sophie. "I made confetti," she said.

Boniface frowned. This unmarried, wedded-to-her-job-and-probably-never-would-be-married lady might have something of a wedding obsession.

"The pages. I shredded them...it gives you confetti," said Sophie, returning to her desk.

"Thank you," said Boniface. "I wonder...could you get me a cup of tea, please?"

"Certainly," said Sophie, already back on her feet. "Milk and sugar?"

"Milk, one sugar," said Boniface, pulling out his phone and opening the drawer as Sophie left.

He fumbled, holding Regenspurger's passport in one hand and his phone in the other as he photographed the pages with the passport control stamps. He put the passport back into the drawer, lying on top of a blue folder, and shut the drawer.

He paused, leaned out of the cubbyhole, and ducked back, opening the drawer and taking out the blue folder.

The icy chill of the Stasi put its fingers around Boniface's heart and gripped tightly, stopping its beat.

He was breathless, winded, feeling physically sick.

He glanced down again at the open folder. Photos printed by a black-and-white laser printer, circles drawn by hand with a thick red pen to identify individuals in the photos.

The building was immediately recognizable. When he saw his own face circled, he knew it wasn't an amusing coincidence: His initial reaction had been right; it was his office.

He turned to the next photo and felt his heart kick. Montbretia. Circled in red. Montbretia. Identified.

He flicked through the remaining photos: His office, people coming, people going, which was to be expected in a block shared with other tenants, but only he and Montbretia were circled.

The sound of footsteps jolted him, and he flipped over the pictures. "Your tea." Sophie put the cup down on the small surface, next to the papers Boniface had flipped over.

"Thank you," said Boniface, realizing the sound he was making was the aspiration of air with no vibration of his vocal chords, which were paralyzed.

He turned back the pages as Sophie spun back to her desk. Surreptitiously, he held his phone, snapping pictures of the photos with red circles. He winced with the sound of the shutter, cursing that he'd never learned how to silence the phone as he held it tightly to muffle the sound, and then replaced the pictures in the folder, slipping it back into the drawer.

"Monty. It's Boniface," he whispered, using both hands to hold his phone. "Call me. Call me immediately."

He stood, hastily scanned the space where he had been sitting, making sure he had left no trace before walking past Sophie's desk without a word.

forty-nine

Boniface strolled down the two flights of stairs, mock saluting to Lennie as he passed his station on the middle floor. With each step he felt his phone—each step a knock against his chest, a reminder of the photos it contained and a distraction when he needed to focus.

At the bottom of the stairs he headed left, following the black-and-white marble tiles. Reaching an open door, he took a breath before entering—a cursory knock as he stepped into the room, hanging just inside the door. "Hey, dude."

The big Canadian looked up, his face sullen.

"I was a bit of a jerk earlier on: I'm sorry. Could I take you to lunch... as an apology?"

Brad went to speak, tilting his head as you would when disappointing a slow child with a basic fact. Boniface continued speaking. "To be frank, I've got something and I'd like to get your advice. It needs your expertise."

Brad's eyes sparked. "Well sure, dude! Of course! I'm always delighted to help."

"Cool, bro." Boniface felt he had exhausted his supply of Brad-isms already. "Are you good to go now?"

"Sure," said Brad, gathering up some papers as Boniface moved fully into the room. "Where are we going?" He dropped the papers into his desk, locking it as he stood.

"There's a great pub down the road," said Boniface. "It's a proper English pub, good food, proper English beer as well as the chilled stuff in bottles. Or if you want something with a bit more flounce, there's a nice French restaurant that I haven't tried yet."

"The pub sounds great," said Brad, reaching up to place something—the key that locked his desk, guessed Boniface—on top of a small glass case containing a hockey puck. "Let's go."

Boniface followed the Canadian. "You like good food? Proper home-cooked food, not something out of a packet or slung in a microwave?"

"Of course I do, dude."

"Of course you do. A big guy like you needs to eat, right, bro?"

They walked through the courtyard garden and out of the gate. Boniface tilted his head to the left, leading his companion down the hill and turning right at the second crossroads. "There we are," said Boniface, pointing to a pub about 100 yards down the street, dropping the pace and wrapping his arms around his stomach. He groaned—a low moan, animal-like—and pointed a contorted face toward Brad.

"What's up, man?" asked the Canadian. "You look in pain."

Boniface looked around, checking they were not overheard. "I got the squits, dude." He winced. "You go find a table, order yourself a beer, and check out the menu. I'll duck back to the office and empty my stomach."

"I'll come with," the big Canadian started.

"No, dude. I'll be fine." He grimaced. "I don't need you holding my hand when I'm...you know... Go and get a good table—I'll be with you in a few minutes, but now I've got to run before I leave a nasty stain." He turned, then looked back at Brad. "Make sure you set up a tab—it's my treat, remember."

Boniface clutched himself, gracelessly lumbering to the corner, checking behind to make sure the Canadian was still heading toward the pub. Around the corner he released his grip on his stomach, stood up straight, and jogged back to Weissenfeld's office. He saluted to Lennie via the CCTV camera as he passed through the outer gate and went straight to Brad's office, reaching to his full stretch to get what was, indeed, the key. He dropped into Brad's chair, unlocking the top drawer and lifting the contents onto the desk.

The top loose sheets of paper were handwritten—at a guess, Brad's fitness log.

He opened the green file below the loose pages. The sheets were neatly clipped inside and had never been turned. The first page was a handwritten note.

Brad

Mr Farrant wanted you to have a copy of this dossier.

T

Boniface noticed the handwriting—he had seen it in Farrant's office. Presumably T was Tamsin Smales-Mainer, Jeremy Farrant's indentured servant cum lawyer.

He opened the next file, a buff-colored piece of card with a few loose sheets with typed notes. He recognized the handwriting:

B

Your copy

T

Then he noticed the heading: Greta briefing.

The note was dated two days ago. Boniface skimmed the contents: a near-verbatim record of his discussion with the CEO about issues from his past that could cause Weissenfeld embarrassment.

Issues that could cause Boniface embarrassment, too.

Boniface pulled out his phone and photographed the pages scattered over the desk before moving to the next file. This was thicker, stuffed with unclipped paper, but with several batches of stapled sheets.

The first was labeled: key talking points. Boniface scanned it. There were two columns. In the first was a list of some of the key dubious behaviors in Boniface's past. The second column appeared to suggest a retort to anyone disagreeing with the "fact" in the first column. Boniface photographed it and placed it face down on the opposite leaf of the folder.

The second sheet was in a different format from the other documents. There was no heading, no footer, no file reference, no date, and the font was one that any modern word processor would default to. All the document contained was a list of questions—questions that had become very familiar to Boniface since the police first mentioned them to him yesterday.

Next was a stapled bundle labeled "people Boniface has upset." The list started with Stan Gadson and his researcher. Boniface flicked through the pages, photographing each one, briefly scanning for details. Some names were familiar. Some he knew had once borne a grudge. Many he didn't recognize.

The next stapled bundle was much thinner: people for background. He recognized a few names as he photographed.

The list of journalists was two pages long and looked more like a spreadsheet printout with columns for name, outlet, phone number, and email address, with a few hand-scribbled annotations that Boniface couldn't figure out. He photographed the pages, then scanned the column of names: not one name he recognized. A similar trip down the outlet column: again, nothing he recognized—there was no BBC, no Times, no major news outlet. Instead, these seemed to be small shipping and transport-related journals.

He placed the list on the left, leaving the final document: a single-page document, dated tomorrow, with the word "draft" stamped in red at the top and bottom. Boniface started to read: "We are hugely disappointed to have been let down..."

fifty

Boniface and Brad walked across the courtyard garden and through the front door of Weissenfeld's office. They stood facing each other at the foot of the stairway to the middle floor.

"So I said, 'Dude'!" Brad threw his head back, laughing out loud.

Boniface laughed. It was the laugh he had honed through several thousand non-funny situations where he was still expected to show empathy and not reveal his true feelings. His true feelings that Brad was the most obnoxious, juvenile misfit it had ever been his misfortune to encounter and all he wanted was never to be in the same room as the overgrown child again. Boniface wasn't even sure what he was laughing at: He'd stopped paying attention ninety minutes ago, when he forced himself to ask Brad an inane question that he knew the dimwit would be able to understand sufficiently so he would think he had given Boniface some good advice.

"They've been looking for you," Lennie stood at the top of the stairs, disappointment in his eyes. "They've gathered in Mister Farrant's room, I believe."

"Dude. I've got work—let's do it again soon." Brad bear-hugged Boniface before turning toward his office.

"Both of you," said Lennie in a flat tone.

"After you," said Boniface, following Brad as they ascended, giving Lennie a pained look, followed by a wink as the pair passed.

Boniface walked behind Brad as they entered Farrant's office to find Greta seated in the club chair and Joanna Baines on the sofa. Boniface indicated to Brad the seat next to the CFO before turning and resting on the overly large desk spanning most of the right wall. As he rested on the desk, Boniface noticed Tamsin Smales-Mainer standing, sentry-like, just inside the door.

"Thank you all for coming." Jeremy Farrant strutted like a professor—an exquisitely and expensively clothed professor—preparing to deliver a lecture to a group of eager students. "I am pleased to tell you that we have been granted an injunction. I won't bore you with the details, but broadly it covers all matters in connection with the Somalia problem, and its scope prevents the UK press from publishing details about the matter."

"Why only the UK?" Boniface was surprised to see Brad asking a question.

Farrant smiled, a thin smile with no warmth. "The UK courts—or should I say, the Courts of England and Wales—can only require parties within the jurisdiction of the United Kingdom to refrain from publishing details. Unfortunately, we can't go round telling those foreign chappies what they should do."

"But isn't that sort of the point that Boniface made?" Brad turned to Boniface. "You don't mind me asking this, do you, bro?"

"Please continue," said Boniface, resting more securely on the desk hewed from ancient wood.

Brad turned back to Farrant. "So surely what we've done is told everyone that we've got a problem—we wouldn't want an injunction otherwise—and now all the foreign papers can print the story, citing us as their source, and we can't do anything to stop it?"

"We can." The lawyer's tone was sharp. Dismissive. "We apply for an injunction in their country."

"Every country? Like, there isn't a central place in Europe or something we could go to?"

Farrant's tone remained sharp. "But you're missing the point. We have applied for, and been granted, what in tabloid parlance is often called a 'super-injunction'." A look of pride crossed his face. "This is an injunction where, in addition to restraining the publication of certain allegations, the existence and details of the injunction may not be legally reported. So there's no source for your foreign newspapers."

"What about the interne..."

The lawyer cut off Brad. "But we've also gone further and included Mister Boniface within the scope of the injunction."

"I beg your pardon," said Boniface. "You've done what?"

The owner of the castle in Scotland frowned, tilting his head. "I think it's quite plain to everyone else, even if it's not apparent to you, Boniface, that there must be a connection between your work for Weissenfeld Shipping, the human reliquiae in your office, and this whole sorry issue in Somalia. Manifestly, there must be a leak or something in your organization, and so for belt-and-braces protection I have made sure there will be no stories about you in the press."

"That's crazy." Greta was standing, her notebook snapped shut. "Do you mean we can't say anything about Boniface and the dead body?"

The lawyer's tone was soothing. "No, it just means the press can't report it."

"So we can't protect ourselves?" Greta turned to Boniface, her tone almost apologetic. "No offense, Boniface, but we might need to throw you to the wolves if you become an embarrassment."

"No offense taken," said Boniface lightly, wondering how painful it would be to be chewed by wolves.

The CEO continued. "The point of an injunction is to ensure that Weissenfeld will be immunized against any publicity during the period

if, or when, Boniface goes down." Her attitude became more conciliatory. "But you are certain that there's no way for anyone to get around
this injunction?"

"A question in Parliament," offered Boniface.

Greta turned to Boniface, frowning.

"Members of Parliament are covered by parliamentary privilege,
which means they can't be prosecuted for breaking an injunction in
Parliament, even a super-injunction, and the press can report what
happened in Parliament, as long as they don't deviate from what was said.
That's right, isn't it, Tamsin?" Boniface stared at Farrant's assistant, who
nodded her affirmation.

"That's not what we agreed," said Greta quietly to no one in particular.

"Now I'm sure there's no necessity to remind everyone to make sure
everything is locked away." The senior lawyer walked behind his desk and
tapped his safe, a smug grin spreading over his face. "The last thing we
want is any sort of leak from this office that undermines our case."

fifty-one

Boniface let the other meeting participants leave the lawyer's office before him.

As he closed the door behind him, he saw two eyes fixing him. Two eyes, radiating hate. Two eyes alive in a dead face of loose gray skin, balanced on a body wrapped in nondescript black clothing.

Boniface could feel no warmth from the man, could smell no odor, could feel no movement of air as the figure approached. All he knew was the two orbs locking him in position.

The figure lifted his hand. "I believe this is your pencil, Mister Boniface." Regenspurger paused before continuing. "I understand the Fraulein instructed you not to touch anything, and yet..."

"I didn't," said Boniface, his throat contracting.

"And yet, I found it. In my drawer. Under my papers." His voice was soft, almost reassuring, and calm—Boniface had never known such menace as the former Stasi officer, and now apparently international jetsetter between some of the most ungoverned regimes, let the silence hang.

"I have put my papers back in order, Mister Boniface, and now I think it's time for you to leave." The eyes pointed to the stairs and Boniface felt compelled to move, walking down the two flights in silence, through the front door and across the courtyard.

The gate slammed shut, and the two men faced each other on the street. The former Stasi agent stepped forward, stopping when their noses were twelve inches apart.

"I believe you have a notebook," he said, snapping the fingers of his outstretched hand.

fifty-two

Montbretia sat on the leather sofa: too low, too uncomfortable.

Somewhere at the coffee shop's head office, someone had decided that this sofa had the look they were after, and then a finance director had pointed out that the unit cost multiplied by the number of outlets gave a big number and so they had bought something that looked similar but could be sourced for one third of the price. Now in every store in the chain—like this one in Fenchurch Street station—there were customers sitting on uncomfortable brown sofas, wondering why the table in front of them was a little too high and worrying that it was quite difficult and rather undignified to get out of the seat.

As Montbretia wondered about moving to a more sensible seat, Boniface came in. She noticed his tie first. He didn't always feel it appropriate to wear a tie, but when he did—as he had been while working with his current client—the tie was always perfect: a symmetrical half-Windsor knot, tightened to his collar, hanging straight, the point reaching a small way over his waistband.

Now his tie was pulled down and hung to one side.

She tried to catch his eye. His usual sharp glint was gone. The usual penetration with which he would inquisitively scan a room was missing. His eyes were moving but not seeing. Montbretia inelegantly rolled out of the sofa to stand and took two steps, positioning herself to obstruct his unfocused gaze. "You looked rough this morning, but you're looking a whole lot worse now."

He looked up, a widening of his eyes suggested recognition.

"Sit down. I'll get you a cup of tea."

She walked to the counter and ordered a tea, looking back at Boniface, now trapped in a seat from which he might never be able to raise himself, at least not without the help of a crane. His hair—short and neat, styled so that you don't notice but you somehow remember, cared for sufficiently that the rules of basic hygiene are met while never being washed more than once a day and never becoming an obsession—was now messy, even more messy than it had been when they talked in Green Park. That wasn't the problem. The problem was that Boniface didn't seem to notice and, more worryingly, didn't seem to care.

Montbretia tentatively placed the tea before Boniface and sat down as he mumbled something that she assumed to be thanks. Feeling like a young child on Christmas morning, she started. "I found Albie...Albie the Albanian."

Boniface's visage remained impassive.

Montbretia tried again. "Albie the Albanian. He saw the two guys.... I've spoken to him.... I would have got more, but your message," she smiled, "all three of your messages, sounded important so I came here. I'll go back and talk to Albie and see if I can video him so that we've got something we can show the police." She held up her camera to show how she intended to video the vagrant.

Boniface sipped his tea, his eyes now starting to move as if under control of his brain, but still he wouldn't make eye contact with Montbretia.

He exhaled through his nose, the air stream rippling the surface of his tea. "I know who dumped the body."

Montbretia was struggling to speak, trying to form a question.

"I can't prove it yet. But all the pieces are there." Montbretia held him in her gaze, eyes wide, nodding for him to continue. "His name's Regenspurger. Garen Regenspurger."

Montbretia fell back in her seat. "Reagan. They all said Reagan-something." She sat straighter. "So who is he and why did he dump a body?"

"He's what you might call a fixer. A troubleshooter. He makes problems go away."

"But he doesn't seem to have made this problem go away—he seems to have created the problem."

Boniface pushed a hand through his hair. It didn't return it to its usual state, but at least the top of his head looked slightly less wild. "You're looking from the wrong end of the telescope. We're the solution to someone else's problem."

Montbretia listened, still not sure what question to ask, but keeping her focus on Boniface.

Boniface met her gaze. "Let me try and explain. I was hired by the client..."

"The super-secret client," Montbretia could hear the grit in her voice. "Are you saying it was them?"

Boniface remained impassive. "You need to hear this. Shouting won't help."

Montbretia shrank. "Sorry."

"I was hired by the client. I was hired before I met you, before I met Ellen, before Nigel, before everything. I was hired for many reasons, including my political connections, and—I like to hope—because I am good." He straightened his tie halfway and continued. "The client had a problem: The story could be newsworthy, but from a business-reputation point of view, it would be poison." Boniface snorted and whispered "poison" under his breath.

"This wasn't your usual sort of corporation in trouble—this wasn't a fire that needed extinguishing, this was a potential problem that would last over years. Five years, ten years, twenty years. Importantly, they didn't think the story was about to break, so what they wanted to do was take control of the situation and have a strategy in place so that when the story did break, they could demonstrate they were already proactively managing the issue." He waited, looking Montbretia straight in the eye. "They were doing the right thing in a difficult situation and wanted me to help ensure that the right message got out there."

"So, Saint Boniface, what was the problem?"

Boniface snorted. "They're a shipping company. A big shipping company who move a lot of stuff around the world. Somehow, a load of toxic waste was taken to Somalia and dumped. Except, it wasn't just dumped—they paid to dump the waste, and the locals they paid moved it to where they drop all their other waste, right next to a squatter camp. Our guys didn't know where it went—they didn't care; they were glad to have got rid of their waste—and nobody in Somalia knew or cared what they had: The people in the squatter camp don't have the internet, and the people who took the cash were busy getting drunk and paying for hookers. You can get a lot of hookers when you're dealing with dollars."

His face turned gray and his speech became strained. "What no one realized was this waste had radioactive materials and all sorts of chemical nasties that got mixed together." He paused, apparently deep in thought. "When it rained, all the poison got washed into the water supply." His eyes misted. "People died. Men, women, children. Some died quickly, some slowly. Some have had their lives blighted—people are blind, there are birth defects.... It's awful."

Montbretia stared at Boniface and started gently. "That's awful, but why are you so cut up?" Then, becoming aware of what she said, with more urgency and even less thought. "It's not that you shouldn't be upset, but you look like it's your fault."

A woman with large gold dangling earrings came into the café and recognized a bleached blonde across the room. Montbretia struggled to hear Boniface's quiet voice over the two women screeching. "The story I was told was that it was beyond doubt that the client was at fault. After all, they paid for the waste to be accepted. But the line was always that no one knew who made the decision. The inference has always been that it was the captain or maybe someone from the local company." He hesitated. "So I was working with the owners, who privately acknowledged their corporate culpability and wanted to make things right."

"Why do I feel there's a however?" asked Montbretia.

"Because there is." Boniface held out his phone. "I've got the evidence. Photographic evidence. Someone knew what was going on. Someone sent the ship to Somalia and then flew there, arriving a few days before the ship and leaving after the waste had been dumped." His voice a whisper. "This wasn't an accident. This was premeditation."

They sat without speaking, becoming consumed in the noise of the café with the train announcements intermittently breaking through from outside.

"That someone," began Montbretia. "Who?"

"Regenspurger."

"Regenspurger? The guy who's looking down the telescope from the other end?" Boniface made no movement as Montbretia continued. "The guy who's responsible for the dumping the body in our office?"

Boniface flicked his eyelids in acknowledgement—apparently tilting his head was too much effort.

"I don't understand."

"That doesn't matter." Boniface hesitated. His voice faded and he continued, his tone almost apologetic. "Some things are not quite as you thought."

Montbretia frowned. "You mean you lied?" It was a tentative question, not a statement.

"No. I told you the truth. But not the whole truth. There are gaps in what I told you, and you've had the impression that things are different to how they really are."

"You had better explain, quickly."

"The work you've been doing for the Global Logistics Forum. Getting it set up, finding contributors, building the website, the benefits of global trade, ethical considerations...all that stuff."

Montbretia tipped her head forward warily.

"Through the work you've done, you know some of the big shipping companies? At least by name and some of the very broad details of their businesses?" Montbretia continued her hesitant affirmation as Boniface kept talking. "So you're acquainted Weissenfeld Shipping."

Montbretia's nodding became far more positive. "Big firm. Lots of different shipping lines with different specializations—have a ship for pretty much every job. Run by Greta Weissenfeld. She's built it from a small family business to what it is today. Determined woman, very smart, very savvy, but don't stand in her way." She wrinkled her nose. "I've seen some photos—always very well presented even if it's not how I would dress. Forty-something. That's about it."

"You know how the Forum has been largely funded by a Spanish trust?"

Montbretia nodded, feeling some foreboding about what she was about to hear.

"Weissenfeld is our client and Weissenfeld has been funding the Forum."

Montbretia thought for a moment. "That doesn't make any sense, Boniface. If they funded the Forum, then why did Weissenfeld make such a stink when that Norwegian guy wrote an article about foreign shipping crews? Surely they could have ignored it; I mean, it's not as if the piece even mentioned them."

"But they had a point: The article went too far. Read in a certain manner, it wasn't far off racist."

"Come on, Boniface, it was accurate, even if you didn't like the style."

"It had some points of fact that were correct, but how it was presented was misleading. It implied that foreign sailors are a safety hazard, where the truth of the matter is sailors from the Philippines, India, Singapore, Panama, Africa, Europe, or wherever are all uniformly safe. The nuance the article didn't bring home is that it's the range of different languages spoken that leads to reduced safety. It's not the fact that crews are foreign, it's the fact that they don't all speak the same language, which leads to misunderstandings and accidents, and against that background Weissenfeld put out a press release criticizing the Global Logistics Forum. But in reality, it was a very mild press release."

"Mild? Did you read the press release, Boniface?"

Boniface met her stare. "Read it? I wrote it."

"You."

Boniface nodded. "Yes. Me."

"But..."

A glint flashed in Boniface's eye. "But what? Tell me, what happened after that press release?"

"There was a piece in the *Financial Times*, a short article on the BBC website, some French sites picked it up. I don't know—there was a lot of shouting—what specifically are you referring to?"

"What happened to your web traffic?"

"It grew."

"By how much?"

"It spiked." Montbretia threw up her hands, almost to dismiss the comment. "For the first three days we averaged fifty times the normal traffic. After that died down, we stayed at about ten times the normal traffic."

"What about the links from other websites, like the BBC?"

"We got a lot."

"A few weeks later, what happened to your ranking on Google, Bing, and the other search engines?"

"We starting hitting the first page of results for key target search terms."

"So take me through this slowly. Where's the downside to you, to the Forum, to the website, arising from the press release issued by Weissenfeld?"

Montbretia sat, moving her lips but knowing that no sound was coming out.

"Can we do the painful bit and join the dots?" Boniface asked.

Montbretia remained still as Boniface continued. "Super-secret client. Weissenfeld. Employer of Regenspurger. Weissenfeld. You and I. Working for Weissenfeld. The Global Logistics Forum. My idea to help as part of a process to manage the press reaction to an accident. In good faith, you thought it was an independent forum. In reality, Weissenfeld's motives may be to use the Forum to help cover up their willful dumping of toxic waste in Somalia."

Montbretia stood, wrapping her arms around herself, taking small gulps of air. "You lied. You lied about who was financing the Forum, you lied about its purpose. You made a judgment call—you didn't give me the information to make my own decision. In fact, you gave me enough information to lead me to one conclusion: the wrong one. Now you're saying that I've been working for a company that has killed hundreds of people by dumping chemical waste, and it's not your fault because you had the best of intentions."

She took a few more gulps of air and pushed her hair behind her ears. "Do you get it? It's not that I feel foolish—I feel like I've..." She stumbled over her words. "I don't feel like—I have been helping a murderer get away with it. The lies, I'll get over. The lack of trust..."

A tear slipped down her cheek. "What is it about you and these dysfunctional domineering women? They're like catnip to you—is it some form of new addiction to replace your old ones?" The people at the next table turned at the raised voice.

"There's one other thing," said Boniface, softly but firmly.

"I don't care."

"You need to. We've been under surveillance. Me and you. Regenspurger's got photographs of us—me and you, separately and together—going into and out of the office, red hand-drawn circles marking us out."

Montbretia felt like a truculent teenager. "Wow. You've put me in danger, too. I might get hurt by a red circle."

"This is serious, Monty. Regenspurger is a dangerous man. Whatever you do, for the next couple of days stay away from the office, stay away from Tilbury, stay away from my place, stay away from your house. Stay in a hotel, go somewhere—I'll pay. Just don't be found."

"What are you going to do?" She paused. "No. Don't tell me. I don't care and I wouldn't believe it anyway." She stepped away from the table and hesitated. "I'll come and collect my stuff—from your place and the office—sometime. But at the moment, I'm too angry to be in the same room as you."

fifty-three

"If I may summarize," Stephen Holding, Boniface's criminal lawyer, looked up. "In making these comments, I am, naturally, taking a harsh view. I don't wish to give you any false hope."

"Naturally," said Boniface without any commitment as he skulked in the corner of Holding's office, looking at the scuffmarks on the desk's modesty board and imagining the thousands of clients—all on legal aid, wearing their best nylon-shell suits—who had come into this room, sat in one of the chairs opposite the lawyer, and then tilted the chair back, resting their feet against the modesty board.

"The nearest you've got to material you could produce in court is some photos that were probably obtained illegally, meaning that they have little evidential value. However, if I'm wrong and we could construct an argument that these photos were legally obtained, then I'm not sure that they prove much."

Boniface frowned.

"Look, Boniface. If this goes to court, the other side would argue that they were fakes, and really, what have you got? Some blurred shots of passport control stamps and a few shots of printed pages. It's hardly proof of a criminal conspiracy. It's not like we've got sworn affidavits or statements from the lawyer—not that we would be able to get hold of them easily."

"But is it enough for you, Steve? Is it enough for the cops? Is it enough for some sort of negotiation?"

Holding leaned back in his fabric-covered chair and swiveled to meet his client's gaze. "Can I make sure I've got the remaining details correct? And then perhaps we can talk about the photos—and how they can be used—in context."

Boniface had his arms folded and rocked; his weight transferred through his left foot on the ground, his right leg bent back with his foot against the wall as he tensed and loosened his thigh muscle. "That sounds like a no to me."

"I'm dubious, Boniface, but maybe there are options." The lawyer picked up his steel-rimmed spectacles and looked down on his notes spread across the brown wood of his desk. "You have made some allegations. Let's start with the one that most directly affects you."

"Please continue," said Boniface, standing away from the wall but remaining with his arms folded as he started to walk along the path crossing on the long edge of the lawyer's desk, assiduously avoiding the two fabric-covered seats that Boniface was sure smelled of criminal.

"You say that this Mister Regenspurger ordered the murder of a vagrant who was picked up in Tilbury docks. The body is the one that was subsequently dumped in your office."

Boniface grunted his acknowledgement as he reached the wall that separated the office from the corridor running outside, standing to the right of the dark-brown wood door—the entrance and exit for the room. The wall was solid to waist height—plaster panels, sheetrock as Montbretia called it, which had been regularly repaired—topped with obscured safety glass to the ceiling. Boniface stared at the metal grid embedded in the safety glass before turning and leaning on one of the pillars between two panes.

The room went quiet. Boniface turned to see the lawyer had laid his pen on his desk and was apparently waiting until he had his client's attention. "Other than a few conversations between Montbretia and these vagrants, Angus, Gerbil, and Albie the Albanian, we have no evidence to prove Mister Regenspurger is involved in the murder, and even less suggestion that he was acting on the direction of a company director or officer."

Holding picked up his pen and continued. "Not to mention, we've yet to establish why you would be the target for such a body dump." He looked back at Boniface to acknowledge his next point. "I know you have a theory—and it's a plausible explanation—nonetheless, it lacks any evidence."

Boniface shifted his weight as the lawyer looked down.

"It seems to me that we may be able to prove that Mister Regenspurger has an extensive collection of frequent-flyer miles, that he may have dubious tastes in holiday destinations, and that he returned your pencil in a manner that you found to be intimidating." He turned a page, then turned back. "If Mister Regenspurger was in Somalia and the other African countries at the relevant times, then there may be a reasonable belief on your part that the chief executive, Fraulein Weissenfeld, may have lied to you, but that's not enough to even suggest a connection with the murder of the guy dumped in your office."

Boniface unfolded his hands and swept his hair back.

"How is Montbretia? How has she taken your revelations?" Holding seemed genuinely concerned.

Boniface felt every muscle in his face sag. "I think if we were to describe matters in terms of how one would present the issue to a court, you would say that our relationship—both in terms of business and friendship—has broken down completely and irrevocably. I mean, how do you build trust and get back from what I've done?"

"But you have made the risks—as you perceive them—abundantly clear to Montbretia. She is in no doubt as to the kind of people who are involved, and she understands that she appears to have been under surveillance?"

"I have tried, but she's angry and she's hurt. But she's sensible—once the initial rage has passed, she'll go somewhere she won't be found."

"So, Montbretia is safe." Boniface affirmed as the lawyer carried on. "As for the photos and this Regenspurger character, I'm glad for the information, but I'm not sure that there's anything we can do—at least, there's nothing we can do at the moment."

"Can't we go to the police?" Boniface felt the forlorn hope he was searching for.

A look of disappointment came over the adviser's face. "What? Lay it all out for them?"

Boniface became more enthusiastic—searching for the hope in the question that didn't seem to be present in his lawyer's tone. "Yeah?"

"You remember what I said that first morning about locking yourself into a story?" He sighed. "If you had said nothing, then we could have done something. But you were quite resolute in your defense of your client, and what you are now suggesting is that you change your story. In other words, you are proposing to stand in a police station and say you lied and wasted police time. Not only that, but you are considering going into a police station and saying that you have obtained information possibly by criminal means."

The lawyer continued tentatively. "We can do it. But there are consequences, and I'm not sure we'll get the results you want.

The two men sat in silence before the lawyer continued. "Go home and sleep on it, and if you want to talk, come and find me tomorrow." He pulled an appointment diary out of his suit pocket and started flicking through pages. "I'm free between 10 AM and 10:30."

"Thanks, Steve. I'll sleep on it."

He felt the office door slam behind him before he yanked out his phone, searching for a number as he followed the nylon carpet toward the stairwell. As he reached the street in the early twilight, crossing between angry taxis, motorcycle couriers running late, and frustrated van drivers, the phone picked up. "Tommy. Boniface. I want some manpower."

fifty–four

Montbretia stood. Head bowed, sobbing.

The keen bite of the estuary wind targeted her damp cheeks as she smeared a tear with her finger. In the early evening twilight, the temperature was falling rapidly, but the articulated lorries dragging their containers still thundered up and down the road leading into the docks, apparently unaware of the ending of the day.

Three figures stood on mud and grass next to smashed pallets, burned-out oil cans, and the detritus left by truckers on a strip of land bordered by the road and a steel palisade fence. Angus, Gerbil, and Montbretia in a triangle.

Montbretia sobbed again as she looked to the center of the triangle. "I would have been here. I should have been here." For the second time that day, she clutched herself, raising her head at the top of her sob, letting it fall as she expelled her animal-like pain.

"If I'd been here he'd still be alive, but instead I was wasting time with Boniface. I could have been here sooner." Her head fell and her shoulders quivered.

"If you were here, you'd be dead." Angus's mournful Scottish accent somehow seemed appropriate. "Whoever did this would have killed anyone who got in their way. If you tried to help, you would be lying next to him."

The inert body of Albie the Albanian lay in the middle of the triangle with the three standing guard at each corner. Even in death no one knew Albie's real name, but then again, no one knew what had killed him.

All that could be said with any certainty was that he had been bludgeoned.

The body was face down—half on compacted earth, half on grass—wrapped in a sand-colored raincoat, now spattered with blood. His right leg was broken. Even someone without any medical training could make that diagnosis—it bent midway down the thigh at approximately ninety degrees, with the bone cutting through the fabric of his trousers. His head was turned long past the point that the human neck will tolerate and was now looking down on his back. Or rather, it would have done had the face not been caved in. The eyes were closed and bleeding, the nose literally flattened, and the right cheekbone caved in.

"That's execution," said Angus. "Murder up close, by people with strength."

"I'm calling the police," said Montbretia.

"No." Gerbil spoke for the first time since the three had arrived at the body, his voice scrawny like him, but commanding. "No police."

"You can't leave his body here to get pecked to pieces by the seagulls. He deserves more than that." She wiped another tear as she tugged out her phone. "Much more."

"This looks like a guy who was bludgeoned in a hobo fight," said Angus. "The cops don't like us at the best of times. You think they're going to be friendlier when they have to pretend to care?"

"Then you go," said Montbretia, starting to walk around the body, taking photos. "And step back if you think that a photo might capture your soul."

She took her fifth snap and stood straight, flicking through the pictures, selecting the one that looked goriest. She attached the photo to an email and typed: "Boniface: This is what Regenspurger did" and hit the send button. "No signal. I'll walk up the road until I get some bars and then I'll call the cops. You boys had better scatter. I'll come and find you later. Where will you be?"

"Walk around—we'll find you," said Angus. "I've seen those guys once tonight; I don't want to be around if they decide they've killed the wrong homeless guy."

"You saw them?" Montbretia was concerned.

"They came looking for Albie. The guy with the missing finger looked ready to take a swing with that lump of wood."

"He had a missing finger?" asked Montbretia.

Angus nodded and indicated his right hand. "Half there."

"I'm going to call the police." Montbretia zipped up her fleece. "I'll come looking when I'm finished, but try and find me—I'm not too keen on being out here alone."

fifty-five

It had cost him 150 quid to borrow a cherry picker.

It was useful having an electrician as a mate. An electrician who worked for Southern Supply and spent every day in his cherry picker fixing broken bulbs in streetlights. Except he didn't call them bulbs—bulbs are what go in the ground, apparently. Lamps are what go in streetlights.

Reg Johnson didn't give a toss about whether they were lamps or bulbs, if he was being honest. He had transport with a lift on the back, and all he needed to do was to wait for this Boniface bloke that Tommy had told him to meet here.

Small job. Nice payday. Everyone can be tucked up in bed before midnight. He checked his watch: 9 PM. Right place: southwest corner of Berkeley Square, under a streetlight. Where was this Boni-who-or-whatever?

Three men walked past—each wearing tuxedos. Reg decided to hate them on sight—it would save time assessing all the individual ways he could find to hate them. A man walked past the three coming down the slope: good suit, hair had a bit too much effort but seemed slightly disheveled. He made eye contact and held it.

It couldn't be: Who wears a suit when you're breaking into a building?

Reg reached for the passenger door. The suited man opened it and got into the cab, holding out his hand. "Boniface."

"Reg." He shook Boniface's, feeling the other man's weak grip and small hands. "Reg. Not Reginald, only my mother calls me that, and definitely not Reggie. That's for the wife." He looked the suited man up and down. "You not got anything else to wear?" He indicated the green boiler suit he was wearing. "That's not a usual getup in my line of business."

"It is in mine." Boniface's face remained emotionless. "If I'm seen, I want to at least have a plausible explanation."

"Suit yourself," said Reg, smiling at his small humor as he turned over the engine, which soon found its rhythmic diesel chug. They took the first left, two-thirds of the way up Berkeley Square, followed the road across a crossroads, took the next left, and the next left, into a mews road heading back in the direction of Berkeley Square.

As they passed the corner, Reg said, "This it?"

"Yup," said Boniface.

They continued toward Berkeley Square along the narrow road of garages and upscale apartment blocks, following the next left and pulling up in front of two wooden garage doors, black, set into a white stucco-fronted house.

Reg looked through the windshield, straining to see the higher floors of the buildings, then opened the door, easing himself out to look behind before he killed the engine. He groped between the seats and pulled out something that he threw at Boniface.

"Put that on." As Boniface struggled to pull on a hoodie and a pair of jeans, keeping his polished black brogues, Reg continued. "Round the block once: We're looking for cameras on the building."

"Right," said Boniface, reaching for the door handle.

"Walk. Not fast, not slow. Be aware of your feet and make the minimum noise possible. Feel like you're gliding. Don't do anything to draw attention. You're a ghost. Don't wiggle. Don't walk funny. Put the hood up and keep your head down."

Reg watched him as he walked up the slope, disappearing as he followed the left-hand corner. Three minutes later, he slipped into the passenger door, closing it behind him without making a noise. "Tell me about the cameras," said Reg.

"Three. One on the gate. As you face it, it's up and right. One to the left of the gate, pointed downhill along the side face of the building. One on the lower face of the building, pointing along the wall covering the entrances to those garages. So if you stand on the bottom outside corner and look up, you'll get hit by two cameras covering the walls."

"Gotcha," said Reg, fumbling to stick a fake moustache to his top lip. "I'll be back in three—keys are in the ignition if you've gotta move."

Boniface was muttering something as Reg got out, putting on his sunglasses and a flat-cap to cover his shaved head. He walked the two sides of the block, then turned left down the hill to pass the target, slowing as he approached the building. Having turned the corner and got clear of the building, he speeded up.

"You missed one." Reg shut the door behind him, removing his disguise.

"Really?"

"Go through the gate and there's a little garden, right?"

"Yeah."

"There's a camera covering that," said Reg, holding his hand up and pointing at a downward angle, as if that explained the position of the camera.

He sat back in his seat, turning to Boniface. "This safe. Where is it?"

"Top floor, center and right window."

"Where's the guard?"

"On the middle floor, but he walks around, hence the suit." Boniface pointed at himself, a single flow from his shoulders to his feet.

"I reckon we should take out that camera on the back wall," said Reg, firing up the engine and watchfully pulling out. The cherry picker followed the route the two had walked, rounding the outside corner and turning in close to the former house which was now an office, drawing up as they cleared the end of the building.

He killed the engine and slipped on his hat again. "Keys are in the ignition," he said to Boniface. "I'm going to take out the camera. If we need to skedaddle, then drive, but remember that I'll be in the basket."

"I can't drive," said Boniface. "Well, I can, but it's illegal. I was banned."

Reg exhaled loudly. "Boniface, what we're doing is called criminal enterprise—we're about to break into that building, and I shall then break into a safe for you. In the scale of things, a driving offense is pretty much a civil matter." He paused. "If you want to piss your pants, we'll go home now."

"Sorry," said Boniface sheepishly, sliding into the driver's seat as Reg got out, reaching for a pair of gloves and a hammer in the door tray. He quietly shut the door before walking to the rear of the cherry picker and sliding into the basket once his gloves were on.

Reg looked around, then pressed the button to raise the basket, cringing at the sound of the motor in the quiet night. When it reached level with the roof he stopped, pleased at the silence, and leaned over, pulling off three slates.

Holding the hammer in one hand and the slates in the other, Reg had a quick look before hitting the descend button with the forefinger of his hammer hand. The motor broke the silence, and Reg dropped the slates, watching them shatter on the ground under the CCTV camera but not hearing the noise above the motor. Keeping his finger on the button, he took the hammer with his free hand and, as the basket passed the camera, he swung, knocking it to point at the wall.

The basket reached the bottom and Reg jumped out, pleased to be surrounded by silence.

He opened the van door. "Over there," he pointed to the far corner across the street from the target. "Sit on the ground like you're homeless and watch. Don't get seen and be grateful it's not raining."

Boniface got out and Reg jumped in. "I'm going to hide the wagon. I'll be back to find you. And put your hood up."

fifty-six

"Anything?" Boniface hadn't noticed or heard Reg approach, but now he was squatting beside him as he sat on the corner of the crossroad opposite Weissenfeld Shipping's London office.

"The security guard came out and looked. He saw the slate, threw his hands up, and went in. That's it; that's all that has happened."

"So in the last hour, no police? No additional security? No one coming or going?"

"A few people walked up and down the street. Maybe residents, maybe people from the offices. They were all in a hurry."

"Okay, let's go."

"We're going in?" asked Boniface, becoming aware that his throat was tightening and his pitch rising.

"I'll go and get the cherry picker. Back in ten. You keep watching here." The shaved head on top of a somewhat rotund dark-green boiler suit with splayed feet departed, walking as if he hadn't made it to the bathroom in time.

Reg and the cherry picker were back in ten minutes.

Boniface found himself like a wild animal, his head twisting in the direction of any noise as he walked over to the vehicle with the basket directly under the right window.

He removed his borrowed clothes and joined Reg in the cherry-picker basket. "Up, in, open the safe, out, down, gone."

Boniface wasn't sure whether that was an explanation or an order from Reg. He nodded anyway, and as he did the motor graunched across the night, lifting the basket to the window. As the basket stopped, there was silence, apart from the metallic creaks as the basket rocked.

Boniface noticed that in the split second he had become aware of the quiet, Reg had opened the wooden sash window and moved inside. He was now offering his hand to Boniface, who struggled through the window, reaching the floor and finding every creak in the several-hundred-year-old floorboards.

He walked to the wall on the left behind the large desk, the room dull with only the ambient light outside. With each step, a creak. Reg followed, each step as if his foot was held by a cushion of air. Boniface pointed to the safe on the wall. "That."

There was a sound outside: someone passing. Boniface took three swift steps, reached the light switch, and flicked it as the door swung open. "Mister Boniface."

"Lennie," said Boniface, trying to remember what normal behavior looked like. "I came in here for a kip," he pointed to the scroll-armed sofa, "but slept for a bit longer than I was expecting. I've just opened the window to get a bit of fresh air." He dropped his voice. "You won't tell them?"

"I thought you had gone," said the security guard. "When you and Mister Regenspurger walked out, he said that you had been suddenly called away and signed you out. I didn't know you were back—I didn't see your name on the log."

"Sorry, Lennie. I must have forgotten when I came back." He grimaced. "Long day and all that."

The guard nodded, pensive. "Did you hear anything? While you've been in here?"

"Hear?" asked Boniface.

"We've had a problem with the camera. Look, I can show you," said the guard, moving forward.

"It's alright," said Boniface. "I know the one you mean. The one just out here."

"Funny thing. It looks like some slates fell off the roof and knocked it. It's no use to man nor beast now." He chuckled to himself, plainly desperate to relay a witticism he had been planning for a while. "Scrub that. It's useful as a pigeon perch."

"Didn't hear a thing," said Boniface. "What will you do—get someone in tomorrow?"

"Tomorrow? You've got to be kidding. They've got a four-hour contract." He checked his watch. "But at this time of night, they're normally here in under two, so hopefully it'll be fixed within the next forty-five minutes."

"That's quick," said Boniface, trying to disguise the tension in his voice. "I guess I should get on—you don't want me still here when they come to fix the camera."

"I'll leave you to it," said the security guard as he closed the doors.

"Next time, Boniface, talk faster," said Reg, noiselessly extricating himself from under Jeremy Farrant's desk. "I'm too old to be hiding under desks—learn to say less." He stretched his legs, turning toward the safe. "But I've got to say, that is really soft carpet. I could sleep on that floor."

"Any idea how long?" asked Boniface.

"Looks old. Shouldn't take long," said Reg, reaching into his pocket and pulling out a bird's nest of pieces of metal.

Both of their heads jerked to face the door. "You carry on. I'll deal with it," said Boniface, straightening his tie and tugging the sides of his jacket to pull it tight around his shoulders. He stepped into the corridor, closing the double doors of Jeremy Farrant's office behind him, and stood where he had been when, several hours earlier, Regenspurger approached him to return his pencil.

"Hey Lennie," said Boniface, seeing the familiar shape of the security guard creaking up the old stairway.

"I thought you'd like to know that I've marked you as coming back into the office at about 5 PM, which is when I was on my break." He leaned in, frowning, his voice conspiratorial. "That way we've got the records straight, in case they check." He winked.

"That's good," said Boniface.

"Did I tell you what little Kayleigh has been up to now?"

"She's the youngest," said Boniface—questioning more than stating. The security guard nodded, standing up straight and beaming. "Listen, Lennie, I've got a few bits to finish. Can I tidy up and I'll come down? We can have a cup of tea and you can tell me then."

"Right you are," said the guard, turning. "You want to hear this story. She's just like her mother."

"I'll be right with you," said Boniface. As he got to the door, he turned back. "Lennie. Is there anyone else still here?"

"You're the last one. Sophie left about ten minutes ago."

"Thanks, Len," said Boniface, slipping back into the office and closing the door. "Sorry, Reg, he wanted to talk about his granddaughter. How's it going?"

"Beautiful safe. Lovely piece of engineering for its day, but someone replaced the lock."

"That sounds bad," said Boniface, pulling out his phone. "How long will this take?" He switched on his phone before looking up at Reg. "If they know I'm here, I might as well have my phone on."

"What do you mean how long?" asked Reg. "I'm in. The new lock is a piece of fluff designed to look good—there's more security on a kid's jewelry box. You could've got in with a wire coat hanger." He let the safe door swing open. "Do you want it all?"

"Let me look at what's there," said Boniface, moving to the open door.

"Pick it up and let's go," said Reg with some urgency. "You can read these at your leisure when we haven't got someone who will notice that there's already a cherry picker where he wants to put his cherry picker."

"We need to lock this back in the safe. Missing papers will cause a big problem." Boniface's phone pinged; reflexively, his hand moved toward his pocket.

"Ignore that," said Reg. "Start looking." He lifted all the papers out of the safe and laid them on top of Jeremy Farrant's desk.

Boniface opened the first file. The content was familiar: Tamsin Smales-Mainer's research on him. There seemed to be a bit more detail and more background, but no surprises. The next file contained a few notes on the application for the injunction. Boniface scanned the instructions to counsel, chuckling as he read the signature of the instructing lawyer, seeing Jeremy Farrant's signature, knowing the document was the work of Tamsin Smales-Mainer.

"Hurry up, Boniface." Reg's eyes burned into Boniface as he flipped over the last file. Boniface was no expert, but as far as he could tell, the documents he was looking at were the legal deeds for Farrant's Scottish castle and the surrounding estate.

"There's nothing here. Put it back and lock it up," said Boniface, pulling out his phone: one email from Montbretia. He felt like he had been punched in the stomach and only became aware of his legs giving way when he found himself leaning on the desk.

"Ready?" asked Reg.

"I've got to go this way," said Boniface, pulling himself together. Reg looked somewhere between shocked and confused. "They've signed me in so I've got to sign out...and Lennie...I've got to listen about his granddaughter." He slipped his phone back into his pocket and looked up. Reg was gone.

Boniface walked to the window and looked out. "You're sure you're not coming?" said Reg, standing in the basket.

"I'm sure I should pay attention: You've had more experience than I have when it comes to making a swift getaway." He offered him his hand. "Thanks. I appreciate the help."

Reg nodded his acknowledgement as he shook Boniface's hand through the window. "Tommy will settle up," said Boniface.

Reg nodded.

"Don't forget to submit a VAT receipt." Boniface winked, lip-reading a stream of profanities as Reg's voice was lost under the motor lowering the basket. Boniface pulled down the window and conscientiously locked it. You never could be too cautious—he had heard there were burglars in the area.

He followed the twisting corridor to Greta's office and entered without knocking. Lacking occupants, the Louis XIV furniture looked even more ridiculous than it did when the queen was in her hive. Without any occupants, it was a swift task to confirm that no papers were kept there, and why would they be—Greta kept all her records in her notebook, which was with her at all times.

Boniface pulled out his phone. "Tommy. One last favor." He reflexively looked around the room to see if he was overheard. "Have you got someone who's quick on their feet?"

fifty-seven

Boniface hadn't slept well. After one night in his own bed, he had returned to the hotel close to the Weissenfeld office, but this time he was paying, not Weissenfeld.

Lennie's chattering had seemed interminable, and Boniface was happy when the engineer arrived to fix the broken CCTV camera. Boniface had made some sort of interested noises—it did seem odd that three slates would fall off, and no, he wouldn't have expected that much damage either, but there you go—and then left, telling Lennie he didn't want to be in the way while the guard dealt with the engineer.

Boniface was sure that Lennie's stories of his granddaughter's exploits would send him to sleep, but with a combination of adrenalin following his first ever break-in, accompanying a professional thief who had served time for safe-breaking—in the good old days, when safe-breaking was an art, said Tommy, before everything happened electronically and you needed a degree in computers just to commit a minor robbery—and trying to figure why a corpse had been dumped in his office, Boniface's sleep had totaled under two hours.

The hotel charged by the night, not by the hours slept, unfortunately.

He checked the time on his phone as he stood up the hill from Weissenfeld's office. Diagonally opposite the office, almost at the precise spot where Boniface had spent an hour last night, watching the reaction to the broken CCTV camera, a figure stood. Looking like a workman waiting to be picked up—oddly anomalous in such a high-end neighborhood—he seemed relaxed but somehow managed never to show himself. All Boniface could make out were running shoes, jeans, and a hoodie with the hood raised. The only other detail: He smoked.

Cars, vans, and cabs passed up and down the hill at irregular intervals. At 7:29 precisely, a large midnight-blue Mercedes turned the corner and started making its way up the hill.

The man in the hoodie—apparently a uniform for associates of Tommy—stamped out his cigarette and started to loosen up like a sprinter readying himself. As the Mercedes passed him, the hoodie crossed the road, looking up and catching Boniface's eye, dropping contact as he started to pull on a pair of gloves. He knew Boniface even if Boniface didn't know him.

The Mercedes stopped outside the gate, which was opening apparently without human intervention, and the chauffeur was out of the car. Boniface recognized the face: Bertrand Scheidling. Despite his resentment at the imposition, Scheidling had driven Boniface to his apartment to pick up his tuxedo and then taken him to the opera, where Gideon had seen him and Greta.

As the chauffeur opened the door, the hoodie started to jog. The chauffeur helped his principal, taking her coat and bag as she stepped out—bedroom-wear heels, and a phone firmly to her ear while she gave orders. The hoodie began to sprint as Greta slipped her handbag onto her arm—the handbag containing her notebook, the book in which she wrote all her notes.

Boniface started to walk toward the Mercedes as the hoodie came level with the group, making a lunge for the bag.

Bertrand Scheidling wasn't young, but he was fast and, like any good driver, had predicted what was about to happen and was already taking evasive action. His kick was perfectly timed and perfectly aimed, squarely hitting the hoodie's ankle as the hoodie grabbed the bag.

The hoodie lost his grip on the bag as his ankle twisted and, slamming into Greta, he went down with the chauffeur jumping on him, hurriedly followed by the security guard who had apparently been behind the gate.

Greta, on her heels, spun and fell backward toward the gate, hitting her head on the corner of the brickwork surrounding the entrance as she went down. Boniface was kneeling beside her before she could scream.

Instinctively, Boniface reached to support her head. "Boniface," was all Greta said as she fell toward him, her arms around him like a long-lost lover, resting her head on his shoulder.

Sophie was there. "Fraulein Weissenfeld. Fraulein Weissenfeld." There was concern in her tone as she continued fast-talking in German.

Boniface released his hand, which had been supporting the back of Greta's head since she clung to him. He held it for Sophie to see: Little clean skin was visible under the blood. "We should get her to a hospital."

"I'll call an ambulance," said Sophie, her usual unflappable temperament flustered.

"Get a cab," said Boniface, twisting his head to indicate the passing taxis. "It'll be faster, and Bertrand is going to be here for a while." He made eye contact with the chauffeur sitting on Tommy's hoodie-wearing associate. "You don't want to move at the moment, do you?"

Scheidling sneered at the hoodie as if to convey his agreement with Boniface's strategy.

Boniface made a mental note to teach Sophie how to flag down a cab in London as he watched her bobbing up and down in the gutter, waving both hands in the air. "He wants to know where you're going," said Sophie as a cab pulled up.

Greta moaned, and Boniface held her head firmly, but not too firmly, as he turned to Sophie. "Tell him we're going where the Royal family goes."

Sophie looked back as if to question whether Boniface was sure. He gave a single nod, and she went to relay the destination to the driver before opening the cab door and returning to help.

"Greta. We need to stand up and help you into the cab and get someone to look at this gash." Boniface's voice was soft, reassuring, as he examined the back of Greta's head, her face still firmly nestled in his shoulder, her immaculately coiffed helmet of blond hair clumped and streaked with a spreading patch of purple-red.

Boniface gently untangled himself from his former principal, taking care that she was supporting her head before he moved away from her. He repositioned himself to squat beside her. "Your suit." Sophie had her hand over her mouth—the other was pointing at the left half of Boniface's jacket, now thick with blood.

Boniface gave a dismissive shake of the head. "Can you stand?" he asked Greta.

"We should call an ambulance and get a stretcher," said Sophie.

Boniface felt Greta cringe and shake her head. "No," he said. "It's far less undignified to travel in a cab. Hold her arm as we stand."

Sophie leaned, her rotund figure and shapeless dress making it hard to see which muscles and which limbs she was moving. Slowly, with Boniface and Sophie each holding an arm, Greta balanced, squatting on her heels.

She indicated to Sophie that she was fine, and the secretary let go of her arm as Greta continued rising, resting on Boniface for support. Greta reached down for balance with her free arm, dropping her handbag as she lifted herself further.

The CEO reached a standing position with Boniface supporting her on her right side as she balanced on her heels. She looked around and saw the hoodie-wearer on the ground by the gate, the chauffeur and the guard sitting on him. Scheidling was eyeing him and holding his arm behind his back, while the guard was making calls.

Greta lunged, aiming a kick at the hoodie's head. She missed. Missed by a long way and twisted on her non-kicking leg, losing her balance. Boniface grabbed her around the waist as she fell, walking forward to push her upright. "You can get him later," he whispered. "Let's get you to the hospital first."

"Boniface," pleaded Greta, gripping onto him. "Stay with me." She took two small steps before Sophie ran forward to hold her other arm, and together with Boniface they helped her into the cab.

"Call the hospital and tell them we're coming," said Boniface to Sophie, sitting next to Greta. "Give me her bag." He pointed to the handbag Greta had dropped, which was still lying where she had dropped it. "I'll make sure it stays with her while she's getting checked out."

Sophie passed the bag, and the cab pulled out as the blue flashing lights of a police car appeared at the bottom of the hill.

fifty-eight

Montbretia pulled the blanket tighter. It smelled familiar, but it wasn't what she was used to sleeping under. She also wasn't used to sleeping fully dressed and wearing a zipped-up fleece.

She tried to figure the time—it was early, but there was light so it wasn't that early. She couldn't see sunlight, so it probably wasn't 8 AM yet. All she could see when she looked up were a few seagulls lazily circling in the dirty sky. Another blast from the estuary, and she drew the blanket tighter, twisting uncomfortably on the hard ground.

She hadn't had enough sleep to make her anything other than tired and grumpy. But there was no way she could catch up on her sleep while she stayed in Tilbury, sleeping rough with a couple of bums.

By the time Montbretia had walked back from the place where she had found a phone signal, she could hear the sirens. The first police response car had arrived about a minute later. The two constables got out, inspected the body, made a few jokes that, in retrospect, were in poor taste, and then said they needed to preserve the scene.

Apparently, preserving a scene means asking the person who called you, and who was standing around the scene, to move about ten yards away. While the first officer moved Montbretia and started taking her details and some background about how she came to find the body, the second radioed in. Twenty minutes later, the cavalry arrived. It was perhaps two hours before Raymond Talbot turned up.

He introduced himself. "Good evening, you must be Miss Armstrong. I'm Detective Inspector Raymond Talbot, and this is DS Kevin Hitchcock." One look at their suits—even under streetlight—was enough for her to understand why these two annoyed Boniface. When they started talking, their forced officialdom and propensity to use words they apparently didn't understand the full meaning of, but that they thought sounded intimidating, was enough for her to agree with Boniface's assessment.

Between the attending officers, the backup, and Talbot, the conversations had been numerous and became repetitive. Talbot more than Hitchcock had difficulty with the notion that Regenspurger should be arrested. "Please. What evidence do you have for your assertion that this Mister..." he squinted at his notes, "Ray-guns-purr-gerr is behind this murder."

Montbretia tried to explain but couldn't seem to find a way to get him to understand. "I'm not disputing what you are telling me," he said.

"All I'm saying is that before I knock on his door, I would like to have at least one single fact that I can present to him that suggests he has some responsibility for this murder, and for the murder of the man who was dumped in your office in Wimbledon. At the moment, the best I have is a weak story from the officers who attended Mister Boniface and found the body, some cock-and-bull from Boniface, and a bit of CCTV footage from that mouthy little brat in the estate agents office under your office."

Montbretia wasn't sure what time she finished talking to the police, but it was late and virtually all traffic on the dock road had disappeared. She walked around for approaching another half hour before Gerbil found her and took her to the place where he and Angus would be spending the night. It was as well appointed as their other residences, but this was farther from the madding crowd, being about five hundred yards past the end of the main dock road.

Angus built the fire, and they spent hours chatting. Talking about Albie, talking about Ellen, talking about the men's lives at sea. Gerbil fell asleep first, and by that time the last train had gone and Montbretia had decided she didn't fancy cycling all the way home, so she decided to stay: Sleeping rough in Tilbury was no worse than sleeping anywhere in Tilbury from what she had seen of the place.

When she went to sleep, she had been sitting, wrapped in her sister's old blanket, with a warm fire next to her. As she woke, the fire was out and she was lying on the ground. At a guess, she'd had three hours' sleep.

She sat, keeping the blanket wrapped around her, aware of how much she needed to pee.

Sluggishly she stood, kicking some life into her feet. Some vagrant reflex kicked in, and both Angus and Gerbil opened their eyes wide, searching for the source of danger. "Sorry," said Montbretia. Gerbil shut his eyes and rolled over.

"What are you doing?" asked Angus.

"I need to pee, and I'd also like to know where I left my bike," said Montbretia. "I know I locked it to a palisade fence somewhere, but it all looks the same to me, so I can't quite remember exactly where it is."

"It's back round there," said Angus. "I can show you later." He settled himself, keeping one eye open. "Find a bush to piss in, then go back to sleep—there's no point in being awake now; it's the safest time of the day to sleep."

"Yesterday was a big day for me. I thought I'd started to find my way, thought I'd started to get things on an even keel after Ellen, but everything kinda got shot to shit, and I found that I wasn't where I thought I was. Then Albie got..." She faded, staring up across the scrub ground. "I'm not sure I'm ever going to sleep again, and I need to...you know, head together."

Angus stared up at her.

"Most mornings, I get up and go for a jog or a bike ride, but I'm not... so I'm going to go for a walk and maybe have a pee at the café. Shall I bring back something to eat—a couple of rounds of bacon sandwiches, perhaps?"

"As long as that won't interfere with my macrobiotic diet," said Angus.

Montbretia smiled. "I'll see you later," she said as she traced the route that Gerbil had led her along last night.

Albie's death had reignited the memories of her sister and her violent death. Boniface had been the person who had told her about Ellen's death—he had been there when Ellen was hurt. Boniface seemed to be the one person who understood Montbretia's anger and the loss she felt at Ellen's passing.

He was also the one who understood that she was living—and enjoying living—a different kind of life. She had been traveling for two-and-a-half years, her financing coming from odd jobs and part-time work as she moved from place to place. He understood that she didn't suddenly want to be tied down and join the nine-to-five brigade, but he also understood that with Ellen's death there was a grieving process, which meant that she couldn't keep moving.

She had to stop and reflect, but she still had to support herself. With that understanding Boniface had offered her a place to live, so she didn't have to stay alone in Ellen's old house, and work when she wanted it. And not just grunt work—it seemed that it was work with real value.

But now it was clear that Boniface had lied to her and hadn't trusted her. Worse, the work she had been doing was a cover for toxic-waste dumping, and now it seemed that her involvement had somehow led to Albie being bludgeoned to death. Her choices, her judgments, Albie's death.

Everything collapsed yesterday. Everything she had built since she had lived in London. Even the memory of Ellen was now tainted because it involved Boniface. Now she was alone and nowhere felt safe, but she couldn't go back to traveling because she wasn't sure anymore that she could trust her own instincts: As yesterday proved, her instincts could be catastrophically wrong.

She felt a tear in her eye as she came to the small section of waste ground protected by a slither of yellow police tape flapping in the breeze and a police officer who, even to Montbretia, looked young. A van pulled up, and two civilians got out. Montbretia watched as they walked to the rear of the van and started putting on bunny suits. She thought of science boy and looked at her phone: lies she told because Boniface had lied to her.

She stared at the phone again—this time reading the screen—remembering how last night she had switched everything off that might drain the battery. Now the battery showed only seven percent left.

Hopefully Trevor would have a charger.

fifty-nine

He knew how to swear, get laid, and get alcohol in most languages.

Where he wasn't fluent, the international language of violence was usually sufficient to communicate his message succinctly and cogently, and with an appropriate nuance that translated perfectly into the local dialect.

At the nurses' station, they had been nervous about talking with him. A bit of subtle—who was he kidding?—a bit of less than subtle intimidation had got the necessary information, although he wasn't sure it was worth the hassle in getting it: Fraulein Weissenfeld had a nasty cut to the rear of her head necessitating stitches, and a twisted ankle. She wasn't in her room as she was being x-rayed. However, they thought that Mister Boniface—do you know Mister Boniface...very nice man—was waiting in her room for her return. Perhaps you Mister...Mister...would like to wait with Mister Boniface.

Regenspurger wasn't fluent in Albanian, but he spoke it well enough to be understood.

Standing outside Greta Weissenfeld's room, English would be overheard, and someone might speak German, but there was unlikely to be an Albanian speaker, and both the guys spoke Albanian. He thought about Vlach or Macedonian—one of those was their native tongue—but he was too weak on those languages, so Albanian was the way to have a conversation in public but keep the details confidential. Then again, more than three hundred languages are spoken in London, so it's best to be somewhat oblique.

He looked at an angle through the window, then ducked under the square of glass to scan the remainder of the room. At about forty-five degrees, he saw Boniface standing, looking hesitant, shifty. He looked harder: Was Boniface hesitant or shocked?

He dialed, momentarily taking his eyes off Boniface but returning them as he put the phone to his ear, talking immediately when it was answered while he surveyed the blood covering Boniface's shirt, tie, and jacket. That would be upsetting for a man who dressed so particularly. It was time for a visit to the tailor—this wasn't something the dry cleaner could sort.

"Find the package. Take it into your possession."

Boniface surveyed the room, his head remaining stationary—his eyeballs doing the work—and then moved closer to the foot of the bed.

"Lock up the package securely, then leave it."

Boniface reached out to the table across the bed. Standing with his back to the table, he appeared to be trying to look inside the bag that was on the table.

"Call me when the package is secure. I need the leverage."

Boniface reached back and pushed the mouth of the bag open.

"If this works out, then I want you both on a ship this evening."

He hung up and dropped his phone back in his pocket, keeping his gaze fixed on his prey. Boniface had turned toward the bag and grabbed the bottom, giving it a quick yank so that some of the contents spilled before he walked away, apparently drawn by something outside the window.

Regenspurger watched as Boniface walked back from the window and helped a leather-bound notebook, which was half out of the bag, to be fully liberated.

The notebook lay on the table as Boniface appeared to scan the room again.

There was a swift movement. Boniface reached inside his pocket and pulled out his phone. He drifted along the side of the bed and flicked through the pages of the notebook. Stopping, he held the phone over the pages and tapped the phone's screen. He turned a page, held the phone over the notebook, and tapped the screen again.

He flipped the page again as Regenspurger pushed the door. "Mister Boniface. Good morning."

Boniface dropped his phone, which ricocheted off the table, landing on the linoleum floor with a single impact. His face went white—even through Fraulein Weissenfeld's blood smeared over his cheeks, it was still apparent that Boniface had lost his color.

Boniface reached for the contents of Greta's bag, spread over the narrow table. "It fell," he stuttered, clumsily trying to return the contents to the bag. He knocked some pieces onto the bed—keys, makeup—and looked down, trying to pick up the items with trembling hands.

Without much commitment, he swept the debris he had created back into the bag and stood it upright, shaking it as if settling sand in a bucket. He scrabbled on the floor, then moved toward the window—to all intents a passerby who happened to see a problem and tried to help.

Regenspurger remained impassive, standing inside the door, observing every move.

"Good to see you, Garen," offered Boniface, his voice still quivering as he slipped his phone into his pocket.

Regenspurger kept his glare on Boniface, who stepped backward as if pushed by the force of the stare, stopping when he hit wall. He put his hand to the back of his head, checking whether he was hurt. "Lucky that wasn't worse—we've already got one person with a cut head." His forced good humor faded as Regenspurger maintained his silence.

"We should have a conversation, Mister Boniface." Regenspurger's inflection was tender, reassuring.

Boniface stammered and stuttered. Regenspurger continued, appearing not to notice. "I am disappointed that you haven't behaved as we expected. I thought I was clear yesterday."

"I came to apologize," said Boniface.

Regenspurger raised his eyes and cocked his head.

"I hoped to get my job back…" Boniface was starting to babble, his speech running like a river in full flood. "I haven't been paid the last installment and hoped we could finalize matters."

Regenspurger took three measured paces across the room and stood, with his hand out, before Boniface. He stilled his breathing, looking into the Englishman's eyes, which darted around, fleetingly making contact but breaking it almost immediately.

He snapped his fingers, once, to draw attention to his outstretched hand.

Boniface's eyes still darted.

"Your phone," said Regenspurger.

Boniface's mouth twitched with small, stammering tics audible.

Regenspurger leaned his body toward Boniface—one or two degrees—relaxing his shoulders and feeling his head lift as his did. He locked eyes with Boniface and whispered. "Your phone, please, Mister Boniface."

Boniface fumbled to find his pocket. Slowly he withdrew the phone and placed it in Regenspurger's hand. Regenspurger broke his stare and returned to his position just inside the door, looking back at Boniface, who crumpled and was now wiping sweat with a handkerchief.

"The last thing Fraulein Driesdorfer said before we put her on a plane back to Hamburg was that she thought you were taking pictures of documents on my desk, but she thought that was too much of a crazy idea to be true." He glanced up from Boniface's phone, which he manipulated with his right hand. "However, apparently she was correct in her observation."

He continued to flick through the photographs. Sometimes frowning, sometimes turning the phone and zooming in. "Quite the photographer, aren't we, Mister Boniface? Maybe you can do it professionally in your next job."

He found what he was looking for—select all, delete, are you sure, yes—then watched as a timer whirred, ending on a blank screen: no photos.

"This morning?" Regenspurger looked up at Boniface: He had uttered two words. Two words that Boniface could interpret in many ways. Two words that he uttered as both a statement and a question.

Boniface stared back. Apparently he was aware of the technique Regenspurger was employing: Say something, leave an uncomfortable silence, and wait for the person you're trying to intimidate to deal with the social embarrassment by filling the gap. Regenspurger knew he was stronger mentally—he knew from firsthand experience that everyone breaks at some point—but at the moment he didn't have enough leverage and he didn't have time to waste, so he was happy to fill in the spaces and leave long pauses to keep Boniface unsettled, scared even.

"It was rather a strange place for you to be."

Boniface looked up, questioning.

The German spoke quickly, dismissing comments with a wave of his hand before the Englishman could say them. "I know, I know...you were there to beg and plead. But why were you there then?" He placed both feet squarely on the ground and faced Boniface. "Why not call and ask for a meeting to discuss these matters?"

"I tried to expl..."

A wave of the hand silenced Boniface. "The point I'm trying to get at, Mister Boniface, is why you were at that specific place at that specific time." He extended his arm with its upturned hand farther toward the mumbling Boniface. "A lesser man might suggest you were there to perhaps point out a target or to give yourself an alibi."

It wasn't a question, but Regenspurger let the thought hang.

"Don't you see how it could look, Mister Boniface?" He kept his glare focused on Boniface, as if to remind him that all questions were purely rhetorical. "The role you played seems odd."

Regenspurger shifted. "This man, who is dressed scruffily, is running fast in the direction of the person you say you wanted to meet. The danger must have been clear to you, but you seem not to have reacted." He snorted. "I can almost understand that: You have soft hands and make a living by telling lies."

Boniface remained impassive, held in place by Regenspurger's menace.

"This man runs up and attacks the person you have come to see while you are a few meters away. What is your reaction? All the men grab this vicious attacker, subdue him, and call the police." He sneered at Boniface, the blood drying on his jacket. "But you? You act as nurse and carry Fraulein Weissenfeld's handbag."

He let the room settle, the only sounds coming from the corridor outside.

Regenspurger snorted. "But here's the interesting part. Bertrand Scheidling, the chauffeur. He's a good man, a loyal man. I talked to him, and do you know what he said?" He glared at Boniface—he wasn't sure what he saw; it could have been anger, it could have been fear. "He said it was as if you knew the attacker."

The room was silent again.

"Tell me. Did you enjoy your visit to the office last night?"

The still was broken by the door opening. "I have insisted on a brain scan." Chlodwig Weissenfeld came into the room, talking to himself under his breath. "Since my sister has had a considerable blow to the head and is already in the hospital, she should be thoroughly checked."

He continued walking into the room and around the bed. "Boniface, I understand you were a great help, thank you." His eyes shifted toward the Englishman, his head moving up and down as if scanning his appearance. "We will reimburse you for the cost of a new suit."

Regenspurger watched as Chlodwig turned to him. "I want to understand how such a thing could have happened."

Boniface looked to the other men. "Gentlemen, matters of company security are beyond my brief, so I'll leave you to discuss those issues in private. And as you can see, I need to clean myself up."

He stepped forward and snatched the phone from Regenspurger's hand as he passed. "Thank you for picking my phone up when I dropped it," said Boniface, his hand reaching the door. "I will, I am sure, see you two later."

sixty

"Can we?" The man in the olive-green army surplus jacket clenched a tight fist, pulling his arm up. "Can we, you know?" He lifted his fist and bared his teeth.

"No."

"But did he say we couldn't?"

"No. But it's too early in the morning, and we need to find her first, and we don't even know if she's here."

"So we grab her, and we can come back later when she's tired?" The scrawny, rat-faced man in the green jacket turned to face the driver. "She'll be tired. She'll be grateful." He sat back in his seat. "Think about it: Have a screw, get on a boat, get something to eat, and have a sleep."

The driver, one hand on the wheel, the other supporting the chin of his greasy face, ignored his passenger.

"Who goes first? We'll flip a coin." He grinned at the driver. "That's not fair on you. You should go first—I've got the big cock. You won't touch the sides after I've finished with her."

The black van lumbered along the main road to the docks, bouncing its passengers with each pothole and rut in the road, its blown exhaust confirming to everyone it passed that the van was as cheap as it looked.

"There." The driver pointed with his left arm, which stretched out of his leather jacket, revealing tattoos up his arm.

Coming out from the pedestrian bridge across the railway was a lone female, dressed in well-fitted jeans and a blue fleece jacket, carrying two bags, which she tried to hold in one hand as she glanced down at her phone.

The van slowed, holding back as the woman followed onto the path beside the road. "Go past her," said rat-face, straining to keep his gaze on her. "Don't blast the engine or you'll spook her."

The van moved forward a short way, following the road as it wound around the docks. "We did well yesterday," said the driver as they passed the flapping yellow police tape enclosing two figures wearing white all-in-one suits. "But we should wait farther down or they might see us."

The rat-faced man kept his gaze on the woman as the van passed. He ran a hand through his dirty sandy-colored hair, nodding. "How are we going to do this? The normal way?"

"Yep," said the driver, accelerating.

"Far enough," said the passenger as the driver bounced the tire over the curb, craning to check oncoming traffic before heading back along the road they had just followed.

"She's not expecting anything." The passenger twisted his neck, trying to keep his prey in his sights for as long as possible. "Wait for her to get past—" he pointed imprecisely toward the taped-off area they were passing again, "where we did some beating last night, and then we move."

They passed the woman, still walking, and when out of her sight, the van turned, again bumping over the curb, and then followed the target. "Slow, slow, slow," said rat-face. "Keep far enough away that she can't hear the exhaust."

She stopped as she came to the taped-off area.

"What do we do now?" There was confusion in rat-face's voice.

"Wait," said the driver, bringing the van to a halt and looking in his mirrors. He slid the van into reverse, moving unhurriedly. "We back off and wait."

The woman whose face had been ringed in red on the photo they were given stood by the tape, watching the men in white all-in-one suits work. Something distracted her—she slipped out her phone, looked down at it, and tapped the screen as if rejecting a call.

"Not too far back," said rat-face. "I want to be able to see her."

They watched as their target slipped her phone back into her pocket and stood outside the tape, looking in. Contemplating. She exchanged a few words with the young police officer who, along with the yellow tape, was the sole protection for the area. "See that?" said the driver, pushing up the sleeves of his leather jacket, the tattoos on his right arm balancing those on his left. He pointed with his right hand—three-and-a-half fingers and one thumb—checking to make sure his passenger had seen. "The cop's aware of her. We need to be way out of sight, and you've got to get her mouth shut tightly, or else the cop will come running."

She pulled out her phone, seemingly in frustration. An exaggerated craning of the neck. An exaggerated stab to the screen, and the phone was straight back in her pocket. "She's moving," said rat-face, a shudder traveling through his body as the driver turned the engine over.

"Easy, easy," rat-face's voice was soft, but still tense. He lowered his shoulder, trying to crouch while he sat as the van glided, its trumpeting exhaust muted. "Slow it, then we can go faster once we're past the cop."

The driver eased the brake.

"Why are we stopping?" asked rat-face. The driver pointed with his head—she had stopped and was going through her routine of pulling out her phone, angrily hitting the screen, and dropping it back into her pocket.

They started moving as she began to walk again, increasing speed past the yellow tape, following until she was about 200 yards past the crime scene. "Are you ready?" asked the driver.

"Willing and able," said rat-face.

The driver pushed the speed up, and as he drew parallel with the pedestrian, cut-and-started, cut-and-started the engine, finally cutting it and then allowing it to drift, bumping across the curb and onto the path as it came to a halt. He got out, miming anger and frustration, and flipped the hood.

He ducked under the hood and watched as the pedestrian approached, apparently unaware of the van in her path. She glanced up, saw the van ahead of her, and continued without breaking step. "Can you see?" he whispered.

"She's in my mirror," said rat-face.

She looked like she had in the photo, although her face seemed worn, maybe tired, and her hair didn't have the sheen or the bounce he was expecting. She glanced at the van with less care than she had glanced at the people working the crime scene, not sensing danger, not slowing, not breaking her rhythm. He stepped back from under the hood, and she noticed him—her eyes completing a mental inventory—but kept walking.

He pushed up his sleeves as she drew level with the van. That was when she noticed: She was staring at his right hand.

She froze.

Rat-face was out of the van. He threw the tape to the driver, his hand continuing in a single movement until it was in place over her mouth. His other arm was around her waist, and he kicked out her feet, falling on top of her. The driver pulled a length of tape, ripping it with his teeth, and put three quick turns around her legs, then ripped another strip.

"Ready?" he asked.

Rat-face kept his weight on the woman and nodded as the driver watched for the other man to drop his hand so that he could place a piece of tape over their captive's mouth.

The woman screamed under the tape and twisted, getting an arm free and kicking the driver with both legs. Rat-face backhanded her across the face, allowing the full weight of his arm to transfer through his hand to her cheek, and then sat on her, one knee pinning each arm.

"Please," said the driver, knowing he was speaking in a heavily accented tone but knowing that he would be understood. "Please do not do that. You will find that while my friend may look scrawny, he is, in fact, stronger than ten men, and any compassion he may have had was brutalized out of him when he was in his army."

The woman struggled, writhing like a bronco trying to buck its cowboy. Rat-face leaned back, slapping his hand on the woman's ass and letting his fingers slide between her thighs. She stiffened as his hand lingered, drifting upward, a dark scream coming from under her taped mouth.

The driver observed his passenger, astride his new ride, and indicated their prisoner's arms, his eyes moving from one to the other. The passenger dragged his hand up, over the woman's jeans, moving it to one arm, and his other hand to her other arm. He moved backward, placing his crotch at the bottom of the woman's ass, grinding as he wrenched her arms together, allowing the driver to wrap tape around them.

With her arms tied, he fell on top of her, allowing his hands to slip under her body.

The driver jumped up and took the two steps to the van, closing the hood and firing the engine, and then backed the van to where the two lay. Leaving the driver's door open and the engine running, he opened the rear doors and turned back to the two on the ground.

The rat-faced man had moved and was now sitting with his legs over the woman, who was still face down in the mud. In his hand, a white-bread sandwich. He grinned as he chewed and offered one of the bags that the woman had dropped to the man in the leather jacket, nodding and looking at the sandwich as he took another bite.

The driver pushed his sleeves back and took out a sandwich, holding it between his thumb and three fingers as he bit. He focused back on the man holding the woman on the ground, nodded his appreciation at the food, before looking back into the bag and pulling out the remaining contents: two more sandwiches. He offered one to the man on the ground and kept one for himself, walking around the two on the ground at a leisurely pace as he continued to eat.

As he finished, he wiped his mouth on his arm and his hands on his jeans. He pointed to the woman on the ground—the dirty, sandy-haired man nodded, pulled his feet back, and squatted beside the tied body. He rammed one hand between her legs and unhurriedly slid the second hand, palm up, under her breasts and lifted her. He took two steps before briskly sliding her headfirst into the van.

The man in the leather jacket jumped in the back, and the doors closed behind him. A moment later, the man who had been the passenger jumped into the driver's seat and revved the engine, trying to take control of the bucking steering as the spinning wheels gained traction.

From his position of discomfort in the van's cargo bay, he reached to roll the woman. As his hand touched her she flinched, trying to move away from him. He moved forward to reduce her space and manhandled her onto her side before reaching into each pocket of her jacket.

As he put his hand into the jeans pockets, he could feel her trembling. There was defiance in her eyes, but he knew that was a mask for terror. He pulled his hand out of the first pocket and slipped it into the one on the other side before triumphantly yanking out what he had been looking for: her phone.

He dropped it beside himself and reached behind for the tape, adding more wrapping to her legs and arms. He then ripped the tape off her mouth. "Listen to that engine. There's no point in screaming." As if to emphasize the point, rat-face hit the gas to exaggerate the roar of the blown exhaust.

"You killed that man." The woman's accent sounded American. "Back there. That was you, wasn't it?" She started to struggle, like someone trying to demonstrate the butterfly stroke on dry land. He slapped her, knocking her head back against the floor.

"You killed that other man and left him in our office, didn't you?"

He placed a thick, dirty finger over her mouth. "Enough." He held it in place, staring at her, waiting for the blink of acquiescence. She sighed—a warm jet of air out of her nose to warm his hand, then the slight nod of her head.

He released his finger and reached for her phone, tapping the face. He held the screen toward her. "Code?" She blinked, her mouth not moving. "Code." He dropped the phone and slapped her again. "Code."

"Three-four-nine-seven," said the woman, a tear forming in her eye.

He looked at the screen. "Has Mister Boniface upset you? He's been calling you very regularly."

sixty-one

There were four newspapers on the counter.

Boniface tried to focus on the pages—forcing his eye to scan the columns, looking for his or Weissenfeld's name.

He had seen neither, but he wasn't sure he had looked hard enough. Each time he started looking, he thought of Montbretia.

Montbretia.

Boniface picked up his phone: Four minutes since he had last called Montbretia. He stared at his phone, watching the clock. It clicked past another minute. He hit redial—straight to voicemail. Until an hour ago the phone had rung—for varying lengths of time, suggesting Montbretia was hitting the hang-up button to forward the call to voicemail—but now, every call went straight to voicemail.

He left another message and tried to focus on the paper.

Instinctively, he reached for his tea—his disappointing tea. Tea is always disappointing in a coffee shop—it's part of the job description of a coffee house to make bad tea—but in between trying Montbretia and focusing on trying to read the newspapers to see whether either he or Weissenfeld had hit the headlines, he had let his tea go cold.

He checked the time again, too soon, but he called again and didn't leave a message again. He stood and looked in the mirror along the side wall and reached up to straighten his tie. As his finger made contact with the dried blood, he forewent the urge to smarten his appearance: How was a straight tie any better when you were covered in dried blood?

He left and started walking, following the backstreets of Fitzrovia toward Oxford Street, the burble of London—the cabs, people shouting, trucks from an industrial age negotiating streets that were built in medieval times following cow paths from centuries before that—failing to distract him.

The arm temporarily blocked his path.

Without looking up, he instinctively moved to go around the obstruction.

The obstruction moved and pushed him toward the railings surrounding the building he was passing, the roar of a van with a blown exhaust covered Boniface's mumbled apologies as he looked up.

The eyes that greeted him told him he was wrong to apologize. The same eyes that greeted him yesterday as he left Jeremy Farrant's office. The same eyes—piercing but held in a loose, gray-skinned face—that saw him this morning as he tried to find what was in the leather-bound notebook.

He turned.

Regenspurger pulled him back.

He turned again. His way was blocked by a thin man, the same height as him with a pointy rat-face; greasy skin; sandy-colored, unwashed, greasy hair with loose curls; and an olive-green military-style jacket.

"Don't be like that, Boniface," said Regenspurger.

Boniface leaned against the railings, grateful for their support, and stared back. He had no inclination to speak and no idea what to say.

"A few words," said Regenspurger, his light German accent piercing Boniface's ears.

Boniface stood straighter, releasing his grip on the railings, and felt the other man push closer behind him.

"I've said all I'm going to say." Boniface's voice was without emotion.

"Really? It seemed like you had a lot to say." He slipped out Montbretia's phone and delicately held it between his thumb and forefinger. "Perhaps I can remind you of what you wanted to say?" He tapped the phone and offered the screen to Boniface, showing a photo. "Your girlfriend. Wearing the very latest fashion in duck tape. About an hour ago."

Boniface grabbed for the phone to find himself gripped by the surprisingly strong man with the rat-face. He struggled, willing himself to stay mute, finally giving up his effort to be free.

The human barricade invading his personal space stepped away. "This way, please," said Regenspurger, his voice a menacing calm tone. Like an unctuous waiter in an overpriced restaurant, he indicated a black van with its near-side wheels on the curb, the man with the green army jacket now standing behind the back doors.

Boniface walked behind the rear entrance to the van—its roof at his chest height. Regenspurger nodded to the other man, who opened the doors. Boniface bent to look into the cargo area. "Monty?" He stood upright. "Where is she?"

"I didn't say she was here."

"Then I want to talk to her." The two men scanned the surroundings like hawks as Boniface became more agitated. "I want to talk to her now. I want to know she's safe."

The younger man landed a blow squarely in Boniface's gut, winding him. Boniface bent forward and felt as his head was shoved, slamming it against the corner of the van's roof, before his legs were kicked away. To finish, the rat-faced man in the green jacket shoved him through the open doors, giving a final push to make sure he was fully inside.

Regenspurger leaned through the doors, holding a roll of tape. "Miss Armstrong needed this. I presume you will remain as our guest without further argument?"

sixty-two

The van doors opened. Boniface felt above his eye where his head had been propelled into the edge of the van roof and wondered if he needed medical attention.

"Out."

Boniface started to slide himself along the van's floor.

A curse was spat out in a language Boniface didn't understand, and the green jacket grabbed his foot and yanked. Boniface reached, grabbing wildly for anything to slow his movement, gashing his hand but finding the door pillars to slow his horizontal motion as his leg was dropped.

His back twisted across the threshold of the van's cargo bay, acting like a pivot as his legs hit the ground and his torso was turned ninety degrees, bringing him to a sitting position as he landed on his coccyx. He flopped forward, putting down a hand to steady himself, where he found a film of oil covering the concrete he had landed on.

Regenspurger clicked his fingers and pointed—the rat-faced man in the green jacket reached for the scruff of Boniface's jacket, yanking it and lifting Boniface, who felt the jacket give way under his arms as it held his weight.

He stumbled, and like a baby animal born on the run, he was walking, taking his first few steps out of the garages under Weissenfeld's offices. The garages under the CCTV camera that Reg had adjusted with a hammer a few hours ago.

The van doors slammed. The wooden garage door creaked on its hinges, then banged together, and Boniface was jostled. Regenspurger led the way along the outside wall, setting a pace that Boniface found hard to keep up with—the green-jacketed man walked behind Boniface, ensuring that he achieved the necessary forward motion as they turned the corner and ascended the slope. The trio passed through the gate—with blood still showing on the brickwork to the left—crossed the courtyard garden, and entered through the front door before taking the first flight of stairs.

"Where's Lennie?" said Boniface as they passed the security guard's desk. A new face, without uniform, stared.

"Who?" said Regenspurger. "There is no Lennie working here."

Boniface cursed under his breath. Someone else who had got hurt because they were close to Boniface.

He followed Regenspurger into the conference room. The same room where he had spoken to Chlodwig three days ago—or was it two days? Boniface was having trouble remembering. Another snap of the fingers instructing Boniface to sit at the far side of the overly large conference-room table with his back to the window: one man positioned at each egress.

"You didn't seem surprised. You didn't seem concerned." Regenspurger stopped talking. He had tried this in the hospital—Boniface was starting to notice a pattern.

Boniface waited, then decided to speak. "Neither did you."

Regenspurger smiled. "That's the first clever thing you've said."

"It's better than saying 'when,' which is how you wanted me to answer."

"You know when." The German's voice was controlled. "When I found you in Fraulein Weissenfeld's hospital room this morning, you didn't seem concerned. You were worried when I came in and caught you, but you didn't seem concerned about her."

Boniface opened his mouth—Regenspurger raised a single finger.

"Spare me, Boniface. You're a man who is paid to lie, and you lie plausibly for a living, and to be honest, I don't need the truth out of you."

Boniface tipped his head, his eyebrows rising.

"Oh, Boniface. You're teasing me," said the German in a mocking tone that sounded more menacing to Boniface. "Look at the basic facts. You go through my desk, taking photographs. You photograph the contents of Mister Phipps' desk. I escort you off the premises, and then you are found, apparently asleep in Mister Farrant's office, around the time the CCTV camera is broken. Broken when a slate decides to dislodge itself from the roof for the first time in two hundred years."

He snapped his fingers again. "I missed the best bit. When the slate fell, you heard nothing, apparently."

Boniface left the silence for Regenspurger to fill. "It doesn't make sense to me. Does it to you, Mister Boniface?"

"I think you've made up your mind already," offered Boniface. "Rhetorical questions rather bother me. Can we talk about Montbretia, please?"

A look spread across Regenspurger's face—for the first time, Boniface saw him smiling with his eyes. "I have a proposition for you, Mister Boniface."

Boniface waited.

"We have a press conference later today. One of your specialties, I believe."

Boniface made no show of emotion.

"I would like you to lead the press conference and make a small announcement."

Boniface calibrated the slight twitch at the extremes of the former Stasi officer's mouth and waited for him to play his card.

"You chat at our little press conference: Miss Armstrong lives. You don't: She dies. One small announcement in return for her life. Five minutes' work, that's all I'm asking."

It was Boniface's turn to remain mute, leaving the other man to fill the awkward social embarrassment—or in this case, the frustration of not seeing an emotional response from Boniface.

Boniface knew the question Regenspurger wanted him to ask: What do I have to do? But it was more fun to imply another question—and the response could be more illuminating. He kept his intonation moderate as he looked up at the ex-Stasi officer. "We know your threat to kill Montbretia is realistic because you killed the guy who you dumped in my office and you killed that poor fellow at Tilbury yesterday."

The pride in Regenspurger's eyes was unmistakable, even with the confusion of the unexpected approach. "You give me too much credit, Mister Boniface. I didn't kill anyone." He took Montbretia's phone from his pocket, deliberately setting it in front of him. "Miss Armstrong seems to take my view: She believes that yesterday's death was your fault."

"My fault, but not my hand. I think that is the point that was being made." Boniface let the silence settle, looking at the man with sandy-colored hair across from Regenspurger. The man met Boniface's glare and locked on.

"As long as you understand that our threat is real, that is enough." Regenspurger's comment distracted Boniface, who broke his stare, turning back to the German.

Boniface went to speak but found no words coming.

"Our friend at the end of the table is a man who enjoys what he does," offered Regenspurger. "For him, what he does is more of a vocation. He doesn't see it as work, but as a pleasurable business with added bonuses." He picked up Montbretia's phone, holding it so Boniface could see as he flicked through to the photograph of her taken earlier that morning. His tone became sharper. "Would you like Miss Armstrong to become one of those added bonuses before she dies?"

Boniface felt his jaw tremble and his eyes moisten.

"You're not a punching and kicking sort of person, Mister Boniface. Even if you were, you don't know where Miss Armstrong is located, and all it takes is one call from me and..." he let his unfinished sentence hang. "Are we clear?"

Boniface wiped his eye. "We're clear."

"Good," said Regenspurger, a flick of emotion distorting the lifeless skin draped over his face. "So we're agreed: You will make a brief appearance at our little press conference this evening."

Boniface remained silent, his head gently bowed.

"Aren't you going to ask? Isn't that big brain of yours curious to know what the press conference is about?" Regenspurger's approach was like he was dealing with an upset child who he was trying to win over with kindness.

Boniface raised his eyes to the German.

"I lied a little bit." Regenspurger put his hand over his mouth. "I might have given you the wrong impression: You will be the star of our press conference. We need you to make a public confession."

Regenspurger sat back in his chair, twisting it in the narrow gap between the table and the wall to face Boniface. "A small confession. A public apology. That's all. You know the drill: I've let my friends and family down. I am truly sorry. I am going to the police station straight away."

Boniface lifted his head weakly as Regenspurger continued. "It's a small confession—you don't have to admit to murder or anything like that." He dragged his hand over his face, pulling the skin tight. "All you have to say is that the body dump was your idea. You didn't murder anyone—you just wanted to dump a body to create a stink."

"That's what you public relations people do, isn't it—create a stink? You say that you asked someone to drop a dead body, but there was an argument about money, and the person you asked to do the work dropped the body in your office."

Regenspurger waited before continuing. "You tell your story and say you are truly sorry for what you did, and that you are sorry you caught up Weissenfeld Shipping in this matter, making it appear that there was a link to their business. You will sit next to Fraulein Weissenfeld and apologize."

"I'll do it," said Boniface.

Regenspurger's head flicked to scrutinize Boniface—his eyes apparently searching for some sort of confirmation of what his ears thought they had heard.

"I'll do it," repeated Boniface. "But you know that the story won't stick. At some point, someone will figure that I'm not the murdering type, and however hard I protest, there won't be enough evidence to even take the case to trial."

"We will help," said Regenspurger. "Do you think we lack the ability to make someone look guilty? While you're talking, we'll fill in some of the gaps."

The German smiled. "A bloody knife in your apartment should help. Even if you do walk away after years of legal proceedings, because you made your full admission to the cameras while sitting next to the CEO, people will only remember that Weissenfeld hired a bad PR adviser."

Boniface sat up straighter. "And as I make the announcement, you flush something through the tubes." He hesitated, his voice softer as he continued. "I'm the chaff while you release details about Somalia."

Regenspurger made the smallest movement of his head.

"Got it," said Boniface. "I make an announcement, you make an announcement. Both announcements are covered by the injunction, making it hard for the press to report, but you put the information in their hands and give them two stories. One about dead people in Somalia, the second about a PR adviser dropping dead bodies as part of his strategy to influence people."

A slow sneer broke out across Boniface's visage. "If I'm a journalist—if I'm an editor—which story will I pursue? Which story can I pursue, being as it's difficult to get into and out of Somalia, and, let's be frank, the public don't care about a few more deaths in Africa? So even if the injunction falls apart next week, by that time, everyone will have stopped caring about toxic waste because they're far more interested in the corpse in the office in Wimbledon."

Regenspurger nodded. For the first time, Boniface thought he saw genuine pleasure reflected in his cold demeanor.

"I publicly sacrifice myself and Montbretia lives?"

"That is the deal, Mister Boniface." The German's voice chilled.

Boniface stood, untangling himself from a chair that wouldn't go back far enough for him to get out without wiggling. "I may not be in a position to negotiate, but may I make a suggestion?"

Regenspurger looked up and nodded once.

"Look at me," Boniface indicated his bloody suit. "My appearance may provoke interest in another story. Can I change? Perhaps have a shower?"

"Yes."

"A quick trip home to sort myself out?"

"I would expect nothing less. In fact, my friend here," Regenspurger indicated the green jacket, "will be pleased to drive you home and then make sure you are at the press conference—which will be held in the Methodist Hall in Westminster—at 5 PM."

"Five PM for a five-thirty news conference. Timed exactly for every news outlet whose lawyers feel they can run any snippets on the six o'clock news, which will alert the editors of the press, getting the story into the newspapers tomorrow morning." Boniface winked at the German. "Good strategy—what I would have suggested."

"In case you're wondering, our friend," Regenspurger nodded at the man opposite him, "doesn't speak English, so please don't try talking to him or negotiating any changes."

"How will I tell give him directions to my apartment?" asked Boniface.

"No need. He already knows where you live."

Boniface's voice was weak as he continued. "Is he the man with the beard?"

"No." Regenspurger bared his teeth, like a shark having his photo taken. "*He* is with Miss Armstrong in case you forget our agreement."

sixty-three

The lunchtime traffic was frustrating the rat-faced driver.

Boniface enjoyed watching his futile annoyance as the van sat motionless before moving a few yards, only to wait again. Each time the traffic eased, the driver gunned the engine, the blown exhaust shouted, and the driver moved swiftly to the next impediment to his journey.

They pulled through the rear entrance behind Boniface's block, an L-shaped building with the horizontal member facing onto Wimbledon Hill Road and the vertical stroke—with the cheaper apartments—overlooking the parking lot and the bins.

As they pulled through the entrance, instead of directing him to the front as he had done when Bertrand Scheidling had been driving, Boniface pointed to the service entrance at the back. "Put it over there."

The driver didn't respond but swung the van round, reversing into the area indicated by Boniface.

He slammed the door as he got out, looking across the low roof of the van at his driver, who seemed hopeful that Boniface would try his luck or upset him in some way so that he could unleash a few swift blows—perhaps do more and go back to Regenspurger to plead that he had no other choice.

Or go back and find Montbretia.

Boniface scanned the brick-built structure, white wooden frames surrounding the doors and windows, and white metal casement windows with three horizontal panes in each section. The man in the green military jacket was staring at him, a flick of his head unmistakably communicating impatience.

"This way," said Boniface, pointing to the rear service door. A lump of brown wood in another white frame with a single slit of wired safety glass running most of the length of the door. He pulled the door open, stepping into the dim hallway.

The rat-faced man in his olive jacket and with his unwashed hair followed behind, at just over an arm's-length distance as the two crossed the polished marble-chip flooring. The light—a dull light listlessly bouncing off the white plaster walls—came from the window over the intermediate landing, where one flight of stairs turned to meet the next, rotating those who ascended and descended through one-hundred-and-eighty degrees.

Boniface put his foot on the first marble-chip stair—the wear in the riser more pronounced than on any of the following stairs. He reached for the dull brass rail and started his ascent with the rat-faced man staying three steps back.

He slowed at the intermediate landing, then stopped, flicking his head back toward the service-entrance door like a wild animal startled by a noise.

Rat-face mirrored his move.

As rat-face began to turn back, Boniface kicked off the wall, aiming his elbow behind the man's eye. He caught his guard's temple, then watched as the other man's reflexes deployed. The man with the filthy hair swung his far arm, fist clenched, toward Boniface, turning his whole body and pivoting on the worn step. His foot slipped, and Boniface kicked out, transferring enough momentum to topple his captor down the stairs.

Boniface watched as the other man fell—his arms still trying to punch as his head hit the step, the next step, and the last two steps as his body slid down the stairs, stopping when his shoulders were resting on the entrance-hall floor.

Boniface exhaled, resting his hands on his knees, unable to look away from the crumpled heap at the foot of the stairs.

Olive-green jacket, jeans, army boots. The body seemed motionless. Boniface became aware of himself panting as he strained to hear over the noise of his pounding heart whether the other man was breathing. He held his breath and looked, too afraid to step closer.

He took two steps down and observed.

Lifeless. Silent.

He took another step and kicked a boot—the highest part of the static body.

No reaction.

Boniface swung his legs—one then the other—over the brass banister and slid down, jumping off before the rail curled at the end. He walked around the inert figure, staying outside the reach of the arm that flopped at a right angle.

He squatted. Studying. The top of the chest was moving rhythmically, but the breathing was light.

Boniface kicked his tormentor's right shoulder and jumped back as if he had received an electric shock.

The body remained unmoving.

Boniface looked down, leaning left and right to see under the head. He leaned down and twisted the head from left to right.

No reaction.

He glanced back furtively, his eyes covering every inch of the dull hallway, then lifted the head and strained to raise the shoulders. He used his knees to prop up the shoulders and reached his hands under rat-face's armpits, bringing his hands together over the man's chest. He gripped his hands together, pulling his body closer to the inert slab of meat on his hallway floor, and rested his head on the inert body's shoulder.

He inhaled and turned his head away. "You could do with a bath," he muttered as he inhaled and started to drag the body backward. The feet thumped down the last few steps, and Boniface found a momentum as he slid the body over the smooth surface. The body dragged over the doormat as Boniface hit the door, pushing it and taking three steps to the van, where he dropped the lump, leaning it against the back end.

Boniface felt the pain is his lower back and became aware that he was outside, in the open, visible to people who he couldn't see.

He scanned the parking lot and the balconies, then reached down, patting the pockets of the man in the green jacket. There was something is his right jeans pocket—Boniface pushed his fingers in, extracted a small bunch of keys, and opened the rear doors of the van, leaning the body forward as the doors swung.

Boniface squatted inside the van and reached, returning his arms under the other man's and his hands to their grip at the front of his chest. "One, two," he whispered, listening as the last few threads at the back of his jacket gave way. "Three." He hefted the torso up and levered it into the van's cargo bay, then slid it until the legs flopping at the knees caught on the threshold.

The body was half on top of him; Boniface pushed it off and slid out of the van to shove the legs in before jumping back in and pulling the doors closed behind him.

He sat, sweating, panting, feeling his muscles ache. Montbretia was right; he should go to the gym or do some exercise.

Boniface stretched out his hand and pushed his fingers into the side of the other man's throat. A pulse. Light but consistent. He hurriedly felt around the back of the other man's head. He could feel no bleeding—and he should be quite an expert on that by now, this being the second head injury for which Boniface could be held culpable that day.

He scanned the van—he knew there was some tape when he had been pushed in, and presumably since Regenspurger had threatened him with it, it must have some function.

He found the roll of silver tape.

Which first? Arms or legs?

He went for the legs, then stopped. Wrong. He contemplated the body—a curled S-shape half on its back. Boniface pulled the feet out the way so they wouldn't stop the body twisting, then reached over and grabbed the olive jacket on the far side, pulling it toward him, using his knees to ensure that the body didn't slide.

It flipped over onto his knees.

Boniface pushed the man off and again leaned over to release his right arm, which he was lying on. He yanked the two arms together and bound the wrists, putting four or five turns of tape around them. He pulled the feet and put five or so turns around the ankles before sitting back to admire his work.

"How much tape do you need?" he muttered under his breath and tried holding his hands behind his back, imagining they were taped. "More than that."

He tore off a strip of tape and pulled the elbows as close together as he could get them before wrapping the whole of the lower arms in tape. He admired his handiwork and then levered the body back across his knees, adding a few turns around the body, taping the arms against the back of the inert body.

He shoved his former jailer off his knees, flipping him onto his back. As he had done with the elbows, he pulled the knees together before encasing his legs in duck tape swaddling in the same way that Montbretia had been bound in the photo Regenspurger showed him, but with more tape.

Boniface grabbed a lump of hair and immediately let go, instinctively wiping his hand on his jacket. "You need a good shampoo, mate."

He sighed, then pulled the hair, lifting up the head so that he could slip a foot under to keep the skull elevated. He took the tape, laid the end of the roll over the mouth, and then wrapped several turns around his head, moving his foot as he was finished.

"Vomit? Suffocation?" He studied the body slumped in front of him. "Fuck you, you took Montbretia."

He felt the vertical bracing in the van, giving it a firm tug. It didn't move. He tore a long strip of tape and fed it behind the bracing several times to make a loop. He flipped the body onto its front again and created a similar loop behind the arms before pushing the body toward the bracing and joining the two loops with more tape.

"Enough," he said and jumped out of the van, slamming the door behind him before pulling out his phone and hitting a familiar number. He jogged into the hallway, scanned the bottom of the stairs—not a mark on the floor—then ran up the stairs to his apartment. By the time he got through the door, his phone was ringing.

"Tommy. One last favor—it's for Montbretia, not for me." He walked to his CD rack and flicked through, pulling one out. "I'll make her appreciate Dutch prog rock," he whispered, returning his phone to his ear.

sixty–four

"It's a bit fucking public here, Tommy." Boniface's eyes were darting like a fly trapped in a bottle.

From the moment Boniface had got out of the battered black van, he had looked agitated. No, not agitated, more than that—and angry. Distraught, frantic, perhaps. The man who was usually so smooth and relaxed was twitching, tightening his own spring, which seemed ready to release at any moment.

"What's the problem, Boniface?" Tommy took a bite of his burger.

"Problem? I've got a bloke tied up in the back of the van."

"Your sexual preferences are up to you," said the big man, trying to bring some levity to the situation.

"Tommy!"

"Did your boyfriend hit you?" Tommy pointed to a cut over Boniface's eye.

"Tommy, Montbretia's in danger, and you bring me out to a place like this to take the piss." Tommy looked around: It seemed like a good place, near the motorway, near to people he could call on, near to Tilbury—where they were going, apparently—away from CCTV cameras, and at a place where you could get a decent burger from a guy who was a mate.

But things were clearly not normal; this was the first time he had seen Boniface not wearing a suit. Business casual might be expected, but old jeans and disheveled hair seemed out of place. A sign that all was not well with Boniface if the phone call he had received ninety minutes ago had not already made the point.

"Calm down, Boniface," said Tommy, laying a father-like paw on his shoulder, stuffing the remains of the burger into his mouth with his other hand. "We're among friends. Talk to me, tell me what we need to do."

"They've got Monty."

"Who?"

"The people who killed that vagrant and left his body in my office." Tommy looked down at Boniface; he was trembling, tears in his eyes. "They killed another man last night. Pummeled him to death and left him. I've spent the last ninety minutes driving a van while I'm legally banned from driving; a van that I'm not insured to drive and that is probably stolen anyway." He wiped the back of his hand across his nose, straining to contain his impotent rage.

"Shhhh," Tommy kept his intonation delicate. "These are small problems. Do you want the van to disappear?"

Boniface nodded.

"The guy in the back." Boniface nodded again. "Alive or dead?"

Every muscle in Boniface's body tightened as he looked up at Tommy. The upset was replaced by shock. "He's alive and he needs to stay alive. He's my leverage."

"Okay," said Tommy, pulling out a phone and starting to dial. "Gary. Tommy. I'm at the burger stand on the A13... Yeah, that's right. Listen, there's an old black Ford Escort van. You can't miss it: beaten to shit with an RSJ for a front bumper. Can you make it disappear? Now."

He fixed on Boniface, who was twitching again. His head moving in small jerks.

"One minor problem—there's someone in the back. Could you keep him alive? Thanks, Gaz. I owe you." He flipped the phone back in his pocket. "Gary will be here in ten to sort the van." He held out his hand. "Keys."

Tommy walked to the van, opened the driver's door, and put the key in the ignition, then leaned over and looked in the cargo area. A figure wrapped in silver duck tape wriggled and groaned. Tommy looked up to see Boniface had opened the passenger door and was retrieving a suit carrier and what looked like a CD. "Who is he, Boniface?" asked Tommy, looking over the van as they slammed the doors.

"I told you," said Boniface with no emotion, "he's my proof, and he's the only leverage I've got, which is why I've got to be back in Westminster by five."

Tommy started walking to his van. "Five? As in 5 PM today?"

Boniface dipped his head once, biting his bottom lip, apparently concentrating.

"Today?" Tommy made sure Boniface understood it was a question.

"Yeah," said Boniface disappearing out of sight on the other side of Tommy's van.

Tommy faced Boniface as they opened their doors, the big man getting in first, rocking the suspension under his weight. "We'd better move." The wheels spun on the loose surface before Boniface was seated as Tommy threw the steering wheel to point the van at the exit.

The engine screamed as the van accelerated; when it reached cruising speed, Tommy shouted to his passenger: "Without wishing to sound rude, Boniface, but you're not much of a fighting bloke—and if I'm honest, you're not really great with the gaffa tape—how did you get that bloke in the van?"

"I figured my only chance was one-on-one on my own turf. I had to hope to get lucky, and I got lucky. I played like I was beaten, and they went along with it. I got onto some stairs, giving me the higher ground, and did that whole 'what's that?' look—he glanced back, I pushed him, he hit his head. Dumb luck. Nothing else."

"So why didn't you call the cops?"

"Because he's the only bargaining chip I've got, but I can't play him until I know that Montbretia is safe."

"About that," said Tommy, his voice sounding serious. "Whatever it is that you've got to do in Westminster, you go and do it. I can drop you at the station; you can put your suit on and go. I'll hang around here and look—I'll call some of the guys to come and help." He snorted. "We could even call the cops."

"Once I start talking in Westminster, there's no incentive to keep Montbretia alive," said Boniface, in almost a whisper. "Montbretia's in trouble because of me, so I've got to sort it out. She's far more cut out for this running and jumping, punching and kicking stuff than I am, but if she can't help herself, I can't leave her, even if I'm not sure what I can do. There is no option to walk away after what I've done."

"Are you sure, Boniface?"

Boniface deliberated, apparently trying to put words in the right order. "They've taken everything from me, Tommy. My business is dead because I'm being forced to admit to something I didn't do. Random strangers are being killed. I've kidnapped someone. I have one option, and that is to break them, and I'm going to break them with Montbretia by my side."

He stared out the window as he kept talking. "I need to find Montbretia. She needs to know that she's safe." His voice cracked. "And I need to say I'm sorry." He turned back to Tommy, wiping a damp smear on his cheek. "Once she's safe, I need to get back to London and..." He scrabbled for the right word. "Vengeance is an ugly word. They killed, they tried to destroy..." He inhaled. "I need to make sure there's no more destruction, and I need to make sure that what I thought I was working on—what Montbretia thought she was working on—is what happens."

Tommy exhaled. "So how do we play this one, Boniface?"

Boniface reached for his CD and held it up. "Dutch prog rock."

Tommy took his eyes off the road and flashed at Boniface. "Are you crazy?"

"We can't shout and holler—we'll draw a crowd, perhaps we'll get arrested, and maybe we'll find his friend."

"His friend," said Tommy, feeling the tension in his voice.

"I knew there was something I forgot to tell you," said Boniface. "We don't know what he looks like. But if we play 'Sylvia,' Montbretia will know it's me and will know it's safe. We can then get to her before anyone figures what we're up to."

sixty-five

"It's been an hour, Boniface. Are you sure this is a good idea?" He leaned up against his white van, pockmarked with rust spots. "Are you even sure she's here?"

Boniface strained, as if looking harder would help him to hear or would help the sound travel to Montbretia. He felt like he had seen every reinforced concrete fence, every piece of barbed wire, every steel palisade fence, every tractor park, every bit of scrub and wasteland, every chain-link fence, every collection of shipping containers—some in designated areas, but most, it seemed, left on any piece of unclaimed land.

Tommy had taken them to the top of the road leading from the docks, killed the engine, put in the CD, and cranked the volume. As the opening power chords of "Sylvia" spread, Tommy and Boniface would start looking—Tommy would then kill the music, and in the comparative quiet, broken by trains, lorries pulling containers, passing planes, seagulls, and any other number of noises, they would both strain, kidding themselves that all they needed to do was listen harder and they would find Montbretia.

"Are you sure she's in Tilbury?" Tommy asked again.

"No." Boniface was noncommittal. "But after the last twenty-four hours, I'm not sure about much. What I do know is that I messed things up, and because of that Montbretia came here, and because she was here they found her and took her, and the very minimum I can do, if I ever want to be able to look at myself in a mirror again, is to get her out of the hole I've put her in."

Boniface held up his hand, commanding Tommy to be quiet, twisting his head as if it would give him the hearing of a superhero. He dropped his hand, straightening. "This is the last place that I know she definitely passed through. If she's not here, then where? Where would they have taken her?"

They got back in the van, and Tommy fired the engine before driving two hundred yards without speaking. Tommy opened his door, reaching for the CD. "It's not that I'm not having fun, Boniface, but would it be easier if I asked Gary and some of his mates to persuade our friend who you so kindly gift-wrapped in silver gaffa tape to tell us where she is?"

"He won't talk and he doesn't speak English."

The melodic power chords played as both men began their survey of the surrounding area. "There was a moment that I thought I was starting to like the track," said Tommy as the melody started. "But now…" He continued scanning. "I get the point of playing *this* track, but is there really nothing else we could use?"

He stopped the music—Boniface was close against a rusty chain-linked fence, pushing his head against the slack as if trying to get closer.

Tommy walked over. "We've covered everywhere obvious."

"Then we'll do the not-obvious," hissed Boniface, sounding like an annoyed reader in a library.

"Sure you don't want to go back to London and do what you need to do there?"

"I want to be in London," said Boniface. "But I need to be here."

sixty-six

The music stopped. Boniface gripped the gray steel palisade fencing, staring through with the look of a man who had been in prison so long that he had lost everything that mattered to him, including his own sense of self.

"Play the music again." There was an urgency as Boniface shouted. "The opening chords."

Tommy half-jogged, half-lumbered the few steps to the van and leaned in. A momentary pause, and the sound of 1970s Dutch prog rock played through tinny speakers filled a small part of Tilbury docks. Boniface kept a hand on the fence, which was now a gilded cage protecting the jewel: Tilbury railway terminal. Anywhere else in Tilbury, and the land would have been a vacant lot, but the rail siding ended here and someone had laid cement so that containers could be stacked, and brought in a crane to move the containers onto the trains.

Nobody knew the value of the contents of the containers, but you don't move empty boxes, so whatever was there needed to be protected.

Boniface drew his hand across his throat, and Tommy killed the music.

Within the yard, quiet—far away, there was banging. A deep sound. Something hitting metal. A big piece of metal—something thick. But there was also a resonance: It wasn't just the impact of a solid object regularly coming into contact with metal; the sound continued to reverberate after the impact.

"Monty! I'm here, Monty," bellowed Boniface.

"Shut up," Tommy reached Boniface as three bangs rang out.

"M..." Tommy slapped his paw over Boniface's mouth.

"She's alive. Let's keep it that way." He released his hand. "She didn't get in there by accident. If the guys inside the fence know she's there, they were bribed. Even if they weren't, remember that we still haven't seen that other bloke you talked about." He wiped his hand. "I thought you didn't want to make a scene."

"You need to get me in there, Tommy."

"Now you're thinking straight," said Tommy. "And I'm glad you volunteered, because I'm not in a state to get over." He looked down at his gut, a gelatinous mass flopping over his jeans and stretching his T-shirt to the limit of the tensile strength of the fabric. "I'll get the van over."

The engine strained as Tommy bumped the vehicle over the curb, backing it parallel to the fence. "Sorry. Can't get it closer," said Tommy, pointing at the rutted ground around the fence as if that was sufficient explanation. "On to the roof, jump down, and you're sorted." He opened the back doors of his van and pushed the younger man's leg as Boniface hauled himself onto the roof.

"It's higher up here than you think," said Boniface squatting, the van rocking as he moved.

"That concrete will be harder than you think when you land on it," said Tommy. "If I were you, I'd get one foot on the top of the fence instead of jumping. That way you can slide rather than adding another big height to your fall."

Boniface moved toward the edge of the roof, the radius pulling away his support. "Have you got a plank or something?"

"Not in the van, but I can look around," offered Tommy.

"No time," said Boniface, focusing on the fence. He hesitated, then launched himself, his back foot sliding on the curve of the roof as he pushed himself, his front foot aiming to make contact with the spiked trident at the top of the palisade.

As his center of gravity passed over the fence, Boniface started reaching down, trying to grab anything to break his fall. One hand scraped the top of a trident defiantly standing guard on the top of the steel. His other made contact as Boniface ducked deeper, trying to roll but finding the fence was burying its spike into his left foot.

He pulled his trailing leg, feeling the pain with another trident spiking his calf, ripping flesh and fabric as he rolled, letting go as his body went into freefall. Boniface held the fence with the one hand that had gripped, trying to slow his fall, letting go as his foot slammed into the concrete, sending shockwaves through his spine.

A twist and his knee broke the rest of his fall, bringing his body to rest on the solid ground.

"Drama queen," said Tommy, standing by the fence, a look of shock registering across his face. "Could you do that again and I'll film it? I'm sure we could get a couple of hundred quid if they show it on the telly."

"Can you break a kneecap? Because I've never felt pain like this before," whimpered Boniface.

"I'll go and tell Montbretia that we won't be rescuing her today," said Tommy, opening the passenger door of the van. He returned, pushing his hands through the fencing. "Is your leg alright?"

Boniface examined his leg—his calf was a mass of ripped flesh, ripped fabric, and blood. "Doesn't hurt that much."

"It will," said Tommy. "That's shock stopping the pain." He pointed down to the objects he had stood on the ground inside the fence as Boniface tried stretching his knee. "A knife and something to drink."

Boniface rolled over to analyze the offering. "Beer?"

"I don't carry water," said Tommy. "This is a work van. The guys that use this van want to feel that they're being rewarded. Water—even your finest foreign water—doesn't say thanks like a beer does."

Boniface put his weight on his ripped leg, pulling himself up by the fence, then gingerly tried resting some weight on his damaged knee. He fixed Tommy with a glare and very calmly, very precisely said, "Ow." He grimaced. "That is my final word until I've found Monty."

"It'll get better as you walk on it," suggested Tommy.

He leaned to pick up the penknife and can of beer, slipping both into his back pockets. "I'll go find."

"I'll grab something to make it easier for you to get out, and I'll make sure we've got a good excuse for parking the van here."

Boniface limped, trying to figure whether it was his knee or his kneecap that hurt when it took his weight.

Stepping more fully into the yard, he surveyed the rows of containers—long rows, each with containers stacked three or four high. He walked to the row on the far right, checked on the passageways flanking each container, then hissed, "Monty."

He moved to the next row, again another shouted whisper. In the next row, he heard a familiar—but this time louder—sound. Metal being struck. He stared up: The containers were stacked three high in this row, all with door seals except the top container. The doors were locked, but the security strip of wire was missing. Keeping his voice low, he said, "I'm coming, Monty."

Boniface positioned himself in front of the stack of three crates, looking up. Montbretia had told him once—and with all the work she had done for the Global Logistics Forum, she should know—that crates were at least eight feet high, and sometimes over nine. He didn't have a tape measure, but he could see that they were above his head height, and when he tried to grab the top of the crate, it was higher than he could reach.

He stood back to observe his task. Before him, two doors, locked. For each door, two vertical bars ran from the top to the bottom, fitting into secure slots at each end. A small way off the ground—Boniface presumed at a reachable height when the container was loaded onto a trailer—was a handle for each bolt. Each handle had a padlock hole, which was empty. Instead, the four vertical bolts were secured by a massive block spanning all four, which was much newer than the container.

Boniface tried the vertical bars: They felt secure, and with some caution he could slip his fingers behind each bar. He lifted his foot onto the lock and pulled to heft himself up.

He glanced down: Two, maybe three feet up, and already he felt dizzy looking at the ground. He stretched—he could get his fingers over the lip of the container. He dug his foot into an indentation in the door and levered himself higher, throwing a hand to grip the top of the container in a slot in the roof's corrugation.

A half turn of his head, and he faced back to the container. "Don't look down," he mumbled as he threw his free hand to grab a vertical bolt on the container above. He grabbed and pulled, lifting his right leg until his foot found purchase on the bottom container.

He panted and felt the tremble in his leg as he slipped his hand along the bar and pulled himself farther, levering his body into a standing position, his toes on the lower container as he gripped the vertical bars locking the middle container.

It was official: He didn't care whether it was his knee or his kneecap— he had a pain in his left leg, and the calf in his right leg was pumping.

He lifted himself by the lock on the second crate, feeling the burning pain as he propelled himself with his right calf muscle. He took a breath, gripping the vertical bars with one hand as he felt behind him to grab the can of beer and then the penknife, moving the contents of his pocket onto the top of his crate.

He risked a glance across the yard and saw Tommy under the hood of his van, black smoke billowing out of the engine, then turned to face the crate and begin the final ascent.

As his toes embraced the second crate, he firmed his grip on the vertical bars, realizing it was him shaking, not the crates wobbling. He moved to the left, standing clear of the door on the right, and leaned across, reaching for the handle.

The handle pulled out to ninety degrees. Boniface then pushed it down, opening the bolts at the top and the bottom, and repeated the process with the second bolt before pulling the door against its tired hinges. The door refused to shift more than a few inches before Boniface gave up and pushed his arm through the door, barging sufficient space for him to slide in.

His steps echoed in the dark as he walked back to kick the door open, keeping firm hold of the locked door as his foot impacted against the unwilling, but slowly moving, metal.

He surveyed the contents of the crate, looking for Montbretia but finding his eye drawn to a fallen white plastic garden chair with a gray roll on it. It took a few seconds to realize he was looking at a person— mummified with duck tape—taped to the garden chair and tipped back, but with its feet against the outside of the crate.

"Monty!"

She moved her head and mumbled something through her taped mouth as Boniface ran over and hefted the chair to the sitting position.

Feeling his eyes moisten, he went back to the door, where he leaned out to reach for the knife and beer before returning to kneel next to Montbretia.

"Listen, I don't know if you're still talking to me." Her eyes crinkled.

"I've got a plan, but do you want a beer first?" The silver roll of duck tape nodded as Boniface opened Tommy's knife.

sixty–seven

Montbretia couldn't watch, so she looked around the metal box that had been her prison for the last several hours.

Corrugated steel walls; they looked rusty, but it was dark. A floor that might have been painted once, but in the light that pushed through the half-open door she could see it was scuffed, scraped, and worn.

"Eeeee." A sharp intake of breath.

"Did I hurt you?" said Boniface, pulling the knife away.

"No, sorry. I'm not used to seeing you with a knife unless you're eating." She felt it impolitic to say "with a knife when you're nervous, shaking, and waving the blade near my arm." Boniface returned to his task: cutting diligently through the duck tape binding her right arm against her body—the unspoken assumption that he was taking care to avoid the flesh on either side and, if possible, without cutting the clothes she was wearing.

Oh, and all major organs and any arteries should also be avoided.

His attempt to cut a hole for her mouth had been almost successful. Almost. He only cut her top lip twice.

And her chin once.

But it's not easy trying to find a mouth when it's covered with duck tape and there's little light. Boniface had spent several minutes feeling the tape, trying to find the precise place to cut—he had been close when he plunged the blade, just not close enough. Maybe it was the cut over his eye that was distracting him.

Then again, maybe it was her fault. He had offered her the choice—he could pull all the tape off or he could cut. She went for cut, knowing the pain of taking sticky tape out of her hair.

"There," said Boniface, evidently pleased with himself.

Montbretia lifted her right arm from the elbow as Boniface shuffled on his knees to the left arm. "What are you doing?" shrieked Montbretia.

"Sorry, did I get you again?"

"No."

"You want me to do the whole of that arm before I do this one?"

"No, Boniface. Go!"

"Not until I…"

She cut him off. "Go! Forget all that stuff about revenge is a dish best served cold. If you don't serve it, it doesn't count. Give me the knife, and I'll cut my way out." She waved her now free hand, splaying and contracting the fingers. "I'll feel safer doing the cutting, too."

He stared into her eyes. "Are y..."

"Yes. Go. This isn't about matching punch for punch and landing a good blow. Revenge is about a knockout punch. I understand the plan; I'll get out of here. You get yourself gone." She pointed to the door with her head as Boniface self-consciously dusted himself off.

She watched as he cautiously sat on the threshold of the crate, dangling his legs outside. He gripped the door, then pulled himself back in and walked over, reaching into his pocket. "Phone," he said, laying his phone on the floor next to her. "Call Gideon and talk about really dirty stuff. We need his help."

He returned to his sitting position at the exit, gripping the closed door. "Are you're sure we can trust Tommy?" she asked.

"I'm sure. I'd trust him with my life. I'd trust him—I *am* trusting him—with yours. He thinks you're great, and he'll save you from any covenants you feel obligated to enter into with Gideon." The last thing she saw before he dropped out the door was a nervous smile.

sixty-eight

Boniface dropped, hitting the concrete and falling clumsily.

He lay where he fell, breathing steadily, taking a mental inventory. Head: hurts, but hit concrete last so probably hurts least, and anyway, was already cut above the eye. Shoulder: new pain from the fall, but probably more the surprise of hitting the concrete. Hip: ouch, but like the shoulder, this was a new injury, not one introduced by Regenspurger's man in the green army jacket, and not added when he slipped, landing badly as he came over the palisade fence.

He raised himself, resting on his arm as he continued his inventory. Having landed heavily, his knees could be filed under hurt-pain-ow, especially the left one, and his right calf, to use the best understatement he could call to mind, was throbbing.

Boniface rolled back toward the container and hauled himself up, using the vertical bars to hold his weight, reaching if not vertical, a sufficiently upright position that a long-ago extinct human ancestor would have been proud to adopt.

He took a few steps—capable of balance, but not yet used to the newly found pain in walking. Somehow the rat-faced man was now firmly in his mind. What would happen if he had got out before Gary reached him? What would happen if someone looked in the van or heard the groaning?

What if he got out? Boniface's head spun, with the pain in his neck it felt like it had turned through 360 degrees, but he knew he had looked left and right, scaring himself about who might be around.

He moved, barely lifting his feet as he followed a path through the crates, unable to get the rat-faced man out of his mind. What would happen if he got free? Would he know how to contact Regenspurger? Would he come back and look for him and Montbretia, and kill them? Was it safe to leave Montbretia here, even with Tommy?

Was this another stupid risk he was taking—this time even more reckless because he knew what was at stake? What chance did he have that his plan would work? He sighed. Too many moving parts, too much risk.

He reached the palisade fence separating the yard from the scrubland running along the dock road and followed until he drew level with Tommy's van, which was still smoking. He pushed his face against the vertical bars, looking for Tommy. Looking for whatever Tommy had found to help him get out of the yard.

It took a while to realize that the figure about fifty yards away was

Tommy sitting on someone. Boniface stared: The lumbering old walrus appeared to be on top of someone who was struggling but still able to land blows from his horizontal position.

Tommy was in control, but he was taking a pounding, and the other guy seemed to have the energy and the incentive to fight.

Boniface focused on the rows of three-high containers running parallel to the trident-topped fence that had nibbled his shoe and chewed his leg, looking for anything to help him get over. Someone, some-where—someone who wore a high-vis jacket—had undertaken a health and safety check and had ensured that all waste in the yard was cleaned up. Boniface was all in favor of reducing workplace accidents, but the lack of any wood or rubble lying around wasn't helping.

There was nothing.

He assessed the containers, trying to gauge their height relative to the height of the fence. The fence looked higher than one container. He positioned himself between one stack of containers and the fence, his arms spread. He touched neither, guessing he would need to extend each arm by around twelve inches to reach.

He cursed under his breath and looked up at the containers: two regular containers and on the top, a specialized brick-carrying con-tainer—the same proportions as its siblings below, but lacking a side wall to allow easy access.

Boniface cursed again, walking to the end of the container stack.

Practice makes perfect. It might have hurt more, but Boniface's second ascent of a container stack was swifter. Halfway up, he figured that the pain wasn't increasing and it was easier to climb without a can of beer in his jeans. He reached the top and edged his way around from the end doors, holding onto the reinforced vertical corner as he turned onto the open face of the brick container, leaning back to rest on the bricks and look at Tommy, who was still on top but was getting hit with greater frequency.

He leaned back, pulling at the heat-sealed plastic wrapping, and eased out three bricks, which he tossed over the palisade fencing, watching how they arced to the ground. He tried to calculate how far he would have to jump out so that he too could arc over the fence.

He lifted himself to a standing position, muttered "gravity, height, distance" and jumped, leaping as far away from the crate as he could. As he started to feel the effect of gravity, he began to wish he'd thought about a landing strategy as he frantically tried to recall the old war movies he had seen when the parachutists roll.

His contemplation was interrupted by his feet hitting the ground. His forward momentum pushed him, and he found his ankles bending, breaking the fall onto his knees, his hip, and twisting as he rolled onto his back.

Again he lay still, waiting for a new pain but not feeling it.

There was a muffled sound in Tommy's direction. He gathered up his bricks and ran to the big man. "Hey, Tommy," he said, holding out a brick.

"Afternoon, Boniface," said Tommy, looking up, a look a pride spreading across his face as he took Boniface's offering while the flailing arms remained weighted under the human ballast.

Boniface gripped a brick in each hand and scrutinized the flesh on the ground. He stepped on one arm, precisely positioning his foot at the elbow where the forearm protruded from a leather jacket. Boniface focused, waiting for the thrashing hand and arm to pause, and then slammed the bricks together, crushing the hand between the slabs of fired clay.

The man in the leather jacket bellowed as Boniface released the arm and walked to the other side. He put his foot down, trapping the right elbow, and closely examined the hand. Three-and-a-half fingers, one thumb. "Where's your beard now?" said Boniface, as the bricks came down on the hand.

Tommy held his brick as if ready to strike the man's head. "Enough," he said as the man lay still. "There's some webbing in the back of the van, Boniface."

Boniface jogged over and came back with the strapping. "Legs first, Tommy?"

"Legs first, Boniface," said Tommy, moving forward on his captive's stomach, still brandishing his six-sided oblong weapon.

"All done," said Boniface, admiring his newfound skill in wrapping.

"We're going to roll you," said Tommy to his seat, holding his brick above the man's face. "It's your choice whether you get hit."

The man nodded. Tommy started to stand, and his captive jerked violently to the left, pulling his legs up. Tommy dropped his weight back onto the man. There was a sound of air being expelled, followed by a thud as Tommy brought the brick into contact with his head.

Tommy stood, taking a second webbing strap Boniface offered. "Where's Monty? Is she okay?"

"She's fine—she's cutting herself free."

"So what are you doing here? Go," said Tommy, pointing toward the station. "I'll take care of her...and him."

sixty-nine

Boniface caught his reflection in the glass panel separating him from the cabbie: hair, shirt, tie, jacket, all straight. Cut over left eye, still nasty, but he had at least been able to clean his hands and face in the restroom at Fenchurch Street station before jumping in the cab, which then doubled as his dressing room during the fifteen-minute jaunt across the City of London, grazing the West End and finishing in Westminster: the heart of British political power.

Boniface kicked his bloodied jeans, T-shirt, and sneakers into the gutter as he opened the door, paid the cabbie, and walked swiftly around the corner to Westminster Methodist Hall.

Most people saw the word Methodist and figured church. Most people saw a church and figured religion. Most people didn't realize Westminster Methodist Hall had a whole range of rooms, from large to small, that could be hired by the day or by the hour, making it a perfect meeting and conference center.

Its proximity to Parliament—topping an oblong with the Houses of Parliament at the foot and Westminster Abbey and a purpose-built conference center along the sides—made it a near daily location for political press launches.

But today, this had been chosen as the site of Boniface's public execution.

"Where have you been, Boniface?" He was six-two and Canadian but had the temperament of a small, angry man. "I've been calling."

"But which phone?" asked Boniface. "I don't have a phone, so it can't have been my phone that you called."

"Boniface, I don't have time. We've got a press conference, and in case you haven't noticed, we're discussing a very serious issue. Now what was that issue?" North American sarcasm never works well on an English ear. "Oh yeah. You. You telling us how you thought you would dump a body." He exhaled. "Geez, Boniface, what were you thinking? This is a real mess I'm going to have to fix."

Brad had turned and was already walking. He hadn't said "yo" or "man" or "dude" once, and somehow Boniface missed that.

"Keep up, Boniface." He didn't look back. "Regenspurger has been intolerable. He thinks it's enough that you're here. He doesn't understand all the arrangements that need to be made. The people to be called, the..." Boniface stopped listening as Brad went through the oak double door into the central reception.

"We're back here," said Brad without breaking step as he led Boniface through a carpeted labyrinth threading around a series of small conference rooms. "We've got a room for the actual press conference with a room where we're meeting before."

"Can we have a look at the room where the press conference is being held?" asked Boniface.

"No time," the Canadian continued at his pace.

Boniface slowed, waiting for the figure in sandy chinos and a blue shirt to notice, slow, turn, and backtrack to where Boniface had decided to stop. "Come on, Boniface."

"Give way on this one thing, Brad. It'll make it much easier for you, and we'll all get wherever it is you're going quicker than if we stand here arguing."

Brad sighed and flounced down the corridor. "Alright. We were going that way anyway."

The tall Canadian pushed a door and led Boniface into a room. A long table, covered in a blue velvet-like cloth that reached the floor at the front and with three heavy leather-bound chairs behind, stood on a low stage. In the main body of the room, there was an island of gilt-framed chairs: four rows of interlinked chairs, each row split with five seats to either side of a central walkway.

A brief flicker of awareness rippled around the room as the two entered. Boniface scanned the faces, looking for anyone familiar, but saw no one. Three young-looking journalists chatted; two older journalists tapped furiously on their phones. Boniface scanned again. Why the recognition? Were they pleased to see anyone or had they been pre-briefed? Perhaps that was how Brad had persuaded them to come. A dumb move, but possible.

Boniface maneuvered himself into the room, looking around and muttering platitudes—"Hi...how are you doing...good to see you"—as he walked to the second row and sat.

Brad sat down beside him, leaning in close and straining to keep his voice quiet. "Boniface. What the hell are you doing?"

Boniface sat up straight, watching as another journalist came into the room. Looking concerned and unsure as she entered, her face burst into life as she recognized one of the older journalists, his head momentarily raised during a brief pause from tapping on his phone.

"If you want me to commit suicide in a religious building, then please let me sit and contemplate, and get a feeling for the room." No one heard apart from Brad.

"Keep your voice down," Brad's voice was air pushed through a clenched jaw. "We need to prepare."

"Then let us go and prepare," said Boniface. "I presume the charming Mister Regenspurger will be there."

"You bet," said Brad, standing.

"I want to come back here before we start," said Boniface as Brad shook hands with another journalist who had just come through the door. "What do these journalists cover?"

"Some are transportation and logistics specialists, like..." He inclined his head toward the man he had shaken hands with. "We also sent the invitation to the business desks."

"That explains why I don't recognize any faces. I used to know the politicos."

Brad led them out onto the corridor—a broad passage that ducked and dived around the rooms—his mop of light-colored hair flopping from side to side as they walked, every five feet passing a fire extinguisher, a health and safety notice, or an exhortation to worship.

Boniface slapped his pocket, his habitual check on his phone. The primeval instinct to panic was rapidly replaced by regret that he had given his phone to Montbretia. He felt his knee twinge as he tried to keep up with the Canadian, and the feeling of regret was washed away by a wave of relief for having made sure the right person had the phone.

"Have you got the time, Brad?" Boniface asked as he tried to keep up.

"Five. Five-fifteen. Something like that," said Brad, turning a corner into a darker part of the passage, then turning back on himself and pushing a door.

A small room. Like the press conference room, it was spartan: a plain but functional carpet and white painted walls. Unlike the larger room, this had no source of natural daylight and no raised stage.

"You see, Mister Phipps. I said he would be delivered at the time we needed him." Regenspurger turned to Boniface, continuing in his precise tone, the German accent scratching at the Englishman. "Where's your friend, Boniface?"

"Parking the van. There were too many cops around, and it's too much of a sensitive location for him to leave it on the street." Boniface paused. "I think he's staying outside. This isn't his sort of place."

Regenspurger nodded.

"I presume Greta will be here."

Regenspurger nodded again. "She is recovered from this morning, thank you for asking, Boniface." The German sarcasm seemed much more effective than the Canadian.

"One more thing," said Boniface without making eye contact. "I want all the executives to be here."

"That's not..." Brad started and was cut off by a look from Regenspurger. "That would not be practical, Herr Boniface."

"Then make it practical. They're all within a mile of here." He moved farther into the room before continuing. "This has nothing to do with our agreement—and as you can see, I'm doing what I said I would." He waited for a flicker of acknowledgement to pass across the piercing eyes. "I want confirmation from all the company officers—from Greta, from Chlodwig, from Joanna, from Jeremy—that after today, our relationship is finished. I want to hear it firsthand from them." He faced Brad. "I apologize if this delays your press conference, Brad, but I'm sure Mister Regenspurger understands my perspective."

The German remained motionless, then flicked his eyelids, pulling out his phone.

"While you two sort that, I'm going back to the room."

seventy

Boniface didn't like to make presumptions based on appearance and stereotypes.

Who was he kidding? He loved to.

Then he'd spend the next five minutes revising his opinion as reality kicked in.

The journalists were starting to arrive with greater frequency now, but their entrance was always the same. The heavy wooden door would open, and the deer-in-the-headlights face would appear. After the initial shock, the eyes would then begin to sweep the room.

Some would skim in circles; others would scan along the rows. Some would alight on a friendly face, and a new playground clique would be formed. Those that didn't find a friend would feign cool professionalism—they didn't need anyone to talk to; they had work to do, and they had phones to tap and stare at earnestly as they hoped someone would come and sit next to them.

Boniface made an inventory—reviewing appearances against his mental library of stereotypes as he tried to assess which were the shipping and logistics journalists: His guess was the just-out-of-university types. The business reporters: His gaze alighted on three somewhat older journalists who dressed better but had that not-on-the-track-to-editorship look. Brad had also mentioned that he had called some crime journalists. Boniface made another assumption based on a stereotype: The guy with the 1970s tobacco-colored leather blazer, complete with belt, suggested Brad might have been successful.

He had been sitting for two minutes, and already the seat was starting to feel uncomfortable. A gilt-colored frame with seat and back padding wrapped in deep-red synthetic velvet may look stylish in the brochure and may be acceptable for a short while, but Boniface could find nothing to recommend the overly narrow human-hating contraption.

He shifted one seat to the right and leaned toward the journalist sitting alone at the end of the row. Young, wearing a suit that Boniface guessed he wore every day—it had that I've-only-got-one-suit-and-it's-a-cheap-suit look. "Could I borrow your phone?"

The acne-scarred face under the flop of greasy hair turned to look at Boniface. Shock registered, as if Boniface had suggested they wrestle naked in the middle of the floor.

Boniface pointed at the gash above his eye. "I got mugged." Some of the fear seemed to drain from the young man. "I just want to check the

BBC; you know they're expecting the big one to break any minute now."

"I didn't," said the young man, reaching for his phone. "What have you heard?"

Boniface called up the BBC news website. Apparently nothing was happening: The president in a central Asian dictatorship was dead, the inflation figures had been seasonally adjusted, which made a 0.1 percent change—the leader of the opposition was trying to argue that this was a very, very, *very* bad thing—and yet another soccer player had been accused of assault. Boniface couldn't be bothered to check whether he assaulted his girlfriend or someone in a bar who supported the opposition.

"Who are you with?" asked Boniface as he refreshed the screen. He didn't listen to the reply or the justification about how, whatever job it was, was a step on the career ladder. "Thank you," said Boniface, handing back the phone and returning to his own scan of the room. Three more journalists had arrived and added to the pockets of tête-à-têtes vibrating in a hive of self-created intrigue.

The door opened again.

There was something familiar in her face.

He watched as she scanned—she was an along-the-rows scanner—waiting until her gaze passed him and then bounced back as some flicker of recognition triggered in her synapses. Her momentary look of confusion morphed into an inquisitive look—a question posed across the room as she frowned, tilting her head, but with her lips smiling.

At last, a familiar face.

The haircut had become less practical over the years. Boniface remembered when it was long. Now it was straight at the front, and as you looked around back the hair was cut up high on her neck, angling down to the straight edge. Very stylish. Looked great. She could carry it off, but it obviously required a lot of work to keep it looking that good and to stop it from going flat.

Boniface got to his feet as she started walking toward him. The clothes had changed, too. They were less fashionable now, but more stylish—classic would probably be the right description of the skirt and jacket combination—and with some more color. If he wasn't after a favor, he would have also noticed that she had added a few pounds. Correct that: a lot of pounds.

"Jennifer." He spread his hands.

"Boniface." Jennifer Quilley met his embrace, politely kissing him on each cheek.

"All grown up," said Boniface, stepping back to admire his acquaintance and putting into practice everything he had learned with Greta about paying a compliment without using words.

"Boniface the bullshitter," said Jennifer, flashing a mouthful of television-ready teeth. "It's rather rude to call you what we called you behind your back, but it does have a certain alliterative panache." Her grin was replaced by a flirtatious pout of her lips, seemingly intended to keep the atmosphere light.

"Alliterative charm or not, it wasn't really true."

"Oh Boniface, it was true often enough." She slowed, weighing her next line. "Alright, you told the truth except when you were protecting Gideon. How is Gideon, by the way? Still got the same...tastes?"

"You mean Gideon who, just this week, stood naked to answer the door to me and then picked chocolate out of his pubic hair?" She nodded, a slight hint that a story was being stored away for later retrieval. "Not a clue—haven't seen him for years." Boniface gave his best look of mischievous inscrutability, stepping back and offering Jennifer a seat.

Boniface sat next to her, his own tête-à-tête. "So you've fought your way out of the political trenches to become the business editor and on television?"

"Slightly more humane hours, or at least more predictable, and more time indoors. But it does lack some of the..."

"Thrill of the blood sport," offered Boniface.

"Thrill? Vicarious enjoyment, perhaps." She tilted her head. "What about you, Boniface. I miss watching your performances. You're...?"

"Sober," he said, cutting in before a question could come.

"Don't apologize," said Jennifer. "Some of my best friends are sober."

Boniface leaned toward the journalist, the muscles in his jaw tightening. "Jennifer, fun as this is, I need a bit of a favor, rather urgently."

seventy-one

Boniface watched the turquoise jacket cross the room. The sharply cut blonde hair seemed an age-appropriate improvement for Jennifer Quilley.

He looked across at Brad, who had been talking to some of the younger journalists—the shipping and logistics journalists, Boniface was guessing. The Canadian seemed desperate to try to keep his attention on the young woman he was talking with, but his eyes were drawn to Boniface's acquaintance as she crossed the room.

Before she could reach the door to the room, it opened forcefully. He watched as Jennifer's hair was caught in the draft. Instead of the normal hesitant journalist, an older man stepped in, immaculately presented in a three-piece suit and oblivious to the inconvenience he may have caused for anyone else.

Jennifer stepped to the right, ducking behind Jeremy Farrant as she left. Farrant had adopted the standard behavior of the journalists and was scanning the room. His eyes came to rest upon Boniface. He made eye contact and gave a sharp backward nod, leaving Boniface feeling compelled to follow the man, who had already left the room.

He was standing across the corridor, obliquely facing the door, scowling, as Boniface exited. "Why am I here, Boniface? I'm told you're making a public announcement."

"Boniface. Why did Jennifer Quilley leave?" Brad seemed unaware that Boniface and the lawyer were in conversation. "You were talking to her, and then she left. She's an important TV journalist—we need her here." He was looking down the corridor in the direction she had gone.

"She's an old friend of mine, Brad." Boniface didn't mind exaggerating somewhat. Well...exaggerating extensively, and without limitation.

"But we're meant to be starting now," the Canadian was whining. "You've been here for nearly an hour, I don't see any reason for the delay—you seem to be wasting time."

"Calm down, Brad. It's not a problem." Boniface held a business card so Brad could see it. "She's got to pop out for something. I promised her that I would personally call her five minutes before we start if she's not back."

Brad inhaled, looking ready to speak, then walked toward the room where the Weissenfeld executives were gathering.

"You were about to explain, Boniface," hissed Farrant. "Why am I here?"

"Good evening, gentlemen." Chlodwig Weissenfeld and Joanna

Baines appeared behind Boniface.

"They are gathering in the room at the end," said the lawyer, pointing in the direction that Brad had gone. The two carried on walking, not breaking step—Chlodwig acknowledging Boniface, Baines staring straight ahead.

"There is one point of law that requires clarification before I speak. I am keen to make sure that my interests are protected and that the Weissenfeld interests are also considered." Boniface dropped his voice to a whisper. "More to the point, this demands someone with your...gravitas. I want to ensure everyone accepts your confirmation—I don't want an ongoing discussion based on ignorance of the law." He stood up straight. "Do you see why I *needed* you?"

"Gracious. I quite understand." Boniface watched as the lawyer took joy that someone had recognized his talents.

seventy-two

"This isn't the sort of car to pick up women. But it is the kind to draw a crowd," said Tommy Newby, pulling his vintage Bentley Speed Six onto Parliament Square. "Let's see how big we can get the crowd." He parped his horn and joined the five lanes encircling the green square fronting the Houses of Parliament.

"Notice how people notice," he said to Montbretia. "You don't get that with a Porsche or a Ferrari, and people don't hate me like they hate those bankers and their flash cars."

Montbretia pulled out Boniface's phone. "I'm going to make some more calls."

Tommy reached for the gear stick, flattening the clutch and praying that the gears didn't graunch in public.

"Political desk!" Montbretia shouted into the phone.

A cabbie drew level with the Bentley, apparently more concerned about looking at the car than he was with his or his fare's safety.

"You heard right," shouted Montbretia. "Gideon Latymer will break a super-injunction on the floor of the House of Commons. Within the next thirty minutes—if the Speaker agrees to an emergency question."

"How many journalists have you got coming?" asked Tommy as Montbretia ended the call.

"Who knows? But a crowd should help: Boniface wants it to make the news." She looked around and turned back to Tommy. "Are you sure you can manage it?"

"It's mechanical—it's easy."

"Remember," said Montbretia. "You need to break down before the barrier so we can get a crowd of people. If you're in the parking lot, then they can't get to you. I'll give you a whistle when your crowd has drawn enough people and you can send them over to us, and it should look good in front of the TV cameras."

"Gotcha. You ready?"

"Yup."

Tommy finished the circuit of Parliament Square, moving into the curbside lane and slowing the Bentley as it passed in front of the Houses of Parliament, the passersby all turning as they heard the thundering beast of an engine. He cautiously positioned the vehicle between the two crash barriers; Tommy knew that they might look inoffensive with their muted brown covering and fluorescent yellow highlighting, but underneath was solid concrete designed to protect Parliament from suicide bombers. In an argument with the barriers, Tommy's Bentley would lose, so he followed the road as the fortifications funneled vehicles into the Old Palace Yard parking lot, pulling up at the security gate and stalling the engine.

Montbretia turned to the police officer who had stepped out of the guard's box behind the gate, apparently unsure as to whether he could stop worrying about the safety of British politicians for long enough to admire the vintage British engineering.

"Gideon Latymer should have cleared us about thirty minutes ago," she said.

The young officer looked down at his clipboard. "He did. Straight through and park...you can park wherever you want with a car like that."

Montbretia started to thank the officer as Tommy turned the engine. It turned but didn't fire. He turned it again, but still it didn't fire.

"I'm off," said Montbretia, jumping out. Tommy tried to keep sight of where she was heading, seeing a cameraman and a sound engineer holding a boom with a long fuzzy microphone at the end, and a third person with the group—a woman, better dressed and checking her face in a compact.

"I'm sorry about this." Tommy acknowledged the policeman. "If you want a car to start first time, don't get one of these." He turned the engine again, shaking his head in disappointment when it didn't fire.

He got out of the beast, removed the leather straps traversing the long nose, and opened the right side of the hood.

"Look at that engine." There was a muttering on the far side of the crash barrier where a small crowd was gathering, apparently preferring to admire the vintage car rather than worry about their personal safety as they stood on the road.

Tommy put his hands onto the engine, pulling faces to suggest he was concentrating on adjusting the machinery, as he watched Montbretia scuttle around in her quest to find journalists and encourage them to gather around the Saint Stephen's entrance to the Houses of Parliament. It had seemed a bizarre plan that Boniface had concocted, but there were several TV cameras standing around, and he knew that some of the political bloggers that Montbretia had spoken with had promised to make sure there was maximum real-time publicity.

Gideon Latymer appeared on the steps outside the Saint Stephen's entrance. Surprisingly for a politician, he appeared not to be talking. Montbretia looked around before being swallowed into the crowd. It was Tommy's cue to move away—apparently Gideon was hesitant about appearing in public with Tommy. Tommy checked and could see the top of Montbretia's head as she emerged from the crowd she had created, walking up the steps and giving Gideon a peck on the cheek before standing next to him, gripping his arm.

Tommy stepped back from the car, closed the hood, and fastened the straps. He then turned to the small crowd admiring the car. "If there are any journalists here, could I suggest you gather over there, where I understand Mister Latymer is about to make a very important announcement?"

He pondered, then continued. "In fact, even if you're not a journalist, you may find the announcement interesting. For myself, I will move the car into the parking over there." He indicated the Old Palace Yard parking lot.

"If it starts," said a voice in the gathering.

"It will start. First time," said Tommy. He surveyed the crowd. "A small wager for anyone?"

seventy-three

A turquoise jacket appeared at the end of the passage.

Boniface watched as Jennifer Quilley proceeded along the passageway. "Can we start now?" asked Brad.

Boniface acknowledged Jennifer as she crossed toward the room scheduled to hold the press conference. She looked to Boniface, nodded her affirmation, and then twisted her head in the direction from which she had walked, returning to meet his vision before giving a slight questioning frown. He mouthed "thank you," feeling the ends of his lips lift involuntarily. She looked perplexed—having been involved in a whole conversation without words, it appeared she did not understand what she had heard.

Brad shuffled as Jennifer disappeared from view, like a teenager being told to wait.

"I want two minutes," said Boniface. "Two minutes with everyone else so that we are all agreed on what is happening."

"I think we know what's..."

Boniface cut off Brad. "Two minutes to make sure it's not a total cluster... To make sure we all give the same message."

"I don't see that it's necessary, Boniface," whined the Canadian.

"You stay here then; I need to talk to the decision makers," said Boniface.

"Well, if that's the case..." Brad followed and passed Boniface, hurrying toward the room where the executives had gathered.

seventy-four

Brad pushed the door and Boniface followed him into the box with no source of natural light, checking to make sure everyone was there: Greta, Regenspurger, Chlodwig, Jeremy Farrant, and Joanna Baines.

Greta stepped forward, swathed in a bottle-green dress, tailored to her preference to imply a full figure rather than suggest the necessity for a diet. Her shoes, also green, were high but not the height of her usual office shoes, reducing her stature by an inch or so. Her hair had returned to its flawless helmet-like shape, and when she spoke her voice was resolute. "What's the holdup, Boniface? Herr Regenspurger tells me that you will be making an announcement."

Boniface could detect no sign of any weakness after her injury that morning, and her reduced height had not translated into a reduced determination.

Chlodwig gave his slightly-disappointed-but-wanting-to-stay-encouraging half smile. "We want Greta to be next to you, receiving your apology, so that everyone understands that this morning's incident was minor. It's important for the share price that the markets understand that the CEO is in control."

There was a burble of agreement around the room. Boniface waited for it to calm and asked, "Before we start, does someone have a phone?" He surveyed the faintly unsettled, frowning faces. "Not for me—we should check the breaking news before we proceed. Brad, you must have a phone."

"Sure. But I don't..."

Boniface stopped him. "Call up the BBC news website and go to the live broadcast feed." Brad remained motionless. "Humor me on this: Let's see what story they're running."

The room focused on Brad as he tapped on his phone, then squinted at the screen with the tinny sound of the small speaker carrying the commentary into the room.

"Perhaps if you could hold the phone up so everyone can see what's happening?"

Brad held his phone with the screen facing outward.

"What is the relevance of all this?" asked Jeremy Farrant, looking at the screen over his half-moon glasses balanced at the end of his nose.

"Maybe nothing," said Boniface. "But could somebody who has got a better view tell me who the journalist is?"

"I can never remember his name," said Joanna Baines, "but he's the

BBC's political editor."

"Political *editor*," said Boniface. "So not a regular journalist?"

Baines mouthed the word "no."

"Can someone squint and tell me what the ticker on the bottom is saying? Or perhaps you could turn up the volume, Brad, so we can all hear."

Brad twisted the phone back and stabbed a button. The volume increased, the tinny speaker distorting with each sibilant and plosive the political editor delivered: "Of course Mister Latymer will not be saying anything here—while he's outside the Chamber of the House of Commons, he's not covered by parliamentary privilege."

"That's interesting," said Boniface. "It seems that Gideon Latymer is about to do something newsworthy. Has anyone read the ticker yet?"

Brad turned the screen back; holding it close to his eyes, he started to mumble: "MP to break super-injunction." He stared out. "It says MP to..."

"We heard, thank you, Brad," said Boniface, pausing as he felt the tension drain from his muscles. "You know about my connection to Gideon Latymer. Indeed, that was one of the reasons for hiring me." He focused directly on Greta, catching a glance as she looked away, her eyes darting, searching elsewhere for reassurance.

He scanned the room: Regenspurger seemed calm, Baines looked angry, and Chlodwig appeared confused, but doing his patrician best to be supportive in a difficult situation.

"I'm seeing some confusion," said Boniface. "You're here because, despite the injunction, you want me to make some announcements to the press, knowing that the press cannot report what they are being told... because of the injunction." Jeremy Farrant stood straighter at the mention of the announcement. "But you also know that there is a sufficient legal gray area that the press will be able to mention my connection with a dead body and will push further because they know I'm one person, and as an individual I won't have the legal resources to fight the matter, especially if I'm in jail."

"Man, they really got you." Brad had a broad smile. "Now I get how it works."

"Don't you see?" Joanna Baines blurted.

Boniface ignored the two and continued. "When the Somalia story comes out, then it will have lost much of its sting because it will already be old news for the press, and you will always be able to remind people that you had bad PR advice."

He caught Regenspurger's eye—a self-satisfied aura possessed his face with the hint of a smile forming at the corner of his mouth.

"A calculated gamble," said Boniface. "One that I can respect, but I have an alternative proposition."

Regenspurger frowned, his voice soft. "But you are not forgetting our agreement?"

"How could I forget?" said Boniface, raising his voice as he continued. "I will not be making a statement this evening. I did nothing wrong. I was not responsible for the death of the man whose body was dumped in my office, and I had no connection to the people who dumped the body."

Boniface saw the confusion spread across Chlodwig's face as he looked to Regenspurger, his eyes asking for an explanation.

"As you can see on the news, Gideon Latymer is about to break your injunction." He glanced to Jeremy Farrant. "I'm sure Mister Farrant will confirm, a Member of Parliament can break an injunction, even a super-injunction, and is protected by parliamentary privilege."

Farrant puffed himself up, gripping his lapels. "That is correct, Boniface."

"The media is then free to report, without restriction, what has been said in Parliament," added Boniface.

"That is also correct," said Farrant. "Although they may only report what has actually been said; the injunction is still in place, so they can't extrapolate any further. But I think you're missing something, Boniface. It would be highly inappropriate for a Member of Parliament to take this action; it would be a complete abuse of his position."

"What? To tell the truth? To announce that Weissenfeld Shipping made a decision at an executive level to dump toxic waste in Somalia?"

"Greta?" Chlodwig turned his disappointment onto his younger sister, who was giving him her best indignant look.

Boniface continued. "As you can see, Mister Latymer is at Parliament, so he can't be diverted." He turned to Regenspurger. "Even you, Mister Regenspurger, with your extensive network of bullies, thugs, and intimidators. You can't stop Gideon."

Regenspurger's countenance remained unstirred.

"But you're thinking that you have some leverage." Boniface saw a momentary glimmer of pride. "Brad. If you look closely, there should be a lady holding tightly to Gideon's arm."

"She's hot," said Brad.

"Would you mind showing Mister Regenspurger the screen?" As Brad passed his phone, Boniface continued. "Some of you were unaware that as well as dumping toxic waste, Weissenfeld has also been involved in kidnapping. But let's not worry about that yet, because as you can see, Mister Regenspurger, Montbretia is free."

Boniface paused, watching Regenspurger's face twitch. "Montbretia free. Leverage over me, gone." Boniface beamed. "In case you're wondering…those pleasant young gentlemen…I've got some friends looking after them, and we'll deliver them to the police later this evening, when I'm sure they will be happy to explain the two murders they committed."

"Murder?" Greta shrieked, turning to Regenspurger, whose face had returned to its customary look of dead flesh draped over a skull.

"You authorized him to procure a body and dump it in my office, but time was short, so he got a body the old-fashioned way," said Boniface.

"Is this true, Greta?" asked Chlodwig.

"I'm afraid it is," said Boniface. "And they beat another man to death yesterday."

He caught sight of Greta: Outwardly, she had aged ten years in ten minutes. Once proud, once strong, she looked broken.

"We can talk over the details later," said Boniface. "First, we've got a press conference with people waiting."

"But we can't... Not if you're not..." Brad was jabbering. "This is very embarrassing, Boniface."

"It's alright, Brad. The press conference is still going ahead," said Boniface. "However, the agenda has changed slightly."

Boniface relaxed his shoulders and stood straighter. "First order of business: Greta, you are announcing, with immediate effect, your resignation."

"Absolutely not." Her retort was swift, but as Boniface observed the CEO, he could see no appetite to fight.

"Greta, there have been two murders." Chlodwig's voice was soft but definite.

"Chlodwig is correct, and that is why you will announce that he will be acting chief executive while a search is made for a long-term successor," said Boniface. "You can explain that regretfully, the head injury you suffered this morning will require surgery, and with the recuperation time you won't be able to devote your full energies to the role."

He looked at Chlodwig. "The first task for you as CEO is to acknowledge that Weissenfeld has been involved in dumping toxic waste in Somalia. While you're making the announcement, Mister Farrant will call the lawyers to have the injunction lifted. You can say that the injunction was sought to give Weissenfeld time to confirm some key facts, which have now been confirmed."

"But this is still..."

Boniface held up his hand to stop Chlodwig. "You will make one other announcement." The patrician German paused, waiting for Boniface to continue. "You're going to announce that Weissenfeld is establishing a foundation for Somali victims of any chemical dumping, and are endowing the foundation with one billion dollars, U.S."

"No, Boniface, you're going too far. We don't have that sort of money," said Chlodwig.

Boniface made an exaggerated shrug. "I'm sure if we ask Joanna and consider the alternatives, we can agree that is an achievable figure." He glanced at the CFO. "It's tax-deductible, too, and it's far less than other companies have paid for spilling oil into the Gulf of Mexico."

"No, Boniface. Absolutely not," said Chlodwig. "You are asking us to change our whole management structure and to commit a vast sum of money. We need time to think about this."

"You've got all the time you need," said Boniface. "But remember, your company has been responsible for two murders, and as soon as Gideon walks inside and reaches the floor of the House of Commons, your options all disappear."

seventy-five

"I do not know where you heard that story; I suggest you check with your sources. It would be highly inappropriate and highly unusual for a parliamentarian to interfere with the judicial process."

Boniface could hear Gideon's explanations to the last few journalists who were questioning him on the steps, framed by the Saint Stephen's entrance to the House of Commons, the splendor of the Victorian gothic architecture rising above him. He stood erect, aware that there could be cameras on him.

A face poked from the far side of the dark blue suit. "Boniface!" Montbretia dropped Gideon's arm, ran between him and the journalists, and threw her arms around Boniface.

Although having the air rapidly expelled from his lungs, Boniface could hear as Gideon continued. "I was not the source of this story. My office was not the source."

Montbretia squeezed tighter.

"I'm sorry," said Boniface.

"Shhh."

"I'm sorry and thank you," said Boniface. "If I'd listened to you, I never would have needed your help."

Montbretia said something that Boniface couldn't hear.

"I know your sex life is none of my business, but I hope you didn't have to promise Gideon too much to persuade him to take your call and to play ball."

"It's alright, he's had me clinging to his arm and staring up at him in front of all those cameras for the last hour. He has had sufficient reward," said Montbretia, looking up at Boniface.

Boniface continued. "I'm not going to make promises that I can't keep; I've learned my lesson. But while I was telling Greta that she was resigning, even though she didn't know it, I had an idea."

Montbretia let go and stood back, staring up at him, mock stern. "Don't you think you've had enough good ideas, at least for this year?" Two tourists walking past stopped and stared at Boniface and Montbretia.

"No, this really is a good idea. I thought, as well as making Greta resign and admit to dumping toxic waste, thereby ensuring that she lost all her power and authority and has had to publicly humiliate herself..."

"That was a good plan, Boniface. As I lay trussed up like a duck tape sausage, it did give me a certain pleasure as you explained what you wanted to do. It also distracted me from my fear of your knife skills."

"It gets better," said Boniface, watching the tourists start to walk away. "I suggested... Well, I told them that they are setting up a foundation to support victims of chemical dumping in Somalia. Doesn't matter who dumped, the foundation will support them."

Montbretia's face had a look suggesting she had just had a pleasant surprise. "That is a good idea, Boniface."

"Wait. That's not the good idea. I also told them that they will endow that foundation with a large establishing grant," said Boniface. "And they agreed."

"That's a very good idea. How much did you suggest?" She stared up at him, expectation in her eyes. "Please tell me you at least said something sensible, like ten million bucks?"

"I said one billion dollars."

Montbretia stood open-mouthed.

"I was thinking on my feet," said Boniface dismissively. "They won't end up paying that much, but they announced it, so it will be a big number."

He stared at Montbretia, her eyes starting to mist.

"Don't cry yet," he said. "I spoke to Chlodwig—he's a good man, and he has a conscience. I recommended that he get a range of people on the board. People who can ensure the money is spent on the people who need it."

"You were full of good ideas today, Boniface."

"I suggested you." Boniface observed as his words registered with Montbretia. "And he said yes."

Montbretia remained stationary. "Really?"

"It's not full-time work; it's board meetings and then supervising the distribution of funds to make sure that the money is making a difference, and that might mean some travel." He looked her straight in the eye. "Can you cope with some travel?"

She turned her head from side to side, as if weighing the question.

"So if it's not too much like a commitment to a day job, will you do it?" He hesitated, then gabbled, stumbling over his words. "Weissenfeld will meet your expenses and pay you a day rate when you're working for the fund."

Montbretia embraced Boniface again, sobbing.

"Don't cry yet," said Boniface. "Wait until everything's in place."

"But what about you?" Montbretia pulled back, wiping her eyes. "Haven't you still got a huge problem—a dead body, police, and all that?"

"Nah. Nothing that I can't lose with a more interesting tale of international intrigue and two foreign killers searching the mean streets of Tilbury, looking for vagrants to kill. As there's no evidence linking me, there's not much to print." He put his arm around Montbretia's shoulder. "Come on, let's go and tell Gideon about your new position. You're going to need all the political friends you can find."

There was the sound of heels behind them. "I thought I might find you still here."

"Veronica!" Montbretia dropped Boniface's arm, rushing back to embrace her. "Thank you, thank you, thank you."

Boniface could feel the involuntary spasm of muscles across his face and knew his former wife would read the confusion. "I was about to say that you should develop good relations with the press, but you already seem on pretty good terms."

"Congratulations, Boniface," said Veronica, embracing Montbretia and facing Boniface over the younger woman's shoulder.

Boniface mouthed "thank you."

"I didn't get it. I thought you let her off lightly." Montbretia turned her head to observe Boniface as Veronica continued. "Then we heard the rumor: They're getting ready for her at Biggin Hill."

"What's that?" asked Montbretia.

"It's an airport—it specializes in executive jets. It means Greta will be out of the country within an hour," said Boniface.

"So congratulations. When I heard she was running, I realized you had got inside her head." Veronica paused. "You bounced her, I take it? Didn't give her any time to think?"

A smirk spread across Boniface's visage.

Veronica tilted her head. "And now the admission that she made will chew away at her brain."

"It will keep chewing and chewing and..." said Boniface in a matter-of-fact tone. "Forever. But they tried to hurt Monty." He let the thought hang before turning to walk over to Gideon, reaching him as the final journalist left to file her story.

"Boniface." Gideon embraced the man standing two steps down.

"Thank you, Gideon," said Boniface. "Without you...well..."

"Me?" asked Gideon. "All I did was stand here with Montbretia."

"Montbretia who has got something to tell you. She's with Vron—go and ask her," said Boniface. "I'm off to chat with Tommy."

He walked across the Old Palace Yard park lot to the Super Six, which still had a small group of people admiring it and asking Tommy questions.

"Boniface." Tommy bear-hugged the thinner man.

"I can't begin to thank you, Tommy, but next time could you hurry up? I strained every sinew to slow things down so you had enough time to get here, and then I find you went home to get your favorite toy."

"I had to take the van back, as it had our friend in it," said Tommy. "I brought the Bentley because people pay attention to a Bentley, and that was what you wanted, wasn't it?"

"Next time, bring it faster," said Boniface with a wink.

Boniface Books

You can check out the latest Boniface books at simoncann.com/boniface

The Murder of Henry VIII (Boniface #1)

As Boniface said when he took the job, how hard can it be to handle the press and publicity for the launch of a book about England's most famous Tudor monarch?

But when the author is murdered, Boniface realizes the job demands more than he expected. And when the man Boniface is talking with is shot, then he witnesses a third person being forcibly drowned, and he finds he is being pursued by a former Russian Special Forces soldier, he runs.

He delays his death by trading the only thing of value he can offer his would-be assassin: proof of a 500-year-old cover-up. The only difficulty in making the trade is that Boniface can't prove what he knows is true—yet.

If he finds and hands over the proof, the murderer has no incentive to keep him alive. If he lives, he has to explain the transaction for his life to his capricious paymaster.

Boniface needs to unwrap what the dead author found, figure out why he was killed, protect his client's interests, and stay alive.

Tattoo Your Name on My Heart (Boniface #3)

Although past his mid-thirties, the teenager that lives inside Boniface's head can't believe his luck when he is hired to help one of his rock idols, Danny Featherstone, and his ex-glamour-model wife, Dawn.

Danny and Dawn are the target of an anonymous internet hate campaign that has led to poor ticket sales and lost television work. Broken contractual terms brought to light by the hate campaign have led the management to freeze the band's assets, cutting off the couple's source of income.

And then Dawn disappears.

Boniface searches for Dawn but uncovers small-time crooks looking for money and excitement who think Boniface has something they can extort. Making his search even more complicated is an angry son looking to destroy the parent he believes abandoned him, and embittered, poverty-stricken musicians trying to regain their former fame and get a slice of the income that was only ever theirs in their dreams.

But most worrying, Boniface finds a husband who loves his wife, unconditionally, and who will do anything to protect her.

About the Author

Simon Cann is the author of the Boniface series of books.

In addition to his fiction, Simon has written a range of music-related and business-related books, including the *How to Make a Noise* series, the most widely ready series about synthesizer sound programming, and *Made it in China*, about entrepreneurs building businesses in China. He has also worked as a ghostwriter on a number of books.

Before turning full-time to writing, Simon spent nearly two decades as a management consultant, where his clients included aeronautical, pharmaceutical, defense, financial services, chemical, entertainment, and broadcasting companies.

He lives in London.

Keep in Touch

If you want to know more about Simon, his books, the background to his books, and what he's up to, then check out:

- His website: simoncann.com
- His Facebook page: facebook.com/simoncannauthor
- His Google+ profile: google.com/+simoncann
- His YouTube channel: youtube.com/simonpcann

The swiftest way to find out when Simon's next book will be published is to join his mailing list at simoncann.com/mail